Copyright © 1994 by Benita Kane Jaro

Library of Congress Cataloging-in-Publication Data

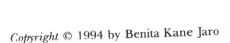enita Kane.
he door in the wall / by Benita Kane Jaro.
p.   cm.
BN (invalid) 1-877946-38-1 : $22.00
. Caelius Rufus, Marcus—Fiction.   2. Rome—History—Republic,
-30 B.C.—Fiction.   3. Rome—History—Civil War, 49-48 B.C.—
tion.   4. Rome—Officials and employees—Fiction.   5. Caesar,
ius—Fiction.   I. Title.
3560.A5368D66   1994   93-36292
.54—dc20   CIP

All rights reserved, including the right to
reproduce this book, or parts thereof, in any form,
except for the inclusion of brief quotes in a review.

Manufactured in the United States of America

First Edition, January 1994 -- 1200 copies

THE PERMANENT PRESS
Noyac Road
Sag Harbor, NY 11963

THE DOOR

b

BENITA KA

Jaro, B
Tl

IS
1
265
Fic
Ju
PS
813'

STATE LIBRARY OF OHIO
SEO Regional Library
Caldwell, Ohio 43724

THE PERMANENT PRESS
Sag Harbor, New York 11963

To my parents: Belle F. Kane and Howard L. Kane
And to MAJ, as always.

Dividitur ferro regnum; populique potentis,
Quae mare, quae terras, quae totum possedit orbem,
Non cepit fortuna duos.
—LUCAN, BOOK I

Then the possession of empire was
put to the arbitration of the sword.
The fortunes of a people which possessed
sea and earth and the whole world,
Were not sufficient for two men.

—TRANSLATED BY ANTHONY TROLLOPE
1815–1882

He was as great as a man can be without being moral.

—DE TOQUEVILLE ON NAPOLEON,
applied by Sir Ronald Syme to Caesar

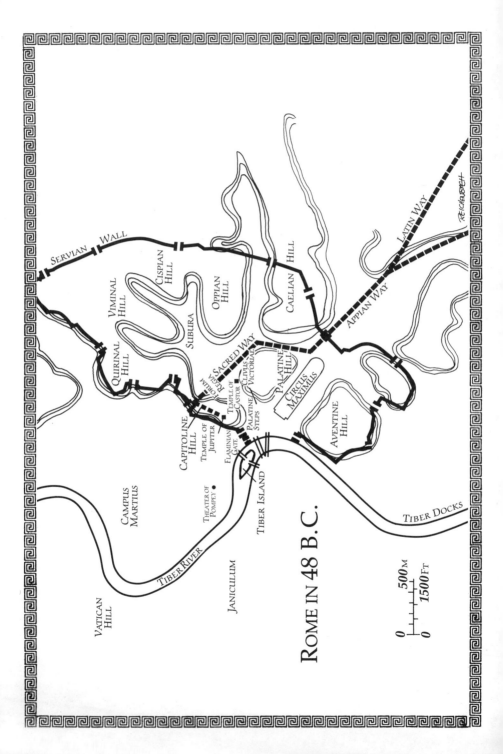

ROME IN 48 B.C.

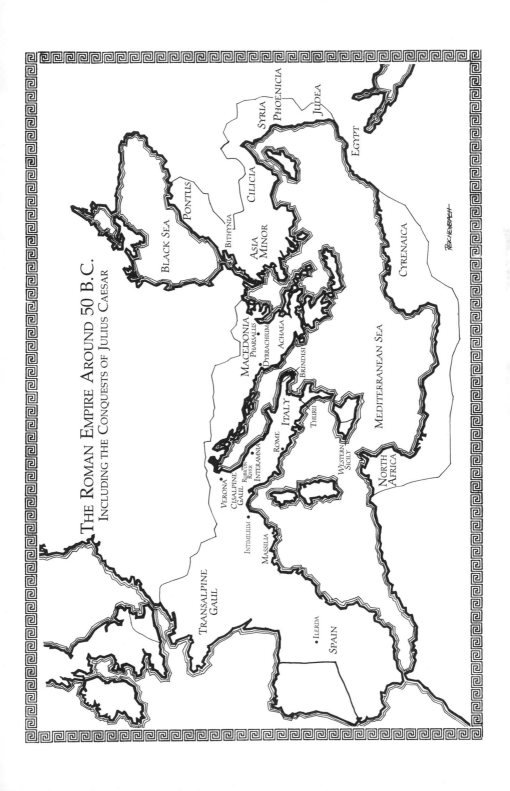

The Roman Empire Around 50 B.C.
Including the Conquests of Julius Caesar

TRANSALPINE GAUL

VERONA
CISALPINE GAUL
INTIMILIUM
MASSILIA
RUBICON RIVER
INTERAMNIA
ROME
ITALY
THURII
BRINDISI
WESTERN SICILY
NORTH AFRICA

ILERDA
SPAIN

MACEDONIA
PHARSALUS
DYRRACHIUM
ACHAEA

MEDITERRANEAN SEA

CYRENAICA

BLACK SEA
PONTUS
BITHYNIA
ASIA MINOR
CILICIA

SYRIA
PHOENICIA
JUDEA
EGYPT

BOOK ONE

This morning when we seized the town, I took this room for my headquarters. It used to be a guardroom, I believe, for it is perched above the municipal gate, and has views in two directions: one over the road, the other across the rooftops to the sea. It is perfectly adequate for my purposes, except that it is entirely empty. "Bring me a table and chair," I order.

The chief magistrate of the town, my prisoner now like everyone else within the city walls, nods violently over his twisting hands. "Very good, praetor. A table and chair."

"I must write a report."

The magistrate goes on talking, bobbing up and down and wiping away the sweat, but I am not listening. I am looking around the room. The sun comes in the windows, bringing with it the heat of an early October morning, the scent of stone baking in the sun, a faint, salt whisper of the sea. Overhead pigeons flutter with muted cries; from the street voices rise, so attenuated by the heat that I can barely hear them. I lean against the sun-dried window frame, and the silence that has surrounded me since I left Rome falls on me again.

The silence. It is true: around me a great stillness has fallen. It is as if sounds cannot reach me any more, as if I were removed from them—or they from me. Once in Rome an apartment house fell down. The noise was so great that for a long time after no one in that street could hear at all, and we went around signalling to one another by gestures, ambiguous and strange, through the dusty air. It is like that for me now. In Rome there was a vast noise. It covered the universe. And now everything is quiet around me, and what people do has little meaning. It isn't an unpleasant sensation, this silence. In fact, I rather enjoy it. There is peace in it. For a change.

In Rome there has been no peace for many years. There has been pulling and shouting, the clash of swords. Men are dead in the streets, and armies have assembled; there have been battles, bloodshed, cries, smells—noise. And the

3

fighting has spread, to Italy, to Spain, even as far as Greece, where two armies—two Roman armies—sit facing one another, across a void and a silence. We are waiting, we have been waiting for months, to hear the outcome. Until the news arrives, I do not seem to hear anything else.

In my time, Rome has produced great men—two of the greatest our country in its seven hundred years has ever seen. Gnaeus Pompeius Magnus, called Pompey the Great, and Gaius Julius Caesar. Conquerors, statesmen, patriots; rivals and colleagues, first one then the other, now they are pulling the city down around their ears in their haste to destroy one another. The noise of it was everywhere. My ears still ring, my eyes sting with the dust, my throat is parched. Yet in this dusty room it is quiet, and I will have a chance to think.

But not if the little magistrate has his way. "Praetor," he wails at me now, twisting his hands together as he surveys the dust-moted emptiness. "For your report? Wouldn't you prefer something better? Something more suitable? My house is at your disposal if you . . ."

"This is fine." I am not interested in the mewlings of an anxious provincial dignitary in a little town hundreds of miles from Rome. "This will do. In a civil war one cannot expect comforts."

"Yes, praetor."

"You have heard of the war here? Caesar? Pompey? All that?"

"Oh, yes, praetor, certainly." But I am by no means sure he has.

"Yes, well, if you will excuse me, I must write—"

"Yes, praetor." He is encouraged, his eyes take on a gleam of hope. A report is something he understands. "Praetor—" he ventures. "I—" But he has not quite the courage to ask me the obvious question. I can see him working himself up to it—he is thinking now, for instance, that I am young to be a praetor, and wondering if he can make something of that. I am young, thirty-four, instead of the normal forty required for the office, but he is wrong: there is no advantage to him in that fact.

I give him a grin that shows my teeth and he subsides into

his normal futility. "Yes, praetor. A table and a chair, as you asked. They are coming. For your report."

"That is satisfactory. Tell me, magistrate—" Again that hopeful light. Perhaps now I am going to divulge . . . ? But no. "Tell, me, magistrate. What is the name of this place?"

Dashed, he mutters, "It's called Thurii, praetor. It's quite an important town in this region. We have a valuable trade in pitch and timber, and the harbor is the best in Southern Italy. Or the best for a town of this size, anyway. . . ."

"Yes, yes. Well, a town as important as . . . what?"

"Thurii."

"Yes, Thurii. A town this big ought to have a garrison, shouldn't it?" I know it should, especially in the time of a war. It is not the kind of thing Julius Caesar overlooks.

A hit. Sweat starts out on the little man's forehead and his weak brown eyes look frightened, his jowls shake. "No, no. We haven't got anything like that. No garrison. You can search the place . . ." But he has no hope of concealing the terror that is turning his fat skin green.

"I have searched it," I say patiently. "My men have been through it from grain cellar to temple pediment. Remember?" I wave my hand toward the window, through which I can see my rag-bag of an army down below, making its bivouac in the dusty little square. "I know there's no garrison. What I *want* to know is why not?"

"Oh, praetor, I couldn't tell you that. Surely that's a decision for Rome? They wouldn't consult me about things like that, would they? I mean . . ." He's lying of course; I expected he would. I don't know quite why, however. He has something to conceal, this fat little creature. Well, he's not alone in that.

This provincial Solon is not as stupid as he looks. "Praetor," he says, still hopeful, "could you tell me . . . ? Who *are* your superiors? I mean . . . I mean, your report that you're going to write? May I ask, who is it for?"

Who is it for? A good question. In fact, another hit, this time for his side.

He knows it, too. Taking heart from his near strike he blurts out the rest of his problem. "Praetor," he cries. "*Which side are you on?*"

5

It is of course the most important question in a civil war.
And I have not known the answer since I left Rome.

There has been too much noise. In my life, there has been
too much. Perhaps in the silence of this place I will discover
the answer . . .

But there is to be no silence. No sooner have I thought
this than the door bangs open, the dust-motes leap and spin,
the little magistrate flings a glance of panic over his shoulder—what on earth is he concealing? I shall have to find out,
and soon. Suddenly the room is full of people. My staff, such
as it is—my freedman, Philo, a dark man with a harried look;
a runaway gladiator who serves as my military tribune—don't
laugh, he was the best I could do, and at least he had some
experience in the army—half a dozen senior centurions, a
clerk with a writing board and stylus, trying to take notes; a
servant trying equally assiduously to remove my travel-
stained cloak and the dust from my boots. Also, four of the
ten members of the town council; a distinguished philosopher—or what passes for one in a place like this—the flamen
from the Temple of Jupiter in the forum down below; and
a retired military tribune who fought with Marius a generation ago and who is therefore the town's expert on anything
military. Three slaves are struggling through the crowd with
a plain wooden kitchen table which they set in the middle of
the floor. A fourth places a beautiful antique ebony chair
behind it. Every one of these people is shouting at the top
of his voice—the philosopher in Greek—waving his arms,
shrugging, gesturing, milling around.

"Get out," I tell them, to a chorus of protests. "But *praetor*
. . . the baggage wagons . . . the issue of grain for the noon-
day meal . . . the hostages from the town . . . the duties of
the Truly Wise Man . . . the time we invested a town on the
Po. . . ."

"Out," I say again, this time slightly raising my voice. "I
must write. I have a report to make." There is a sudden quiet
as if a theater full of people had turned to stare at me. In a
surprisingly short time the room is clear and I am alone with
the sunlight and the dust-motes, the birds on the summer air.

I like this empty room, with its unfinished wooden walls and the names of the young men who served in the guard carved into them, its unswept floor patched with sunshine from the translucent sky outside . . . Through the window I can see the town. From here it is no more than a collection of roofs in every color that tile can take: rose, ivory, amber, garnet, rust, falling in a long, arrested tumble down to the swept blue curve of the sea. The shadows hug the walls, unwilling to venture further into the empty morning streets, the fountain plays alone in the sunny little forum. Pigeons fly up, the sunlight on their turning wings; a squad of my soldiers marches through, raising the dust near the temple . . . So this is Thurii, my possession.

Closer at hand, on the other side, is the road. It passes under the wall, just beneath my window. Its heavy white stones, slow and rutted, are thick with dust, but as it slips away, it gains momentum. Out past a clump of straggling oaks wilting in the heat, it picks up speed sliding through the dark blue shadows as if they were a pool of water, out into the golden fields, the tarnished silver olive groves, heading for the forests and the mountain slopes to the north. As the road runs it gathers speed. It leaps a gully on a single stony foot and stretches itself out, lean and empty, racing over the countryside towards the place where the sky comes down to meet the earth. There it joins the highway, the Via Appia, and disappears, free at last, on its long journey north to Rome. Rome . . .

The silence. The summer air. The sea.

I have drawn a piece of paper toward me, over the nicks and scars of the kitchen table. I must write. And it must be paper, not the wax boards used for notes, for this is an official document—as official, I suppose as any in my life. Though to whom I ought to address it I do not have the least idea.

Once there was a man who would have cared. Gaius Julius Caesar, the most remarkable man I ever met . . . Well, enough of that. He is not the only man in the world who might have wanted to know what has become of me. I have friends, I even have enemies, who would want to hear from me. There

7

are the boys I grew up with, the men I served or served under, and the ones I fought against: I could write for them. But most of them are dead in this terrible war. And the others . . . ? I cannot tell. Scattered, discredited, destroyed, or gone on to be heroes and remembered forever. I do not know. It is part of the silence that surrounds me that I can get no news.

The thing to do is to write my report, beginning at the beginning and leaving nothing out. Perhaps in the end it will show which side I am on.

And in the meantime, writing itself will be enough. It has its own reality, its own rewards. For instance, the paper they have given me is beautiful, made from papyrus as soft as new leather and thick as cream. A few threads at the edges glow where they catch the sunlight. It is an object of the same order of beauty as the plain bare room, the kitchen table, the shapes and colors of the parched landscape outside. It is a long time since I have had a chance to notice such things.

The shadow of wings tumbles across the paper, a drift of air floats through the window, bringing with it the vast, drowsy hum of the summer morning, I must make my report. There will be time enough later to decide who it is for.

DOCUMENT APPENDED

THURII   OCTOBER 1, 706 YEARS FROM THE FOUNDING OF THE CITY

REPORT OF MARCUS CAELIUS RUFUS PRAETOR PEREGRINUS OF ROME

No, that's wrong.

LAST REPORT OF MARCUS CAELIUS RUFUS PRAETOR PEREGRINUS OF ROME . . .

I

Someone laughed in the dark under the archway. "Shut up," another voice said and the laughter died away. I heard Clodius swear.

"What's the matter, darling?" the first voice continued. It was my cousin Catullus', rusty on the cold night air. "Is your dress too tight?"

"By the Dog," Clodius mumbled, but a drift of music from the building silenced him. I looked out into the Forum where the first brightness of the sky had extinguished the stars, though it had so far failed to reveal the earth below. A breeze had begun to blow off the Tiber, bringing the smell of silt and damp, chilly stone. I felt cold and sober, robbed of the wine I had drunk during the evening. A sadness as of loss gripped me, and I wandered a few steps into the open space. "If we're going to get him into the festival, you'd better hurry," I said over my shoulder. "It's almost dawn." From the house behind the archway the music came constantly, a thread of sound over the muffled rumble of the drum. "The women must be getting ready for the sacrifice in there," I urged them, rubbing the stubble on my chin. I wouldn't mind a bath, I thought. It had already been a long evening.

"By the Dog, I'd like to know what they're doing now," Clodius hiccupped. He was standing in front of me—weaving a bit, it was true—looking at me with ludicrous solemnity out of his large black eyes. I could just make them out, hollows in the pale oval of his face, his mouth another. He had his finger over his lips to warn me to be quiet, but he was trying to talk around it. "No one's allowed to know what the women do in there on the night of the feshtival."

"But you're going to find out, aren't you, darling?" Catullus said, coming up beside me. "How does he look?"

The light in the sky must have been growing, though I

9

could see no difference in the slow seep of grayness overhead, but against the east now I could make out the roof of the Temple of Castor, and when I looked down, there was Clodius in a woman's dress.

"Great Gods," I said.

"He'll be better when we get the wig on—put it on, will you? Good. See?" Catullus passed me the wine jar he had had the foresight to bring with him, and I felt better at once. The wine did not seem to reach my stomach at all, but to go directly to my head. I laughed. "The Pontifex Maximus' wife is going to love him," I said, and drank some more.

"She already does," Clodius boasted. "Point of the whole operation." He closed his eyes and shook his head, but he was so drunk he forgot he was making these gestures and while he talked his eyes remained closed and his head went on bobbing. "They're having a feshtival there. Women's goddessh. All the men have to leave—even the slaves. Good time for me. Opportunity. Won't meet her husband in the atrium, see?"

"Yes," I said. "We know." I was laughing. We had arranged this in a bar after a party. To Catullus I said, "He does look pretty good. You think he'll pass? That wig . . ." It was strange how completely the wig disguised him; he really did look like a woman. He was a grown man—nearly thirty as far as I could tell, which made him almost ten years older than I— but he was short and slight. That helped his disguise, I suppose. I could never have gotten away with it myself, for I am tall and strongly built. But it was more than that—there was something strange about Clodius. The dress did not create it, it only seemed to bring it out.

"He'll do just fine, won't you, darling?" Catullus was crooning in his grating voice. I could see that he recognized Clodius' ambiguous character, too.

"There'll be a lot of women in there." I was thinking how unreliable—and how drunk—Clodius looked. "I mean, do you think it's a good idea? It's not just his girl-friend, you know, but her husband's female connections—the whole clan, I wouldn't be surprised. Plus the maids, the musicians—"

"The musicians!" Catullus cried, hunting busily around him. He seemed to wink in and out of the darkness of the arches on the Pontifex Maximus' house. Clodius, muttering, lurched back and forth on his feet. "You're not going to fall down, are you?" I asked, making a grab for his arm.

"There." Catullus reappeared and shoved a lyre into Clodius' hands. The strings gave out a startled cry of protest. "All set then? Let's go." He took Clodius' arm, gesturing me to take the other. We led him back under the darkness toward the music, but he shook us off. "Go alone. Perfectly shober now."

"Come on." Catullus dug his elbow into my ribs to force me to be quiet, for the door was opening. The light from inside spilled out toward us, making the darkness around it deeper, but showing Clodius in its brilliant glow. His slim figure looked graceful and feminine in its flame-colored dress, his head under the saffron-dyed wig was as proud and delicate as a statue's. He turned and I saw his profile. "Great gods," I whispered to Catullus. "He's a handsome man." Even the wig could not disguise that: his skin was white, his eyes black; his features were arrogant and aristocratic and stamped with so pure a beauty that this little prank all of a sudden seemed silly and rather tawdry.

Catullus at my shoulder gave me his irregular grin. "Nice for the Pontifex Maximus' wife."

Clodius had disappeared into the doorway to the sound of flutes and finger-cymbals. "Like the god Dionysus," I said, and Catullus nudged me again in the ribs. "Yes. And he's escorted by two drunken satyrs, just as in the traditional pictures." He laughed and handed me the wine-jar. It was a big one. He must have persuaded the bartender to part with half the evening's supply. Clever Catullus. Holding it in my arms very carefully I wandered into the Forum.

The sky had lightened again, and the buildings, as if dawn were creating them, appeared as unfinished shapes against the gray. The air was very cold, and I could hear the rattle of leaves in some laurel bushes nearby, the first startled cheep of a sparrow waking under the eaves. Catullus leaned against a pillar, his arms crossed on his chest, his head back. He had a wrestler's stocky body, with heavy muscles dragging down his neck, and forearms that looked bunched and layered. His face was no more than a cluster of ill-assorted features, but his forehead was intelligent and his mouth sensitive. He was twenty-one, two years older than I, and while I had not yet grown into my height and was still awkward sometimes, he was already a man.

He was also either asleep on his feet or deeply absorbed in thought. He did that often—disappeared into himself— even in the middle of a discussion. I wondered what he was thinking of, but his face gave no indication. I sighed and drank some more wine.

"The Forum of Rome," I said, drawing in my breath. I don't know why it moved me, for it was scarcely more at that moment than a sense of space opening out around me, a touch of cold air, a gauzy drift of breeze. All the same I walked out into it with a feeling of elation. The gray in the sky had spread and imperceptibly deepened into a rich wine-blue. Shapes of buildings, recognizable now, were cut against it out of some substance not like stucco and stone but cool, liquid, and dark. wavering on the point of disappearing back into the night, like reflections on black water. I thought if I touched them my hand might pass right through; I even laid my palm on the stone of the Pontifex Maximus' house and was surprised to discover that it was as warm and rough-textured as an animal's hide.

I stepped out farther, hugging the wine-jar to me like a baby. I was a little uncertain on my feet and thought I might drop it. It seemed a sad thought. "Here," I muttered. "I've got you. Don't worry, I won't let you fall."

Out in the open Forum the air was still quiet with the silence of night, made as it is of small, distant sounds: the murmur of water tumbling into a fountain, the whisper of leaves, a low thrumming of the wind passing among the columns of a temple porch. But in the side streets it was almost morning. I could hear footsteps on the stones as someone hurried to be the first to wait on his patron; a baker rolled back the shutter of his shop, releasing the smell of bread into the air; smoke from the morning sacrifice eddied out into the darkness, stinging my noise with the pungent cleanliness of incense.

A voice spoke near at hand, and I turned to look at Catullus, but it had not been his. He was leaning where I had left him, a dim shape in the darkness of the archway. His eyes were still closed, and I wondered if he knew how to sleep on his feet, like a horse. It would not have surprised me. He knew a lot of things, a fact which I envied. He was my distant cousin, but we did not, at that moment, seem very much alike.

The voice spoke again. I whirled around, still clutching the wine-jar. Catching myself off balance, I tripped and stumbled against someone, falling heavily on top of him. He thrashed under me like a fish; I could feel the hard bone of his hips grind against mine. I hugged the wine-jar tighter. "Herc, what do you think you're doing?" I bellowed, but his legs were tangled with mine, his elbow punched in an undirected way at my mouth.

"Ouf," he said as the breath went out of his lungs. Immediately other hands gripped my arms, pulling me upright. I caught the bluish shine on the edge of a helmet, the blackened flash of a crimson cape. "Great Gods!" I cried. "Lictors!" I had knocked down a magistrate of some kind. I tried to lean down and see who it was, but the hands tightened on my arms, digging into the muscles so that I winced. "Hey, watch out," I protested. "You'll make me drop the wine."

"Name?" a second lictor demanded, planting himself in front of me in a threatening way. He carried his bundle of rods; he was fingering it, waiting for the order to take one out and beat me. I tensed my shoulders, but the arms holding mine did not relax their grip. "Name?" the lictor repeated.

From the ground their magistrate said: "That's all right, Andreius. It was an accident. Let him go."

They were well-trained, these official bodyguards. Immediately they released me and stepped back a pace or two. "I'm sorry," the man in front of me said, "but this is the City Praetor. I thought you might be trying something. The light's poor and I didn't see you were . . ."

"I am a Roman knight, a member of the Equestrian Order," I said, feeling I might burst with anger. "My name is Marcus Caelius Rufus. If you have any questions to ask me—"

"No, no. Sorry."

"Marcus Caelius Rufus, is it?" the magistrate said, getting up from the ground. He dusted himself down, taking a lot of time over it. I could see he was a tall man, handsome and slender, and very elegantly dressed. I thought he looked about forty years old. He looked annoyed, too, as I suppose he had a right to be, but he spoke to me kindly. "So, Marcus Caelius Rufus is your name?"

"Yes. And my father is a knight, really. He's a wheat and grain broker here in Rome. We're from Interamnia, over the mountains . . ."

"I know Interamnia. And you live here, in the city, yourself?"

Yes. I'm studying here."

"Oh?" He raised one eyebrow, I stared at him, wishing I could do that.

"Yes. With Marcus Tullius Cicero, and with Marcus Licinius Crassus . . ." I was trying to knock him down again with these respectable, not to say distinguished, names, though in truth I had not been anyone's pupil for a while. I had left my principal teacher Cicero's care, and gone back to my father's house on the Oppian Hill—a fact I was not going to mention to this magistrate, whoever he was.

He did not seem overly impressed by these sponsors in any case. "How old are you, Marcus Caelius Rufus?"

"Twenty. But I'll be twenty-one in a few months . . ."

He smiled. "Twenty is a good enough age. You don't have to be in a hurry. Is there any wine left in that jar?"

I passed it to him, and he drank. I could see the strong, fluid muscles moving in his throat. "So. You drink your wine neat, Caelius Rufus?"

"We were on our way home from a party. I was going to give this to . . . to my . . ." I cast around for someone who might plausibly receive a gift from me.

"To your parents, of course. Isn't that nice? But you don't seem to have left much for them."

"Well, my . . . my friends and I had some on the way . . ."

He laughed. The growing light showed him to me clearly now; a man of about my own height with a long face, broad at the cheekbones and hollow over the temples. The early breeze lifted his thin, pale hair and he smoothed it hastily. I could see that he was a man who cared about his appearance, for his toga gleamed like thin milk in the bluish light and

14

the tunic beneath it had elegant long sleeves embroidered half a foot deep with purple and gold.

"Your friends," he said. It was not a question and I did not answer. I was fingering the hem of my own tunic, wondering where he had gotten that embroidery done.

He took the wine-jar again. "What are you doing at the Pontifex Maximus' house at this hour of the morning? Here, have some wine. He's not at home now, is he?"

"No, he's not home. At least I hope he's not. It's the festival of the Women's Goddess. Men aren't allowed in the house at all."

"That's right." The first true daylight was slanting into the Forum, showing the pale, lemon color of his hair and touching the corner of his dark brown eye. "Well," he said, "if the Pontifex Maximus isn't at home, what are you doing at his house?"

There were people in the Forum now: artisans on their way to open their shops or hurrying to their patrons, school-children escorted by their pedagogues with bundles of books and stacks of wax tablets, servants from the big houses chattering in groups, waiting for the markets to open. Here and there a lantern still gleamed in the shadows, but overhead the sky was full of winter color. A flight of pigeons crossed it; the statues on the roof of the Temple of Capitoline Jupiter gave it back in beams of gold. Excited and happy and still quite drunk I suppose, I said, "A friend of mine is visiting his lady friend in the house."

"Really? But I thought you told me no men were allowed in there tonight."

"Hah, that's the beauty of it." I was nearly doubled over with laughter. "He's disguised as a woman."

Behind me one of the lictors stamped his feet restively and the laughter died on my lips. "Good gods, " I mumbled. "I . . . I . . ."

I looked up to see the praetor grinning at me. "Disguised as a woman? Who's his friend? One of the maids?"

A sheep is as good as lamb. "The Pontifex Maximus' wife," I said.

"No." He had fine, clear skin except that a scarlet flush had appeared across the cheekbones. I thought he might be angry, but he was smiling at me, and I liked him very much. "Oh, yes, the Pontifex Maximus' wife," I assured him.

"That will be news to the Pontifex Maximus," he said. I laughed. I was going to dig him in the ribs with my elbow, but at the last moment remembered the wine-jar and clutched it tighter instead. He winked at me. "And who's her lover?"

"A man called Publius Clodius Pulcher. We met him in a bar tonight. He says she's in love with him."

"Is she indeed?" He straightened his toga, preparing to go. His lictors stood to attention, watching him under their shiny bronze helmets.

"Well, Marcus Caelius Rufus, if you ever need anything, come and see me. You understand what I'm saying. I'd be glad to help—"

I did understand. He was offering to make me his client, if I felt the need of another patron. "Thank you," I said, genuinely grateful. He was, after all, the City Praetor.

"And try to keep this business quiet, will you? After all, a scandal about the chief religious officer of the state isn't going to do anybody any good. No bragging in bars, or—"

Under the archway from the house a confused noise was issuing. Women's voices in it, raised in cries of anger or fear, followed by a loud thump or slam. I saw Catullus open his eyes and duck quickly out of sight behind a pillar.

"You'd better attend to that," the City Praetor said, but he stood a moment longer beside me, watching as the door flew open and Publius Clodius, his yellow dress half torn from his body and flying in rags around his shoulders, shot out into the archway. His wig was dangling from his ear, his lyre was gone. He panted, looking once behind him, but he had slammed the door and the women, in their panic and confusion, were having trouble getting it open again. He turned, and seeing me, waved his arms. "Run," he screamed. He made a grab for his wig and darted past me.

"Goodbye," I shouted to the City Praetor and dashed after Clodius. Behind me I heard the tramp of the lictors departing, but the sound was swallowed by the voices of the women, now pouring into the Forum, shouting after Clodius and me.

The sun was up. We dodged through long, slanting bars of light and cold blue shadow, around the circular Temple of Vesta. I could hear the priestesses inside and smell the smoke of their altar fire. "Wait," I shouted after Clodius, but he did not seem to hear.

I jolted along after him, the wine-jar impeding me. Near the Temple of Castor a crowd of about a hundred men was escorting a senator toward the Curia. It slowed Clodius down, and on its fringes I managed to catch up with him. He gave me a startled look from under his long, black lashes. "I thought you were arrested. Where's your friend Catullus? They take him too?"

I explained about the man I knocked down. "It's all right. The praetor was very nice about it. I told him about your affair with the Pontifex Maximus' wife, and he just laughed."

Clodius was leaning against the steps of the Temple of Castor, catching his breath. Above us, the Palatine Hill rose in green pines and grape-blue shadows, I could see the corner of a wall, its yellow stone basking in the sun and some rich man's prized palm tree rattling in forlorn magnificence in the garden behind.

"Do you know who that was that you ran into?" Clodius demanded. He swore at me, a vile stream of words out of his beautiful, feminine mouth. He didn't seem to be drunk any more. My fingers clenched. He was small, hardly up to my shoulder, it would be dishonorable to knock him down. "Of course I know," I sneered. "His lictors told me. He's the City Praetor."

Clodius laughed bitterly; he was cursing me again. "That's right. He's the City Praetor. His name is Gaius Julius Caesar. He's the Pontifex Maximus, too."

"The what?"

"He's the Pontifex Maximus," he repeated, blinking his black eyes wearily at my stupidity.

"Great gods," I cried, and dropped the wine-jar.

**LAST REPORT OF MARCUS CAELIUS RUFUS
PRAETOR PEREGRINUS OF ROME ...**

That was how it began: three young men dodging through

the Forum in the frosty sunlight of a December morning, nearly fifteen years ago: Catullus, the rusty-haired poet from Verona; the drunken, and though I did not know it then, dangerous, Clodius; and me, Marcus Caelius Rufus. Not one of us was much more than twenty, and we were out for a good time. And now two of us are dead, ashes in a vault somewhere, blind to the beauty of the morning, all warmth and laughter gone. Dead. How long can it be before I join them?

REPORT . . .

And for whom?

I have been outside. The glare dazzled me, the heat beat down on my head. In the streets the sun redoubled, reflecting off the pavement and the walls. It was like walking through a village of bronze. On the hot air the odors of the town lay in patches, never mingling: the smell of wet paving near the fountain, a garden nearly gone to dust with its roses and its herbs. From behind a shuttered window a woman's perfume; from another, garlic, oil, pepper, wine. A small town, provincial and quiet. Behind its doors it is waiting . . .

Near the main gate I found a disturbance. One of my soldiers had accosted a woman. Her father or perhaps her husband was protesting while the soldier thrust her behind his back. She had modestly drawn her cloak over her face, but her eyes were wide with terror. I had to laugh at her man, a tiny pigeon-breasted creature, but brave, waving his fist under the nose of the legionary and shouting at the top of his voice. The soldier, growing hotter, was reaching for his sword.

He looked, like most of my troops, ragged and unprofessional, dressed in some old leather bits and pieces his grandfather must have taken off an Iberian chieftain in Spain or Gaul, with, by the gods, a handful of feathers stuck in his helmet—which was African. He had a hard, uncivilized look on the edge of an outbreak—I have a number of the roughest kind of ex-slaves, herdsmen and runaway gladiators among my troops, and I guessed that this man was one of them, though I could see no brand to be sure. He had neglected to shave, and his hands were dirty, but when he saw me he drew himself up in a well-meant but poorly executed attempt at military smartness.

"What's going on here?"

The soldier, nearly mutinous, began to explain. Seeing me, the woman's diminutive companion cut in. "Oh, I'm glad you're here. This lout has tried to seize my wife. Order him to let her go. A respectable matron. I don't know what the army is coming to . . ."

"You misunderstand the situation," I said to the man. I was in a hurry; my business there was urgent. "This is not a training exercise; this is a civil war. My troops have invested this town." I nodded to the soldier. "It is theirs. If they want a woman, they'll take one. Is that clear?"

The man's face went white and the woman started to cry. At the gate the rest of the guard was laughing; my gladiator, who was still standing at some kind of attention, looked at me with new respect. "Furthermore, I gave orders that you people were to stay indoors. If you can't keep your women at home during a siege, you have only yourselves to blame."

I shoved him aside and started for the gate, but he fell on his knees in the dust, moaning and gabbling. "If he doesn't shut up, run him through," I said, disgusted at this display.

"Yes," the legionary cried, but as I went I saw him thrust the woman at her husband with a gesture of irritation. Laughing, I passed out onto the road under the skimpy shade of the trees.

There the scouts were waiting for me, a rabble of tired and dusty men, locals whom I had engaged to patrol the roads and bring back a report of movement in the area. Now they stood holding their exhausted horses in the golden dusk of the shadow of the wall.

"Well?" I was still worried about that absent garrison.

They didn't want to tell me, that much was plain. Their eyes went everywhere—the white stones, gleaming ferociously in the heat, the landscape shimmering under the brutal sun. I said gently, "If you tell me, then we'll both know."

They rustled like leaves in the boiling air, but no one spoke. I waited. Finally the head scout said, "Praetor, there's an army on the road. It's coming this way."

"An army? Are you sure?" A foolish question: an army is not the sort of thing anyone misunderstands. The scout, in fact, did not answer.

"Well," I said after a pause. "How many men?"

"A detachment of cavalry," he admitted uneasily.

It was like questioning a slave on the rack, though I don't know which of us was suffering more. "A hundred men, would you say? Something like that?" My army, rough and ill-trained as it is, can handle a hundred horsemen . . .

"More, praetor. A lot more. I don't know how many exactly."

"Veterans?"

"Yes, praetor. Very well trained and completely equipped. From Spain and Gaul. Roman troops, though. I am sure of that. Roman troops are unmistakable . . ."

Roman cavalry, well-trained and well equipped. I doubt he could have brought me worse news. "Whose cavalry is it? Milo's? Pompey's?"

I was wrong. There was worse news.

"Caesar's," he said.

Caesar's. Of course. "Where are they?"

"On the Via Appia."

"Coming this way?"

"Yes, praetor. They're being sent to garrison this town. Replacements for the troops that were here before."

"So there was a garrison here before?"

Their eyes gleam like mercury in the heat. "Yes, praetor. There was."

The little magistrate had a secret after all. No wonder he was sweating. I can feel the dampness start out on my own body. A garrison of Spanish veteran cavalry. On its way here.

"How long do we have?"

He does not like me to put is so bluntly. "Oh, praetor . . ."

"How long?"

"About a day, or—"

"Or a little less?"

"Dawn tomorrow," he whispers. "Not later than that."

On the way back I ordered the guards at the town gate to close the huge double leaves. "No one is to go in or out," I told them. It was a precaution to keep the fact of our being here a secret as long as possible. I don't suppose it will make any difference, but it never does to neglect any detail. I climbed the stairs to my room, thinking of this. It never does to neglect any detail . . . I know where I learned that, and who I learned it from.

The grateful silence of my room, the golden motes, the hot, still air. The paper is waiting for me, and the voices from the past . . .

LAST REPORT OF MARCUS CAELIUS RUFUS . . .

That was the beginning. Three young men in the Forum, the Pontifex Maximus, the long, cool sunshine of the breaking dawn. In a way it was the beginning for all of us, though I did not find that out for some time. For Catullus that was the day he found the woman he loved for the rest of his life, for Clodius the day he first confronted his most implacable opponent. For me, who met Caesar that morning—well, I suppose that whether it was friend or enemy that I met still remains to be seen.

All I knew then was that I was running, flying down an alley between large villas and high garden walls, somewhere at the top of the Palatine Hill. I was laughing out loud at the thought of the Pontifex Maximus' face. Water from a gutter splashed up around my feet, a dog barked, a servant came out of a house and emptied a bucket of slops. Down the way in front of me, between the blue shadow of one wall and the sunlit gold of another, two figures dashed, one in a white tunic, one in a yellow dress.

"Why are we running?" I panted, coming up to them. "Is someone after us?"

They had opened a door in one of the walls. Inside, a woman's voice said a word I didn't hear. I caught a glimpse of a garden—white paths and winter shrubs, a row of cy-

21

presses . . . Clodius, tipping his wig over one eye, slipped
inside and disappeared into greenness.

"His sister's house," Catullus said, giving me a grin as he
prepared to follow.

"Wait. What's happening?"

He shrugged. "Who cares? It's fun. Come on."

"You know there may be repercussions about this."

He pursed his lips dubiously. "What do you care if there
are?"

"He knows who I am. There'll be trouble . . ."

The garden was more important to him; I had to put my
hand on his arm to keep him back. "Just think for a moment.
People are going to know about this . . ."

"Thanks to you."

"All right. All right. But it's done now, and we have to
think of the future. There might be a prosecution. Did you
ever think of that? We need an alibi . . ."

From inside the garden the woman spoke again. Catullus
seemed to tremble as if a chill had gone through him. His
rather battered face lifted, his gray eyes shone. He leaned a
little toward the open door.

"Come away from there," I said. "We've got to figure out
what to do."

"Clodius isn't worried."

"No, why should he be? He's an aristocrat, a member of
the Claudian family. Do you know who they are? He's related
by birth or marriage to just about everyone of importance
in the entire city. Do you think anyone will bother him? Of
course not. But we're not in the same position. We're out-
siders, from provincial towns . . ."

"We have connections too," he objected. He came from the
provincial aristocracy; he knew people. But for me it was
different. My father was a grain broker, and a knight.

"But your father has friends," he said. "You could ask them
for help."

"My father!" That was a thought. Cold, distant, preoccupied with making money—when I was little I had thought
him as tall as the statue of Jupiter in the Temple at home.
Even now, it wouldn't have surprised me to learn that he was
hollow and made out of bronze as well.

"All right. Not your father, then," he conceded. "Someone else." He was nearly dancing with impatience.

"Who?" I shouted, but he was not listening. Giving me a distracted grin, he slipped into the garden.

I looked at the open doorway a moment longer. Then I turned and ran down the alley to where another passage cut into it. I had remembered another door. And an alibi.

in all my toys, and set them where I could see them. All the same, when the pedagogue lit the lamp and left me alone, I felt like a prisoner, abandoned and condemned. One of the maids brought me my dinner and gave me a kiss, and another came to be sure I was in bed at the right time. I cried a little when she left, for she blew out the lamp and I had to lie in darkness—a thing which had never happened to me before.

I stayed awake a long time, waiting for something, I don't know what. Not my mother—I had no hope there. Not my father—that would have been worse than nothing. A hero, I thought. A great bronze man out of Homer with a sword, and a shield that covered him from his shoulder to his knee. He would run them through—all of them. Then they would know. My father especially. He would learn . . . But I had no idea what adults knew and what it was my father might change . . .

Or perhaps it would be a bear that came, down out of the mountains. A huge furry creature with bright, kind eyes and long claws. He would snatch me up and take me back with him. I would live in his cave, on berries and spring water and do what I pleased. My mother would be sorry when I was gone.

The door opened, the line of light widening into a triangle and rising to fall across the bed. A figure blocked it and I thought for a moment that the bear had really come. But it was Crito, the pedagogue, carrying a small clay lamp. He set it on the shelf and sat down on the bed, looking at me with mild dark brown eyes under a fall of silver hair.

"Trouble getting to sleep, Marcus?" he asked. He put his hand on my arm, stroking me gently. It felt warm and friendly, as if it anchored me to safety. He smiled, and the silver hair glinted in the light. "It happens sometimes." His hand went on, over my shoulder, my neck, my chest. "Don't worry," he said. "Everything is all right." He moved his hand along my ribs, and his dark eyes smiled kindly. His hand slid lower and rested for a moment on my penis. it made me uncomfortable, and I flinched away. "All right, Marcus," he said in his gentle voice. "It's all right. I won't do that if you don't like it."

"No," I murmured, but his hand was warm and soothing, and outside the circle of light it was very dark. Presently I allowed him to touch me there again.

After that I do not remember any more. I fell asleep, I think, to the rhythmic movement of his caress.

So passed my seventh birthday. The next day I went to school.

Until that time—I have almost written "Until the end of my childhood," as perhaps it was—the idea of money had never come into my head. I had heard adults talk about it of course, and an uncle of mine—Catullus' father as a matter of fact—had given me some silver denarii for a present. But of money in the larger sense, of richer or poorer, plebeian or knight, I had not the smallest notion. I knew, of course, that we Caelii were knights, but I think it meant no more to me than to say that we were free men. In the stories that my mother read to me such things did not figure, and I suppose my parents did not discuss money in front of me. In my innocence I would have said that it did not matter very much. Well, that it did was the first and most lasting lesson I learned when I went to school.

The morning after my birthday, Crito came to wake me. I put on my clothes under his vague and gentle eye, and gobbled down the porridge he had brought for me. It was still dark when we left the house, though I could feel that it was going to be a beautiful morning. It was near the end of May. Crito carried a lantern and a bag with writing materials and books, and walked two paces behind me. I was excited to be out, away from the house, so early, and alone: everything seemed delicious to me, the cool touch of the air under my thin toga, the powdery dust on my bare feet . . .

The school was a room built into the wall of a house. It jutted out into the narrow street near the center of town. Next to it was an entry to the habitation behind, beyond that a bakery giving out a smell of fresh bread so that my mouth watered with hunger. My parents did not believe in overfeeding children. The fourth wall of the school was open to the street. The boys were waiting outside, their servants in a cluster behind them. They had games and toys I had never seen before: carved wooden boats to sail in the gutters, jointed dolls on strings, small bronze horsemen and soldiers. They stopped their play and looked up as I approached. A big boy stepped forward and put his hands on his hips. "Who are you?"

"Marcus Caelius Rufus."

"And your father?" another flung out from this big boy's shadow.

"My father is Marcus Caelius Rufus, too," I said, innocent and proud.

"No, he's not," the first boy asserted.

"He's not?" I couldn't understand what he meant, but his confidence overwhelmed me, and I was already uncertain.

"There's only one Caelius Rufus in this town," the big boy said. "He owns the grain brokerage. He's a rich man. There's a warehouse on Pomegranate Street, and an office near the Temple of Jupiter that belongs to him."

"That's my father's," I said eagerly, glad to have impressed this large and competent boy. I wonder now how old he was. Twelve? Fourteen? I thought he was a man, as old as my father, or the friends who came for dinner parties.

"He's not your father," the big boy insisted. "He's rich. He has enough money to get himself listed as a knight. You're poor." He touched a fold of my toga. "Threadbare," he snorted with contempt. "And you have only one servant."

"How many do you have?" I felt borne down to the ground by his certainties.

"A pedagogue, a boy to carry the boards and styluses, another for the lantern, a fourth to wait on them and serve us the lunch."

"Oh," I said.

"You aren't wearing any shoes." This last he said in a terrible voice, as if it were the most convincing proof of all. I began to cry.

"I *am* Marcus Caelius Rufus," I wept. "My father *is*—"

"Your father is nobody. And you're a little liar, that's who you are." The other boys, all of whom had stopped whatever they were doing to watch this, burst out laughing.

"*No,*" I shrieked. "I'm telling the truth."

They gazed at me wide eyed, surprised, I imagine at my

vehemence, but I was desperate with fear. I could not imagine what they were talking about, except that there was something wrong. My clothes, my servant . . . My father was not my father, and I had told a lie . . .

"Perhaps he is telling the truth," a smaller boy ventured, timid and well-meaning.

"Yes," the big one said. "Caelius Rufus got him on some freedwoman and is training him to be a clerk or some such thing . . ."

At this they all laughed again. I stood in front of them sobbing now uncontrollably, silenced by a shame I could not understand. When I look back on it now, I still do not grasp what was quite so amusing. They must have known perfectly well who I was—my name certainly showed them that I was the child of my father's legitimate marriage, and my mother's people were very well-known in Interamnia. Perhaps it is only that anything different and new seems laughable. Perhaps they would have mocked any boy who appeared among them. And again, I really was remarkably badly dressed and outfitted, by any standard, let alone those normal for the son of a knight.

I do not remember the rest of the day. When we got home the pedagogue unrolled my books on a table in the garden and set me to work on the lesson, but he was a lax old creature, and did not pay much attention. Presently I got up and wandered away to find my father. He was in his study, going through a roll of accounts with his secretaries; he looked up briefly.

"Hello, Marcus. Back from school already? How was it?"

I had no hope of telling him. "Father," I blurted out, my heart squeezing in terror. "Are we poor?"

"Poor?" he looked down at the roll of accounts and his mouth tightened. "We're doing well enough. Why do you ask?"

"The boys said. Father, I don't have any shoes. And they said my toga was . . . something. And I have only one servant, and no boats or soldiers or anything like that . . ."

He held up his hand to stop me. His face had closed and his voice, when it came, was angry. "I do not care for the kind of ostentation you're talking about, Marcus. That kind of showing off about money. I never wore shoes to school, even in winter. Neither did my father, and his father before him. It is against our traditions. The Roman way is simple and plain. All this luxury and idleness are destroying our country. I will have nothing to do with them, is that clear?"

Very little about it made any sense to me at all, but I understood that once again I had angered him, though once again, I did not know how . . . "Father," I muttered, looking down at the floor, "am I going to be trained for a clerk or something like that?"

"We'll see, Marcus. Don't bother me now. I have work to do, if we're not going to be as poor as you think we are. Run along now. I'm sure you have lessons to do."

I must have been the ideal subject for teasing, for the boys at school did not give up. Every morning they waited for me: as soon as the servants' backs were turned, they began. They called me "The Clerk" and "The Freedwoman's Son," and they mocked me for my poverty. I answered them as well as I could, shouting all the epithets that I had ever heard in the servants' hall and inventing others, but I was still very young, and my childish voice could do little to protect me from them.

I began to dread going to school; I had nightmares that woke me long before dawn and I was too nervous to eat breakfast. My mother was concerned and summoned a doctor, who probed me with gentle fingers and soft questions and patted me on the head when he left. After that my father called me into his study.

"Marcus," he said after some hesitation. "Is it true that you don't like school?"

His voice was sad and kind, and I answered honestly. "Oh, father, it's horrible. I hate it."

"I see. You're certainly not doing as well as I expected there."

"No." It was true. My problems with the boys kept me from concentrating on the lessons, and because I slept badly I was always tired.

"What's the matter? You're not a stupid boy. You should be a good student." His voice was still kind, but he had drawn his brows down in a terrifying frown. I saw I had displeased him again, and I stared at him helplessly.

"Look, Marcus. You are a Roman, just as I am. Sometimes we have to do things we don't want to. Do you see?"

I shook my head.

"When I was about your age, my father told me the story of Regulus. Have I ever told it to you? No? Marcus Atilius Regulus was a Roman, like you or me, but he was a great general, too. He fought the Carthaginians, almost two hundred years ago, and he won. Oh, yes. Roman armies are always victorious," he cried, his eyes shining. "No one can defeat us—or, not for long. Remember that, Marcus."

"Yes, father."

"Good. See that you do. As I said, Regulus defeated the Carthaginians, but they would not surrender, and later in another battle, they captured him. They intended to torture him, and they would certainly have put him to death, but he asked for time to go home and put his affairs in order and say goodbye to his family. He gave his word as a Roman citizen that he would return when he had done these things. The Carthaginians agreed, and they asked him to arrange an exchange of prisoners and give their terms to the Senate in Rome.

"So Regulus came home. And he did what the Carthaginians had asked, though he advised the Senate not to accept their terms. He visited his family, very briefly. Within a short time, he took ship and sailed again to Carthage, as he had promised to do."

"What happened?" I whispered, but he was angry again.

"They tortured him to death like a slave," he said, staring hard at me. I believe I wanted to protest that I had nothing to do with it, but I wasn't quite sure this was true. Perhaps in some way I did not understand, I had. He was my father, after all, and he seemed to be telling me so.

"That is how a Roman behaves," he said. "Do you understand now? He does what he ought to, whether he wants to or not. That's what I'd expect of you, too. There will be no more complaints of ill-health, no further sign of reluctance. You will go to school, you will apply yourself to your studies, and you will succeed. That is what I expect of my son."

31

My son. *Was* I his son? And if so, did that mean that my mother was a freedwoman? And what did it signify if she were? "Father," I cried, "is mother . . . ?"

"Your mother expects the same of you as I do. That's all Marcus. I don't want to discuss it any further. You will go to school, no matter if you like it or not. Your parents want it: that should be enough for any decent Roman boy. Do your duty. Like Marcus Atilius Regulus."

"Yes, father," I said, and went back to the garden, where the Carthaginians waited.

I struggled on, but the teasing did not stop. My dreams grew worse, until I dreaded the fall of night, and the lonely journey to my room. The walk to school was like the march to execution; the old man plodding along behind me might have been conducting me to my death. He knew it, too. Sometimes I would feel his touch on my shoulder, my neck, the top of my hair. I had no power to refuse these caresses, the nature of which I did not fully understand. Nor did I turn him away at night, but endured his gentle love for the sake of company in the dark.

But, of course, whatever passed between us in my little bedroom, it did not help at school. At last there came a morning when I could not go. When Crito's back was turned I slipped away and hid myself behind the arbor in the garden. Crito wandered around calling my name, now near, now far, among the bushes and the flowers, by the pool, along the walk of espaliered plum trees. At last his voice was silent. Peeking out between the leaves, I saw him sitting with his head in his hands. I sneaked away and spent the day playing with the children of the bath-house slave.

It was the slave who gave me away. Well, you cannot expect much of these people, they fear their masters too powerfully. Late in the afternoon, she saw me, and in spite of my threats and promises, led me to my tutor. He was still sitting in the same place, at the stone table in the garden, with my school books in a heap before him and our uneaten lunch in a basket at his feet.

He looked up when we approached, tossing the gray hair off his forehead. His eyes were like the coursed deer's when the dogs have chased it all day . . . "Marcus, have you . . . have you been in school?"

"No, he has not," the maid exclaimed. "I found him in the kitchen garden with my own two, if you'll believe it."

"Oh, I believe it." Crito sighed, and I saw in his eyes the extinction of his last hope.

"Well, Marcus," he said heavily, waving his hand to dismiss her. "Sit down. We must think what to do about this."

Cold with fear I lowered myself onto the stone bench. He must have seen that I was frightened, for he put out his hand and rested it on my arm. It was large and pale against the peeled-willow whiteness of my arm, and it felt warm.

I don't know what I expected him to do. Once or twice when I lived with my mother I had been punished—sent out of the room, or deprived of a treat. I didn't think that was going to meet the case now. And in spite of Crito's kindness, I knew he could be strict. But he only sat there for a long time, looking at me abstractedly. Finally he said, "If I tell your father—"

I swallowed hard. I hadn't thought of this.

"If I tell him . . ." His own throat was working. "Marcus," he said brushing his pale hair back and wiping his face. "You know that I am a slave, don't you? Do you know what that means?"

"That he can tell you what to do."

"That's right. And do you know why? Because he owns me. I am his possession. Like—like this table. If it displeases him, he can throw it away. Or sell it and get a new one. It is his. Do you see?"

"Yes."

"Good." His hand stroked my arm in a gesture of approval. "*He* can also punish me, if he wants to. Do you understand that?"

I held my forearm still. "Yes," I said, watching his hand.

"Well, he can punish you, too. You are his possession as well."

"He can punish me? I thought it was only you."

"No. You owe him your obedience just as I do."

"Why?" I jerked my arm away in a spasm of rage. "I hate him."

He sighed. Perhaps he hated my father, too. But he was a a scrupulous man, and had his duty to do. "Don't talk like that, Marcus. It's against the gods, and they dislike such impiety."

"The gods want me to obey my father?" In that case I was prepared to hate them, too.

He nodded. "They want you to. Just like me."

"Am I slave, then?" I asked, my anger eaten up by a vast astonishment.

"No. You are his son. That is why he owns you. He can do anything he likes to you. Sell you, even. As he could sell me. As, I'm afraid, he very well may . . ."

"*Sell* me?"

"Oh, yes, if he likes. He owns everything here. The house, the servants, the animals, everything. We all belong to him."

I was so shocked I could hardly understand what he was saying. "He could sell me?"

"Yes," he said patiently. "Any of us. Your mother—"

"My . . . my mother?"

"Oh, yes, certainly. He owns her too. And you."

"But he wouldn't, would he?" I asked with a confidence that I did not feel. "Not my mother and me."

"He might. If he were angry enough. There was once a Roman general who put his son to death, for treason . . ."

"Was it Regulus?"

He smiled. "No, not Regulus. Another general. But that is why you must obey your father. Whether you like it or not. Whether you hate him or not. You belong to him, and you owe him your obedience, as his possession. Now do you understand?"

"Yes," I said, dry-mouthed.

"You are an intelligent boy. I thought it would be better to reason with you than to punish you. You may go to your room now, and think over our discussion."

"You won't tell my father?"

"Not this time. But Marcus . . . Marcus, please don't. Don't do it ag—" He shook his head, and his pale hair across his wrinkled forehead. "Just go to your room."

"Yes," I whispered.

But I did not go. I wandered around the house, avoiding the servants' eyes. My mind felt tender and bruised, as if it had been beaten, and no idea would stay in it for long. For a while I dangled my feet in the pool, later I lay down on my stomach and tried to catch one of the big gray mullets in my fingers; I climbed up behind the wickerwork supports of the grape arbor and watched the swallows hunting in the windless air. But none of these things helped. In the end I found myself standing, very small and frightened, in front of my mother's door.

"Why Marcus," she cried, when she had embraced me, and called the maids to see that her son had come to visit her. "What's the matter? Are you crying?" There was a note in her voice that I did not understand; it made the tears come faster so that I could not speak. I buried my head in her lap and sobbed.

She allowed this for a moment, but very soon she stopped me and wiped my face with a square of linen from her dressing table. "No. Tell me."

I tried. Words burst from me: the school, my pedagogue, my clothes, the boys, the teasing, my father . . . "So it's the school that you don't like?" she asked, understandably puzzled by this list. All my pain and fear flooded from me. "I hate it," I screamed, and my eyes and nose streamed with the fury of my unhappiness. "I want to stay here with you."

"Marcus," she said. Her voice was like a slap. "That's enough. You can't stay here with me. Only girls stay with their mothers at your age. Boys go to school. You don't want to be a little girl, do you?"

I shook my head. I believe I was more confused than anything else.

"Of course you don't." She raised her hand and gestured to a maid to take me away.

"No," I shrieked. "I'm a boy. Don't . . ."

"You can't stay here. That's final."

"Mother, let me. I'll be good. I'll . . ." I screamed, but she had turned on me a face so closed and angry that, cold with terror, I could only stare back helplessly. The servant took my hand and led me, unresisting, back to my room.

That night I lay awake a long time. Crito did not come. Once, heart pounding with a fear I did not acknowledge, I got out of bed and looked at myself in the light that came in under the door. I touched my body: my arms, already long and straight though thin, my ribs, the shallow curve of my hips. My hand went lower, to my penis. For a long time I looked at it, a small object, darker than the rest of me, dangling from me. An afterthought. But that notion was too fearful, and I did not pursue it. I got back into bed.

I thought of the bear that I had dreamed of once, that would come down out of the mountains and destroy the boys at school. It would even, if I asked, use its great paws to— but I no longer had any confidence in dreams, or in anything else—and I let the idea lapse. I would buy a slave in the market place, a great bronze soldier, and have him kill my enemies. But I had no money to buy anyone. I was poor. I had forgotten that. Well, then, Crito. He was nice. He would kill the boys for me. But I knew that he was too humble, too gentle, to do violence to anyone.

Towards morning, I resolved to run away. I slipped out of my room and through the sleeping house. It was still dark; only a glimmer came through the hole in the atrium roof; the columns stood up like the boles of trees in a forest. Here and there a doorway loomed, a darker shadow on the dim stucco walls: my mother's rooms, where she slept, bound in a cocoon of darkness; the maids, all together, with their children; the other women servants; the gardener and his boys— all the inhabitants of the house, confined in the still, chilly air. Only I had escaped. I moved through the night like a mist, leaking away on silent feet.

Out behind the kitchen garden I came to the door. It was low and small, the right size for a child, but old and unused. The hinges cried out in elderly protest as I pushed it open. Heart racing, I waited, but even the bakery servants were not up yet and no one came. Trusting to my luck, I slipped through.

I stood outside the door for a long time, wondering where to go. It could be anywhere. I was free. There were no limits on what I did now; I could do anything that came into my

mind. No one would forbid me anything, no one order me
to do anything. A breeze was blowing, travelling towards me
over a vast distance. The smell of the mountains was in it,
the snow on the tallest peaks, the pines, the cold, the cry of
eagles in the high, bare places. The grasses bent as it passed
and my feet trod them down again, as I raced towards it. In
the wind there were hints of places even beyond the mountains, rumors of freedom I had never heard before. I thought
there was a message in it for me, a summons coming to me
on that enormous wind, full of mystery and joy. And by the
gods, when I remember it, I think so still.

That was the day I discovered the road. It was far from
the house, and it was full morning when I saw it, raised on
its artificial ridge above the plain. Its white stones gleamed
as if they were polished, the curbs and gutters were cut with
a beautiful precision. I stared at it from the reeds below for
a long time before I dared to clamber up onto it.
When I did, I could not believe what I saw. The whole
country seemed to lie at my feet, the little villages and farms,
the trees, the fields, the little streams foaming white as they
dashed down from the snow-covered mountains. Far away in
the other direction a haze shimmered on the horizon. I knew
it was the sea.
After that I went often to the road. There was always something happening on it. Farmers herded their sheep along to
the market, women with jars on their heads swayed gracefully
behind them. Once a praetor went out to his province in the
east in a chariot painted with scenes of war out of Homer.
Behind him marched what I thought was the biggest army
in the world. Perhaps two thousand men—four cohorts, now
that I think of it—tramped after him with measured steps,
singing. I hid in the reeds and watched them. Their weapons
were polished so brightly the bronze shone like gold, their
leather breastplates gleamed. After they were gone I climbed
up on the road. They had left it scattered with their posses-
sions—a buckle, a scrap of fringe, even the rind of a fruit I
had never seen before. I gathered them up, all these trea-
sures, and I kept them for years. The buckle might be in our
house in Interamnia still.

I knew that the road came from Rome. I imagined the city, sometimes. It was filled with men like the praetor, pale and clean-shaven and scented like a garden, and others like the soldiers, with faces as hard and bronze as their uniforms. I knew it lay over the mountains somewhere, but that it was far, for my father's business took him to the city now. I did not have any hope of going there myself.

One day when I returned to Interamnia, I was met by some herdsmen. I recognized them as my father's men, and I wondered what they were doing practically at the gates of the town. They were armed, too, with thick cudgels or iron-tipped pitchforks. I did not have long to wonder: they swept me up, setting me on the shoulders of the tallest, a rank-smelling, thatch-haired Thracian. It was like riding in the crotch of a tree. All around me they exclaimed about my welfare, but their dialect was so barbarous I had trouble understanding it. They were arguing about a reward, I think.

My father was waiting in the atrium. My mother was nowhere in sight, but he had Crito with him. The old man's head was lowered and his lips were moving. My father stood so tall he seemed to touch the painted ceiling. "Well, Marcus," he said. "Where have you been?" He was furious with rage. I swore in my mind that no matter what he did, I would not tell him.

"Well, Marcus?" I had never heard him so angry before. I looked him in the eye and spat at him, as hard as I could.

At that his face congested and he unbuckled the belt of his tunic. "Bend over," he said. He had never beaten me before, but he made up for it now. My back and legs burned with my father's violence, my heart swelled so that I thought it would burst my chest. Screams shot from me, like the spittle that dotted the floor. Presently he stopped, and I heard a voice sobbing with mine. It was Crito. He sent me a terrified glance as a servant conducted me to my room—he had reason to, poor fellow. My father beat him, too, this time with a metal-tipped whip. I know because he ordered all the doors in the house left open, so that everyone could see. Crito grunted when the iron touched his flesh, but he was a better man than I for he never once cried out, though my father's anger lasted for a long time. When it was done, my father sent for the slave-broker from the town and had him taken away. I waited for the man to return for me, but he never did.

III

So it comes back to me. The odd thing is that I had forgotten it, not just after I became a man, but almost immediately, perhaps within a few days. I don't believe I've thought of it from that moment to this.

How could I have forgotten, you will ask, and I have no answer. It had gone from my mind as if it had fled, and my life continued much as before. Truly a child must be a mysterious sort of creature; he spends his days among the very people who have harmed him, without overt fear or hatred, indeed even with affection if that is allowed him; he studies and plays, he eats and sleeps and talks; he goes on living, though in the blackest darkness of the night, he has sworn that he will not.

I have had to walk around a little, for my thoughts have driven me to motion. I feel a kind of tension, a tremor runs though me as if I were a tree that has felt the axe. It is anger, as new as if I were still seven years old, transformed into this shaking. My ears hum with it, and my muscles tense. "He goes on living, though he has sworn that he will not." Gods!

Outside the windows the sun pours down its poppy somnolence on the roofs of the town, on the feathered silver of the olive groves along the road, the gold and purple of vines in the fields. Peace, simplicity, calm, the whole landscape is drenched in them, saturated. The air smells of tranquillity, the clear violet distances dream. Nothing moves anywhere . . .

I have said that I forgot, and that is true, yet all the same, I was changed. I no longer went to my mother's rooms, or played with the servants' children; I grew solitary and withdrawn, and seldom spoke at home unless I was addressed. I had a new pedagogue, younger and more alert and a better teacher when we did lessons at home. My father must have paid good money for him. This new tutor intervened, and presently the boys stopped teasing me. I think he spoke to my father about it, too. Yet I did not take this as a sign that my father was concerned in my welfare.

On the contrary, for some years I continued to believe that he might still sell me. In the first place, he was always short of money, or so he said. Certainly he did not spend any of it on us. As I grew older I became aware that our house was really very small and shabby and not in good repair, and that my clothes were really worse than those of the other boys in the school. I still went barefoot all year round like the schoolmaster's son, who sat in the back, alone.

Yet in those years my position grew, and I found myself accepted, even popular, at school. Undoubtedly this was due to my father's growing importance in the town. His business had prospered; he was elected to public office; he had friends everywhere. A lot of men respected his frugality, thinking as he did that it reflected the best of our ancient Roman tradition, and their sons correspondingly took it more for granted in me. I had friends, too; eventually we were the oldest and biggest boys in the school, and did pretty much what we wanted.

At home, too, things were easier. Since my father's business was doing so well, he often found himself obliged to travel. Usually it was over the mountains to Rome, but once in a while he had to go even farther than that—to Sicily or North Africa, where he was buying farms to produce wheat and barley for the markets in Italy, especially for the voracious mouth that Rome, swelled with a huge and growing population, was becoming. It meant that for long periods he was away.

In those years I started going back to my mother's rooms whenever my father was not at home. My mother was always glad to see me, and to hear about my day in school, or listen to the recitation of my lessons. It was pleasant, but as I grew older another attraction began to seem more important to me. The maids were friendly, as they had always been; indeed they were more than that, and finally—sometime in my fourteenth year, I think—one of them hinted unmistakably at a different sort of interest. When she came that night into my bed, I was pleased, but I can hardly say I was surprised. I had been waiting in feverish excitement for what seemed like hours.

I was not disappointed. Her arms were soft and strong, her body full of movement and a sense of life. At the climax I cried out and buried my head in her shoulder, holding on to her as if she were a spar in a shipwreck, and afterwards I lay comforted in the circle of her arms. She was not a pretty woman, nor was she young. She smelled of linen and steam and the faint scorch of the iron.

On my sixteenth birthday, my father cut off my hair and offered it, along with my boy's striped toga and the amulet I had worn since birth, on the altar of our family's gods. My mother cried, my uncle made a speech, my cousin Catullus, two years older than I and down from Verona for the occasion, winked at me from the back of the crowd of relatives and local dignitaries, and we all trooped into the garden for my coming-of-age dinner.

There we encountered a pause as we all took our places and waited expectantly. But the servants remained lined up under the colonnade with their hands at their sides, and the plates on the tables were empty. I wondered if my father had been too parsimonious to provide any dinner, but of course that was not the case. Not with all his fellow magistrates and business men from the town to impress. After a while, he glanced across the garden to the door from the house, gave a faint shrug, and signalled the servants to begin.

Of the meal I can recall nothing, except the man who arrived just as the first course was being served. He was a Roman, a senator, and obviously someone very important, for I saw that we had been waiting for him. The place between my father and me on the head couch had been reserved for him, and a place set beside my mother for his wife. He came in with a smile for everyone and a bouquet of flowers for my mother, a strong-looking man in young middle age, with fine, regular features and warm, brown eyes. His smile was friendly, but he carried himself with great dignity and weight. I saw that it was not just to my father that this man was important.

"Well, Marcus, how good of you," my father cried, standing up to clasp the visitor around the shoulders. "It's wonderful of you to find the time to come."

"It's a pleasure to share such an auspicious occasion," the newcomer said. He looked at me with what I could only imagine was approval.

"He's had a sound upbringing," my father said, seeing the direction of his look. "You won't be disappointed. His teachers report that he is the brightest boy in the school, and I think I can say that I have brought him up with the discipline proper to a Roman citizen."

I was surprised to hear myself praised, for I do not think it had ever happened before. I stared at the man who had elicited all this from my father. "I'm sure he'll do very well," he was saying. Suddenly cold, I wondered if my father had decided to sell me to him.

I did not recognize the thought, for I had long since forgotten the old pedagogue and everything he had told me. Still, the idea came to me with compelling power, and for a moment I was blinded and deafened by it. My father was going to sell me. I was sure . . .

When the food came in I was not sure again, for it seemed obvious that no one would put on such a banquet for a son he intended to get rid of. It was elaborate and very delicious, and I could see that it had been expensive as well.

The man called Marcus was very friendly, leaning over to talk from the place next to me on the couch, where he reclined on one elbow. He made it look elegant, as it is supposed to. Reclining at table is the privilege of a free man, after all. "Ah, asparagus," he said. "Are you fond of it, too?"

"Yes." His voice shocked me. It was the most beautiful I had ever heard, a low growl full of music and warmth, suggesting depths of feeling and intellect he was only waiting to be able to share.

"Yes, I like asparagus. It's my favorite."

"Naturally, naturally. It's your birthday, isn't it? Well, when you come to us we must have asparagus whenever we can. Terentia," he cried raising his voice to his wife, "make a note

43

of it," and the fashionable lady at the end of the table smiled at me in a very kindly way. He bent the same smile on me. "Are you interested in politics, oratory, that sort of thing?"

"Yes. I'd like to be an advocate and have a career in public life." I spoke warmly, for this had been my dearest wish for many years now. Indeed, it was the hope of every boy in my school—to go to Rome and make a name for himself in the law courts. From there a man of talent might launch a career in the Senate, and even in the higher magistracies, though there were not many boys from provincial towns like ours who had managed that. Still, we dreamed, and talked about it all the time.

"It's a worthy ambition for a Roman," the man said, as if he were agreeing with my unspoken thought. "Every man has an obligation to serve the state, just as each woman does to raise strong children. We must all fulfill our obligations as citizens,"

"Yes, that's what they say at school." He was listening with such flattering attention—indeed, that was one element in his almost phenomenal success, his ability to listen—that I confided without a second thought my deepest wish. "I want to be one of the consuls in Rome, some day."

"Ah, so do I. So do I." He laughed. "Perhaps we'll both be lucky, if we work hard. What do you think?"

I thought it was very likely, and in my own case I did not see that it was a matter of luck at all, but politeness prevented me from saying so. Someone was calling his name from down the table—"Marcus Tullius Cicero—" and asking for his opinion of some current scandal in Rome. I stared at him, rudely, I'm afraid. I had heard of him. Indeed, the whole world was beginning to do that.

Marcus Tullius Cicero was what they call a New Man, a plebeian, like the Caelii, with the money to qualify for the equestrian class and be called a knight. He was not a patrician, and like us he came from a country town. He had a few connections in Rome, but not many. Even so, he had risen in the city, rapidly and far. He had started as an advocate in the Forum, trying cases of disputed wills and water rights—anything anyone would give him. But in the time of the tyrant Sulla, he was the only man in Rome willing to protest the abuses of the government, the murders under the form of law, the violent seizures of property. His courage was a byword, like his eloquence, and his fame grew, reaching even to a place like Interamnia.

By the time he was in his forties, long after Sulla was dead and democracy had been restored, he had held every office but the very highest. He was a praetor now, and everyone said that it was only a matter of time before he travelled higher still. In fact, the consulship was as close to him as his wine cup on the table. He had only to put out his hand and take it.

So I went to Rome, to be Cicero's pupil. I remember every moment of the journey: how we jolted along on the road in three wagons loaded with our household goods, for my father had bought a house on the Oppian Hill and was moving to Rome to be near his business interests. I remember the thin blue air on the heights of the mountains, the great square cliffs, the eagles circling so high in the sky you could hardly make them out, their thin cries floating back to us. Flowers starred the grass when we came down onto the plain, and the air was mild and crisp. Then one evening I saw under a flaming sky a dark city massed on seven hills, a river of gold running through it. Rome.

I was Cicero's pupil. and I lived in his house. Far from treating me like a slave, he behaved to me as if I were his son. I took my meals with him and his family—the lady, Terentia, and their two young children; I sat at his feet in his study when he interviewed his clients; I followed him to the law-courts in the Forum if he had a case to plead, and to the Curia if the Senate was in session. I copied his notes and speeches, I listened to the debates, I gave my opinion when asked and kept it in reserve when not.

He was a splendid teacher, even on such unpromising material as an adolescent boy whose idea of speechmaking was primitive in the extreme. Patiently he educated Interamnia's idea of eloquence out of me. He corrected my irritating expressions, my wildly fluctuating voice, my overdramatic and boastful gestures. Slowly he polished me into something acceptable to Rome. For the rest, his political and legal work, he taught without seeming to, merely commenting on what he did and why, but this method too was effective, and I felt myself learning every day.

For a long time I enjoyed my life with him. But he lived for his work, pouring all the tremendous energy of his nature into his writing and speeches, his arguments and discussions and debates. And I had thought my father drove himself. But work was Cicero's joy: his bright brown eyes sparkled and snapped, his intelligent mouth twitched into a smile, his heavy shoulders leaned forward with the intensity of his pleasure in every idea he considered, from the finest technical points of philosophy or jurisprudence to the grossest methods of electoral politicking. When he encountered something he did not know he laughed aloud and sent his secretaries to look it up. Daybreak, midday, dinnertime, even the deepest hours of the night were all the same to him. He worked, and though I do not think he knew it, he was entirely happy.

But I was not. I was young, free of my father for the first time in my life, living in the greatest city the world had ever seen. News of it reached me constantly: the ink that shuddered in its jar when a heavily laden cart rumbled by outside, the voices of other young men in the street, the cry of a vendor, a breath of perfume as a woman went through the Forum in a curtained litter, all spoke to me imperatively, taking my attention from work as if they held it captive on the point of a spear. Some days I thought that if I looked at another wax tablet of notes for a speech that someone else was going to give, or listened once more to instructions on how to raise my arms to emphasize a climax in an argument, I would go mad.

Of course I had some freedom: I went to parties and lived the life of a well-brought up young man in the city. And my father gave me an allowance. At first it seemed to me a very large sum and I didn't know what to do with it. I bought clothes and small items for myself, gifts for Terentia and the children, I visited women from time to time, I got drunk when I could.

In my free time, I roamed the streets. I saw the temples

and the offices that were attached to them; one afternoon I watched the slaves striking coins in the Temple of Juno Moneta, on another I saw them conveying them, guarded by a magistrate and a dozen lictors to be stored in the Treasury at the Temple of Saturn. I watched the Vestal Virgins pray before the sacred flame of their Hearth; I spied out the secret cache of weapons at the Temple of Castor in the Forum.

I visited the workshops: I would stare for hours at the sandalmakers, potters, ropeweavers, masons, though what so fascinated me about these lowly occupations I cannot now remember. A boy is interested in everything, I suppose. And there were whole streets of each of them, all selling the same thing, shop after shop of armorers all hammering at the bronze, or perfume-makers, drugging the air for blocks with their competing scents. Catullus lived in a street in which they sold sandals, nothing but sandals. How could people buy so much? It was certainly not like Interamnia, where we thought we were lucky to have one flyspecked little shop that sold everything we didn't make at home.

There were street festivals around the little corner shrines where the priests danced, or processions in which gods were carried through the neighborhood. At one the statues lay out in the forecourt of their temple on couches like guests at a dinner party, at another—some foreign cult—the swarthy men and women beat themselves with whips until the blood fell like in dots and splashes in the street for the honor of their god.

There were political meetings, the big public ones in the Forum, where the orators made their speeches, gesturing from the Rostra like statues against the open sky. But there were others too, dark and smoky, like conspiracies, where men with seductive voices spoke of the destruction of the government and the abolition of debts. My cousin Catullus and I watched one night with a silent crowd outside the prison when five of these soft-voiced men were executed. That was later, when Cicero had indeed become consul, just as he had always wished. He was their target, and with great courage he had captured them and convicted them. They meant to kill him, and to arm the slaves, inciting them to set fire to the city.

I found that out afterwards. At the time I only heard them speak of their desire to help the ordinary citizens of Rome, and what they said seemed true and valuable to me. Certainly I had never seen such poverty, such desperation, at home in Interamnia. In Rome families lived five or six to a room in the slummier tenements, and water was two blocks away; men stood on street corners all day because they had no work. I did not understand how that could be. How can a man have nothing to do? Can he not just do something? Surely anyone can weave a basket or make a brick? But it was not so. Catullus explained: they could not have sold their goods if they had created them, and in the end their despair would have been the same.

Yet there were riches in the city, too. I had been right when I first saw it, dark on its hills—a river of gold ran through Rome. Up on the heights, away from the slums, there were mansions bigger than the temples in Interamnia, and people who dressed like kings and lived like gods. I saw them at parties when I went with Cicero or my parents. The men had a sleek, well-cared-for look, and the women were so beautiful I almost groaned aloud with desire.

There were plenty of women in the city, and even a few accessible to a boy kept as short of money as I was. I must admit though that sometimes I had to resort to the ones who cluster around the statue of Marsyus and bare their breasts to passers-by, shouting obscene remarks. I was lashed to the mast often enough by my poverty, though they cost no more than admission to the baths. Even so, I spent more than I could afford on them, and on their more elegant sisters. My allowance was beginning to seem smaller to me all the time.

As for men, I could have had them as often as I wanted, for I was already a handsome boy. Sometimes they followed me in the street, or made pests of themselves in the baths. A few even hinted that they would have allowed me the aggressive part—well-born men, I mean, not even slaves or freedmen—forgetting their dignity and position in the urgency of their desire. Their lack of Roman self-control disgusted me, and I would jeer at them and run away. As for the others, I used to pretend I had not heard.

It seemed to me that there was everything in the city, all the things that I had dreamed of in the world. One night I saw the Homeric heroes I had read about as a child: wild men from the mountains of Asia dressed in the huge, blind-eyed helmets of archaic Greek warriors. But they were slaves, a line of them, magnificent men, short, powerful, oiled till they gleamed in the torchlight, gladiators being paraded through the city to a new barracks under the eye of their trainers and guards. Roman armies had captured them. My heart swelled with awe to think of it.

The next day I saw the bear. He was dancing alone in a square in the loud and plebeian section of town known as the Subura. He wore a muzzle and a little cap of some dark red material that fell over his eye, and he stared out at the crowd as if he did not like us very much. His owner, a dirty little Phrygian, kept chattering as the bear performed its solemn dance—a vulgar distraction. The bear seemed to know it. He danced without music, and without plan, and at the end he dropped down on all four feet and looked at us calmly. If he knew what he was waiting for I did not, but I thought that when it came it would be remarkable, some fate worthy of a hero, some gift from heaven. The city seemed full of such wonderful destinies in those days. Even a bear might represent one; he might stand in for a god.

My life at Cicero's went on in this way for nearly three years. I can't say that I was really unhappy, though my need for money grew as I found more places to spend it, and my sense of confinement in the hard-working routine of Cicero's life began to stifle me. It was my father who rescued me, though if he had known what he was doing, doubtless he would not have. Pleased with my progress and having had good reports of my work, he decided to expand my edu-cation.

He had recently made the acquaintance of Marcus Licinius Crassus, the richest man in Rome. Crassus was an aristocrat and a political figure; in addition to a business man; he had been consul with Pompey the Great some years before. A useful man to know, my father said, and he knew him well. So, two or three times a week I crossed the valley from the Oppian Hill to the Palatine, from Cicero's modest mansion to Crassus' amazingly opulent one, followed by my freedman Philo with a stack of books and supplies under his arm. There, for three hours or so, I listened to Crassus talk to his clients or lecture under the topiary yews in his garden.

A number of young men also attended: his own son Publius, Gaius Scribonius Curio, an aristocrat to his finger-tips; a boy of about my own age called Mark Antony; another called Calvus who was a friend of Catullus' and was already becoming known as a poet; some others, all of whom I liked the look of. At the conclusion of the lecture Crassus stood up, bowed to us, and disappeared into his house. The first time he did this I prepared to follow, but Publius Crassus put a casual hand on my arm. "We usually go out for a bit now."

"Go out?"

"You know. Have a few drinks, go to the baths, see what's happening. Curio has a little friend who usually gives us dinner. She might be able to find someone for you—she has lots of friends." He nudged me in the ribs to be sure I understood.

"I'm expected at Cicero's." I glanced over to where Philo my freedman was waiting. At that moment he looked more like my jailer than my secretary.

"Just tell your man you'll be staying late with my father. Cicero won't object."

"No, of course he won't, m-my dear," Gaius Scribonius Curio fluted at me in his exaggerated upper-class drawl. It was so effeminate it was hard not to laugh. I wondered if his friend was actually a man, but Curio, I found out later, had elegant tastes and liked men and women both. There are some like that, I know, though I do not understand them. The older generation doesn't either, and sometimes complains, but they complain about everything we do. It has never seemed enough reason to make me drop Curio's company.

"Really, m-my dear," Curio assured me. "Cicero will think it's an excellent opportunity for a young m-man. You'll see."

"A young man should benefit by his elders' instruction."

Mark Antony let out a wild, ramshackle laugh. "At least that's what my old man says when I tell him. Not that I do, much. He just expects me to be late by now."

"Thus we see the value of a precedent." Publius Crassus chanted, imitating his father. We all laughed, and somehow, when we stopped, I saw that it had been decided.

There remained one last and most crucial embarrassment. "I haven't any money," I said, knowing that what I had was going to be inadequate.

"I'll lend you some," said Publius Crassus.

So began my real introduction to the city, the second, and secret part of my education. It was an expensive one. Curio's little friend had an endless supply of ravishing acquaintances, each of whom had to be entertained with meals and parties, trips on the river, new clothes, jewelry, servants. I needed new clothes myself, so as not to look like the poor cousin in from the country who has no idea how things are done in Rome; I had to treat my friends as often as they treated me.

Then there were the bets on the gladiatorial games on holidays, there were wagers on dice and on chariot races and on the game of holding up your fingers and shouting "How many?" so that the one with the most showing wins. But we did not stop there. We also bet on other things: how many bricks there were in a builder's yard, or how much wine Antony could drink in one swallow, or whether the respectable matron we were following home from the market would smile or struggle when we accosted her.

There were bribes to servants for admission to their mistresses' rooms, to irate husbands for their silence, to Philo to tell lies for me to my father, and to the doorkeeper at Cicero's not to say what time I came in. There were musicians to hire, and caterers and entertainers for parties, there were gymnastic trainers and jockeys and retired boxers; there were bills for damage to property, and for cleaning my clothes. I bought a pair of carriage horses—it was almost as cheap as hiring them, and anyway the rented ones never look as smart as one's own. Soon it seemed economical to buy a racehorse as well.

My allowance from my father did not cover all this, of course, and he would not extend it, though his business was flourishing. I tried to explain to him. "Father, you know it's expensive nowadays in Rome, especially if one wants a career in politics. I mean, one has to have friends, and keep up with them. They will be a help later on. Besides, it doesn't look right to act as if we're poor."

"It's good for young men to learn to manage money," he announced and turned away to his accounts.

"Very well, I'll learn," I said through my teeth, and went straight to the money-lenders. By the time I was nineteen I was well over million and a half sesterces in debt.

It was nothing by the standards of our crowd. My father, if he'd had any memory at all of what it was like to be young, would have recognized that. Curio owed about ten times as much, and he was rich to begin with. But he had been involved in an accident, in which the wagon he had been riding in with a free woman had gone off a bridge and turned over. The woman had been killed and Curio had paid a large sum in compensation to her parents to prevent a scandal. I heard that it cost him almost a million and he had not even been very drunk at the time.

Antony was the worst of us. He owed money everywhere. He did not seem to set any limits on himself at all. Once I saw him in the slave market, bidding on a pair of adolescent boys. Curio was with him, and they were nearly swooning over the pretty twins. Don't ask me why. And the expense! Women are nothing in comparison. That day alone Antony paid two hundred thousand sesterces for those two boys, and he and Curio crowed about it all the way to the Forum. You'd have thought he had gotten a bargain. Antony had them out at parties for months afterwards, too. I got sick of their simpering faces and their servile manners. I'm afraid I wasn't very tactful about it, I could see Curio and Antony eyeing me sometimes as if they wondered what was wrong.

They were very good friends, Curio and Antony. Curio countersigned Antony's notes—I don't think he quite realized the size of the bills Antony was running up, or perhaps he didn't care. Perhaps for Curio there weren't any limits either.

I was present the day the bills came due. We were lying

around in the garden at Curio's house—alone for a change. It was mid-afternoon, and none of us felt like working. Possibly the heat had gotten to us, for we sprawled on the couches as if we had been beached there, washed up by the storms of the night before. Antony was picking at a design on a wine-cup with his thumb-nail. It seemed to absorb all his attention. From time to time Curio murmured something: we could go and see what was happening at the baths, if anyone felt like it? Did anyone want any food? There were bees in the garden—busy little things—and their hum was putting me to sleep.

All of a sudden Curio's father was among us, waving a fistful of papers. "Do you know what these are?" He hurled them into Curio's lap.

"Bills?" Curio bleated as if he had never seen such things in his life.

Antony let out his long, ropy laugh. He sounded as if he were still drunk.

"Don't you laugh!" Curio's father turned on him like an enraged ram. Well, Curio looked like his lamb, with his protruding teeth and his large, round eyes. They were fixed on his father now, who was shouting at Antony. "These bills are yours. My son has backed them."

"I . . . I know." Antony stood up very straight, a Roman soldier about to take his punishment. We all were. Curio had tears in his eyes, I swear it. I don't know what I expected—the whip perhaps. Curio's father looked furious enough for that.

"What did you expect me to do about this?" he cried, turning on his son again.

It was not tears in Curio's eyes, it was laughter. Oh, no, I thought. Don't laugh; you'll make it worse. "What did I expect you to do, father? Wh—why, pay them, of course."

I waited, hardly daring to breathe, but Curio's father only said, in a wondering voice, "Do you know how much they come to?" His anger seemed to have evaporated.

"I have n-no idea, father."

"Six million sesterces."

Curio's eyes widened in surprise. Antony, unable to help himself, rattled out his laugh again.

"Very well," Curio's father said, ignoring Antony. "I will

pay. But I want you to understand that I will pay no others. Is that clear?"

I was gasping, my heart was racing. Six million sesterces. Just like that. Very well, I will pay.

"And you," said Curio's father, turning to Antony. I was wrong when I thought he was no longer angry; it was just that he could not be at odds with his son. "You are not welcome in this house. Get out now, and never come back."

"But," said Antony who was giving his imitation of the general Regulus in the hands of the Carthaginians again.

"Out. Now."

Antony looked around, a little wildly, as if he feared the servants might come and throw him out. Indeed, I thought they might myself. What was passing in Curio's mind I could not tell; his face was a perfect blank, and he looked foolish and ineffectual. There was certainly no help there.

"Yes." Antony reluctantly picked up his toga. He glance once more at Curio's impassive face. Really, Curio, who looked so silly and childish, was the most Roman of us all.

"All right. I'm going, just as you say." A grin touched Antony's mouth. I saw, though Curio's father did not, that Curio tipped him a sly little wink.

I seized the opportunity and slipped out myself. I did not want to be present while Curio's father told him off. Besides, Curio had countersigned a lot of my notes too.

It got to be a regular thing: when we went to call on Curio I went in at the front door while Antony climbed in over the roof. Pretty soon we were all living just as we always had. I spent what I needed to, and borrowed what I could, feeling perfectly justified. I hadn't spent anything like six million sesterces. All the same I began to wake up at night thinking about what would happen if my father found out.

Catullus thought I was crazy, but he was never really a part of that crowd anyway, and had no political ambition. All he liked were sordid little bars where he could write his poetry undisturbed. Cicero never knew. Right up until I finished my apprenticeship with him I continued to sneak out of his house every night, going over the roofs like Antony or bribing the servants to let me through the door into the alley.

Among them, the servants had enough off me to buy a small farm, and the doorman could have financed the public games. And I borrowed from everywhere—Curio, Antony, Publius Crassus and his father, anyone who would lend me anything. Even after my three years were up and I had moved back into my parents' house, no word ever got back to my father. In time I ceased to wonder why not.

IV

So it was that on this morning in January when Clodius and Catullus and I broke into the Women's Festival, I stood in front of the door of Clodius' sister's place, and tried to think of an alibi. It took me some time to remember my student days. The first rays of sun were flooding into the alley, dissolving the cool shadows left from the dawn. I could feel the warmth on my face. I blinked once or twice. Inside the garden a woman spoke, and I heard Catullus' grating voice answer her. A drift of smoke, blue as chalk, brought the scent of burning leaves; I heard the first rattle of shutters at an upstairs window. The house was waking up. I turned and ran.

It was no trouble finding Cicero's place from the alley. When I was a student I had climbed over the back wall often enough, coming home in the first light of day, just as I was now. I even remembered a place where a heap of broken roof tiles and discarded boards made it easier to climb . . . There it was, no one had troubled to remove it from the alley. I put my foot on it, and hoisted myself over into the garden—not the beautiful formal one in the center of the house, but the kitchen plot with its grape arbor and fig trees, its rows of vegetables and herbs, its heaps of compost in the corner. I dashed through, ducking into the main part of the house.

There I halted, hiding behind a column in the peristyle where the sun had not yet reached. The formal garden lay in shadow, its hedges dark against the curl of mist from the pool, the bare branches of the ornamental trees black scrawls on the cool, pale shadows. I held my breath and waited for someone to come.

Presently a slave come out of the house, yawning and scratching his head. Tiro, Cicero's secretary.

"Oh, there you are, Tiro," I called, stepping out from behind the column. "I've been looking for you for hours."

The secretary gave a start. "Oh, I'm sorry. I must have overslept. What time is it?"

"Never mind. We'll let it pass this time. But your master does need you—this morning of all mornings. Something important has come up."

"Oh, dear gods," Tiro cried. "And I'm late. Well, thank you for telling me."

In Cicero's study there was chaos—as usual. Paper and waxed boards were heaped on every surface; clerks and secretaries ran in and out. "Where's your master?" I demanded, and a clerk, grabbing at a pile of boards as he looked up, missed his catch, swore, and jerked his head in the direction of the front of the house. Tiro turned on his heel; I dashed after him.

In the atrium we found Cicero sitting in a chair surrounded by at least fifty men. He was always busy in the mornings when his clients and political friends came to pay their obligatory calls on him. "Hah, Tiro, there you are," he shouted. "I need you. Who's that with you?" He was peering nearsightedly through the shafts of sunlight that lanced from the hole in the roof. His eyes were crinkled at the corners, a smile of welcome curved his mouth when he saw who it was. "How long have you been here?" he cried, standing up to clasp me around the shoulders.

"Oh, heavens, it's my fault," Tiro cried. "I don't know what happened. I must have overslept—Marcus Caelius has been here for hours, looking for me."

"Hours? That's too bad. I apologize for my household. But by Hercules, I'm glad to see you," Cicero shouted in his vibrant growl as I stepped forward into his embrace.

It was a good thing that I had an alibi, however tenuous it was, for the scandal that followed our exploit in the Forum was tremendous. You'd have thought Clodius had seduced the Chief Vestal, instead of merely the Pontifex Maximus' wife. There was talk in the Senate of a trial—those flatulent old hypocrites claiming that the state might take some harm from Clodius' impiety. I don't see how. The house was purified and the rites performed again; if the gods weren't satisfied they gave no sign.

But nothing would satisfy the conservative oligarchy but a

trial, and Clodius had to stand in the Forum and hear himself indicted for sacrilege. Caesar divorced his wife—well, how could he avoid it, with the fuss the conservatives were creating?—but, graceful as ever, he avoided giving offense to Clodius, who was something of a popular hero, and had important relatives as well, by saying that he did not think his wife was guilty of adultery with Clodius. It was simply, he explained, that Caesar's wife had to be above suspicion.

I saw Caesar that day in the Forum, when he was asked about Clodius and his wife. He looked so elegant in his beautiful clothes, and so witty and charming—in fact, such *fun*—that I could not see why anyone could dislike him. But some people did. There were rumors that he was ambitious—that in fact he would do anything to get ahead. They said that when he was a young man in the east he had allowed a king to whom he was sent as an envoy to make a use of him that would be disgusting to relate. It may not have been true, for it was rumored that he liked women, at least as much as Publius Clodius did. The boy Marcus Brutus was said to be his son, which would have been news to Brutus' mother's husband—or perhaps it wouldn't have been. Caesar had been pretty openly her lover for years.

He interested me: those were all interesting facts. I thought about them for a while, and then began to ask around. It was odd how well-known he was—I mean for a man with little in the way of family distinction or political achievement behind him. Yet Rome was full of rumors of him, and everybody knew something.

The first person I asked was Catullus. "Caesar?" He took so long to look up from his papers I thought he wasn't going to answer at all. "Yes, I know him. He used to dine with us when he was stationed in my province. My father knows his family." His voice trailed away and his eyes wandered back to the poem he was writing.

"Well, what's he like?"

"Who? Oh, Caesar. Listen, Caelius, what do you think of this poem? I wrote it to her. To Clodius' sister. Have you ever seen her? I met her the day we broke in to the festival. It was her house that Clodius took us to, in the alley there. You ought to see her, Caelius. She's the most beautiful woman I ever saw." He handed me a piece of paper on which he had copied out a poem. "I wrote this to her."

LAST REPORT OF MARCUS CAELIUS RUFUS . . .
DOCUMENT APPENDED

Sparrow, my girl's delight
whom she plays with as she holds you in her lap
giving you her fingertip
and teasing you to bite . . .
Bright-shining, my desire and my love.
I believe she feels her passion like a weight
and solaces her pain.
If I could play as she does
my drooping spirit would rise in flight.

"Why, it's good," I cried, absolutely astonished. "You're a real poet."

"Oh, it's not much. Do you think she'll like it?"

"You've seen her, haven't you?" I was suddenly sure he had. "I mean since the morning of the festival."

"Twice," he admitted, glowing. "Oh, Caelius, she is so beautiful, so elegant—"

I had to listen to his rhapsody about Clodius' sister for the rest of the morning. "You're a made man," I said, enviously. "She's a powerful woman in this city."

He cared nothing about that. She hadn't even promised to sleep with him.

Finally I managed to get him back to the subject of Caesar, very briefly, it's true.

"Caesar wrote poetry, too," he said, his eyes widening as he remembered. "It was pretty good. I mean, actually quite good. He's a fine speaker, too. Very eloquent, in a simple way."

"So he's got talent."

"Oh, yes. He's intelligent. Tells witty jokes. Effeminate though."

"No, he's not," I cried, angry for no reason.

He shrugged. "Caelius, do you think Clodia will like it if I give her this poem? I mean will she . . . ?"

I got out of there before he dreamed himself into real trouble.

"He's intelligent," my father said, "but he wastes it. He certainly comes from a good family, descended from Aeneas of Troy and the Goddess Venus. One of the few original Trojan families left in Rome. They haven't done much for a few generations, but they have connections. He could do something with them, if he wanted. He's clever enough." He looked irritated. He had come down to the warehouse to inspect a shipment; we were strolling through the shadowy space, peering into the jars. I had risked a question about Caesar only because I was so bored.

"Well," I argued, "he hasn't entirely wasted them. He's the City Praetor. That's something."

The grain slid from my father's fingers, falling through the light like sparks of gold. In the mouth of the jar it darkened and disappeared, leaving behind a tiny pattering sound, like drops of rain. "Kernels are very small," my father said, worried. "Water problems, do you think?"

"About Caesar," I prompted.

"A lightweight. Effeminate. This jar, too? What do you think?"

It was typical of my father to dismiss my concerns with contempt like this. My anger surged up in me. But I wanted more information. "A lightweight?" I asked, managing to be civil.

"Thinks about nothing but his love affairs. Dresses like a peacock, acts like a goat. Gold fringes, long sleeves. So much purple dye he looks as if he fell in a vat of wine. In debt, too. I have it on good authority that before he even held public office he owed forty-five million sesterces. I know he spent millions on the public games when he was aedile. Which he had to borrow, because the Julians may be an old family, but they are certainly not rich."

In the gloom of the warehouse his eyes glittered with anger; he hated anything that seemed to him financially unsound. "Of course, an aedile has to put on adequate games. Otherwise he would be failing in his duty to honor the city and its gods. But to use the occasion to aggrandize himself from pure extravagance and frivolity, and with money that isn't even his in the first place . . ." My father turned on me in the semi-darkness. Motes of gold swirled around him, his eyes and teeth glittered like silver. "You stay away from him, Marcus. He's a wastrel, a fop, an unstable character. Do you understand me? Stay away. That's an order."

"He's the City Praetor. Doesn't that mean something?" Anger was stiffening my shoulders and making me look him in the eye.

"Not so much as this." The snap of his fingers echoed in the dust space like the crack of a whip. "He's extravagant, he's a fool, he's wasted his talents and his opportunities. If I hear that you've been near him, I'll cut you off without a sesterce. Is that clear?"

That was a laugh, considering how few of his precious sesterces he dispensed anyway. I flung a word at him as I stalked out of the building, so furious I was nearly blinded by the light.

"Caesar?" my mother said, smiling slightly to herself. "He's a very charming man. At least many women think so. Pompey the Great's wife did, while her husband was in the east, and so did Servilia, whose boy Brutus is supposed to be Caesar's. Well, that's what they say. Caesar has very beautiful manners, you know." She sighed. "But his morals aren't very good. You don't have much to do with him, do you, Marcus? Because I don't really think—"

"Don't worry, mother. I don't move in those circles at all." I said. I didn't tell her that I thought it would be a very great pleasure if I did.

"How much does Caesar owe?" Publius Crassus repeated my question. "About forty or fifty million sesterces, I believe."

"Fifty *million*?"

His smile faded. "My father considers it a good investment. I don't see it. He's frivolous and effeminate . . . I can't see that he'll go far . . ."

Oddly enough it was Cicero who had the highest opinion of him. Or the most definite anyway.

61

"Caesar isn't quite what he seems," he said, putting the letter down on his desk and rubbing the bridge of his nose. His eyes were tired all the time. "He seems to do nothing but play, doesn't he? Play at politics, play at love. But for twenty years there hasn't been a seditious political movement, or a dirty business deal, he hasn't had a hand in. He hasn't a scruple in the world, and he's been involved with some very unsavory characters . . ."

"Who?" I cried, fascinated.

He shook his head. "I shouldn't say. I never had any proof. I'd have arrested him, if I had. But I'll tell you this: he's a very ambitious man. The display and the fooling around are only to cover it up, like a marble front on a stucco building. Except that the building's architect puts on falsity to look more impressive, while Caesar is trying to look less."

"Surely that's a very peculiar thing to do?"

He rubbed his eyes again. "Unusual, but not peculiar. It serves his purposes: it brings him a great many contacts, and it prevents the powerful from taking alarm at his progress. And he doesn't mind—he doesn't care what he does to gain his ends. A delightful person, but not a very nice one." His voice became a sad growl. "You can't blame him. When he was young he had terrible experiences . . ."

"What experiences?" I couldn't have turned away from this conversation now, if the house had been on fire.

"Oh, you're right, that is interesting. When he was sixteen Caesar was married to the daughter of a political opponent of the dictator Sulla. That was the old popular hero, the general Marius. I'm related to him myself. Well, anyway, Sulla wanted Caesar to divorce the daughter—to prove his loyalty, I suppose. Caesar was very young at the time—not yet out of his teens. All the same, he refused. He has always kept his allegiance to Marius and to his popular faction very clear in everyone's mind. I'd honor him for that, if I didn't wonder what advantage he saw in it for himself.

"In any case, he refused, and Sulla was enraged. He hounded Caesar so badly that the boy had to go into hiding. His father was dead, and he was all alone. He lived very dangerously in those days, never sleeping in the same place twice, keeping his identity concealed. It was a courageous thing to do. Not many people refused Sulla, or challenged him."

"You did." I knew he had first won fame in the city by trying a case against the dictator's freedman—and winning, in spite of the risk.

"Well, yes. And it's always been a bond between Caesar and me. That and our relation to Marius. We had to resist Sulla, because of that. But many people gave in—Sulla's power was really very terrible. I hope our country never sees anything like it again.

"Sulla kept lists of the people he disliked or feared, you see, and if your name was on it, you had lost your citizenship. Anyone could kill you without fear of penalty. Thousands died that way, out of envy or spite or a desire to curry favor with the dictator. Or for their property, if they had any. When they were dead, Sulla posted their heads in the Forum on poles, to terrorize the rest of us. Believe me, it did.

"So the risk Caesar ran was very real. A night of moonlight, a servant corrupted, and his head might have been one of them. As it was, he caught a fever in the marsh country, and Sulla's soldiers caught up to him. It cost him a lot of money to bribe them to let him get on a ship out of the country. Sulla was very disappointed. 'You'll regret it,' I heard that he said: 'There are many Mariuses in that boy.' Long afterwards, and I have never made up my mind if this was an irony or a deliberate plan of Caesar's, when his first wife was dead Caesar married Sulla's granddaughter. Sulla was dead too of course, so I don't know. Strange, isn't it? But I have always thought that this encounter with Sulla was the real beginning of Caesar's career."

"How?"

He shook his head in sorrow. "It made him feel that there were no limits in the world, I think. That there is nothing a man in power may not do, and nothing a man without it may not suffer."

"And that's not true?"

"I don't think so. There is morality to limit us, and the gods, there is even the natural goodness of human beings . . . Well, not everyone agrees. We must try to help those who don't to see things in a better light, eh, Caelius?"

Perhaps we must, but that was not what I wanted to hear about. "Caesar was changed by his experience?" I asked. I had an idea there was more he could tell me.

"Yes, indeed. For one thing, his health was broken. He's had epilepsy—that's what the Greeks call the falling sickness—ever since."

"I never heard that."

"He keeps it a secret. He's afraid that it might interfere with his ambitions."

"Which are?"

"Oh, I don't think he sets any limits on that." He smiled, a melancholy twitch of the lips, and I thought with astonishment that he felt sorry for Caesar. "The thing is," he said, "I don't think he sets any limits on the means he will use to accomplish them either."

That was what I knew of him then—Gaius Julius Caesar, son of Gaius, deceased, forty years old, Pontifex Maximus and outgoing City Praetor of Rome. It was only what the rest of the city knew, which was everything—and nothing, of course. I think what chiefly impressed me was what I have already said: that he was so well known to so many people. He inhabited the city the way a nymph is part of her forest, a Nereid her stream. He was everywhere, glimpsed in the corner of your eye at public meetings, in the temples just leaving as you arrived for the sacrifice, talking with a group of older men on the other side of the exercise grounds. At a party he had been there earlier and gone on elsewhere, where you were not invited; with a woman, he had been her lover while you were still at school.

A movement has caught my eye, distracting me. I don't know what: a pigeon fluttering past the window, a branch moving in a puff of air. Nothing now. I look around the room.

There has been no change. The silence that encloses me is as deep as ever, the heat of summer is no greater, no less. The army the scouts reported—a wing of cavalry, veterans, heading this way; I have not forgotten—well, there is no sign of it. The road stretches away, empty and white, the town crouches as fearfully behind its shutters as before. On the air come gusts of summer scents: hot stone, baking grass, the salt of the sea, all exactly as they were when I came. But the square of sunlight on the table has moved. Time is changing. Time is growing short.

V

The scandal around Clodius grew, and finally there was a trial. Clodius got off, but only by bringing in a lot of very heavy-looking slaves from the country and intimidating all the jurors. That and the money and promises Crassus paid out in bribes did the trick, in spite of the fact that Cicero testified against Clodius, and broke his alibi. The jury didn't care. Caesar kept very quiet, and hardly allowed himself to appear involved at all, a policy that I imitated.

There was one exception, a party that I went to around this time—a huge bash out in the Subura that Caesar gave to celebrate his taking up a military command. Now that his praetorship was over he had drawn lots with the other senior magistrates in the traditional way, for the commands in the various provinces. Caesar had drawn one of the two Spanish ones.

"Thank you, yes, I think something might very well be done with them," he said, flicking a thin, cool smile at me when I congratulated him. He stood in the atrium of his house—not the official residence in the Forum, but what I guessed was his family place out in that rather plebeian quarter. It was a smallish house, not much nicer than the one my father had bought, though it was festive enough now, with lamps everywhere and well-wishers trooping through all the rooms. I had heard that Caesar was so exigent that he had once torn down a whole villa on Lake Nemi because a single detail of it displeased him—it was one of the things that made my father think he was such a dandy—and I wondered how he could live in this dim and unattractive place. But then I remembered his formidable family pride. It had led him to make a spectacle of his connection with the exceedingly unaristocratic general Marius; no doubt it led him to keep this house, and use it, no matter how cramped and out of style it became. "Something might be done with the Spanish provinces?"

He raised one eyebrow. "You never know."

Perhaps he meant that there might be trouble there and he could hope for a military adventure, with all the profit and renown such things can bring. Perhaps he had something else in mind. It was never very easy to tell, with him.

"I'm so glad you could come, Caelius," he murmured with great warmth, looking me in the eyes. We were the same height, I noticed, two tall men, whose heads rose over the others in the room. Our height isolated us; we spoke as if we were alone. "Look, Caelius," he said, putting his hand on my arm. "Why don't you come with me? There's room on my staff—"

I had turned away, but I could still feel his gaze resting on me like a touch.

"Oh." I was confused. "I . . . I'd like to. But I couldn't leave Rome. I mean, thank you very much, it's a great honor, and I'd love to, but the city. . . I only just got here, you see. I have a lot to do . . ."

"I know. I'd rather not leave Rome myself."

He looked so elegant and sophisticated, so urbane and charming, I could not imagine him on campaign. What would happen to his beautifully arranged hair, his rich and complex perfumes, his manicure? It was unimaginable. It was even funny. I smiled at him. Immediately he smiled back.

"Sir, can you tell me? Why did Crassus get Clodius acquitted? I mean Crassus is your friend, isn't he? And though I know he didn't mean it, Clodius did insult you . . ." With your wife, I meant, but managed not to say it. I was already impertinent enough. He had every right to have me thrown out of the house . . .

But Caesar laughed. "I asked Crassus to."

"*You* did?"

"Of course." He seemed to be waiting for me to say something, but I was too surprised to think. "But your wife—" I blurted out. I was very conscious of his hand, still resting warmly on my arm.

"My ex-wife."

"But Clodius—" I persisted.

"What about Clodius?" He waited, his eyes still on my face with an almost palpable force, not warm now but cool and assessing. I couldn't think of anything to do but to turn the moment into a joke. "Something might be made of him?" I said, remembering his comment about Spain.

Amazingly it was the right thing. He laughed again and patted my shoulder. "It's a pity you won't come with me to Spain. We could do some great things."

I smiled.

"Well, if it can't be, it can't. Enjoy the party, Caelius. Help yourself to anything you want."

There was indeed anything I could have wished for—the best entertainment, the most brilliant collection of people in the city. The food was of such quality that it took my breath away. He must not have cared at all what he paid for his supplies, and his cook must have been the best in Rome.

It's odd to think that at that moment, while he laughed and joked with his guests, he must have been nearly frantic. He owed so much money; his creditors were even threatening to prevent him from leaving Rome.

What would have happened if they had? Who knows? But it is possible that the world might never have heard of Julius Caesar. He might have died as obscurely as his ancestors. I believe this thought occurred to him, and even as he was teasing me, exerting on an obscure young man the charm for which he was so widely liked, he was thinking, worrying, turning over in his mind his choices and possibilities . . .

In the end Crassus paid some sort of installment on Caesar's debts—I heard it was around thirty million sesterces—and promised to take care of the rest. Caesar was allowed to depart for Spain.

"My father will get his money back, you'll see," Publius Crassus insisted to me. "The Spaniards will pay. Between the taxes he can collect—and it's pretty much up to him what he can get out of them, once he's paid the Treasury his share—and the favors a governor has at his disposal, Caesar will do all right."

"He'd better."

"He will, don't worry. He'll be ruthless enough when it

comes to the moment." He picked up the end of his toga, and we went down to the gate to see the departure, with its priests and omens and all the pageantry. It was fun, but I came away feeling oddly bereft and abandoned. I don't know why. The sight of that pale yellow head in the sunshine did something to me, and I had to turn away.

I got drunk that night, but it didn't help much, and two days later my father summoned me into his study.

He was sitting behind a table he used for a desk: a tall, handsome man much like me in appearance, though his hair was graying at the temples. On his desk were several letters and a pile of half-unrolled ledger books, but he pushed them all aside except for a very small stack of notes. His large, well-shaped hand was treading these down like an ox's hoof, holding them flat as if they might struggle under his power. His face was grim and his eyes sharp with bitterness.

"Marcus. What is this?" He held up one of the papers. I recognized it, of course; it was from one of my creditors.

"A bill."

"What? Speak up."

"It's a demand for payment on a loan," I said, very loudly.

"Yes. And this? And this?"

"The same."

There was a silence, for me suspenseful, since I did not want to look down and see what he was doing.

"You owe money all over town," he said at last.

"It's only one and a half—" I felt like a legionary, standing at attention in the general's tent. If he had had any feeling for me at all he would have asked me to sit down.

"Are you telling me that your debts only amount to one and a half thousand sesterces?" He sounded sad. I looked down, but all I could see was the top of his head, and his strong fingers turning over the notes. Gods, I thought, he's in a rage.

When I was little I had thought he was as big as the statue of Jupiter in our town's most impressive temple. Somehow he didn't look any smaller now. "A million and a half," I admitted.

He stood up, a process that seemed to take hours. When

69

he had reached his full height our eyes were on the same level. I had no time to reflect on this, for his were narrowed and brilliant with anger. "It's time you understood something about money," he said.

I thought, Oh, I understand a lot about it. That you keep me short when you can well afford to give me more. That you want me to have a career, but you don't want to pay for it. You want me to remain dependent on you, to come begging for money like a slave, like a woman . . .

"Nothing to say?" he asked. I thought he was mocking me. For a bronze farthing I would have picked up the stack of papers and thrown it at him, I would have told him what I really thought . . . but he was my father, and I could not. I remembered Curio and his father. "I think you should pay those bills," I said.

His face flooded with rage; a vein hammered behind his eye. "You what?" he roared. I clenched my fists and stared into his eyes.

Slowly he mastered himself. "Enough. I told you once that you didn't know the value of money. Well, you are going to learn. I'm sending you to North Africa to work on the estates there. Perhaps that will teach you."

For one light-headed moment I thought he was telling me he was going to sell me as a slave.

"I want you to take a look at the farms there, and the shipping business." He knew perfectly well how I felt, but he didn't care. "I expect a detailed report. I will want to see the books, so be sure they are properly prepared, just as you have been taught." He turned away as if that was all he had to say—no farewell, no father's advice, not even a friendly warning, say about the dangers of fast company in the provinces—if there is any fast company in the provinces.

I supposed I was dismissed, but he had something to add. "I want to be sure you are properly supervised. Therefore, Marcus, you will travel in the escort of a friend of mine, the propraetor Quintus Rufus. He is to be the new governor of the province." He waited, expecting something from me, his hand poised on the edge of his desk. I did not answer. It was all I could do not to smash my fist into his face. Properly supervised.

"Marcus, this man is powerful and important. He can do a lot to advance our interests in Africa. Do you understand anything I'm telling you at all? No? Well, think it over. I want you to treat him at all times with the respect due his position. If he tells you to do anything, do it at once, without question; if he—"

"But father," I cried, finding my voice at last. "What about politics? What about my career in Rome?"

He snorted. "Your career in Rome? You haven't the sense or the maturity to administer a dog kennel. What makes you think you have anything to offer the voters of Rome?"

He would have gone on; I could see the muscles of his jaw working, and his color beginning to rise again.

"When do I leave?" My anger was near to erupting from me, a scalding flow that would have burned us both.

"As soon as possible. The sea lanes become rough in October. Be gone by then." He turned to one of his secretaries and began to instruct him in some other matter. I knew I was dismissed, erased from his mind as if I had never been born. I left without saying goodbye.

I began to devour the city, like man who is going to starve filling himself with bread. Bread? It was a banquet. I went everywhere; I scarcely slept. No acquaintance gave a party I didn't attend, bringing with me a dozen people from the previous one, or if it was the first of the evening, from the bars where I had been drinking before. Freedmen, aristocrats, actors, women from the porticoes, it made no difference to me as long as they wanted a good time. Once I even brought the dirty little Phrygian and his dancing bear.

Sometimes, going towards someone else's bed very late at night, I would find myself alone in the silence. The tall buildings that cut angles into the field of stars overhead, the slats of a pigeon loft on an apartment roof, the crimped edges of tiles on the baths, called out to me like friends. The gods gesturing on the temple roofs were like family.

I walked tirelessly on those nights, for it seemed to me that around the next corner there might be something wonderful to see, and I could not bear to miss anything. In the baths I listened to the gossip as if it were the talk of philosophers, I

71

prowled the shops buying anything: perfumes, Greek pottery, antiques, gemstones, glass. When there were games I went to them, betting on gladiators or horses with Antony and Publius Crassus, and keeping out of the way of the aedile, who would punish gambling if he saw it. I crossed the river and went to swim at the popular bathing spots; I threw the javelin and the wooden balls on the exercise ground in the Campus Martius. I was saying goodbye.

I waited until Pompey the Great had celebrated his triumph—a spectacle I did not want to miss for Pompey was the most famous Roman who had ever lived. He had conquered most of the known world—North Africa, at least the part that didn't already belong to us, and a large portion of nearer Asia as well. He had chased the pirates that used to plague the Eastern Mediterranean like mosquitoes into hiding or crucified them, he had brought millions of people under our rule, and millions of sesterces into the Treasury. People said he was a new Alexander the Great come back after three hundred years. Well, there hadn't been anybody in between him and the famous Greek to challenge them.

In those days the city could refuse him nothing. The Senate granted him a triumph, under pressure, because they feared him and were jealous of his popularity. But Cicero, who was Pompey's oldest friend made them do it. It was supposed to be the most magnificent triumph in the history of the city. It would take two days, one of which was Pompey's own birthday. I couldn't miss that.

I was invited to watch the parade in the company of Cicero and his friends. For two days the loot and captives and armies filed through the Forum and up the Capitoline Hill to the Temple of Jupiter, where dozens of sheep were sacrificed in a cloud of incense so thick and aromatic that the dignitaries in the temple courtyard choked and gasped. Pompey flashed by in a golden chariot, his scarlet toga embroidered with scenes of his battles billowing out behind him, his face blazing with red paint under his crown of laurel. He looked like Mars himself, fiery and proud.

A great man. A magnificent one. He laid his spoils at the feet of his city like a hero of ancient days, giving without stint to his country. At night a public feast was held, with thousands of couches and tables, and wine pouring out as if an aqueduct had sprung a leak.

I ran into Curio in a temple courtyard, where whole sides of beef were roasting. He had already provided himself with a plate, having had his people clear some plebeians out of the way to secure it. "I thought you'd be with your friend Catullus," he said. I explained that Catullus was having an affair with Clodius' sister. He was like a man who has fallen into a jar of honey—he was happy, but it kept him busy.

"Really?" He laughed, a short baa of pleasure. "Well, frankly m-my dear she's too m-much for me. They say she's a beauty though."

I took my own plate and chased some people away from a couch so we could recline there. "I heard something about this Clodius business. I heard that Caesar was the one who persuaded Crassus to get Clodius acquitted of the break-in. What do you think of that?"

His round eyes opened and his lips puckered. "Oh, m-my dear. Can that possibly be *true*?"

"Caesar is the one who told me."

He let out a bleat of surprise. "Really. He is the oddest man, isn't he? I m-mean his own wife. He's very *cool*, isn't he?"

"That's what I thought. So I wondered . . ."

"I m-mean, im-magine seeing that your wife's lover is ac-quitted of the very pretext he used to get into your house. I m-mean, *im-magine* . . ." He bent his face over his plate and studied it for some time. With his round eyes and curly hair, he looked like a lamb watching a beetle crawl up a stalk of grass. "Well, I would believe it of Caesar. He's done it before."

I thought he wasn't going to tell me, but something must have decided him, because after a while he began to speak. "M-my dear, take m-my advice. Stay away from him. He's a very dangerous m-man."

"Don't be silly. He's very nice, quite a charming person. He must be the friendliest man in Rome, always willing to put himself out—"

"So the pirates who captured him thought."

"Who?" I could hardly hear him over the clatter of plates and the hiss of fat in the cooking fires.

"It's not a very well-known story," Curio said softly. "M-my father heard it from a cousin of his who's related to the Servilii, Caesar's m-mother's family . . ." He poured some wine and passed the pitcher to a man who did not bother with a cup, but drained it from the rim. "I wish I could do that, don't you, m-my dear?" Curio whispered. The man's friends were cheering.

"About Caesar."

He smiled around his large yellow teeth. "Yes. Well, when Caesar was a young m-man he went to the island of Rhodes, to escape some political trouble at home—he had managed to make an enemy of the dictator Sulla, I think. He's related to Marius, the popular leader . . ."

"I know about that."

"Well, when Caesar was on the way there his ship was captured by pirates—this was in the old days, before Pompey cleared them out of their little hole in the east. The pirates took Caesar to some island they used for a hideout—there are hundreds of them over there you know, and they kept him a captive. They asked for twenty talents in ransom." He gave me a look from under his eyelashes. Perhaps they were one of the reasons people thought Curio looked like a girl, for they were as long and thick as whiskbrooms and rested modestly against his cheeks as he looked down at his plate again.

"M-my dear, you must understand who the Julians are. They're a very old family, of course, but not very well off, or very distinguished. If we were talking about the glory of Rome, Julius Caesar is not a name that would spring to your lips. If you see what I m-mean. And Caesar was young, and rather, you know, *charming*—"

I knew immediately what he meant. The tall, slender figure, leaning gracefully—very gracefully—against a pillar, the delicate gesture as he scratched his head in a pantomime of elegant puzzlement . . . "Are you telling me he's effeminate?" I demanded."

He shrugged.

"Really, Curio," I said, beginning to get angry.

"Oh, m-my dear, what difference could it *possibly* m-make?

Who cares if he is? And anyway, we were talking about the pirates."

"Yes, we were."

He smiled to himself. "The pirates called him 'the boy.' He was young, you know. Our age, or less. About twenty, I'd guess. As I said, they asked for twenty talents ransom. I'm not sure about Greek m-money. All those foreign currencies never seem quite *real* to me, if you know what I m-mean . . ."

"It's about fifty million sesterces."

"Really? That m-much? That's quite a respectable ammount, isn't it? Especially for a m-man in his position. I m-mean, he didn't *have* any position. 'Do you know who I am?' he asked them, and when the pirates, quite naturally, said they had no idea, he called them fools and told them to ask fifty talents."

"He wanted the pirates to *raise* his ransom? Why?"

"M-my dear, I just don't know."

I was laughing. "Well, you're right, Curio. That's a very bold and cold-blooded thing to do."

"M-my dear, that's not the end of it. He stayed with those cutthroats for about a m-month and during that time he never showed the slightest sign of fear or concern over his fate. He treated them like *servants*, ordering them to be quiet when he wanted to take a nap and so on. He even wrote poetry to pass the time, and forced them to listen to him read it aloud. If they didn't like to, he told them they were illiterates and barbarians. He took his exercise with them, and played ball on the beach, and when he was fed up with them he used to tell them that when he had escaped from the island he would come back and crucify them all. Go ahead, laugh. I'm sure they thought it was funny, too."

He wasn't amused though; he looked sad. His soft eyes and gentle mouth might have been ready to cry. He studied his plate for a long time. "Curio?" I said.

"Well, anyway, m-my dear," he answered in a heavy voice, "Caesar raised the m-money, all fifty talents, from his friends and from his wife's family, and the ransom was paid. As soon as he was released, he armed some ships and went after the pirates. They were still on the island where he had left them, so he captured them and took them to prison. He confiscated their m-money and ships and so on, and went to the Roman governor of the province, whoever it was that year, and demanded that his prisoners be executed. The governor kept saying he'd study the problem—"

"He wanted the money for himself," I interrupted. "After all, it must have been a considerable amount. Not just Caesar's fifty talents, but a lot more than that. He was probably trying to figure out some way to seize it legally."

"Probably." There was another of his silences, then he sighed. "Well, anyway, when Caesar couldn't get any satisfaction from the governor he just took the pirates out of prison and on his own initiative crucified them all."

I shouted with laughter. "Just as he'd promised. He must have told them to raise the ransom because he knew he'd get it back."

"No. He can't have known that. It was far m-more likely that they would kill him. He might have seen the possibility— just the barest hint of a hope—of escape some day. No m-more than that."

"Well, I told you, he's very bold."

His head drooped again. "The pirates liked him, you know."

"Yes, you can tell that. It's a good joke. They must have laughed when they saw the crosses going up. I'll even bet they thought he liked them, too."

Curio's eyelashes swept up and his eyes grew round. "But that's why he's so dangerous."

"What, because he made a bunch of thugs believe he liked them and then crucified them when he had the chance?"

"Not at all, m-my dear. Don't you *see*? What Caesar did was worse. He didn't *pretend* to like them. He really did."

I saw Catullus just before I left, at a little dinner I gave to introduce him to a woman I had been spending quite a lot of time and money on. Her name was Flora, no doubt not the name she was born with for she was one of the *libertinae*— an accomplished courtesan with an interest in poetry as well as the arts of her profession. I thought Catullus would admire her since he was a man of taste, but he wasn't very impressed. Desperate at one point for conversation, I told him Curio's little story.

"Think how brave Caesar must be," I said. "You wouldn't guess it to look at him, I mean he seems so elegant and so . . ." I waved my hand because I couldn't think of another world to describe him. "I mean he did just what he said he would with those men. He didn't let anything stand in his way. And he didn't allow himself to be afraid, or to be deterred by any other feeling—not pity or anger or anything. I think it's really an amazing story."

Catullus shuddered. "I think it's a very sad one."

"Why?"

But he only shook his head. "That's not courage. It's inhuman coldness."

"Well, call it what you like, it's very unusual," I said angrily, and on that note we parted. The next day I sailed for North Africa.

VI

The square of sunlight has moved again; part of my paper shines in it now. Against the scarred wood it makes a brilliant edge, a division, light from dark, the present from the past.

LAST REPORT OF MARCUS CAELIUS RUFUS
PRAETOR PERIGRINUS OF ROME . . .

My report. For whom?

Out in the town under the porticos and in the dusty little Forum, my men are cooking the noon meal. Before each eight-man mess the braziers are set out, bread is baking, those who can afford meat or who have taken the trouble to secure it in some other way are turning the pieces on the grills. For myself the town council has sent in something: do they imagine I would be fool enough to eat food from their hands? I gave it to the servants, who were glad enough of it: it was a whole poached mullet, I think, and a roasted chicken and some other things—Thurii's rather pathetic best. For myself I have asked for a plate of beans and a jug of wine. They will be bringing it up from my officers' tent soon.

The fat little chief magistrate carried Thurii's offering to me in his own hands, sweating copiously in the morning heat, which did not make the lunch any more appetizing, let me tell you. His jowls were already blue, though he must have been shaved before we arrived. The scent of aromatic herbs came from him, the sort you would find in Rome, though not in the best houses. His toga, somewhat hastily draped, flaps over his little round belly; his legs are short and fat, like an overgrown baby's. He has small, anxious, rather intelligent brown eyes, like plums. They are too soft in his puffy face.

He is the sort of man who is perfect for his job—he can manage the grain warehouse and the harbor master, he can cope with the publicly owned slaves and keep the prostitutes and the municipal market honest, the baths clean, the festivals ritually correct, but three hundred soldiers occupying his town on a late summer morning is more than he bargained for. He twists his hands and moans, and annoys the one man in the world he has to please . . .

"Praetor, what is happening? I mean, our town . . . we . . . we have a right to know. If you're going to . . . You took hostages, you see, and . . . Oh, praetor, what is going on?"

"Magistrate, I don't have time to explain the civil war to you."

"Well, we know about that. We've heard of Caesar and Pompey."

"Oh, you have, have you?" I have to try not to laugh. The whole world has heard of them, I should think.

"Oh, yes. We're no backwater here. Thurii is very up-to-date. We hear all the latest news." He stands straighter now, and beams at me. Only his little eyes shift anxiously as he says, dropping his voice, "Praetor, which side are you on? I mean . . ."

"What exactly do you want to know?" I am striving for patience, but it is beginning to elude me.

"Oh, praetor, everything. Whatever you want to tell me."

"You tell me. What do you already know?"

He looks around the room for a chair, but there is only mine, and though I am standing by the window, I do not invite him to sit in it. I remain leaning against the sill, my legs crossed at the ankle, watching him. He amuses me; he keeps the silence at bay.

"Well." He puts his hands behind his back and takes up an orator's stance, as if he were going to recite a speech. "Pompey and Caesar. Two very great men, very great." He is watching to see if I will react to one name or another, but I have been trained in a harder school than a provincial town council, and, defeated in his hope, he is forced to go on uninformed. "Well, we heard that Caesar, who felt that his rights had been abused, had crossed into Italy from his province with an army, and that the Senate in Rome had appointed Pompey to defend them against him."

"That's right."

"Is it true?" His small bright eyes search my face. "Did the Senate really try to refuse Caesar his rights?"

You won't catch me like that, I think. "Some people say so."

"Yes, praetor," he agrees unhappily. "Well, we heard that there was fighting in Italy—"

"Practically none."

"Really?"

"Really. Caesar took a few towns up north when he first came into Italy, but there was little resistance. And Pompey sailed to Greece to raise more troops, while Caesar went to Spain to fight Pompey's friends there and avoid being cut off from behind . . ." On the summer breeze the memory comes back to me, the bitter Spanish soil, the rivers bursting from their banks, men shouting, the screams of drowning horses, armor torchlight, trumpets. Later, mountains, bare as bronze and as cruel, long marches, and a terrible thirst. "Yes, magistrate? You were saying?"

"I just said that we'd heard that Caesar had made a new Senate in Rome, and a new government."

"Just so. A new government. But of course, the old one escaped with Pompey to Greece where they say they are still in charge."

"Of course. Of course." The sweat is practically pouring off him in his haste to agree, and his mouth is moving so quickly his words come out in a gabble. "And the armies are all drawn up facing one another now, in Greece. Caesar is there, and there's going to be a battle. Oh, yes, that's what we heard. Everything will be decided at this battle, when it comes."

"Or nothing will."

"Yes, praetor," he says, but he does not really understand. Apparently he does not realize that the battle he is talking about is long since over, with a great victory for Pompey. Though, as I have told him with scrupulous honesty, nothing is settled, for Caesar has escaped, and taken his army—or what's left of it—with him. No one knows where he is. At least, no one *I* know does. Caesar's whereabouts, the fate of my friends and acquaintances, all are part of the silence that has fallen around me. I have no news. But I am sure of one thing: nothing is settled, nothing at all.

"So you see," the magistrate says earnestly, matching my candor with his own, "I want very much to know what is happening. Praetor, why are you here? Why do you need my town? Is it to help in the war? In that case, of course we are anxious to do our best for the distinguished gentleman you represent—"

I have said nothing. I am waiting to hear how far this little man will go.

"Only, praetor, *which one of the gentlemen is it?*"

All the way.

"Praetor," he whispers, "can't you tell me? Which side are you on?"

I raise one eyebrow and give him the sight of my teeth. "Why, the government's, of course. And see that you keep it in mind. Any help you give us will be remembered favorably by the authorities. Of course, any hindrance . . ."

"But . . ." He is nearly shouting, forgetting himself entirely. "*Which government?*"

My patience is at an end. "Good morning magistrate," I say, indicating the door with a nod.

"Sir, I'm going, I'm sorry to trespass on your time. I know you're busy. But, don't you see? My town. I'm responsible . . . Praetor, couldn't you just say, *which government?*"

"Why, I didn't know that was worrying you, magistrate. Certainly I can say. The *legal* one. Of course."

Defeated, he bows his way out, closing the door on my laughter.

The legal one. Only the outcome of the war will determine which that is. That is what a civil war is about. Of course.

I have had another interruption—the first scout. They showed him into my room practically on the heels of the little magistrate. He is a different horse altogether, brisk and to the point.

"Praetor, I have seen the cavalry again. They are certainly from Spain, and just as certainly Caesar's. Their strength is nearly four hundred men. I got this figure from one of the auxiliaries who is marching with them. He thought I was a centurion with the main body and he gave me the figure. It is, in my judgment, almost certainly accurate."

"I see. They are coming this way?"

"Yes."

"And they will get here when?"

"If nothing delays them, by first light tomorrow." He does not know for sure if he is telling me good news or bad, but he too is peering at me through the glowing shadows of my room.

"What might delay them?" I ask.

He shrugs. Of course. What could delay a full wing of cavalry on the march? "They seem in control of the region. I don't see any opposition . . ."

"No. What were they doing when you saw them last?"

"Praetor," he says, coming to attention and looking at me squarely. "They were singing."

VII

LAST REPORT OF MARCUS CAELIUS RUFUS
PRAETOR PEREGRINUS OF ROME . . .

It wasn't the end of the world out in North Africa, but only because ships came occasionally with letters from Rome. There was no one to talk to—the praetor I travelled with was far too self-important to gossip with a young assistant, and provincial society, such as it is out there, was entirely occupied with local matters. They might never have heard of Rome at all.

My interest in the municipal elections or the marriage of the town headman's daughter being limited, I waited eagerly for news of the city. Cicero wrote once in a while, Curio rather more often. Catullus' friend Calvus sent a note to say that he was concerned, because Catullus' love affair with Clodius' sister, Clodia Metelli, appeared to be over. It seemed she had found other young men to interest her. "What did he expect?" I wrote back. "She has money, power, connections. She doesn't need a poor boy from Gaul who hasn't even made the beginnings of a career for himself in Rome."

I might have been writing that about myself, for out in the dust of North Africa I had begun to fear that I would never succeed in politics, never hold office or win glory on a battlefield or see my name carved into stone in the temples as one of the consuls for the year. Here, in this little town, I would remain, forgotten by everyone. I did not like to think whose fault it was. The gods punish such thoughts. Once, long ago, someone had said that to me, I couldn't remember who . . .

In that time I was troubled by nightmares. In them, my father—it was always my father—died in bizarre and humiliating ways, while I watched, paralyzed with horror, or tried to save him but failed. From these dreams I woke, panting and dry-eyed. I felt so ill, though I did not know why, that I even went to see a priest of Aesclepius. All he could do was give me a drink to take at bedtime, but it left me so heavy the next morning that I threw it away.

So I accepted my affliction and lay awake at night, listening to the dry rattle of the wind scraping the palm tree outside my window, hearing the jackals call over anonymous remains out in the desert.

A strange little echo of this trouble came to me in a letter from Curio which I received about this time.

DOCUMENT APPENDED

"I heard from a friend of mine in his escort that Caesar is doing very well in Spain. He's been putting down rebellious tribes and setting the government in the pacified areas on a rational basis. Still, there are some curious tales going around, my dear, that you'll want to hear, since you take such an interest in Caesar.

"For instance, my friend says, that on their way to Spain when they were riding through a little village in the Alps— you know the kind of place I mean; they keep the pigs in the square, and the only running water is the melting snow in the street—well, my friend said to Caesar, 'Can you be- lieve that even in this place there are ambitions and jealous- ies and struggles for power among the important men, just as if they were all in Rome?' My friend was laughing, but Caesar gave him a peculiar look—have you ever noticed, he has *very* unusual eyes—and said, 'I'd rather be the first man here than the second in Rome.' He meant it, too.

"Another time, in Spain, Caesar was sitting in his tent after supper reading the life of Alexander the Great when of all things he suddenly burst into tears. My dear, imagine the consternation. The general wailing, the servants run- ning around with hot towels and cups of wine, and I don't know what. His staff was thunderstruck. 'Well, don't you think it's worth crying over?' Caesar asked them. 'At my age Alexander had killed so many people, and I have done nothing important at all.' At his age, Alexander was *dead*,

**my dear, but don't let that spoil the story. Perhaps history
isn't Caesar's strongest point."**

I laughed and put this letter aside, but from that moment
the vivid dreams stopped, the wind ceased to trouble me and
the jackal howled over someone else's bones.

Cicero, too, wrote about Caesar. "He's doing very well—
surprisingly so if he were at all the man he seemed to be.
You will know what I mean, I'm sure. A life on campaign is
nothing like the life he led in Rome. but Caesar seems to
have adapted very well. They say he drives himself physically
very hard, and his men respect him for it. And he's having
some success as a general—an unexpected talent, wouldn't
you say?"

And another time: "I could never see what Caesar wanted
this command for, unless it was to challenge Pompey by an
equal accumulation of power. Now that Caesar is back in Italy,
with the Spanish war successfully concluded, he's demanding
a triumph, which he may get. It was a popular victory. With
that and the loyal army behind him, he may be in a position
to rival the Great Man after all." Cicero always called Pompey
"The Great Man" though it was only half a joke.

"I don't like it," he added later, "The situation seems to me
to be dangerous." He did not elaborate. Still it was a typical
Ciceronian comment, and for a moment I saw him at his
desk, his fingers massaging his nose, his eyes closed and his
heavy shoulders slumped with weariness. It reminded me of
the city, the lights winking on the darkened hills, the golden
river flowing under the sky. I groaned aloud with loneliness
and put this letter aside too.

Cicero wrote again, a month or so later:

DOCUMENT APPENDED

**"I was not the only one to dislike Caesar's ambition, or
let us say to distrust it, it seems. He has petitioned the
Senate to let him run for the consulship *in absentia*, because
if he came into the city to campaign he would forfeit his
right to a triumph. The Senate refused, saying that cam-**

paigning *in absentia* is unconstitutional. which in my view is unfortunately correct. So Caesar will have to choose: the triumph or the consulship. Just in case he chooses the consulship, the Senate has already assigned the provinces the next-year's consuls will govern when their term of office at home expires. Whoever is elected will have 'the forests and cattle paths'—an assignment hardly requiring a consul at all. Indeed a junior magistrate like an aedile could handle it perfectly well, if they were ever assigned duties outside of Rome.

"Still, it is traditionally a proconsular assignment, and it's perfectly legal to give it to next year's consul, if the Senate wants to. No doubt Caesar was hoping for something more attractive: a rich and lootable place like Syria, for example, or a troubled one like Gaul, where he could win more victories and command an even larger and more devoted army. No, this move on the Senate's part is designed to make the consulship less attractive than the triumph, that's all.

"Well, we shall see which one Caesar picks. I'm betting on the triumph myself. It offers more certainty, and Caesar is no fool. He knows that without the Senate's favor very little can be accomplished. And the Senate has certainly made its opinion plain.

"But enough of this. I hope things are going well with you . . . Terentia and the children send their love . . ."

A few days later he wrote me the outcome, though I had to wait for the next ship to find out what it was. Caesar had chosen the consulship, in spite of its disadvantages; he was campaigning very actively. I wrote to Cicero that it had been my guess, which was true. "Caesar strikes me as very intelligent, in spite of what he pretends," I said. "I think he will always prefer the reality of power to its appearance." Perhaps I was beginning to understand something out there all alone in the wilderness. I certainly had plenty of time to think.

At the elections in July, Caesar was returned as consul, along with a very rigid conservative named Bibulus. Curio wrote and told me about it:

My dear, the amount of *money* Caesar spent. The Senate, as nervous as my auntie Scribonia, went around saying that if Caesar was elected without a strong conservative colleague, he'd be impossible to restrain, so they all got together and agreed to put up Marcus Bibulus as their candidate, pooling their money to back him. My dear, it was like the scramble to back the favorite at the chariot race. I'm not partial to Caesar, you know, but this was—it was *unseemly*. Even Cato got caught up in it and actually said, in a public speech, that bribery in a good cause is morally justified. Really, my dear, I'm not making this up.

Not that any of this bothered Caesar. He just went on splashing his money around. Hercules alone knows how much he spent. In addition he paid Crassus back everything he owed him—twenty-five million sesterces. I wonder if he left those poor Spaniards with a rag to their backs or a crust to their tables. But they seem absolutely to adore him, so perhaps there's more to this provincial administration business than meets the eye. Have you left anything behind for the rest of us in North Africa? You must be doing *splendidly* out there yourself. Come home soon and tell us all about it.

I had not done so badly; I had applied myself and made some contacts and some money. My chests were packed with cash, and the few good things I managed to find in the shops. I thought vaguely that they would go to furnish an apartment or a little house, if my father could be persuaded to put up the rent. I did not think this very likely, but I resolved to try. Every night I passed the crates and boxes stacked in the atrium waiting to go. My longing for the city revived with all its original force; my nights were as bad as my first ones in the colony. But I felt different. I was older and more mature. Something had changed for me in North Africa, though I couldn't have said what.

I arrived in Italy at the end of October and spent some time with my parents in the country, a duty visit. It shocked me to see how old they had become. My mother had lines around her eyes and mouth and a rather shorter temper with the maids than I remembered; what there was of my father's hair was now entirely gray, and he had grown a beard, which made him look like one of our ancestors.

He nodded rather abstractedly over the account-books from the North African farms and businesses, but he said nothing at all. I had expected criticism, and so was not surprised at this grim silence, though I was disappointed. I had done, I thought, rather well. The farms were much improved: yields had increased and expenses were down. The businesses were all showing healthy profits, some of them for the first time.

In addition I had a letter from my propraetor Quintus Rufus, which I handed to my father with the seal unbroken. This was not quite as virtuous as it sounds, for Rufus had told me he was writing that he had found me a very satisfactory assistant.

Still, my father might have said something. It made me angry all over again, in spite of my resolutions not to allow myself to be drawn into my old rage. I waited in silence, however, clenching my fists as if I were clutching at my self-respect, but my father merely hummed a little to himself and stared off into space.

So, thinking I had nothing to lose, I raised the question of an apartment. To my astonishment, he agreed, even allowing me some money toward the furnishings. "Get a good address," he said, with all his usual disdain for my projects. "You'll need it."

"Why is that?" I asked, incautiously, knowing I was asking for a flight of barbed comments on my life and my habits.

"In the first place, the value of the lease will appreciate. And in the second, if you're going to make a career in public life you'll need to be visible, and accessible to your clients."

I think my jaw must have dropped. Hadn't he destined me for a clerk's life, practically a servant's, in his offices and warehouses? Why had he wasted my time for a year in Africa if he hadn't? He had as much as told me he didn't think me worthy of a slave's position. "*Am* I going to have a career in politics?" I asked, biting off my words sharply to keep my fury from bursting through.

"I thought you wanted one."

I could not trust myself to speak. "Well," he said, "it's what

I always wanted for you. Why do you think I spent so much money on your education? And had to call in so many favors? Cicero and Crassus don't take just anyone for pupils, you know. I've been working for your career for years." He gave me a look I had not seen before. I only realized later it had been intended for a smile.

I paid my calls in the city when I arrived there: the obligatory one on Crassus who embraced me briskly and gave me a small stack of legal matters to attend to for him; on Cicero, who was working, as he had been when I left, on a bill in the Senate to get a grant of land as a reward for Pompey's veteran soldiers. Though he was genuinely glad to see me he scarcely had time to talk. He was very grateful for my offer of assistance.

Next I sent a note to Catullus and invited him to call. He was absorbed in his love affair with Clodia—now apparently hot again—and not much interested in my plans. His poetry had become famous and was recited all over the city. In the Argiletum, the street that runs behind the Forum, the booksellers painted their doorways with advertising for copies of his lyrics. Well, they were very good, anyone could see that.

DOCUMENT APPENDED

> Mourn, O Venuses and Cupids
> and all who love what's beautiful
> my girl's sparrow is dead
> my girl's delight is dead
> which she loved more than her eyes.
> He was as sweet as honeycake
> and knew her as well as a girl knows her mother.
> He never left her lap
> but hopped around now here, now there,
> chirping all the time to greet his mistress.
> Now he goes along the dark way
> from which they say no one returns.
> O curse you, you vile shades of Hell
> that devour all beautiful things—
> Now you've taken a pretty little bird.

O cruel, o poor little sparrow
Because of you my girl's sweet eyes
are red and burn with tears.

Catullus himself still had his old air, slightly shabby and slightly tough, but his battered face was twisted with anxiety. He talked for two hours about Clodia Metelli, and only remembered to ask about North Africa when I was already showing him out the door.

I went to see the rest of the crowd, too. They were busy with their various pursuits—not very different from the ones they had been after before I left. Antony, grown if anything handsomer, was as wild as a lion on a mountainside; Publius Crassus was preparing a speech for his father against his father's old enemy Pompey the Great; Calvus had become quite the budding young orator; Dolabella, one of our gang from Crassus' lectures, looking aged, turned out to be worried about a marriage his father was arranging. He was afraid he would have to accede to it to pay his debts. Even Curio, though he invited me to dinner and listened very politely to my stories about North Africa, was really more interested in what had been going on at home.

Finally I called on Julius Caesar. This was not as bold as it may seem, for on my return from the provinces I had found a message from him asking me to do that very thing as soon as I got back to the city. With the message was a present—a handsome trophy of spears and shields from Spain, carved with the sinuous almost fluid animals of the Celtic tribes. Obscurely flattered by this gift I set the trophy aside, planning to hang it in my new place when I got one.

Caesar received me in his official residence in the Forum, for in addition to his election as consul he was still Pontifex Maximus. He had a beautiful office, with cubbyholes for books built nearly to the height of my chest, and dark gold walls above. His library must have been a good one, for I could see the leather-bound rolls neatly stacked with their pretty scarlet tags hanging down, showing the titles stamped in gilt. He had two or three secretaries, to all of whom he dictated at once, and a number of clerks copying letters or tallying accounts, but these he sent out of the room when I arrived.

"Well, Caelius. Tell me about North Africa."

I told him what I could, and rather more than I imagined I would, for he asked me questions, his eyes glinting with interest. His thin mouth curled as if he were tasting what I said. It gave him pleasure, too, though I couldn't see why exactly. I found myself relating things I had scarcely noticed that I knew: matters of local political and social life as well as of business and agriculture. He was even interested enough to inquire about philosophy and art.

"It might be useful some time," he said. His eyebrow rose, and he laughed. "You never know."

"You don't, do you?" I smiled back, thoroughly at ease.

"And what are your plans now?"

I looked around his beautiful room. "I want to get started."

"And what do you have in mind to do?"

"Anything," I said.

I saw him nod, a tiny movement as if for himself alone, and his brilliant dark eyes rested on me, weighing me. "I see." His grin flicked again, quick as a knife. "You've changed, Caelius."

"Africa's a good place to think. There isn't anything else to do there."

I was entertaining him. He was smiling. "I know. So is Spain. Well, we ought to be able to find something—for a man who is willing to do anything."

"Thank you."

"I usually have something to eat around now. Would you care to join me?" I remembered the dinner he had given to celebrate his assignment in Spain—the most extravagant and at the same time the most refined and elegant meal I had ever eaten. "I'd be delighted," I said with considerable enthusiasm.

But his lunch was only bread and cheese, and some very weak wine. I looked at him in surprise when it was set before me, waiting for the rest of it to appear, but Caesar was already eating. It was obvious that there was to be nothing more.

As he ate he read me a petition he had received—he wanted my opinion. I ate my own meal, wondering at the contrast. His austerity impressed me, but I could not understand it. It was not Roman, somehow. If I had owned such a cook, I would not have been so Persian as to use him for a banquet for half the city, nor so Spartan as to ignore him when I was alone.

VIII

I heard that Publius Clodius had a flat to let: the ground floor and garden of a house he owned on the Palatine Hill. He wanted thirty thousand for it, which I borrowed from Crassus. It was certainly expensive, but nobody could deny that it was convenient to the Forum. It was the best address in the city. Cicero lived down the street, as did Clodius himself; his sister Clodia, Catullus' mistress and the wife of the outgoing consul Metellus, was next door. Crassus had built a mansion in the same street. It was the first building in Rome constructed entirely of marble. Pompey the Great lived nearby, and Curio shared a bachelor establishment with his father at the other end. Even my father was pleased, though he blinked when he heard the price. I thought he was going to shout at me, but he swallowed his anger, if that was what it was, and agreed to reimburse Crassus for the rent.

So I distributed my purchase from North Africa around the house, I hired a cook in the Forum and brought in some slaves, I hung up the Spanish trophy, and considered myself moved in. Very soon clients began to show up in the mornings, people my father had sent from our farms and businesses, or tenants of the buildings he was beginning to buy in Rome.

I went to call on Crassus yet again and got some more work from him; Cicero sent me out to the country with a letter of introduction to Pompey the Great. I waited in his house among the hundreds of petitioners until at last I was shown in to him. He wasted about the time it takes to swallow twice on me and my letter, but he gave me some jobs to do for him too. Most of the time I spent trying not to stare at him, for although I had been hearing about his greatness since my childhood I had never been this close to him before. It was like standing in front of Achilles or Alexander.

Pompey was a big man, handsome in a florid way, with a flat face and heavily lidded eyes, which he seldom opened all the way. When he did, the effect was startling. His gaze was bright blue and very blank, like a statue's. He had the traditional Roman dignity of manner. Combined with the stare and with a certain sense of his own importance that emanated from him, he seemed less like a man than like a monument to himself.

I don't know if you understand the kind of jobs I was given in those days. They were typical of a young lawyer's when he's just starting out. I don't mean to complain—nobody ever humiliated me over them, or not deliberately—but they were pretty grubby all the same. Basically, I did errands; there's no way to get around that. I did whatever no one else wanted to do. I interviewed clients and took depositions, I went to meetings, I tried cases so insignificant they might have been disputes between two flies. One I remember dealt with a quarrel between shopkeepers over an intrusive sign, another over an accusation of theft of a hundred sesterces worth of goods. My biggest case concerned an inheritance worth about three thousand. And so on. But those jobs obliged great men, whose constituents these little people were, and it put the great under an obligation to me. You never know when that will come in useful.

I did political favors, too. More than once I carried money to one or another poor plebeian in the depths of the city. "This is a gift from Crassus, who thanks you for your support," I would say. Or from Pompey or Clodius or Caesar. It didn't matter to me, and I don't think it mattered much to them. They got the help they needed and I got a reputation as a useful young man, who could be relied upon to do anything to get ahead.

From these encounters I sometimes took back information to my patron. Sometimes it was of a kind it is degrading even to know, let alone repeat. Once in a while I was sure I was paying for other than the normal services—intimidation, for instance, or extortion. It was a revelation to me that almost everyone did these things. In view of that, was I going to let squeamishness get in my way?

I also got an extension of my education in other ways. In those months I discovered a part of Rome I had never seen before. When I think of it now I am struck by that, for it was by far the largest part of the city. Yet it had been until then nearly invisible to me.

This was the city of apartment houses and small shops, of casual labor employed by the day in brick yards and smelters and at the Tiber docks. It was inhabited by actors and musicians, caterers and cooks who hire themselves out for dinner parties, by bakers and weavers and leather workers, armorers and greengrocers and vendors of fish, baskets, or yard goods. Retired legionaries live there and new recruits not yet sent to join their units. So do construction workers, and night watchmen, and hired bodyguards.

They live as I say, anonymous and invisible lives, crowded with their families five or ten to a room in crumbling tenements in the deepest parts of the city. They go to the baths and games and the political debates; they wait on their patrons in the great houses when they need help and contribute their few extra coins to their trade associations, their temple sodality, and their burial association.

Yet they are citizens, freeborn Romans like you or me, though in many cases they are poorer than slaves, and live much worse. Many would not survive at all if it weren't for the grain and cooking oil the city distributes to them at reduced prices, and for the fact that they have one thing the rich will buy: their vote. At elections they lose their invisibility; then even the blindest politician can see them.

They turn out by the thousands in their tribes to cast their ballots into the urns as faithfully as they know how, for whoever has helped them in their desperation. It takes all day for them to pass through the Forum, and you can hear the heavy tread of their feet on the gangways for hours after they have left.

They are the vast unconsidered force in the city. They fight the wars, they elect the officials, they manufacture what we use, and sell what we buy. They do not know their power; even now they are scarcely aware of what they could do. But in the time that I spent among them, they were beginning to get an idea.

It was not the plebeians who understood that they were powerful, exactly. It was the most patrician of the aristocrats who saw it first: Gaius Julius Caesar and Publius Clodius Pulcher. I mean, of course, everybody does something for the poor—ever since the days of the Gracchi in my great grandfather's time that has been the sign of intelligence in a politician. Crassus, never a dull-witted man, was very generous, and Pompey was fond of showing himself at large meetings and haranguing his supporters in the old-fashioned style.

They liked to listen, too—I suppose amusements are short among the poor. I remember one speech of Pompey's that had to be held in the Circus Flaminius because so many people wanted to come. Cicero was popular too. He never had the wealth of the others, but he had a fine and dramatic reputation as the defender of the constitution during his consulship and of the rights of individuals in the courts, so he could always draw an enthusiastic crowd. That was all traditional. But Caesar and Clodius were different.

At first I couldn't see how. They did not seem to be doing anything that powerful aristocrats in public life have not done before. They made the speeches, they visited the neighborhoods, they kept their own doors open every morning to hear the complaints and petitions, and they sent people like me around to the slums to help out where we could. But gradually it dawned on me. These two, independently I think, had arrived at a new idea. They were *organizing* the process.

When I took money from Crassus for example, I went to the Porta Capena or the Subura or some other district and I called on all the people that Crassus had told me to see, climbing the stairs to the miserable, stinking flats, or hunting up the men in the bars or on the street corners. But when I took money to Caesar's clients or Clodius' I went directly to the workmen's association or the temple and saw a man there, who distributed all my commissions for me, like a centurion in the army. Like a centurion, he probably took a cut for himself. Why not? The new system was very efficient.

It was expensive though. Both Caesar and Clodius spent money at rates I had a hard time bringing myself to believe.

Clodius did it, I think, because although he was a drunk and a wild man and a sullen, undergrown bully, he genuinely liked these poverty-hardened creatures, and in some way felt himself to be one of them. Caesar—well, Caesar was a different case. Why should he cultivate the poor? He had already been elected to the consulship; indeed his term was about to start. Beyond that there is very little for anyone to aspire to, and nothing that is in the gift of the mass of voters.

Yet Caesar was everywhere. If I had thought before I went to North Africa that he inhabited the city as a dryad her woods, now he was like rain among the leaves: constant, unavoidable, not unpleasant but noticeable, and finally taken for granted.

I would see him coming down some squalid street in his chair carried by the handsomest porters in the city, waving his hand at the crowds that never failed to gather. His gesture, I had to admit, was a little limp, but no one ever seemed to think the worse of him for that, and the people yelled his name enthusiastically as he passed. Or I would catch him at the end of a speech—perhaps a very informal one from the steps of a temple that happened to be handy. There too the crowds were thick. Caesar's eloquence was in its way as fine as Cicero's and getting to be well known. His style was simple, straightforward and plain.

I saw him everywhere, stopping at a bar for a drink, pressing people's hands at a street festival, coming out of tenements or going into the public baths; not infrequently he stood over my shoulder while I gave out his money, greeting his clients and calling every one of them by name. Why? All I could think of was Curio's voice, "M-my dear, just on the off-chance, don't you see?" and Caesar's own, "It might come in useful some time." But I wondered if it were more than that. I wondered if he had some sort of plan, though I couldn't imagine what it could be.

Once in a while I saw him with Clodius, but I could not tell if their meetings were accidental. In the great houses up on the hills—up on the surface, I nearly wrote—they were sometimes at the same dinner parties. Their aristocratic connections made that inevitable, though the scandal about Caesar's wife made some hostesses chary of inviting them both at the same time. Down among the poor they were both popular, and I suppose they might have run into one another once in a while by accident. There are ways in which Rome, mighty as it is, is as small as a village after all.

Just before he took office, in the dark days of late December, Caesar gave a party for the Saturnalia. I went, along with what must have been half the city. Though the winter day was rapidly closing in there were still crowds in every street. Amid laughter and shouting I heard music. Long lines of dancers were threading their way over the rutted stones, their arms on one another's shoulders. You could not tell slave from free man, for all wore the soft cap that is traditional for the holiday; it flopped up and down as they moved.

Down in the Forum tables had been set out before the Temple of Saturn. The remains of a great sacrifice to the god—whose holiday it is—were turning on the spits. Free men and slaves alike reclined on the couches, eating and drinking while the musicians played and acrobats and mimes entertained the crowd. Near one table, I saw a dancing bear; at another an actor recited passages from a comedy. On the steps of the temple there was a game of dice in progress. A magistrate walked by and did not even give it a second glance. I walked on under a sky all smoke and embers, like the sacrifice, arriving at last in the first true darkness at the door of Caesar's house.

It was the Saturnalia, when all the rules are suspended and the world is turned upside down. Caesar answered the door himself.

"Caelius. Come in." The noise of the party flowed out around him into to the entryway. He looked magnificent, dressed in his best. Well, the Saturnalia is a joyous holiday, it is good to dress up for it. Caesar wore a tunic of fine heavy wool dyed an icy green and embroidered with gold. He did not of course have on the toga. That is not for the Saturnalia. On his head he wore the traditional floppy Phrygian cap, but he had added a wreath of holly to it. Brilliant red berries winked among the dark leaves and his hair shone under it as gold as the embroidery of his clothes. I thrust the package of wax candles that are the usual gift for the season at him.

"Thank you." He gave me his thin, mocking smile. "Come and join the party. It's in here." He put his hand on my shoulder to guide me. Like all his gestures it was warm, friendly, steady. I felt the outline of his palm and five outstretched fingers all the rest of the evening whenever there was a lull or the wine ran low. It made me smile. He was so easy, so pleasant. More than a patron, he made me believe he was my friend.

It was an enormous party, as Caesar's tended to be. I don't know why: he liked to show his friends off to one another perhaps, or he thought it enhanced his prestige if they saw how many he had. In every room there were crowds of people; among the holiday garlands and the tiny points of flame from the candles, they murmured and joked, talked and laughed with each other or with the servants as if it didn't matter at all. No one minded. I saw one dignified old senator burst out laughing when a kitchen boy called him "an old trout." I wanted to laugh myself—it was very apt, for the man's mouth opened and closed and his eyes goggled exactly like a fish's, but even in the Saturnalia I could not take the same liberties a slave can allow himself, and I held my tongue.

In one room I ran into Catullus, talking to his friend Calvus. "What are you doing here?" I cried. "I thought you didn't like Caesar."

He tilted his head toward the wall, where under a mural of Perseus and Andromeda, Publius Crassus was getting very drunk with Antony. A moment later Crassus' father appeared, lean and hollow as a blasted tree. "Oh-oh, here comes Medusa," I said, but he did not freeze us with his melancholy eye. Instead he actually smiled.

At that moment a crowd of about ten young aristocrats had swept through the room, shouting at the tops of their voices: the whole group from Crassus' lectures. On one foot I hesitated, not liking to leave abruptly. But Calvus and Catullus had fallen into a very technical argument about the origins of the holiday; they did not even look up when I went to find the others.

Everyone was there, except Curio and his father, of course. I looked everywhere for him, but I knew all along he wouldn't have come. Some animosities are too deep even for a festival

to heal. I don't know the reason for it—the Curios were supporters of Sulla, and of Clodius, but there is more to it than
that. Some offense given or taken—who knows? But the re-
sentment was of long standing, and they would not have
come.

I missed Curio. I wandered around a little at a loss, for
everyone else seemed to be busy. At one point I saw Cicero
talking to a Spanish financier. I leaned against a pillar and
watched. Presently Caesar came up. He and the Spaniard
spoke earnestly to Cicero, trying to persuade him of something—or to something. Caesar was bending all his silvery
charm on him, cajoling, touching his arm, looking into his
eyes. His body was shaped into a curve of desire, leaning
toward what he wanted so urgently, but held back by his
usually disguised discipline and self-restraint. The Spaniard
moved his arms in the air and showed his white teeth, Cicero
protested loudly that history would not think well of him if
he compromised his principles . . . How? Who knows? I
laughed and moved away. It was as good as a mime.

A long time later, there was the dinner. I lay on the couch
next to a slave, who also reclined, like a free man. He was
the librarian of Caesar's household, an erudite fellow with a
passion for Greek philosophy. He told me several interesting
facts about lions. Did you know that the North African kind
have claws in their tails? Neither did I. But it seems it's true:
the philosophers say so. At least some of them do—

Down in front a fellow was beating on a pot bellowing,
"Let's everybody get into the spirit of the holiday and HAVE
A GOOD TIME." He looked like a cook with his fat belly
and his face shining with good humor. He was beating on a
copper basin, trying to call the room to order, but the servants were all shouting. In the back a huge voice called out
for quiet. It was Pompey the Great, beaming like a new
bronze shield in the sunlight. A large, sleepy smile curved
over his face as he lay down again in the now much subdued
room. Well, I thought, it's a step up for Caesar to have gotten
The Great Man to come.

The servants were calling down in front for a king. "We
must have a king for the festival." And of course they must,

it's the tradition. The servants chose one in our house in Interamnia, and we do nothing that has not been done for several hundred years.

Here there were more of them, and they were conferring among themselves, for it is their right to choose. In our house they always took the gardener's assistant, not exactly a clever man, but very sweet-natured. Here I thought it might be the cook, who was obviously some kind of natural leader. In fact he was hammering on his pot again. Over the din he shouted, "It is the tradition for the servants to choose a king from among themselves, but tonight our choice rests on one of our masters. A distinguished man, a man worthy of every honor—" I craned my neck and saw Pompey smile in secret satisfaction, all by himself on his couch.

"So will you please welcome the Deputy for the Ruler of the Underworld, the King of the Saturnalia, the Lord of Misrule . . ." A flourish on the copper basin. "Gaius Julius Caesar."

I didn't see Pompey's face again, for from the couch beside him, Caesar was rising, graceful as a willow. "Well, friends," he said, "I'm very honored by your choice. Now let's see if I can pay you back."

From that moment the party got wilder. He made the guests wait on the servants during dinner, he ordered that the wine be stronger, and he gave out funny assignments and penalties to the people between the courses as a kind of entertainment. Crassus had to give everyone in the room a silver denarius, but better than that was the way his face grew longer when he heard the news; He made Pompey, "who like Atlas carries the conquered world on his shoulders," carry a flute girl around the room while she pounded on his sides as if she were driving a reluctant horse. I thought Pompey was not entirely displeased, for the girl was pretty, and even Crassus could not have thought that a hundred or so denarii could mean much.

All the time the wine and the music flowed; we got drunker and drunker, the decrees got rougher. People were beginning to get up and move around. A table overturned with a crash. Up in front, Caesar, a brilliant spot of pale, cool green, gave a great shout of laughter and plunged into the crowd.

I did not see him again until very late. The party had disintegrated into chaos. In the atrium not only tables were overturned now, but couches as well. On the ones that remained couples were getting very close to one another: men with men, men with women, groups all together. In one corner where it was very dark a cluster of very conservative senators had cornered a huge silver tray of sweetmeats and were sitting over it discussing politics with all the gravity and decorum they would have shown in the Forum, except that they had taken off all their clothes. Cicero was not among them. He disliked wild parties and had probably gone home.

In the kitchen there was a food fight, in the bedrooms unidentifiable noises, and shouts to join in or go away. Out in the garden there were people lying under the bushes, passed out or otherwise, I couldn't tell and didn't look too closely. A line of dancers tripped among their feet. There was no music, but the dancers did not seem aware of this.

I stepped around them, ducking out of their way behind a topiary hedge. A man's body bumped mine, Caesar's voice spoke in my ear. "Ah, there you are Caelius." His hand gripped my arm, making a warm spot in the darkness. "Come here. I want a witness. I think you can be discreet." I heard him move off. As best I could I followed, arriving at an arbor in the back of the garden. There between the leaves I saw Caesar's pale, cold face leaning forward over a small lamp on a stone table. As I watched he blew it out, and I heard his voice say lightly, "That's better isn't it? We don't want the whole world to know our business."

But I knew it. I had seen in the last golden shine of the flame who his companions in the darkness were. Pompey and Crassus. It struck me as interesting. I was not too drunk to remember that Pompey and Crassus were as close to enemies as politicians ever allow themselves to be, and that Caesar had never been a particularly warm friend of The Great Man, nor on the sort of terms with Crassus that would lead you to expect a conference. Yet here they were, heads bent together in the darkness, talking quietly among themselves as if they had been friends since childhood. It was not a conference, but a conspiracy.

They sat for a long time, and I listened. I have a good head for wine, and I remember even now how Caesar spoke. He was an eloquent man, and he used all his arts on the two men opposite him. He made promises and bargains, he reasoned and pleaded. It was like his discussion with Cicero, only ten times more forceful. By the time the chill of the late December night had seeped into my bones he had gotten them to agree.

He would use his consulship to further their aims—a grant of land for Pompey's veterans, to enhance his prestige and bring him the loyal support of thousands of voters; a tax-revision for Crassus' friends among the knights. They too would be grateful, and Crassus needed their support. There would be military commands for all of them. All Caesar asked in return was a real command for himself. "Forests and cattle-routes," he cried, and for the first time his voice slipped out of control and I saw how angry he was. Or perhaps he wanted them to see it; no man has ever calculated his effects the way Caesar did. Like a great actor, he could seem to be anything he wished.

Pompey and Crassus nodded solemnly and agreed. Caesar did not even smile. The starlight fell on his face, carving the planes into wedges of light and dimness. No flicker of expression crossed his features,

He had brought wine and food to seal the bargain. As he was giving them out, he made a little motion, and I knew he had dismissed me. I faded off into the night as quietly as I could.

It was dark and I was much drunker. I had wandered back into the house and was lost in the maze of rooms off the kitchen. A girl ran past me; I reached out and grabbed her, holding her squirming against me. "Here, pretty. What are you running away from? Don't you like me?"

It was the flute girl Pompey had carried around the house. Her dress had come off her shoulder and her little breasts moved under the thin cloth. There was something charming about her dishevelment, and I bent down to kiss her. It was the Saturnalia, and she kissed me back. Well, well, well, I thought and took her under the elbows to put her back to the wall. Her pointed breasts rose under the cloth and the nipples stood up. I could feel them against my chest.

"That's right, pretty," I whispered, sliding my tunic up over my thighs.

A hand fell on my shoulder and a voice said in my ear, "Enjoying yourself, Caelius?"

It was Caesar. Under the shadow of his cap his mouth stretched in its narrow grin.

"Yes. Yes, I am. A good time," I managed to say. It was very dark in the hallway; I don't think he was aware of the flute girl, though he was standing very close to me. I smelt his clean freshness and the cool mountain scent of his perfume.

"Is everything all right? You're seeing everything, are you? Had enough to eat? To drink?"

"Oh, yes, yes. Just fine. Thank you very much. Wonderful party."

"I was very glad of your help. You're a good friend, Caelius." His breath tickled my ear.

"Glad . . . glad to have been of service."

"You never know what the Saturnalia will turn up. Of course none of it counts—it's all just between friends, isn't it?" The grin widened and his hand gently squeezed the muscles of my forearm. "But I owe you a favor. I'll pay it back, too. I never forget my debts." His eyes were looking into mine, holding me. I caught my breath, and tried to think of something to say. I seemed to be have a lot of trouble. My heart was pounding and my throat was closed. I could feel his hand. He leaned closer to me, and his lips opened slightly.

The flute girl, seeing him for the first time, gave a gasp and wiggled out from under me.

"What's that?" Caesar cried.

The girl shot him a panicked glance and tried to duck away. But he was quick—in everything his physical conditioning showed, like a thoroughbred horse or a fine hunting dog. I hardly saw the movement. Then he was holding her by the arm; she was wiggling like a fish in a net and sobbing.

He held her to the light. In our encounter her dress had slipped farther and her naked breasts stared back at him . . .

I suppose that made it obvious what we had been doing. If he had looked at my own condition he would have seen that too. He laughed, a short, bitter sound, and I thought he was going to be angry, but he threw her in my direction, saying, "Here, catch," in a very good-natured way."Good night, Caelius," he said moving off into the darkness.

"Good night," I called after him. I thought for a moment he had sounded, I don't know—angry? Disappointed? But that seemed very unlikely. I never got a chance to ask him— he was long gone when I looked up from the flute girl again.

I saw him one more time that night, standing up to throw a hand of dice in the crowd of his guests. Someone held a burning candelabrum above his head; the holly wreath give out dark sparks of light; his pale hair and the richer glint of his embroidery flashed like gems. He looked every bit the king of the Saturnalia, the stand-in for the dark god.

He laughed with his head back and his throat moved. His arm, raised for the toss, drew his body into one long line, from his gold-strapped sandals and his lean and elegant legs, to the arch of his ribs and the whippy straightness of his arm. His slender fingers were curled around the little cubes of bone.

He was not beautiful like Publius Clodius, whose features a god had touched at birth in a dream of perfection, but he was as handsome as nature and the human will can make a man. The gloss of him, the polish, the coordination: more than once they had recalled an animal to my mind. Instead they ought of have reminded me of an Olympic athlete, trained to the last moment and strung up like a bow, ready for his race. Caesar was ready, too. You could see it as his arm swept down and his body followed through, his back curved low over his bent knee, and he came to rest. The new shape he made was as fine and taut as the old.

The dice made a tiny clatter on the mosaic floor. His friends murmured; Caesar laughed aloud. He had won the toss, too.

BOOK TWO

IX

For at least an hour nothing has moved on the road. The scouts have not come back. Only the heat and the quiet have invaded my room, only the past with its voices and faces, its images and sensations, all recorded so faithfully by the memory, all so little understood.

In a way it is not surprising that I cannot sift the truth of what I saw from what I believed I was seeing. A deception was worked on me by a great magician. Well, it was worked on the rest of Rome as well. When I remember him as he was then, his lean elegance and polished suavity, his animal beauty and distinction, I see him as I did at that moment, in the depths of the Saturnalia. The winter darkness hovers just beyond the brilliant candlelight; he seems to attract some of it to him, for the glow of his golden hair, the polish of his skin, are shadowed, deepened, made richer and more significant by the deep forest green of the holly wreath and by his dark, shining eyes. The King of the Saturnalia. The Lord of Misrule. Indeed.

He began quietly. At the first meeting of the Senate in the new year he made a speech announcing that although he was committed by his heritage from the general Marius, and by his own convictions, to serve the interests of the people of Rome, and most especially of the plebeian class, still he saw it as his duty to do whatever the Senate wished. His colleague in the consulship—"Elected to restrain Caesar," Cicero murmured to me under his breath—his colleague Bibulus, whom, he, like everyone else in the room respected so deeply, was trying to keep their joint administration a model of harmony and cooperation. He, Caesar, approved this effort with all his heart. The senators on their benches before him would be surprised and delighted to see how he cared for *their* interests.

"Well," said Cicero coming out blinking into the sunshine afterwards, "you couldn't ask anything more accommodating than that, could you?" His breath went out before him on the cold January air as if it screened his words, hiding them from unfriendly eyes.

"You don't like him, do you?" I asked.

"Everyone *likes* Caesar. He's the most charming man in Rome."

"Oh, yes," I said softly, but he did not hear. Or perhaps he did. He looked at me out of the corner of his warm brown eye and his mouth bent gently in a smile.

"I don't trust him," he said. "This isn't the real Caesar."

It certainly seemed to be. He was so careful not to offend the conservatives it was painful to watch. In February when his co-consul Bibulus took possession of the fasces for the month Caesar was so punctilious he made his own lictors walk behind him. I don't suppose any senior magistrate has bothered with this courtesy for a hundred years. He took it upon himself, too, to post a daily notice of the proceedings of the Senate in the Forum—"So that the citizens can see the care that their senators take for them," he announced, apparently without irony.

"He's trying to show them that they were wrong to fear him," Cicero said.

"Does he think they'll change the proconsular assignments, then? I know he wants something better than the Forests and Cattle-paths."

He weighed this with his fine, experienced judgment. It was like watching a jeweler examine a stone. "He is desperate," he said at last.

"*Caesar*? How could he be desperate? He has everything: public office, popularity, admiration . . ." I could not think of anything I would rather have myself.

"He owes so much money. He must owe more now than most people see in a lifetime." He meant rich people—he was well-off himself. "But I don't know. Sometimes I wonder. He has something else in mind—beyond recouping his debts on the backs of poor provincials. He wants something. But what? What could the Senate give him?" He smiled. "Well, we'll see, won't we? He'll make sure we do."

He was so shrewd, so clever. He must have divined all that by the private augury of his own intelligence, for he could have had no idea of the bargain Caesar had struck with Pompey and Crassus. Indeed, though Cicero was close to Pompey, for he had been trying to get him the grant of land for his veterans for over a year now, he complained often that Pompey did not confide in him. He worried constantly that Pompey might be vexed with him for his lack of success; I do not think the possibility that Pompey was contemplating treachery ever occurred to him.

But in March it was plain for everyone to see. In the first meeting of the month, when Caesar was again presiding in the Senate, he announced that he was introducing a bill for the redistribution of land. He admitted at once, with all his famous charm, that proposals similar to this one had been made to the Senate before. This one would be different, he assured them.

They stared at him, totally hostile. Land reform always bothered them. Yet the veterans returning from foreign wars needed places. Well, everyone knew it had to come some day.

Caesar paced back and forth before them, coaxing and gentle, holding out his palm as if they were so many horses wary of the bridle. His voice murmured seductively. "A land bill," Cicero gasped. "Does this mean that Pompey has . . . ?"

It certainly seemed to. "Those men deserve it," Caesar was saying. "Serving in a long war, obeying our orders. We ought to show them some generosity. And what good will it do them to come to Rome and sit idly on the street corners when the poor fellows could be bringing in money to the Treasury from the proceeds of their farms?"

It wasn't getting a very warm reception from the Senate. They sat on their benches as if they had been turned to stone, and not one so much as inclined his head toward Caesar. Even Cicero was motionless, though I could hear his breath coming hard, as if he had run a long way.

The next day Caesar introduced the bill itself. Like everything else he had done since taking office, it was conciliatory, tactful, careful of the sensibilities of the conservatives. The provisions were very fair: only public land was to be used and no private property seized, no matter how unclear the title. Since a lot of them had been buying land in anticipation of exactly this, that should have pleased them. If so, they gave no sign. In addition, Caesar went on, it would all be paid for out of Pompey's booty, so that no one would have to worry about an increase in taxes, or anything of that sort. And to make it perfectly fair, he would change anything in the bill that they didn't like.

He proposed a commission of twenty men—distinguished people, like themselves, he said—to administer the new law. And so everyone could see that he had no intention of profiting by this himself, he would write into the bill explicitly that he would not be one of the twenty.

Again the Senate listened in silence, but by now Caesar had their range and dismissed them without allowing a debate. "Think it over. Tomorrow I'll ask for comments and a vote." Then he repeated that he would change anything they couldn't approve.

"Anything?" a voice called from the back. Caesar never blinked, though he must have felt a moment of triumph. It was the first sound anyone had uttered all day, and it was in his favor.

"Oh, yes," he said calmly. "Anything at all. What's more, I'll take it out altogether if we can't find some compromise that satisfies you. I'm here to obey the Senate's wishes." He bowed. Among those stolid, stony-eyed men he was like an ambassador from a suppler, more accommodating nation. His polish and fine looks were like a mark of foreignness. Yet he felt himself entirely at home. He watched them file out, leaning against the railing of a section of seats, completely relaxed, a small, contented smile on his lips.

That night Cicero called on Pompey, a meeting from which he came back looking grim. He did not stop at home, but went directly to his neighbor Metellus Celer's house, where he and Cato and several other leaders of the conservative faction had convened. From this encounter he returned so late that I, grown bored waiting for him, had long since left. Tiro his secretary told me the next day that his master had been so exhausted he had drunk two cups of hot wine before he could speak at all, and then he had only dismissed everyone and gone to bed.

For myself, that night I walked down into the Forum past Caesar's official residence, then out into the Subura to his family home. Both houses were quiet, silent and withdrawn under the moon, as if everyone were asleep. Wondering if Caesar was really so confident, I stood for a while by the corner watching, but nothing moved, no one came, no light showed anywhere, and presently I went on my way.

The next day Caesar called on the senators one by one to give their opinion of the bill. Each senator stood up when his name was called, but no one responded to his questions. The most conservative of them would not speak at all; the others contented themselves with a few words of vague neutrality. "Please," Caesar pleaded with them. "Please. If there's anything, anything at all that you don't like, just say so. What is it? What is bothering you?" I thought at one point that he was going to go down on his knees to them. It was not even that they were hostile; they weren't. They simply wouldn't say anything at all. Under Caesar's receding hairline fine beads of sweat were beginning to show.

At last it was Cato's turn. He got up slowly, clutching his toga: he never wore a tunic, nor for that matter, shoes, for he said they were contrary to the practice of our ancestors. He was like my father in that, and indeed my father, like most Romans, admired Cato. He might have been one of the great men of the past come back, my father said; he was like his own ancestor, the Cato who destroyed Carthage. If all men were like him we could expect the Golden Age to return. Cato was honest, disinterested, scrupulous to a fault; he allowed nothing to interfere with the exercise of his duty, which to him was the highest pleasure in life. Well, looking at him, I could believe he had few others. He peered around the Senate over the bridge of his narrow nose, his nostrils pinched and the lines carved down to his mouth. He was young but he looked old. His lips pressed together as if he saw something to disapprove of everywhere he looked.

The Senate waited in tingling silence.

"Cato," Caesar said, friendly and straightforward. "Tell us what you think of the bill. It's a good one, isn't it? Fair to everyone. And you must agree that we need it."

Cato's voice had the carrying quality of a buzzing bee. "The bill? It's good enough." He didn't like admitting that, but his incorruptible honesty made him do it; you could see by the darkening flush on his face that it made him angry. "It's not the bill that's wrong. It's the unconscionable power the law will give to those men who sponsor it, men who are right now enticing the people, leading them to hope for extravagant and unRoman rewards. It should be enough for them that they have served their country." He glared with brilliant and bird-like eyes at Caesar, who, quick as ever opened his mouth to speak. But Cato was quicker. Taking an orator's stance, he turned to the senators. "I will now speak until sunset," he announced, meaning that he would prevent the bill's coming to a vote by this method.

"Oh, no you won't," Caesar muttered, but Cato heard him.

"Yes, I will," he answered, and began. "This bill was brought to you by a man whose father and grandfather . . ." and he went on to detail the history of the Julians—an ancient enough family to make it a long recitation. The Senate happily settled down to listen.

Caesar, plainly puzzled, listened, too. Once or twice he tried to interrupt, once crying, "But what has this to do with helping the poor?" But Cato had the floor, and just plowed on. He had a harsh voice and a plain style, but his candor had a certain charm, and you could listen to him without displeasure. He had good lungs, too—he trained with the javelin on the exercise ground in the Campus Martius—and he was plainly prepared to go on, as he had threatened, until evening closed in. Just as plainly, the Senate was prepared to listen to him.

He had finished the history of the Julians and was going on to a consideration of the public land available for distribution, reeling out hundreds of facts without difficulty, when Caesar, his patience at an end, waved his lictors forward and said disgustedly, "He's disrupted the Senate long enough. Take him to prison."

There was a moment of shocked silence. Even Cato paused.

Then, unanimous, the massed senators opened their throats and roared their disapproval. Caesar, impatient, waved the lictors forward. They marched in good order up the aisle to where Cato stood, regarding them with something like satisfaction out of his small, shining eyes. The lictors seized his arms. The Senate gasped.

"Can he do that? Is that legal?" I whispered to Cicero, but he was so deeply disturbed he could not speak. Well, after all, a senator, and a *Cato*: I would have said it was not only illegal, it was unthinkable.

The lictors were bringing him down the aisle. In the silence I could hear the stamp of their feet like heartbeats, and among them Cato's brisk, barefoot slap and shuffle. I could not look at Caesar. Nobody breathed.

At the back of the room a man rose slowly to his feet. He was a general, very hard-bitten and military in his appearance, and a little uneasy. You felt he wished he were in uniform. It would have emphasized, somehow, his extreme disgust.

As deliberately as he had risen he marched down the aisle, toward the retreating backs of Cato and the lictors. "Marcus Petreius," Caesar shouted after him. His voice was as clear and unperturbed as if he had hailed him in the Forum. "Don't you know where Cato is being taken?" he asked.

"Yes. I know. And I would rather be in prison with Marcus Cato than here with you." The old soldier spoke simply, stating an obvious fact, and it had more power than anger or a denunciation. As a man the Senate rose and flooded out into the aisles, following the little procession. I was on my feet too. I couldn't help it, for I was swept along, behind Cicero, in the crowd.

"Stop," bellowed a voice behind them, and I had to turn and look before I realized it was Caesar's. I had never heard him speak in anything but a calm and rather light tone, very even and unruffled. I had not imagined that his voice could be harsh and powerful, or that it could carry to the lictors at the door, who released Cato as if he burned their hands.

Nor had I ever seen Caesar angry. I had thought him icy, deliberate, cerebral—to tell you the truth, rather lacking in the normal human passions—but here he was, as furious as a man can be and still retain his sanity. He was shouting. The cords of his neck stood out, his face was crimson, his eyes glittered, hard and black. He cursed the Senate and the lictors, the law, the gods of the state—his language would have done justice to a gladiator's barracks. "Very well, release him," he shouted at the climax of his rage, ignoring the fact that the lictors had done that already, and Cato was calmly taking his seat. No one laughed.

Caesar stood in the middle of the floor, watching him. He was still furiously angry, but now his voice was quiet. "I accept that," he said very carefully, as if he were drunk or drugged by his emotion. "But since you have seen fit to obstruct me without any reason but your hatred of change and your fear of your fellow citizens, do not expect me to consult you again. I assure you, I will not."

He paused and looked into their eyes, one by one. I think that no one in that room dared to look away, though most of them hated and feared him and none of them would forgive his insult to their sense of decorum. He knew it, too. "The Senate is dismissed," he said and his voice was like the breath hissing off a glacier: slow, and freezing with contempt. "Go. I will not trouble the Senate again."

So Caesar announced that he was going directly to the people. He convened the Plebeian Assembly and put the matter to them. At least they were prepared to listen; he had made sure of that. All those gifts and speeches and appearances, all that river of money he had poured out, had not been wasted. He had never concealed what he was doing, either. Now that I think of it, that's the oddest thing of all. He operated in the daylight, and yet, when the results were seen, people were surprised.

The first shock was that he got Pompey to bring his veterans to Rome. From all over Italy these men sifted down the roads, thousands of them, swelling the city so that the streets near the Forum were nearly impassable. They camped in the temple courtyards at night, singing their campaign songs around their fires. Caesar called on them there, friendly and concerned; by day he made speeches to them in the Forum. Pompey and Crassus stood with him.

Once he asked Pompey if he too wanted the land bill to pass. Uncomfortable, the Great Man nodded.

"And if someone opposes it with the sword?" Caesar asked, smiling at the unlikeliness of this.

Pompey flushed scarlet with rage. "I'll take up my sword against him. And my shield." The soldiers cheered until the echoes rang.

"Pompey was there? At a public meeting?" Cicero said, when I told him about it.

"Yes."

"I thought he didn't like Caesar much. Are you sure?"

I said nothing, but watched him working it out.

"And Crassus?" He spoke with sudden hope. "What did Crassus say?"

"Only that he supported the bill, too."

"I see." But his eyes were turned inward, and had gone as blank as if he were blind.

The day before the Plebeian Assembly was to vote the co-consul Bibulus stood up in the Forum and announced that in his official capacity he had been watching the heavens for omens. They were bad. It was an inauspicious time. Therefore, no meeting of the Plebeian Assembly could be held, indeed no public business of any kind could be transacted—it was against the will of the gods. He doubted it would be possible to convene the Assembly for some time to come, since as consul he was taking the opportunity to declare the rest of the session a public holiday.

That afternoon Caesar summoned me to his house. The sunlight slanted through the hole in the atrium roof, the ripples from the pool spread across the ceiling. The place had a deserted air, like a hall normally used for public meetings, too large for the three or four men half-hidden among the lights and shadows who watched me as I crossed the mosaic floor.

Presently Caesar came, pushing aside a tapestry. He was brisk, he rubbed his hands together and the dry little sound filled the atrium. It no longer seemed too large, too shadowy.

"Gentlemen, those . . . supplies. We need them immediately. Can I count on you?" They nodded. A couple of them were tribunes I think, and another I recognized: a young aristocrat who used to hang around with Antony.

"Caelius, good of you to come." Caesar gave me a welcoming smile. "It's obvious the opposition will try to prevent the vote tomorrow. Don't you agree?"

"Is there going to be a vote tomorrow? I thought the omens were against it."

The atrium rang with their laughter. "A shabby trick," Caesar said. "A cheap attempt to prevent the citizens of Rome from exercising their rights. Don't you agree? I see that you do. Well, we're going to see that they have their chance. That is you are, you and Vatinius here—" he gave a smile to one of the tribunes, one of the ugliest men I have ever seen. In the gloom he looked like a frog with a pocked skin and stretched mouth, and eyes that bulged under a low forehead. Yet he fancied himself a dandy; his hair was oiled and curled, and powder had settled in the creases of his cheeks. I wouldn't have trusted him to hold a horse, but Caesar had more confidence in him it seemed. "You and Vatinius will see to it that our own people occupy the Forum tonight. We don't want Bibulus and Cato and that crowd to bring in their own support in the morning, when the voting begins."

"Then there is going to be voting?"

"By Hercules, there is. You and Vatinius will see to that." And he smiled into my eyes.

It was a wonderful night. That's all I can say about it now. Even after all these years, with all I know or can guess, it is still that. Perhaps it is the best night of my life.

The moon was full; the light drifted into the Forum like scraps of silver mist, trailing among the dark shapes of the buildings. It was bright enough to see the markings on a set of dice, and for a while I played, with Vatinius and some of the others, but tiring of that, I gave it up to go out into the light. In a garden a few streets away a young owl called; the river sparkled as if someone had tossed silver coins on its current, and I heard its liquid chime as I strolled around. From somewhere the scent of almond blossom floated on the

118

air as if the moonlight itself exhaled a fragrance, cool and intoxicating. On the great square stones of the open space thousands of men, Pompey's veterans, Crassus' numberless dependents, members of the workingmen's clubs Caesar had patronized, sat in groups talking quietly or lay wrapped in their cloaks to sleep. In the deep shadow of the Curia a few voices sang softly, the notes of a flute dropped like petals into the quiet air.

That's all there was. There was no incident, no excitement. Just thousands of men, all citizens of a great city, all with one purpose. And I was part of it. I was one of the leaders . . . Yes, with all I know, or can guess, it was still a wonderful moment.

All I know or can guess. Well, that's a lot. For instance, the "supplies" Caesar sent that tribune to fetch were not food and charcoal and blankets, as I had supposed. They were arms. In the Forum. And Caesar intended to use them if he saw any reason to. He never had the slightest qualm about things like that. He was far too clever at putting his enemies in the wrong to bring out weapons before there was a reason, but he was not going to be caught without them. Indeed, he considered what he was doing no more than a reasonable precaution. I didn't guess it then, but now it stands out on that moonlit night like the bulk of the Rostrum itself.

More difficult is this one: did Caesar plan all along that the Senate would refuse him, and he would have an excuse to go directly to the Plebeian Assembly, which he certainly controlled? I don't know; I don't believe anyone does. Caesar did not have the habit of confiding in anyone, and I do not think that if he writes his memoirs they will be any more informative about his motives than his books on his military campaigns. Perhaps the only thing to say is that he didn't care if the Senate backed or refused him. He was happy to go to the plebeians, just as he would have been content to resort to arms. Any way of accomplishing his ends seemed equally good to him. The only thing that was wrong was to fail, and that he did not intend to do.

He came to see us during that night in the Forum. He had been working in his office in the official residence, he

said, but I think he was unwilling to sleep while his friends
were wakeful on his behalf. He lounged around the Forum
as if it were his own atrium, chatting to the men who were
still awake, or exchanging a few words with Vatinius or the
others. I could see that he was in an elevated mood. The
moonlight silvered his hair but hid his eyes in deep shadow.
His hollow cheeks were stretched in a grin; the long, thin
lines of his body were drawn more elegantly than usual. He
seemed to give off sparks, like the river. At the time it seemed
to me only a part of the beauty of the night, but now I am
not so sure. Now I think there was something more at work.
It was the beginning of something for him, something he had
waited for a long time. He was about to make his first move.

In the morning the trouble arrived. With the first light,
Bibulus came into the Forum, surrounded by his lictors and
a huge mob of his friends. Most of the Senate was with him.
Bibulus led them towards the Temple of Castor, where Caesar was making a speech on the steps to a large number of
men. Bibulus' lictors shouted their warning and waved their
bundles of sticks but the press was so great that their progress
was impeded and the consul's bald, freckled head was sweating by the time he arrived. I was standing next to Vatinius,
a couple of steps above Caesar; I saw it clearly, gleaming in
the rosy light as he mounted the first steps; I saw his companions, Cato among them, surge up after him.

He needed his friends, for when he began to speak, cutting
into Caesar's remarks, the crowd yelled and there were angry
shouts to let Caesar finish. Bibulus ignored them and went
on and Caesar, willing to play the same game, continued his
address. The shouting grew louder. Presently a stone landed
at Bibulus' feet, bursting apart with a shocking sound.

There was a moment's silence. Bibulus looked down, Caesar looked around, the crowd watched them both. I think I
may have been the only man not in on it to see Vatinius lift
his hand. Immediately the noise was everywhere, the crowd
was roaring, stones were flying. Someone smashed a basket
of filth down on Bibulus' rosy head. Out of the Temple of
Castor armed men were streaming, swords drawn, cudgels
waving.

"Gods, where did they come from?" I cried, but no one heard me. They flowed past me, and I saw them meet Bibulus' friends with a shock like two currents meeting together in the open sea. Sticks and shards and swords rose like flotsam, cries and thumps thundered all around me. Someone was moaning. Cato shouted to rally Bibulus' men. In the midst of it all, Bibulus' body rose up over the boiling mass and sailed down the steps to land with a sickening crunch at the base of the platform below. In the sudden silence everyone heard it.

I think the whole Forum paused to watch. After all, a consul . . . If he were dead . . . I don't think anyone's mind was capable of finishing that thought. I saw Cato, his mouth hanging open, staring at the crumpled figure. Vatinius had been arrested in mid-motion, his hand outstretched. Even Caesar stopped and fixed his glittering eyes on Bibulus.

Slowly the figure stirred. I think a sigh went out of every body in the Forum.

Bibulus, shaking stumbled to his feet and lifted his head. "All right," he shouted, straight up into Caesar's face. He was furiously angry. "All right. If that's what you want, why don't you murder me here and now?" He yanked open his toga and pulled his tunic from his shoulder. "There," he cried, showing his bare chest. "Do it. Now. What's the matter with you? Are you afraid to kill me?" His friends gasped and rushed toward him, leading him, still shouting back over his naked shoulder, out of the Forum. His lictors, one holding a bloodied arm, another limping badly, followed him. None of them had their *fasces*, the bundles of sticks that symbolize their magistrate's power. In a moment, I saw why. Vatinius had them, and they were broken in half. He gave a shout of laughter, and threw them after the departing men.

There was one more incident. Cato tried twice to make a speech, climbing up on the steps and cawing like a raven over the noise. The first time, Vatinius and his men escorted him forcibly out of the Forum, but he came around by some back streets and popped up again. This time Caesar laughed. Cato, not the least frightened, glared at him with his bird-bright eyes. "This is an outrage. It is completely illegal. No vote may be taken here." He was still shouting when Vatinius led him away a second time, this time for good.

So they set up the urns and the walkways, and one by one the tribes voted. There was no further opposition, and the bill passed by a very large majority. The next morning in the Senate Bibulus appeared with a bandage around his head and a swelling over one eye, and asked the Senate to annul the land law and declare a state of emergency.

The senators looked everywhere around the building, at the painted ceiling, the marble floor, the rows of seats on three sides—everywhere but at Bibulus. There was a long, dusty pause. I saw Bibulus glance at Cicero who shook his head very slightly; in the back a man got to his feet—it might have been the old general Peterius—but before Bibulus could call on him he sat down again. The silence stretched itself out. Presently, without a word, Bibulus nodded to his lictors and strode angrily from the building. The Senate, still unspeaking, got up and followed him out. I did not see Cato anywhere. Last to go, strolling out from a dark corner where he had been leaning against a column, came Caesar. He did not show the slightest sign of triumph, but as he went out into the sunshine outdoors I heard his followers let out a cheer.

He went out into the sunshine to the cheers of his friends . . . The image stays in my mind, the graceful shape, dark against the brilliant, stinging light, the voices of the men outside. Even from behind I could tell that he was smiling.

122

X

I have gotten up and walked around, easing the tightness in my legs, for I have been sitting over this report for hours. The shadows have lengthened outside, the quality of the light has changed. It is heavier now, thick and golden, like honey. A spray of oleander glows against a wall, where before there had been only the luminous dimness of shade; the interior of a room—a table with a jug of water cooling on it—appears out of darkness in soft, earthy hints of color, intimations of a rounded form.

Out on the road a bar of sun between two trees catches the dust suspended in the silence of the afternoon and makes it glitter like a net of gold. Has someone passed? There has been no announcement here. More likely it is simply that the changing slant of light has revealed what was hidden before . . .

The night of the vote in the Senate—or of the failure of the Senate to vote, I should say—Curio came to me, all urgency and concern. "C-caelius," he stammered, "what are you getting m-mixed up in? Can't you see what's going on?"

"Going on? Why? What do you think is happening?"

He looked at me sorrowfully. "We conservatives aren't stupid, you know. I m-mean the senior m-men, like m-my father. They see that Caesar hasn't any scruples at all over politics. Well, he doesn't, you know. They don't like the way he's trying to am-amass power. The plebeians—"

"He's going to do some things that really need doing for the plebeians."

"He's going to use them." He spoke with a firmness unusual for him. He was really angry. "And you're getting the same kind of reputation yourself."

"What kind of reputation is that?" I poured a drink and did not offer him one.

"It's no good. You don't understand. M-my dear, I came to *warn* you, don't you see?"

"I don't need any warning, thank you very much."

He bent his head and his eyes grew round with sorrow. "Goodbye, Caelius," he said gently. "Don't bother. I'll see m-myself out."

The next day when I was walking in the Forum Catullus' friend Calvus cut me dead. Marcus Brutus, who was with him, gave me the ghost of a bow, which he quickly checked when Calvus spoke to him. I laughed and went on. In the cloakroom of the Curia, Cicero took me aside and asked me if I was sure I knew what I was doing. "I thought you wanted a land law," I retorted. "You've been working for one long enough. I thought you were Pompey's friend."

"I doubt if Pompey's benefiting much by this," he said, and indeed I could see many senators who had once been enthusiastic supporters of the Great Man now moving to sit with the conservatives. "Poor Pompey is not coming out of this well," Cicero said. "People believe he's responsible for the violence. Those were his soldiers out there, in the Forum. And whoever persuaded him to make that fatuous remark about his sword and shield?"

"Well, at least we have the land bill."

He shook his head. "Yes, we have the bill, and yes, Pompey will probably feel that he's gained something, so, yes, I will have to support the bill to avoid alienating him, but the cost is too high. Left to myself I would say so. Caesar is splitting the city, putting class against class—a thing more responsible politicians have been trying to avoid for years—"

"Well, perhaps they shouldn't have. Perhaps it should have been done sooner. Then we'd have had some legislation to relieve some of the conditions of the poor."

His mouth twitched as if he were going to laugh, but the face he turned to me was grave. "Look, Caelius, you're getting involved in this, I can see; I think you ought to realize that a lot of people are going to be put off by Caesar's behavior. You run the risk of getting the wrong kind of reputation. You don't want people to say you are the kind of man who doesn't care what he does to get ahead. You are young, and

124

a lot is forgiven to young men—a lot was forgiven Caesar, if it comes to that. He made some rather radical political choices in his own younger days. But don't go too far. Think about it, that's all I ask. Consider your father's wishes—"

"My father's wishes," I said. "Thank you very much for your advice. I have thought about it. I'll do what I believe is best."

Catullus was more blunt. "You're a fool," he said, twisting his mouth into a bitter shape around his wine. "Don't you see what Caesar is?'

I shrugged. "He's a patrician with a lot of brains and charm, and he wants to succeed, to do something for his country. Help the less fortunate, put some of the system on a more rational footing—"

He called the barman and ordered another drink. "He's the most unscrupulous man in Rome," he said in his flat, grating voice.

"Oh, gods, Caelius, can't you see? He uses people, he doesn't care how. Look what he's doing to Pompey. Making him look like a fool, or a criminal—that great soldier. And all the while Caesar lurks in his shadow, doing what he pleases. He'll do the same to you."

"The same as what? As Pompey? He'd have a job to do that—I don't cast a wide enough shadow for a pigeon to hide behind."

But he was not amused. His eyes had a hunted look, there were deep furrows over his broken nose, and around his mouth. "He uses people in other ways."

"Oh, really? How?"

He shook his head. There was something bitter in this gesture, something sick and uneasy, and he looked like a man who had eaten bad food. His skin looked green. "Here, are you all right?" I asked, but he shook his head. His body was losing its strength, too; he was getting thin, and there was a patch of roughness over his cheekbones as if he had been rasped by wind or bad weather. I changed the subject. "And how is the beautiful Clodia these days?"

He jumped as if I had touched him with cold iron and shot me a scowl from under his brows. "Fine," he snarled.

"She's just fine." He threw down some money on the counter and without another word stalked away.

I understood some of it later. Clodia was making a noise in the city just then with her support for Caesar, though her husband, the former consul Metellus Celer was one of his firmest opponents. She gave parties at which her brother and his friends sat at Caesar's feet—or sprawled there in a drunken stupor, from what I heard. Her husband was unable to discipline her or prevent these assemblies, but his disgust was evident.

Catullus seemed to be caught in the middle of it. He was no friend of Caesar's—he had known him since he was a child up north in Verona when Caesar was stationed in that province, and he must have had some kind of aversion to him. Perhaps it was only the unease a man who is primarily attracted to women sometimes feels in the presence of one who distributes his affections as indiscriminately as Caesar.

In any case, Catullus had joined the retinue of a well-known patron of poets called Gaius Memmius, and was often seen at his dinner parties or walking with him in the Forum. Memmius was one of Caesar's most outspoken critics.

If this displeased Clodia, I couldn't be sure. She no longer felt the same about him, that was obvious, but why is hard to guess. There were a lot of young men around Clodia just then, and rumors about them all. It was hard to tell if one of them was a new favorite.

XI

There was so much disaffection in the city that Caesar must have feared that the conservatives would manage to harm the land bill in some way. He was as nervous as a ferret at a rat hole and kept asking us what we heard from our friends.

But what we heard was nothing to the purpose. People muttered, and I had a feeling that their anger was growing, but there had been no outbreaks of actual resistance. Not after what happened to Cato and Bibulus.

Perhaps Caesar had access to sources that gave him more cause to worry, for he convened the Senate and told them he would require them to swear to uphold the law. It had been done once before, so there was a precedent, but all the same, the outcry was violent. Cicero had to spend the entire night persuading Cato and his friend Metellus—the same Metellus who was Clodia's husband—before, very grudgingly and with many expressions of disapproval, they agreed to take the oath. Cicero told them frankly that if they didn't there might be a civil war.

I laughed to myself to see their faces when he said this. They looked like men who had bitten down into green apples. But they couldn't deny that Caesar would go that far—even I couldn't be sure of that—and they swallowed their sour portion and the following day, when the Senate convened, they took the oath.

Caesar laughed at their dismay. "Next time I'll sit on your faces," he said, letting the grossness of the expression show his sense of triumph. Then he dismissed them and went back to the Plebeian Assembly, where he quickly passed the rest of his legislative program. This included a law ratifying all of Pompey's treaties and arrangements in the conquered territories in the east and Crassus' much desired revision of the tax contract.

It is the right of the equestrian class to bid on the contracts for collecting taxes in the provinces. After they pay the government the contracted-for amount, they collect whatever they can in the foreign colonies and territories. That they keep for themselves. It's a good business if you have the capital to put up: my father had money in Crassus' deal. But this time the knights had overestimated what they could squeeze out of the poor provincials, and they wanted their bid lowered, though they still wanted the contract. In effect, they expected the Treasury to make up the short-fall.

It was a gift Caesar had promised during the Saturnalia, and he got it for Crassus, just as he had said he would, through the Plebeian Assembly. His friend, the saurian Vatinius prepared the way for him with speeches and bribes, and got a number of shares in the company as a reward. I didn't do much though I helped where I could, but Caesar always paid very well anyway—he knew the value of keeping his friends happy—so I got a few shares myself.

I didn't tell my father where the money came from, but I used it to buy a litter and eight slaves to carry it around. Well, really I couldn't be seen around town on foot any more, like a servant going on an errand. It was my reward for having understood something difficult, I thought, for being willing to work for what I got, for being willing to do anything. "Where will it all end?" Cicero muttered, rubbing his tired eyes, but I was not tired, and I didn't want it ever to end.

XII

On the first of March, New Year's Day in the old calendar, Vatinius came to call on me. "You'd better come with me," he announced in his plebeian accent.

"Trouble?"

He wasn't dressed for it: he was elaborately curled and oiled and smelt like a woodland in springtime. He had powdered his shiny skin, but the pockmarks and warts still showed, and nothing could disguise his flat, frog-like eyes and his wide mouth.

"I think you'd better come." he said. "Caesar wants you."

"All right. Just a moment—"

He was a tiresomely vulgar man. "No, now. Snap to it. Caesar—"

"I know. Wants me."

"That's right."

Outside, it was a crisp day under a drenched blue sky and a chilly wash of sunlight. Vatinius oozed along, trailing a cloud of violet perfume. I followed, my feet ringing on frozen stone. Presently he stopped before a black and silver door.

"This is Metellus Celer's house. What are we doing here, Vatinius? Celer hates Caesar."

"I know. Makes no never mind. He's here."

The door man let us in and waved us silently though the atrium. In a room at the back of the house, Metellus' wife Clodia sat on an ivory chair, alone in the midst of a crowd. She was as composed as a statue from her smooth dark hair to the white dress crisping around her feet. Her head was turned; I saw her profile, clear as a cameo. She was so beautiful I caught my breath, and a strange little pain pierced me in the chest. The men in the room murmured around her like the sea foaming around a rock, but she did not move.

I looked around for Catullus, but unless he was hidden behind someone's back he was not there. "Is it a party?" I whispered to Vatinius, but he was not there either. He had moved forward and was bowing over Clodia saying something in her translucent ear that she did not bother to acknowledge. All her attention was fixed on a cluster of men with their backs to me, huddled over something on the far wall.

At that moment the group she was watching broke apart, and I saw what she had been looking at. Against the wall a man lay in a plain narrow bed, the blanket drawn up to his chin. His head was sunken on the pillow, his eyes hollowed into caverns. The great blade of his nose, as bleached as a bone, seemed to scythe an arc through the air, though he was motionless. From time to time his lips fumbled with a sound and all the men in the room turned to watch him.

"Metellus Celer, the former consul," said a voice at my elbow. It was Cicero, slumped in a chair, his best toga crumpled around him, his hair disheveled. "This is a catastrophe, Caelius. Now there will be no one to restrain—well, let us not name names in a crowd." But he tilted his head toward the corner. There Publius Clodius, as beautiful as his sister, glared back at him out of his wide dark eyes. Then he saw me and grinned, and his hair flew up in a flash of black as he tossed it off his forehead.

"What happened?" I asked Cicero.

"Metellus collapsed in the Forum this morning. We're waiting to hear what the doctors say." I looked over at Metellus. It didn't seem to me that they needed a doctor to tell them much. Even I, who had never seen a death, could recognize this. As I watched Metellus raised his head. His mouth opened, but all that came out was a spume like the spray on a wave. His face was the color of the winter sea, his flesh was stiff, his skin pearly, his eyes shone with a dull mineral gleam. Drop by drop life was leaving him, and in its place were seeping stillness, colorlessness, rigidity, cold.

From the corner someone let out a high-pitched giggle, instantly cut off. I looked up. It was Vatinius, his white-leaded features congested with embarrassment. Beside him stood Publius Clodius, not in the least put out by Vatinius' behavior.

And talking to them was a tall, elegant man with wheat-colored hair.

"Caesar with Publius Clodius," said Cicero under his breath. "What now?" his face crumpled into sadness, but I did not think it was for the dying man.

The doctors were bending over Clodia. She rose from her chair and went toward her husband. There she paused. From a table by the window someone picked up a cup—I thought it was Caesar—and handed it to Clodius. He stepped forward and put it in her long shell-colored fingers.

For a long moment, nothing happened. She bent her long neck so that her profile drooped over Metellus like a lily; she sniffed the cup, wrinkled her nose, swallowed a little of the medicine. Then she held the cup to Metellus' lips. Over by the window, Caesar, moving slowly, almost idly, went and stood beside Clodius. Together the tall man and the short, beautiful dark one, turned their eyes on Clodia. There was a gasp, a sigh from the bed, a sound like sea-water dashing on a rock. The quiet of the room shattered into a thousand disordered fragments and the cup rolled across the floor.

"Gods," Cicero swore.

"Is it an omen?" someone cried as the room burst into talk.

I moved away to escape the bustle as the maids rushed in to clean up the mess. The visitors shifted and swirled, the doctors settled like vultures at the head of the bed, eyeing their patient with unseemly eagerness.

Metellus lay choking and sputtering on his pillow, his face darker than before. He's worse, I thought. A man in the corner of the room said, "It won't be long now," in an agonized voice, and another answered, "He was well and strong this morning." Someone else, closer to the window muttered, "He's not old. He'll hold out a while longer," but no one agreed with him. He was a man with the high curved nose and large dark slanted eyes of the Clodians, so I murmured some conventional phrase—"a great loss," I think—as I brushed past him. Over by the window Caesar rested his arm briefly on Clodius' shoulder. It might have been a gesture of consolation. By the time I arrived Clodius was gone, and Caesar leaned alone against the wall, his arms folded across his chest, his lips curved in a thin smile.

"A sad occasion," I said, coming up to him.

"But one that opens certain possibilities."

"What do you mean?" Metellus was sleeping now. His breath rasped through the room like a wave, back and forth, flow and undertow. The visitors had composed themselves in postures of waiting; someone had brought some chairs and a tray of food, but no one had touched it.

"Whatever is going to happen is going to take a while," I said.

"When Metellus dies," Caesar said, "his province will become vacant."

I suppose I should have been shocked, but there was something in this candor that appealed to me. I smiled; I believe I would have laughed had the solemn hum of voices around me allowed. "What province is that?" I asked, keeping my voice low.

"Nearer Gaul," said Vatinius, sliding up to us. "The region between the Po and the Alps."

"Not a very big prize. Or a very rich one." I couldn't figure out why Metellus had wanted it.

"Something might be done with it. There's an army stationed there—the governor has the command." Caesar lifted his shoulders in a graceful shrug. "Anyway, it's better than the forests and cattle-paths."

"Well, who will get it, if Metellus can't take it?"

"Ah, that's the question," Caesar said.

"He will. Oh, Caesar will. You can bet on that," Vatinius said, and he laughed out loud in the quiet room.

"Yes, if I can prevent Cato and those old women in the Senate from blocking me," Caesar agreed equably. His cool, shining eyes rested on me and this smile remained untouched. He might have been talking of nothing at all.

I was saved from answering. At the door there was a sudden flurry of movement and noise. Pompey stood in the entrance. He seemed to radiate heat and power. His blue eyes swept the room from under his eyelids. Under his gaze the crowd fell silent. Caesar had gone as still as a carving on the wall.

The Great Man swept into the room, followed by a retinue

of consuls, senators, magistrates. "Look how those important people fawn over him," I said, impressed. "He's like a prince."

"And he wants to be a king." It was Caesar's light, pleasant voice unexpectedly answering me from his place against the wall.

Pompey's red face was bending over Clodia Metelli's chair. "My dear lady, we are so sorry. Such a loss to us all." There was blaring note in his voice, like a trumpet call; heads lifted all around him and on the tray the silver wine cups shook.

"We," I said.

Pompey was progressing around the room; it looked like the parade at a triumph. People smiled, eyes shone, there was a murmur of conversation. Many of those men were his enemies; they disliked him both personally and politically, yet they smiled under his influence.

Except for Caesar. That was so interesting I stepped back a pace to look as Pompey came to a halt in front of him. Caesar had not moved, but still leaned against the wall, his arms across his chest. They made an odd contrast: Caesar, slender, silvery, cool, Pompey all scarlet and gold and twice his bulk. It was as disquieting as if the moon and the sun stood in the sky at the same time, confronting one another.

"Good morning, Gaius," Pompey said. Caesar removed himself from the wall and bowed. It might have been respectful, and it was—I'm certain it was—but there was something in that smooth, small inclination of the head that was so precisely measured, something so assessing in the chilly greenish eyes, the tiny, cruel flicker of the smile, that suddenly Pompey's size and color and magnificence looked tawdry and overdone, and for an odd moment, I felt sorry for the Great Man.

Metellus was shouting on the bed, sitting upright and roaring unintelligibly, like a storm at sea. Silver spray shot from his lips, his cavernous eyes flew open blindly; waving incoherently he struck his hand against the wall with a shock felt everywhere in the room. The doctors swooped in flight around him, the men in the room moved, even Clodia had swept down and was pressing his shoulders back into the pillow. Metellus bellowed constantly, like a bull unwilling for the sacrifice, and in the corner a man cried out in fear.

"The crisis has come," Pompey said solemnly.

"Yes. So it has." Caesar leaned back against the wall. It didn't amount to much, a gesture, a pause no longer than a heartbeat, but it was as plain as if he had spoken it aloud that he had issued a challenge to Pompey. I saw the Great Man's blue eyes go blank, and he turned on his heel in a blaze of scarlet and gold, and swirled away.

XIII

Well, it was only a tiny moment, and perhaps I was wrong at that, for after Metellus' death they seemed to be better friends than ever. Caesar still hovered in Pompey's shadow, while Pompey threw away with both hands the good will he had earned by his conquests in the east.

I heard in the city that they had taken a bribe from the Pharaoh of Egypt. This man, a Ptolemy, had been driven out of his country by the hatred of his subjects. Egypt is not under our control—alone among countries of the Eastern Mediterranean since Pompey's wars, I might add—but Egypt was too big a nut for us to swallow, and it remained powerful, independent, infinitely old, wealthy and fat, simply waiting for the Roman whose imagination and courage are up to taking it. He will come, of that I am sure. Egypt is destined to be ours.

Well, in those days it wasn't yet, though this Ptolemy thought that we would be able to help him regain his throne, and he was willing to pay for it. Curio, who told me about it, nearly strangled on his disgust.

"It's a disgrace. The foreign policy of the Roman people put up for sale as if we were . . ." He couldn't think of anything low enough. "As if we were fancy boys in the slave m-market. And those two—those—" His voice failed him altogether for a moment. "They can do anything they want now, can't they? How can Pompey allow it?"

"How much was the bribe?"

"Oh, m-my . . ." but he did not want to call me "my dear" any longer. "I don't know. It was Greek m-money." Then, as ashamed as if he had taken the money himself, he admitted, "Six thousand talents."

"Oh, great holy gods. That's over a hundred and forty million sesterces."

"That's right. That's what we were sold for." His head drooped, and he looked sad and bitter, and not the least like a lamb.

It was true, too. I heard it twenty times that month. A little poem of Catullus' went around about it, causing gusts of laughter which people smothered if a friend of one of the principals went by. In addition you could see that something had happened. There was money everywhere. The clubs were prospering, groups of plebeians were in the streets all the time now. A number of senators were suddenly free of debts, or had their mortgages reduced or cancelled. Cassius had a new carriage and horses, Mark Antony's mother a pearl worth six million sesterces; Vatinius was building a house. None of this was proof exactly, but it was getting pretty close.

Around that time I had a conversation with Caesar. We were walking in the Campus Martius near the exercise ground. Stakes and strings were laid out everywhere; a crew of surveyors was tramping through the springtime mud, shouting back and forth.

"Pompey's going to build a theater," Caesar said, pausing to watch them. "It's a gift to the city."

"We need it. It's a disgrace that some country towns have permanent theaters while we're still sitting on benches in the Forum every time the games require a performance."

"So it is. Well, Pompey will remedy that. He's financing it with his profits from the east."

Well, I suppose he was. Egypt is in the east.

"Nice of him," I said.

"Pompey has always been a model citizen, always done his duty by his country."

"Like Regulus," I murmured out of some half-forgotten memory.

"Regulus?"

"Yes, you know. The general who was captured by the Carthaginians and came home on a sort of parole. He went back because he had given his word that he would, and they tortured him to death."

He laughed. "Dear gods. Don't tell me you believe that story?"

The small clouds drifted like puffs of smoke overhead, trailing their shadows on the new grass and the soft rust brown of the budding trees. Blackbirds were singing near a temple; three women in light spring dresses passed us, the dresses pressed against their bodies as they moved. "Believe it? Of course I believe it." A door was opening somewhere; a breeze was blowing through. "Why? Isn't it true?"

"No, it's not true. Of course not. Regulus' widow put that story around to justify that fact that she had some Carthaginian prisoners of war tortured, that's all. The rest is just a nursery tale to frighten children into good behavior."

As soon as he said it, I knew that it was true. I laughed. Suddenly I felt liberated, as free as the day, lighter. It was as if it had become spring in me. "Gods," I cried happily.

"Listen Caelius, I want you to go and see Pompey. Will you do that for me? He has a job for you to do—a kind of reward for your help with the land bill. You understand that, don't you?"

"Do you know anyone in Rome who doesn't?"

He laughed again. "Everybody is entitled to his reward," he said, giving me his laziest, most intimate smile. But he was watching me; his eyes seemed to stroke my face, so intense was his concentration. I wondered if he was telling me that the story of the bribe was true.

I went out to Pompey's house in the suburbs, and stood among the crowd of petitioners and clients who waited on him. Finally I was shown in. The Great Man was seated in an ebony chair; his slave behind him whispered my name in his ear as I approached, and Pompey studied me with his flat gaze.

"Marcus Caelius Rufus," he said. He had a pleasant voice, though rather loud. You could imagine it on the battlefield or in the Forum. The conqueror of the east. The consul. The man who had celebrated three triumphs. He was grave and dignified, and sat in his chair with calm authority. In many ways, Pompey was the perfect Roman. But looking into his eyes was like staring at a freshly painted wall.

"You're Marcus Crassus' student, aren't you?"

"Yes, Gnaeus Pompeius, I was."

"And a friend of Julius Caesar." It wasn't a question, so I said nothing. "Crassus mentioned you to me," he went on in his slow, stately, thorough way.

"That's very kind of him."

"He says you were useful. Caesar says so, too. Cicero says you're clever." He seemed to be talking to himself, working something out—whether to trust me, perhaps. "I have a job for you. I understand you're an advocate. I want you to prosecute a case for me." He did not move, but a secretary, obeying some signal I could not see, slipped a paper into his hand. "Yes. Gaius Antonius Hybrida, governor of Macedon. That is, a former governor. You will prosecute him for corruption during his term in office there. Cicero will defend. Here is the information you will need. Are you willing?"

"Yes."

Pompey was speaking. "Julius Caesar said you'd be a good man for this job. He said you could win." Well, I thought, relieved, at least I wasn't being told to lose the case, though with Cicero to defend I probably would, no matter what I did.

"It's a compliment," Pompey added. "Caesar prosecuted Hybrida himself once, what? Ten years ago? Fifteen? Something like that." He looked impatient now, his tongue came out and passed over his lips several times.

"He did? What for?" I thought I could risk just one quick question, but Pompey had already turned his blank blue stare away.

"Gaius Antonius Hybrida served as consul the same year I did," Cicero said. "I'll have to defend him—it's a kind of obligation to a former colleague." He seemed worried. The afternoon sun slanted down through the shutters and lay in slices on his desk. "Why does Pompey want Hybrida prosecuted?"

"It's in everyone's general interest to prosecute corruption."

"That's true. But nobody does it unless it's in his specific interest, too." He brooded on this idea for a while, his dark brown eye glowing in the slant of light. "Pompey has no interest in Hybrida. Now if it were Caesar . . . Caesar has always hated him." He was following the idea, tracking it down like an animal in the forest. "Why should Pompey want to do favors for Caesar?" He shook his head.

"Do you think I shouldn't take the case?" I asked, very softly.

"Why on earth not? It's a *splendid* case. The accused is guilty, the backing is sensational, the opportunity fabulous. You mustn't offend Pompey and Crassus you know. You're too young for that." He shook his head again. "But it's puzzling. What are Pompey and Crassus doing on the same side?" His nose twitched, as if it were warning him of something.

"I'll try to win."

At that he smiled. "Of course you will. I wouldn't have taught you very well if you didn't, would I? I expect a hard-fought battle, Marcus, my boy. Do your worst." He smiled at me and his eyes glowed with affection, but as I left he was already sunk back in thought, blowing out his lips in an ecstasy of concentration. I wondered if he would figure it all out.

I had two colleagues in the case, a friend of Caesar's called Quintus Fabius Maximus, a man of a freezingly patrician family, and one of Pompey's most enthusiastic supporters, Caninius Gallus. He was older than I and seemed to feel entitled to run the prosecution.

Perhaps I would have conceded this, but his plans did not include allowing me more than a few words. I did not argue—he was too senior for that, and Fabius was so remote in his glacial dignity that I did not think he would support me, but I went home that night in a rage, determined to make a bigger impression with my speech than anyone expected. I thought I could. Nothing I had seen of either Fabius or Gallus led me to worry much about what they were going to produce.

Of course, there was Cicero, the greatest orator Rome had ever heard. Well, there wasn't a thing I could do about that but forget it and work on my speech, which I did. Gallus had left the most trivial part for me, the actual charge: Hybrida's behavior in his province when he was sent out there after his term at home as consul. It was as if they were saying that it didn't matter. Well, I had one or two things to show them that might change their minds.

The day of the trial came, dark and wet; the streets were thick with a fog that brought with it the silted, vegetable smell of the river. Water dripped from the eaves, torches spat sullenly from brackets on the walls but gave almost no light, I walked in a hollow globe of dirty, yellowish air that reeked like wet wool. I could see nothing but the glistening paving stones in front of me. People suddenly appeared out of the dimness, preceded by vague sounds that might have been echoes from another street; buildings loomed up unexpectedly, as if they had moved during the night.

In the Forum it was a little better. Togas glimmered among the benches as the lawyers assembled; the jury was already filing in. Around the three-sided square a crowd had collected, coughing in the acrid damp, but waiting patiently enough to be entertained. The edges melted into dripping blackness, so I could not tell how many there were. Enough, I hoped. Enough.

I had been right about the talents of my fellow prosecutors. Their speeches were nothing to worry about—though there were one or two comments that made Antonius Hybrida look uncomfortable. Caninius Gallus made rather a lot of Hybrida's flirtation years before with the seditious group around Catiline, while Fabius talked, at some length and to some effect, of his one-time expulsion from the Senate, for, of all things, grossness and brutality. They must have been pretty bad for the Senate to expel one of their own over them, and Fabius made a good enough job of them.

By the time I got to my feet for my turn, the fog had closed in again; its sulfurous folds had drawn down over the crowd, so that I could not see beyond the first rank of faces. The noises of the Forum came to me as a dull booming from a great distance. From the bench beside Hybrida, Cicero gave me an encouraging grin; Hybrida stared at me with a glare that Medusa might have envied.

I looked at the jury. To my surprise they were regarding me intently, waiting for me to begin, just as if I were an advocate like any other who had every right to appear before them. It came to me suddenly that I had.

My mouth went dry and my palms wet. I was afraid my voice would croak like a frog's. Well, I thought, it's the right weather for frogs; in fact, the Forum is looking a lot like the bottom of a pond right now. So it was that, grinning to myself, I made my first major speech.

"Gaius Antonius Hybrida was governor of Macedon, a position of honor and responsibility which you, the citizens of Rome entrusted to him. Now you are asking him for an accounting of his conduct as your representative. Well, let me tell you how Gaius Antonius Hybrida discharged the duty, the sacred obligation, that you laid upon him."

Out in the yellowish dusk I could see faces; there was Julius Caesar, smiling and relaxed, surrounded by friends. He raised his hand to me, a salutation, an encouragement, a sign of approval. "When Gaius Antonius Hybrida went out to Macedon," I said, biting back an answering grin, "there was trouble there. Disturbances among the tribes on the border that threatened our settlements . . ." Caesar had strolled off, but he was back before long with more men in his train. I couldn't see who they were.

All Rome seemed to be coming into the Forum to hear me. Curio wandered by, but wouldn't stay; Publius Crassus slipped into a place on the prosecution bench. I caught a glimpse of Catullus, standing in a group of aristocrats around his patron Memmius, and at one point I thought I made out Pompey among the vague figures passing just beyond the visible fringe. Listen to this, I called to him in my mind. You gave me this job, but you've never heard anything like this before.

"Let me tell you how Gaius Antonius Hybrida defended the people you sent him out to protect," I cried, raising my voice so that it would carry. "He sent no help to the frontier, and it was not until the enemy was actually in Macedon that he took to the field. The enemy was not intimidated, and they attacked. They stumbled upon him, this degenerate, lying in a drunken stupor, snoring from his chest and belching all the while. The most distinguished of his tent-mates—because, *let* me tell you, it was women, not army officers who were his, what shall we call them?—his comrades-in-arms? Well, the most distinguished of them were stretched out on the couches, and the rest lay scattered nearby on the floor.

"Nevertheless, when, half dead with terror, they became aware of the enemy's approach, the poor women tried to rouse Antonius. They lifted his head, they called his name—in vain. Another whispered something in a seductive voice in his ear. One of them went so far as to slap his face—hard.

"At last he recognized their touch and their voices. He reached out to embrace the closest around her neck. He couldn't sleep—they cried too loudly, and he couldn't stay awake—he was too drunk. So he lay in a drunken doze in the arms of centurions and his concubines."

I could hardly see to the last rows of the benches now. I didn't know who was there. Did Pompey stay? Did Caesar? Who else? I don't know. I never asked and he never said, so I have no idea if my father ever troubled to look in at all.

Certainly my speech was a triumph. I knew it even before I sat down. Antonius' face was as yellow as the fog, Cicero's eyes were shining, the jury hung, open-mouthed, on every syllable. Neither Fabius nor Gallus would look at me at all, but when I sat down it was among cheers and shouts, and a man in the back raised his joined fists like a victor in the Arena.

But my speech was not the only sensation of the day; there was Cicero's as well. Slowly he lumbered to his feet, looking, as always, completely at home. He swung his head from side to side, peering near-sightedly into the dimness. But when he spoke, his voice was beautiful. Every head turned toward him, and every face opened like a flower in the sun.

"It is my unhappy duty to defend Gaius Antonius. Unhappy not because he is guilty, which of course he is not, but because this prosecution should never have been brought in the first place. That is the work of three unscrupulous men, who have not the honesty or the candor to appear before you themselves, but have sent two men and a boy to do the job for them. They wish to conceal from you the fact of their compact, their concord—dare I call it what it is?—their *con-spiracy*."

My mouth fell open and I stared at him. He had figured it out. To this day I don't know how. He was so intelligent, so intuitive, so aware of the city and every breath that moved in it, perhaps nothing could have hidden it from him for long.

"Who else is behind the trouble we have had recently? Who is responsible for the violence that has disrupted our government and brought our communal lives into disorder, perhaps beyond repair? I do not have to tell you. When our consul threatens a man with prison for exercising no more than his right to speak in the Senate—right, did I say? His *obligation*—and when that man is a Cato; when a consul allows his henchmen to assault his colleague in office; when the same three men disregard the legal safeguards and pass legislation by bribery, by threat, and in defiance of all tradition, all law, all religion, what have we to do here with a man who has done nothing wrong except to annoy these men? It is a dangerous thing to do, it seems. Cerberus who guards the gate of Hell has three heads. By the gods, so docs the tyranny that is being prepared for us today."

There were shouts and cheers, mixed with cries of "No!" or "Lies!" or more ominously, "Get him out of there." Cicero did not flinch. "I have said there are three of them," he cried, his voice rising effortlessly over the noise. "Well, perhaps I am wrong. Perhaps our betrayal is not complete. It may be that the greatest man our state has ever produced has not yet abandoned us.

"Who can believe that Pompey would stoop to treason? He never has before. Yet he could have: he has had opportunities denied to lesser men. He could have brought his army into the city when he came back from the east. There are many who would have welcomed him, even on those terms, and some who were sure that those were the terms he would offer. Yet he was too great for that then. Let us hope he is too great for it now."

A vortex had opened in the fog, and through it I saw the backs of a crowd of men disappearing across the paving toward the Pontifex Maximus' residence. A flash of silver-gilt shone at their head, an arm was raised. Caesar.

"And because Pompey was away so long," Cicero was saying, "it may be that he does not realize how his name and his prestige are being used. Unscrupulous, did the prosecution say? In all my long life in this place, standing before you with one tale or another of greed or violence, cruelty or betrayal, I have never had to report the equal of this.

"That a man, gifted himself and in addition the bearer of an excellent and patrician name, should put on like a cloak the fame, the accomplishments, the nearly god-like greatness of another so that he may hide his crimes in the dark . . ."

There was more, but I don't think anyone heard, so great was the uproar. And he deserved it—I don't think Cicero had ever been more impressive. All the same my heart sank to my shoes as the jury began to vote. I heard the voices of the aediles reading the ballots, but to me they sounded like so many seagulls, plaintive but meaningless, in the damp air.

It was not until my friends were all around me, clasping me by the arms, embracing me, shouting congratulations in my face, that I understood. "By Hercules," Cassius bellowed. "You've won." Catullus was pounding me on the back so hard he nearly knocked me over.

Across the way I could see Cicero. He was standing alone. No one in all that crowd had dared to come up to him. "There's the man who really won," I said, but my friends were leading me off to the taverns in the streets behind the Forum. The last sight I had of him was as he stood by himself in the abandoned court. He looked tired; his heavy shoulders slumped and his head sank toward his chest, but his mouth had twitched into a smile.

After that my day dissolved in glimpses. A bar, full of roistering young men, and Catullus demanding the best wine in the house. There must have been a lot of it, because later I was making my way—unsteady, alone, and rather apt to find myself up to the ankles in the gutters—toward the Pontifex Maximus' house. There, lamplight and Julius Caesar's ice-blond hair, as he congratulated me. But he was angry. His eyes were bright with rage and his teeth glittered.

He wasted no words on it. "Come with me, Caelius." He

had gripped me by the shoulder, so that even if I wanted to I would not have been able to decline.

He led me to, what? The Temple of Castor in the Forum, I believe. There in the building as dim as night and wispy with fog, a meeting was in progress. A large gang of men stood in the middle of the multi-colored marble floor like counters in a board game. I laughed.

Pompey very splendid in a bullion-encrusted cloak, and purple with affronted dignity, Caesar, cool as a fish, and as silvery. Lictors, I don't know whose, their bronze helmets gleaming dully, their cloaks rusty in the gloom. There were a lot of them, too, more than I would have expected, but by then I was too drunk to say how many.

Publius Clodius was there, black hair polished, skin pale, mouth like a rosebud. I thought he was the god of the place for a moment—you always forgot until you saw him again how beautiful he was. Beside him was a spindly creature, so young he had not grown out of the angularity of boyhood. He was signing a book.

A book. There was one, unrolled on a stand. Pompey was leaning over it. Was he going to write? Someone was saying, "Do you, Publius Fonteius, adopt Publius Clodius Pulcher as your son, according to the law, and with all the rights and privileges of a son of your house?"

I let out a bray of laughter that rang off the walls, startling everybody. I couldn't help it. Publius Clodius must have been ten years older than this Fonteius, and the fellow was plainly a plebeian while Clodius came from one of the most aristocratic families in Rome. No wonder I laughed. The only surprise was that no one else did.

"Here," I said. Several men in the shadows looked at me. "What's all this in aid of? Why is Clodius trying to get adopted as a plebeian?"

Caesar was busy with Pompey in the middle of the colored marble floor, kneeling over something, I couldn't see what. Togaed men and lictors loomed over him. "What are they doing?" I demanded, my voice getting louder.

"Quiet." Vatinius was swimming toward me in the half light. "They're taking the auspices. It has to be done if the ceremony is to be legal."

145

"You're not serious. Legal? What could be legal about this?"

"Quiet, please. It's legal enough for our purposes."

"What purposes?"

Caesar looked up from the floor. In the dimness the marble was the color of blood.

"You have to be a plebeian to run for the tribuneship. The office isn't open to patricians." Vatinius shook out a cloud of his horrible perfume. "Please. Keep your voice down."

"Does Clodius want to be a tribune? What on earth for?"

"Shh," Vatinius hissed, frantic. "You're disturbing the—"

Down at the end of the room the door was opening. Mist swirled around the heavy panels. I could see a short distance out. A column gleamed, a breath of filthy air came in. Catullus stood in the opening, his red hair dripping, his toga limp on his shoulder.

"Get him out of here," Caesar shouted, leaping to his feet. "This is a private meeting."

Catullus, not having taken this in, said, "Oh, Caelius, there you are. I've been looking for you." His voice was thick with wine and his gray eyes wandered around the painted space.

The lictors looked uncertainly at Caesar. "Wait," I shouted, suddenly understanding. "Wait. Don't. I'll take care of it. He's drunk, he won't remember anything . . . It's all right." Out of the corner of my eye, I saw Caesar nod, or thought I did.

"Gaius," I cried to Catullus with all the urgency I could put into my voice. "Please. Go on ahead. I'll catch up to you at my house. Please."

His eyes drifted back to me. "Your house?"

Caesar had covered the distance between us in a few long strides; he stood beside me now with his hand on my arm. I could feel it, heavy and warm, a friendly grip.

"Oh," said Catullus drunkenly. "Yes. Your house. All right. Sh-see you." He lurched out, yanking the door shut behind him with a hollow clang. The noise seemed to go on for a long time in that dim place, shaking the air.

"You handled that very well," Caesar said, holding my eyes with his. I thought I felt movement behind me, men going toward the door. I must have been wrong; it was probably the wine I had drunk myself. Caesar was talking to me, smiling with dazzling pleasure into my eyes, and I could not look away to make sure.

"Why does Publius Clodius want to become a tribune?" I asked.

"A good question. By the gods, Caelius, I always thought you were a clever fellow. Well, a tribune can be a lot of help. Look at Vatinius there. He's useful, wouldn't you say? And we've got a problem, don't we? I mean, since this afternoon? We can't have people calling us tyrants. It's bad for the city. Sows discord, makes it difficult to get things done."

I had a vision of Cicero, glimmering whitely in the murk of the Forum. "Clodius hates Cicero," I said.

He smiled again and patted my shoulder. Somewhere behind my back the air in the temple expanded and compressed, as if the door had opened, and then shut again.

Catullus was waiting for me in the atrium of my little flat; the servants had brought him wine, and a towel for his hair. He looked much soberer now. "Gods, what a foul day," I said, slitting the seal on an invitation to dinner from someone who had heard my speech.

Catullus had never had much use for small talk. "What in the name of the Underworld was going on in there just now?"

"It was private."

"Oh really? Private?" His eyes had gone brilliant with anger. "Well, I can tell you, whatever it was for it was Hell's own purpose. Pluto and his attendants playing dice on the floor of Hades."

I revised my opinion. "You're drunk."

"Of course I'm drunk. What difference does that make? What was it, some conspiracy to arm the slaves and take over the city, like last time? Or only to murder honest men in their beds?"

"Nothing like that. You wouldn't understand."

He pulled himself out of the chair. His sturdy body looked bunched and compact, as if he were getting ready to fight. His eyes blazed in his lumpy face. "Great gods, I understand perfectly. What do you two do when you're alone?" He minced over to me in an exaggerated parody of Caesar's

147

elegant stroll, and squeezed my arm. "You don't care, do you? Anything he wants. Before, behind, it's all the same to you."

He was shorter than the man he was mocking, but all the same it was a savage caricature. He was shorter than I, too, and I had to hit downward and very close. Even so he staggered and blood shot out of his nose. He wiped the back of his hand across it, smearing it. "What do you think that proves?" he asked. "That I was wrong? Gods, it's as obvious as the sun in the sky. You're getting a reputation as a man who'll do anything to get ahead, and he . . . well, everyone knows what he is."

"Get out." I was panting. I felt as filthy as if I had fought a match with him and not won cleanly, though he was in the wrong and I was right. Certainly I was right.

"I'm going," he said. "You needn't expect to see me again."

"Good."

"But let me tell you one thing. You're my cousin after all, and I have an obligation to the family. You are making as big a mistake as you ever contemplated in your life. Caesar is the most cynical of men. He cares nothing for you. He will use you and discard you like a boy he buys and sells in the market."

"Oh, spare me," I shouted. "Get out of my sight." I raised my voice to call the footmen.

"Caelius, you're making a mistake," he cried, looking back over their shoulders as they led him away. "I'm sorry I was rough—I was drunk, I guess. But you've got to understand—"

"Put him out on the street," I said. "I never want him admitted to this house again."

It was a disgusting suggestion. Stupid. He must have been jealous of my success. He was two years older than I, and what had he ever done? A few poems, highly praised, it was true, but what was that beside a speech that all of Rome would talk about? Yes, he was certainly jealous.

Not that it gave him the right to spew any filth that came into his head, I thought as I plunged my face into a basin of hot water. Just because a powerful man like Caesar had the kindness to take an interest . . . And to accuse *me*, me of all

148

people, of some sexual . . . Well, let it go—I really couldn't be bothered with this sort of thing. The absurdity was obvious. Any woman in the city could tell him. . . .

The note I had received was an invitation from Clodia Metelli to come to dinner. She had been Catullus' mistress but she was obviously looking elsewhere now. In the circumstances, it gave me considerable pleasure to accept.

Down the way, near Clodia's house, a crowd had collected. As I came up I could see the lanterns bobbing in the mist, the long yellow tails of their light smeared across the stones. Men were stooping or kneeling over something on the ground. For an instant it recalled the meeting in the Temple of Castor, and I wondered what auspices anyone would want to take in the middle of a public street . . . The floor of that place had shone like blood, too.

There was blood on the stones and this time it was real. The lantern light shone on it like gold, but in the shadows where it had collected under the dark red hair, it was as deep as night. There were bruises, bad ones, like patches across his eyes; his mouth was broken; his arm lay twisted at an angle that made me sick to look at. He had lost his toga altogether, and his tunic was twisted. Someone twitched it down to cover his thigh. That was where the blood was coming from. A sword had pierced him nearly to his knee . . .

"Catullus," I said.

Half the street was there, partly hidden in the fog. Cicero was saying something under his breath, Publius Crassus had brought a doctor, Clodius had sent his doorman to see. A woman was peering through the curtains of her chair, a banker had come up from the Forum. The doctor had finished and was gesturing to have Catullus taken away on a stretcher.

"They say he's still alive," Cicero said, rising to his feet beside me.

I shrugged. It was like the Temple of Castor all right. There was Vatinius, pop-eyed as usual; Julius Caesar grinned behind him, savagely pleased. The fog tore apart soundlessly on a current of air, and I saw the men they were with. They had been in the temple, too. Big men with battered faces and hard eyes. One of them was sucking a knuckle; blood had splotched another's clothes.

My eyes went back to Caesar. I thought he gave me a quick nod of approval, but the fog had come together again, seamless as a shroud, and I could not be sure. I waited until the doctor had led the stretcher party down the street, then I went on my way to Clodia Metelli's house.

BOOK THREE

XIV

While I have been sitting here, the long afternoon has drawn itself out into evening. On the road the shadows have flowed together into gray. Swallows cross the pale translucence of the sky, hunting the late insects. Dying, the breeze has left the leaves silent on the trees, the tall grass beside the road hardly whispers.

Already there is a coolness in the air. The strong scents of day have faded leaving behind a hint, featureless but unmistakable: the first suggestion of the dew. In a half an hour, perhaps a little more, it will be night.

The great square stones of the road will hardly show their whiteness to what little moon we will see; the countryside will lie in darkness under the stars. Everything that is hunted will be hidden, safe. But until then the colorless light reveals us. And somewhere out there, a wing of cavalry has found a place to stop—fresh water, some farmer's level field—and the leather tents are going up. It cannot be very far away.

A group of men is crossing the square below. It is the town council. They are nothing but bald heads and vague shapes in the dusk. I hear their feet on the stairs, the voices of my guards. Then they are standing in an untidy clump, frightened, in front of my table.

"Gentlemen, I have brought you here to inform you of the regulations for tonight. Those I have already made remain in force. No one is to go out. No one is to visit from one house to another or to go out into the street for any reason. No fires are to be lit, and no other light may show. Is that clear?"

My fat senior fellow, the chief magistrate, pulls himself up to his full shortness and says, "But praetor, what are the women to do about cooking if there are no fires? How will we eat? Are we to starve?"

153

"If necessary. That is your problem. Really, magistrate, you do not seem to understand. If the whole pack of you died during the night, it would only mean one less irritating problem for me."

"Yes," he says unhappily.

"Good. Now. In addition to those rules I am increasing the number of hostages. I want one more from each of you."

At this there are, of course, wailing and tears One man goes down on his knees to me.

"Be quiet! I can't hear myself think."

Instantly they are silenced, though some cannot stifle their sobs. "Praetor," the chief magistrate ventures, "what if we have no more people to give?"

Really, I cannot be bothered with this kind of thing. "If you have no one you must be a hostage yourself. Birria!" My senior centurion troops in with his squad. Immediately the townsmen are silent. Well, Birria is enough to frighten anyone. An ex-slave, a former criminal and gladiator, a veteran of every brawl and battle for the last twenty years, he has the scars to prove it, and the demeanor. "Birria, take these men away. Escort them to their homes and receive from them one family member—a blood relation, not the maid or the kitchen boy. If anyone gives you any trouble, kill him. If anyone fails to produce someone, take him himself. Bring the hostages, chained, all of them, to the square out there, where I can see them. You'll need a squad to guard them. I also want the patrols increased—come and see me after you've set this up and we'll work out a pattern."

Birria salutes, smartly enough, and leads the town elders away. They are crying and pleading, wringing their hands and moaning like seagulls on a beach. I suppose a number of them have only their wives and daughters left at home, and they fear for them more than they did for the more distant relatives they gave up before. That, of course, is why I demanded them. I cannot risk a signal to that cavalry out there in the gathering night.

The colorless dusk has deepened to blue, a tint so powerful it seems to hum like a note of music, in every visible object. The walls of the houses glow like sand under water, windows and doors have a secret look, as if they had withdrawn themselves into the dark. Out in the square the hostages have assembled, wavering like seaweed in the diminishing light, their voices coming to me like thin curlew cries. A lantern is lit, then hastily extinguished, its pale glimmer already too visible. Far away, the harbor sighs, and in the gardens the last breath of evening stirs the trees and shrubs, now massive and indistinct against the sky. The swallows have gone, the pigeons under the roof have ceased to coo, but out on the road, an owl begins to call.

LAST REPORT OF MARCUS CAELIUS RUFUS
PRAETOR PEREGRINUS OF ROME . . .

So I became Clodia Metelli's lover and celebrated on her beautiful and far from passive body my arrival at the heights of power and prestige. Gods, it was strange how easy everything suddenly became. I was famous, everyone wanted to know me. I had invitations to every great house in the city— even some where Pompey himself was no longer received.

My connection with Caesar still did not seem to be generally known—I was thought of as working for Crassus or Pompey, It was all right with me, and certainly Caesar never cared. One more young man trailing him down to the Forum was of far less importance to him, in spite of the augmentation to his prestige, than someone he could use without everyone's knowing his business. He had enemies, who would have been glad to know what he was up to. Even Catullus, recovering from his injuries in Verona, still sent his little verses to circulate in the city. They did a lot of damage.

For me my success was a pleasure. The moneylenders honored my drafts, aristocratic women flirted with me at parties or slipped me little messages, until I had a collection to rival even Caesar's. Important men listened when I spoke. My atrium was crowded with clients. Many were sent by Caesar, but many came on their own, because they had heard of me, and men said in the city that I knew how to get things done.

That was what it meant to have a powerful patron. That Caesar himself was an extraordinary man was only just beginning to appear, but it was true that many people found that if they went to him their paths were suddenly made clear, while those who opposed him encountered obstacles and delays.

There were, all the same, many who did oppose—Catullus was far from solitary in that—and in the months before the elections in July they grew stronger. Bibulus, of course, kept to his house, issuing his boring proclamations and generally trying to put Caesar in a bad light. Most of the Senate called every morning to hear him. There they would be, hundreds of them jammed into the street—for they brought their trains of clients and friends with them. In the cool light of dawn Bibulus would appear, look solemnly up at the sky, and announce that the day was inauspicious and no public business could be done. Then, satisfied that he had put a stop to Caesar's plans, he would go back into his house, and the senators would finish their progress to the Forum.

Caesar was annoyed by this farce, and took it seriously enough so that at a rally of his supporters he once suggested that Bibulus should be burnt out. The mob cheered at this but in the end nothing came of it—no one had the courage to do it, I suppose.

Caesar was busy and did not propose it again. He had Vatinius convene the Plebeian Assembly again and pass the law that had been a foregone conclusion since the day Metellus Celer had died—I mean the award to Caesar of the province of Nearer Gaul to administer after his term as consul expired. He had taken the precaution of bringing in Pompey's troops, and the Forum was lined with them. He made an odd contrast with their sturdy ranks as he paced up and down while the voting was going on, his elegant clothes floating around him, his long stride full of energy and suppressed force.

He convened the Senate, too, under the eyes of the soldiers, and made a speech to them. They had to come—he was the consul—but they were frightened. The Curia is a dim and musty place at the best of times: with a hundred armed men ranked in the aisles, and more just outside, it was a place of dread. Men sat white-faced and shaking while Caesar harangued them, laughing in their faces and strutting like a peacock in his brilliant clothes.

He made them add a second province, the huge and practically unexplored Further Gaul, where the tribes live unknown to the civilized world. His appointment would last five years, he told them, and shaking in their seats, they voted that, too. Outside a mob shouted Caesar's name, and the tramp of military feet made an accompaniment.

When the Senate had finished its vote, Caesar stood up and looked them over. His fine head was thrown back, his teeth shone in a grin. His contempt rang out like a bright coin in the gloom. "You thought you had blocked me—" For the space of a heartbeat his anger showed. "Well, you haven't, have you? If I ever want you again, I will call you."

I remembered that he had said once before that next time he would force them to service him. He had used an expression of considerable grossness, which the senators had plainly not forgotten. It struck me now that he had made good his threat. They looked frightened, disgusted, sick with themselves, like free men who had been forced to act like slaves and take whatever he chose to give.

He watched them, cool and smiling again, as, heads down, like men who had been beaten, they filed out. I'm sorry to say that they were not respectfully treated by the crowd outside. Well, it served them right.

He did not call the Senate again, but used the Plebeian Assembly for all his business. This was principally the extension of the land law, which made thousands of the poor eligible for grants of farms in the country. They did not even have to be veterans.

It may have been too much: not long after it passed a reference to Pompey was booed in the theatre. Caesar, coming in like an actor on his cue caught a share of it, too. He reacted with his typical speed and boldness, threatening to take away their privileges if order was not restored, and what might have been a very nasty incident was averted.

To me it was principally interesting because it showed that people still thought of Caesar as Pompey's representative. In reality . . . well, it was hard to see what reality was. It was like peering through a fog, there were only shapes and darkness and it was hard to be sure of anything. But I had seen the flicker of challenge in Caesar's eyes the afternoon Metellus died, and I was watching . . .

I have an idea that Pompey might have spoken to Caesar around this time, expressing some uneasiness at the situation. Curio and his father had been making speeches—you heard their nearly identical voices braying on what seemed to be every second street corner. They got good audiences, and their speeches did a lot of harm. One of the things that must have bothered Pompey most about the incident in the theater when his own name was booed was that immediately after, Curio and his father, happening to come in, were cheered like heroes.

"Pompey doesn't like to be unpopular," Cicero said, anxious himself, for Publius Clodius had been uttering threats against him. But Cicero was ignoring his own danger and trying to think about his friend. "No," he said, "Pompey didn't spend years of his life in the east to be hissed in the theater on his return. Caesar had better be careful. Unpopularity is the one thing Pompey will never forgive."

Caesar was careful. Gods, when I look back on this time, I cannot believe how cleverly he maneuvered. He was an amazing man: he could be as brutal and coarse as anyone—his treatment of the Senate shows that—but he could be as gentle as a dove and as subtle as a snake.

First, he studied Pompey, and there was something behind that great, red, round face, that dignified and rather pompous demeanor, he saw that no one else did. A love of women and ease, a sensuous longing, a desire for tranquility and domestic pleasures. So Caesar gave Pompey his daughter in marriage, though she was already betrothed elsewhere and he had to scramble to break that contract without alienating the other man's family.

It was a political alliance of course, just like hundreds of others among important families in Rome. But Julia was intelligent and well-bred and had the Julian good looks. She was also twenty-four years old; Pompey was forty-seven. There was no doubt that he fell in love with her. He was wild with happiness; his flat blue eyes sparkled and his face shone; he was like a boy himself. Well, Pompey had been a soldier for a long time. A home, a wife, the possibility of children, all that must have seemed very wonderful to him. And Caesar knew it, though no one else would have guessed.

The next thing he did was to speak to Cicero. Speak to him?—he flattered him outrageously, all in the most straightforward, here-we-are-two-men-of-the-world-social-equals-let's-talk-frankly sort of way. He wanted Cicero's support, he said; he regretted the misunderstanding that had made Cicero feel he had to speak so harshly at the trial of Antonius Hybrida. He knew they wanted the same things, he and Cicero and Cicero's old friend Pompey.

He knew, too, that Cicero had been having problems with Publius Clodius Pulcher. These personal animosities were one of the hazards of political life—he knew from his own experience. Perhaps it would be useful to Cicero to get out of the city for a while? He, Caesar, would be honored to offer him any number of positions. Perhaps he'd like to be an envoy somewhere? Or the head of a study commission? If he wished to go to Gaul he could come with Caesar—he would be delighted—no, *proud*, to have such distinguished company.

This was clever, for Caesar, of course, had encouraged Clodius in his attacks on Cicero, was encouraging even as he offered Cicero this way to escape his enemy. There is no way Cicero could have known this. The circumstances of Clodius' translation to the plebeian class were still secret, and the connection between Clodius and Caesar not apparent.

I think Cicero suspected it, for though he was vain enough to be pleased by Caesar's offers, he was courageous enough to refuse. "What would history say of me in six hundred years, if I compromised my principles out of regard for my safety?" he asked me as he pressed his ring down on the wax seal of a very civil note he was sending to Caesar to decline.

Caesar's offer did have the effect of making Cicero go to Pompey though—like everyone else he still thought of Caesar as Pompey's subordinate. So Cicero asked for Pompey's protection. I don't know if Caesar had found some way to tell Pompey what to say, but in any case, Cicero's fears were allayed, and though he continued to feel that the partners were doing great harm to the constitution, he did not press the point as hard as he might have. So perhaps Caesar accomplished what he set out to do, in spite of Cicero's shrewdness and bravery.

Neither of these two moves silenced all the opposition, but I do not think they were intended to. Now that I am a soldier myself, I recognize what Caesar was doing. He was consolidating his position, bringing into line his support, trying to neutralize at least the first stroke of his enemy's attack. These two moves, the marriage and the offer to Cicero, were prudent and conventional means to this end. The next was the most *unconventional*, the most amazing, imaginative and boldest political maneuver I have ever seen.

He needed an audacious move, for the situation continued to deteriorate. Curio and his father were making headway with their speeches; there were disturbances at political meetings and ugly incidents in the streets. The soldiers Caesar had brought in to intimidate the Senate were visible in the city too, when they weren't needed in the Curia. Meetings of the Senate had resumed, though they were sparsely attended. Caesar once, incautiously, asked the elderly Quintus Considius why.

"They're afraid of your troops," the old knight's son told him.

"Pompey's troops."

"You're the one who brought them in."

Caesar never pushed a point. "I had to keep order. And if the soldiers were really such a threat, would you be here yourself, Considius?"

Considius looked the consul in the eye. "I'm too old to fear death," he said, and stamped out of the Curia. Caesar let him go. The mood of the city was too inflammatory to take any steps against him.

Pompey's uneasiness had increased and he had several talks with Cicero about getting out of the situation. I was present at one of them. We sat in Pompey's garden nibbling his lavish sweets and drinking his wine, while the Great Man regarded us out of his hooded eyes and tried to tell us what was on his mind.

"Well, Gnaeus," Cicero said, as one who speaks to a child, "are you saying that you don't want to ally yourself to Caesar any more? Surely that's not so difficult. Just have the Senate convened and tell them so. Say that you cannot acquiesce in what is being done in your name, and you do not wish to associate yourself with it any longer. You know the kind of thing. And send your soldiers home."

"He . . . he gets things done," Pompey said, passing his tongue over his lips as if tasting a sweet. Cicero said nothing but stared at him in disbelief. "He does," Pompey insisted, looking very blank.

"Well, then you have no problem, do you? I see it's getting late. I won't trespass . . ."

"His methods!" Pompey cried. Caesar's methods might have been strangling him; his face was congested and a purple vein beat in his forehead. "I can't allow . . . any more . . ."

"Yes, well, Gnaeus, I understand, and I sympathize, but unless you're willing to separate yourself from Caesar by some definite act, you're going to continue to be seen as responsible for what he does. And rightly so. After all, what is he? An ambitious consul like dozens, hundreds, the city has produced. But you are Pompey the Great."

"But," Pompey said, his eyes disappearing behind his lids. He sat very still for a long time, blinking. Cicero, patient, waited on his feet with an equal stillness. In the end he left without another word. Pompey never looked at him, nor did he ever explain why exactly he wanted to break with Caesar. And very soon after, Caesar took steps to make sure he never would.

Oh, it was elegant; gods, it was as economical and unexpected as the solution to a problem in Euclid. Caesar must have known that Pompey was anxious and uneasy—indeed, I'm sure he did. I came on him one day in the Campus Martius, studying the excavations for the foundation of Pompey's theater. They seemed to fascinate him, his eyes travelled along the deep trenches.

"He's worried," he said, and I knew who he meant. I wasn't sure he even knew I was there, so absorbed was he, but he smiled and invited me to a party, so I suppose he must have.

161

I left him, still contemplating the vast, criss-crossed, muddy tract with a light like speculation in his eyes.

He did not reassure Pompey. That's the first thing. You'd have expected him to soothe the Great Man's feelings, make sure Pompey was content. But Caesar did no such thing. Indeed, he appeared to do nothing at all. But a few days later, early in July, a man appeared in the Forum when the scaffolding for the seats for the approaching gladiatorial games was going up. He demanded to be taken to the consul and the Senate. A man named Gabinius was supervising the construction; too busy himself, he called over a tribune to take charge. No doubt Gabinius was chosen for just that reason: he was running for consul for the following year, and was much preoccupied. Besides, he was a close friend of Pompey.

In any case, the tribune who happened to be handy was Vatinius—surprise, surprise—who then led the fellow through the crowd of idlers into the Curia. Everyone could see that Vatinius was not *connected* with him in any way. Of course not. Nor was Caesar. It was Pompey's friend Gabinius who had introduced him to the Senate. Everyone could see that.

Inside the Curia the man identified himself as Lucius Vettius, a knight from Picenum—which just happened to be Pompey's home town. He had, he said, information to lay before the Senate. "Again?" someone called out, and there was laughter, for Vettius had tried once before to give information against the rebel aristocrat Catiline. Cicero in charge of that investigation had found his information totally worthless.

After that we hadn't seen much of this fellow; I could just remember him, hanging around the fringes of Catiline's crowd, if I tried. He had been fat and shiny, like a well-basted capon; he was if anything, glossier and rounder now. Though there was nothing obvious about it, the way he gave his evidence struck me as odd. He was too eager, too interested, not very coherent. Altogether I thought it was very strange that Caesar was paying such close attention to what he said. Vatinius kept glancing at him. He spoke in a well-trained voice—someone had spent money on his education once. Even so his manner was very peculiar, as I said. He was nervous, of course, but that wasn't all. Something was haunting him, like a cold breath on the back of the neck. He was afraid as well.

"Senators," he said, hiding his eyes behind his eyelids like a woman about to faint. "Senators, I have here . . . I have evidence about a conspira—

XV

I have broken off my narrative to record ... No, it is too much. I cannot say ...

I must write. This report must be completed, for whom no longer matters. It is the information that counts now ...

**LAST REPORT OF MARCUS CAELIUS RUFUS
PRAETOR PEREGRINUS OF ROME ...**

It is odd. I thought that the road was the way that news would come, but in the end the stones were silent. The word has come from the sea. An hour ago. The darkness had begun to stain the air, like wine in a bowl of water. The fields had melted into blackness, the cypresses thrust their slender shapes into the sky. Over the town the roofs were a pattern of cut and countercut, but down below houses, streets, squares had gone, drowned in the deep well of the night. Only the sea still had color and movement, a nacreous glimmer, paler than the sky, as if the memory of light still lingered there. And in the harbor, gliding on the pearly shine, a trireme folded its oars like wings and slid toward the quay.

My first thought was for the cavalry on the road. Here then was the solution to the problem they posed, my escape from the trap they were about to spring. A ship. I would go to Pompey, then, and take my chances with him. Pompey would welcome me, he would be glad to have anyone now that he was winning. And even at the most unlikely, even if after all Caesar won, what happened to me would be no worse than what would happen if I stayed. It was like a sign from a god, a promise that I would be free. Filled with joy, I sent my people down to the harbor. In a very brief time the ship's captain stood at attention in front of my desk, very correct in his leather breastplate and short woolen cloak, his helmet under his arm.

"They told me there was a praetor here from Rome. Is that true?" His eyes went around the bare room.

"Bring some light," I said to the servants. "I am Marcus Caelius Rufus, from Rome. I am a praetor. What can I do for you, captain?"

In a moment we had lamps on the table and a chair in front of it; someone had brought food and wine. The instrument of my deliverance ate hungrily, his yellowish teeth tearing at the bread. "Sir, this couldn't be more fortunate. I have an urgent report. And then, at the first harbor I can find there is a praetor. Surely a god is smiling on this meeting."

"Oh, yes indeed, captain. Yes, indeed. Well, make your report. Tell me what is so urgent that you came out in a ship without even adequate food on board, and had to put in to the first harbor you found."

He gave me a startled look, then a comprehending one as he looked down at the ravaged plate. "Yes, praetor, you are right. I did come quickly. The Senate will want the news. There has been a battle. In Greece."

"Has there? Since the confrontation at Dyrrhacchium, where Pompey defeated Caesar? Because if that's all you've got, it's stale news. We've already heard."

He opened his eyes at that. I could see him thinking how much he would have to tell us. "Oh, no praetor. Another battle."

"Go on."

So the captain put down his wine cup, wiped his hand across his two days' growth of beard, and destroyed my future before my eyes.

When Caesar had fled from Dyrrhachium, and Pompey pursued him, they went east across the bare, lion-colored fields of Northern Greece, until they arrived at a point where the great plain of Thessaly is crossed by a little stream. It is near the town of Pharsalus. There they faced one another on either side of the little water: victorious Pompey and his huge army, accompanied by hundreds of senators and dignitaries, all well provisioned and luxuriously housed, and Caesar and his veterans. They were depressed and disheartened by their defeat and full, as troops are in such circumstances, of panic and guilt.

Yet for a long time there was no battle, for Pompey's advisors were so sure of victory they spent all their time in argument over the spoils, and Pompey, always deferential to the nobility, allowed himself to be ruled—overruled, I should say—by these important men. In this way he spilled out his chances like water into sand, for Caesar used the time to let his troops recover their health and their courage. He never punished them, though at Dyrrhachium, when Pompey had broken their line, they had run away like green recruits. Instead he told them that a new engagement would wipe out their disgrace.

When the two lines finally did meet, Caesar held back his best troops and at the crucial moment, threw them at Pompey's cavalry with orders not to hurl their javelins in the usual way, but to use them like spears to stab the horsemen in the face. Well, cavalry troops do not come from among the Roman soldiers—we fight on foot as we always have. They are Macedonians and Alexandrians, Thracians and so on. They can be very brave, but you can't expect the same steadiness under pressure that Romans would show. Indeed, in the assault the horsemen broke and ran. The rest of Pompey's legions—two of which had once been Caesar's—gave way.

In a short time the battle was a rout. Pompey retreated to guard his camp and waited in his tent. When the end was obvious, he took off his scarlet cape and the other signs of his rank, and fled. He rode all night, stopping only to pick up a few friends, until he came to the sea. There he boarded a grain ship and set out to raise another army in the provinces of the east, where he had been a conqueror many years before.

"In this battle, captain," I said when I could trust myself to speak, "were there many lost, among the officers and the—?"

He nodded.

"Who? I mean . . . Cicero?"

"Cicero is safe in Dyrrhachium, praetor. He never went with Pompey. I heard that he had been ill."

"Thank a god for that illness, then. And . . . Antony? He was there, I'm sure. Caesar's shadow, that's Antony."

"Mark Antony commanded Caesar's left wing. He served with distinction and was not wounded, as far as I know. Another young man, Marcus Brutus, fought with Pompey. Do you know him, too, praetor? They say that Caesar gave orders before the battle that if any of his soldiers encountered him they were to be careful not to harm him."

"Caesar was always very fond of him. He is a friend of the family," I said neutrally. That, of course, is one way to put it.

"I see. I suppose in civil war . . ."

"Just so. In civil war it must be common enough. And Pompey? What happened to him?" He was looking at me closely—I suppose my voice was strangling in my throat. Well, something was dying there: my chances, my hopes. It was more than ever important that no one should guess which side I am on.

"Pompey went from one place to another," the captain said. "He was trying to decide what to do, but people had heard about the battle everywhere he went—all those little kings who owed him allegiance, that he had put on their thrones or kept there when they were threatened by their enemies, all those cities he had freed, and made friends of Rome. But now they were afraid of Caesar, and not one of them would help him. The island of Rhodes wouldn't even let him land."

I could not even say aloud, "Poor Pompey," though it was in my mind. "What happened?" I asked, as emotionlessly as I could.

"He went to Egypt, praetor. The Pharaoh there owed him a favor."

"Pompey took a bribe to put him back on his throne. A hundred and forty million sesterces. I'll say he owed him something—they were more than friends, they were partners in crime."

He let out his voice in laugh to keep mine company, but over his open mouth he was watching me. "Of course," I added, to be fair, "Caesar had a share of that money, too."

He blinked. The whites of his eyes were laced with tiny veins, the rims were red. He had come a long way to tell me this news. A god was smiling on this meeting, he had said. Laughing, more likely.

"The Pharaoh and his chief eunuch conferred, when Pompey's little fleet came in sight," he told me. "They were afraid he might have too much influence with his old soldiers—a lot of Pompey's retired troops from the eastern wars live in Egypt. And if Caesar ever heard that the Pharaoh had helped Pompey, he would be angry. This Pharaoh has problems of his own right now. His sister Cleopatra has raised an army against him, and he is faced with a civil war of his own. If Caesar—"

"Never mind that. What has happened to Pompey? You have said that the Pharaoh owed him a favor. Owed. Why the past tense? Isn't he in Egypt now?"

He gave me a little nod of acknowledgement, but he did not allow my questions to turn him from his story. He was so tired, perhaps he couldn't think. In his mind he had arranged to tell it in one way, and now he was following his plan. "The Pharaoh sent three men, one of them a Roman military tribune, named Septimius, who had served with Pompey as a centurion. They went out to Pompey's flagship in an open boat."

"So Pompey had a fleet?"

"Yes, praetor. A man I know told me that when Pompey saw how many ships he still had he cursed the men who had told him to fight Caesar on land. He had raised a little army by now too, and his wife and son had come out to join him.

"So Septimius, this military tribune, went out with two others to fetch Pompey. Pompey's wife was crying that it was dangerous, but there Pharoah and all his court were lined up on the quay and there were ships in the harbor, and Septimius was saying that there were sandbars that made it impossible for a big warship like Pompey's to come any closer. Though I know Alexandria's harbor like the pool in my own garden, and I can tell you that there are none. Near the lighthouse there's some debris from construction—"

"So Pompey got into the boat? Is that what you're telling me?"

"Yes, praetor. He said something. Here. Someone wrote it down for me, but I can't read it. It's in Greek."

"'He who enters a tyrant's door, becomes a slave, though he was free before.' Pompey said that?"

"Yes, praetor. What does it mean?"

"It's a quotation, from Sophocles."

"I see. Well, he was an educated man. A good man, praetor, a fine Roman soldier."

"So he was. What happened to him?"

"Once in the boat he asked Septimius, who was still standing up as they went toward the shore—to show respect, you understand, praetor—if he knew him. 'Didn't you serve with me?' he said. Septimius nodded, but he wouldn't answer. No one in the boat would say anything, so Pompey studied the speech he was going to make to the Pharaoh. Oh, it was smartly done. I would call it a well-planned operation." He paused, and his fatigue or his emotion overcame him again, and he wiped his eyes. "When they arrived at the quay, right in front of the court and all the dignitaries, an old client of Pompey's came forward to help him out of the boat, And as Pompey stepped up, Septimius stabbed him in the back."

"In the back?" I cried.

"Yes, praetor. But he didn't die immediately. He looked around at the other men in the boat—"

"Stop," I said. "I can't listen to any more of this." I pulled my cloak over my head and sat for a moment catching my breath. My chest burned as if I had been running, my eyes stung. Gods, what a death. I remember the Great Man in the days when he was powerful, in the Forum, his round face fiery, his hundreds of clients and supporters trailing after him like the tail of a comet. He had such splendor, such dignity, he was more like an image in a temple than a man.

"When did it happen?" I asked.

"The twenty-eighth of September."

"Gods. It was his birthday."

"I believe so, praetor."

"And the anniversary of his triumph when he came back from the east."

"Yes."

"Oh, gods." I closed my eyes with my hand and the tears splattered hotly on my fingers.

Presently the captain said, "The Pharaoh gave order that

169

Pompey's head was to be preserved to give to Caesar. They know how to do that in Egypt. Then the court and the crowd went away, leaving Pompey's headless body on the shore. That night two of his old friends—his client and an old man who had been an ordinary soldier in Pompey's army built him a pyre and stayed with him all night, until the corpse was burned and the rites performed."

I uncovered my eyes. "They saved the *head* for Caesar?"

He nodded.

"I don't believe it. No one, not even a barbarian, would do such a thing."

"They did do it. They thought Caesar would be pleased. But when he saw it, Caesar—"

"Yes?" I was still hungry for news of him, though we were no longer friends.

"He did what you did just now, praetor. He turned his head away and drew up his cloak, and those near him said that he wept."

"Yes," I said, "he was a good man after all." I don't know which of them I meant, Pompey or Caesar.

Pompey is dead. I have been sitting here while the evening has deepened into true night, alone, trying to take this in. The burning in my chest has subsided to dullness, as if my heart has grown too heavy for my body; my lids droop over my eyes so that it is an effort to lift them. Pompey is dead, and I cannot tell if my grief is for him, or for myself.

There was more, before I had a chance to be alone. "Praetor," the captain said, leaning over my desk in his eagerness. "Have you ever seen him? Caesar, I mean?"

"What? Oh, yes, frequently. Both of them."

Like the rest of the world he was prepared to forget Pompey now that he was dead. "Is he human? Caesar, I mean?"

"Why on earth shouldn't he be?"

"I don't know. I just thought he might be—a god."

"A *what?*"

"Well, praetor, he just doesn't seem like other men. He does things that normal people couldn't. When he was chasing Pompey after Pharsalus, for instance, he came to the

Hellespont and found that there were only a few rowboats on the shore. So he took them, and midway out in the straits he met an admiral of Pompey's with ten war ships coming up from the Aegean.

"I don't know if you've ever seen a war galley from a rowboat, praetor, but let me tell you it's a sight, with its huge sail bellying out and all the ranks of oars moving in time, and the marines drawn up on the walkways with their spears glittering in the sunlight. And this admiral had ten ships like this.

"Well, Caesar just stood up in the rowboat and shouted up to the admiral to surrender to him. And the admiral did. He must have thought Caesar had a fleet behind him. All right, praetor, laugh, but you must admit it's a very remarkable thing to do."

"He's a very remarkable man."

"Yes," the captain said, but there was so much reserve in his voice I could hear him adding, "if he's a man at all," as clearly as if he'd said it aloud.

I sent him away with a reward to sleep in a house in the town, telling him I would get his message through to Rome. I paid him enough honor that he will not notice that he is being isolated, and his news confined to me alone.

When he was gone the night seemed to come back through the window, bringing with it the town and the fields, the exhalations of plants, the bronze dampness of the dead leaves, the tick of sunwarmed stone cooling in darkness. I blew out the lamp.

Presently I could see the road as it ran glimmering through the night. The town was no more than the shape of its roofs against a few white stars, opening like flowers in the field of heaven; the sea was reduced to a whisper on the shingle. But out in the harbor, riding on one winking light, the trireme waited, reminding me that I will have to decide now where to go . . . Well, never mind. I have until morning to think of that. And in the meantime I must finish my report.

XVI

Silence and the night breeze, coming to me from far away, over the fields and forests, and a door opens into the noise and color of the past . . .

LAST REPORT OF MARCUS CAELIUS RUFUS PRAETOR PERGRINUS OF ROME . . .

Where was I? Oh, yes, Vettius and the moves Caesar made to assure the adherence of Pompey, to neutralize those who were growing dangerous to him. He was already planning for when he was going to be away in Gaul.

Vettius. Well, Vettius stood up in the Senate with a list of men he claimed were part of a conspiracy to assassinate Pompey—yes, Pompey. And at the head of the whole thing he named Curio. The man who was supposed to give Curio the dagger was none other than Bibulus. How's that for a neat summary of all the troublemakers?

"Do you think I couldn't buy a dagger for m-myself?" Curio shot back when Vettius accused him, and the whole Senate burst out laughing. Well, it was nonsense. Bibulus had warned Pompey publicly back in May, to watch out for a plot, and Pompey had thanked him for it, too. Curio had heard rumors and had gone to his father. The two of them had paid a call on Pompey to warn him. The man who was supposed to organize the murder—another friend of Pompey's—was in Macedon at the time. The Senate laughed and put Vettius in chains, declaring that any magistrate that released him would be guilty of high treason.

The next day Vatinius and Caesar had Vettius brought before the Plebeian Assembly, where he repeated his story, though during the night the names had somewhat changed. Curio's still headed the list, but young Marcus Brutus' was now absent. "Well," said Cicero, "a night of *passionate* appeal has intervened, hasn't it?" Cicero's own name was on the new list, but it had not, it seemed, impaired his sense of humor.

He meant that Caesar had gone to Servilia, his mistress and Brutus' mother. When the Senate got through laughing at this they sent Vettius back to prison to wait for his trial, where it was expected that he would talk freely in exchange for immunities and guarantees. Cicero was more worried than his joking showed. "There will be more prosecutions, and a spreading scandal. Once this sort of thing starts, it's very hard to stop it. It's such a convenient way to get rid of people, you see . . ."

The city was so uneasy that the elections had to be postponed, though Caesar and Pompey—and Crassus, when he could be induced to say anything—wanted them carried out on the normal date. They prevailed for the tribunician election, and Clodius was chosen, making Cicero more anxious than before. "More trouble," he muttered, blinking as if the light hurt his eyes. "And on top of it all Vettius is going to speak—"

But Vettius never did. Early one morning a few days later Vettius' body was found on the stones outside the prison. The official report said it was natural causes, but I saw the body myself, and there were marks on it, bruises as if from blows and around the neck the signs of a rope.

Many people saw it; it lay on the stones until some slaves came to take it away. Most people felt that someone had gotten rid of an embarrassment, and no one dared to point a finger at the man most obviously involved. And after a while the whole thing was forgotten.

Yet the point was made. The stink of murder had penetrated as far as the Forum, an acrid odor of conspiracy, false witness, proscription, exile, death. It caught at the back of your throat when you took a deep breath.

Everyone felt it. Curio developed a flutter under his eye and a habit of turning his head as if he thought he might be followed, Cicero took an extended visit to his country houses. The person most affected was Pompey. He disappeared.

Well, that's an exaggeration. He retired with his new wife to his beautiful, sprawling villa out in the suburbs and did not come into the city any more. He posted armed men at his gate, and there he remained, to the snickers of the entire city, leaving Caesar and Vatinius with their hands free, to do whatever they liked and say he supported it.

So Pompey was more dependent on Caesar than before. Yet many people blamed him for the entire incident. He brought in one of his own clients from Picenum, and suborned his testimony, they said. To gain sympathy. But why would he do that? Pompey didn't need an elaborate plan. All he ever had to do was renounce Caesar, and people would have come flocking back to his door. The demonstrations around the Curios prove that, and if they didn't what happened later, when the split finally came, is ample evidence. Or so I would have said.

No, it was Caesar who chose that weapon, one that lay so close to Pompey that the Great Man could not fail to understand what he meant. And understand he certainly did. Tarnished like a silver shield in bad weather, the Great Man retreated behind his gates, and there was no longer any possibility that he would ever pull free of the man he thought was his friend.

Left to themselves Vatinius got through the rest of Caesar's legislation. By the time October came . . .

That damned light. It winks like a star in the wind, drawing my eye so that I cannot concentrate, pulling me back out of the past to where the ship rides at anchor in the harbor, and far away in Egypt Pompey the Great has been snuffed out like a lamp.

. . . By the time October came, and the postponed elections, Pompey and Caesar, together with Crassus and all his millions had had enough time to get two friends of theirs elected to the consulship for the following year. One of them was Caesar's new father-in-law. Cato objected, and at one of his speeches there was a riot and Cato was nearly killed. After that there was no trouble.

On December the tenth, Clodius took office as tribune, and immediately announced a very radical program—free food for the poor and so on. When on the last day of the year, the outgoing consuls laid down their bundles of sticks, he would not allow Bibulus to make a speech, though Caesar made a long and very eloquent one.

The next day two praetors—one of which was Catullus' patron Memmius—stood up in the Senate and began a denunciation of Caesar's consulship, saying that his legislation had been passed illegally and by force. They talked for three days. Caesar must have felt that an axe was being put to the root of the power he had spent so much care in cultivating. It's hard to say; his animation and charm effectively disguised his thoughts, and besides he never wasted a moment on anything that had already happened. He took steps, as he always did, to deflect any possible blow to his future. He took up his command outside the city walls, thus making himself immune to prosecution, but he kept close enough to be informed of what went on in the city.

I know about that because a few times I reported to him, riding out to his camp where he received me very cordially in his usual relaxed and informal style. Though he listened with attention to everything I told him, he never confided his own plans or ideas. I used to look at that wide-cheek-boned face with its long, thin smile and frost-green eyes, and wonder . . .

He fought back: his outward calm was not cowardice or resignation. He published three speeches against the praetors, and when one of them tried to challenge his immunity I was one of the people he asked to argue on his side. When I won the point for him, he thanked me, so that my head was pleasantly inflated with his praise.

If Pompey is dead, it means . . . No, I must not think of that. I must write. It is my duty now. I must record . . . The truth . . . Oh, gods, that light . . .

Others helped Caesar, especially Clodius, who was a tribune now. Clodius offered Cato a job he couldn't refuse—to go out to Cyprus as an envoy of the Senate, and supervise the transfer of the island's assets to the Treasury. It was public service of the most finicking and difficult kind, requiring unimpeachable integrity. Everyone in the city knew that no one but Cato could do it.

Cato knew it, too. He accepted. There was no one in the city who could get rid of an enemy with greater economy and elegance. It was not Clodius who thought of that. It was Caesar.

The other danger was Cicero. I know that Caesar had not forgotten his speech at the trial of Antonius, and was aware of how dangerous Cicero's tongue could be. He said so—indirectly, to be sure. He praised Cicero's eloquence and his amazing power to move a crowd. That was all he said, but it was enough. When Clodius stood up in the Forum and announced that he would pass a law condemning to exile anyone who had ever put a Roman citizen to death without a trial, it was plain that it was only a matter of time before Cicero had to go.

Of course, Clodius hated Cicero quite enough on his own, but I do not believe he dreamed this one up by himself. No, of course not. Why, Caesar waited outside the city for nearly three months until Clodius could force Cicero into exile. He must have wanted to see it very badly, for he nearly missed his great opportunity in Gaul. A day or two later and the vast migration of the Helvetian tribes down out of their Alpine pastures would have gone too far. Our own province across the Alps would have been overrun and Caesar would have lost everything he had so patiently worked for all those years in Rome.

Yet he waited until the last possible moment—or even beyond that—to the hour when Cicero himself left Rome. Then he was gone himself. His army, already obeying him as if it were his own swift and disciplined body, had pulled up and disappeared almost before we realized it, and all that was left on the plain were a few holes from the tent pegs and the long sigh of dust settling to the vacant ground.

It's no use. That light.

"But, praetor," my freedman Philo objects when I order him down to the harbor to have it put it out. "It wouldn't be safe without a light . . ."

"Put it out," I roar, banging my fists down on the table. The paper jumps, the pale square fluttering like a moth in the darkness; Philo's flesh leaps on his bones, too. Good. "See to it." There is pressure in my head, my face is on fire. Gods, that ship . . .

I ought to put a guard on it, just in case. "Philo," I shout, and my voice echoes like brass in my ears.

Too late; he's gone. I'll have to do it myself. I can't have some passing fisherman wondering what's going on. In fact, for all I know, the light might be visible from the road. Besides, it keeps reminding me: Pompey is dead, and my hopes with him. I have nowhere to go. I am trapped here, waiting. It is so unjust. I had a right to better, I had hopes . . .

The room suddenly feels too full of stale air. My report will have to wait. I slam out the door, flinging a word to the sentry as I pass, and hurl myself down the steps two at a time. Out into the night, where there ought to be a breath . . .

But it is close and hot here too. The wall of the town rears up, cutting off the breeze; in the gardens only the highest branches move gently against the night sky. The stars are confined to a channel overhead, racing like spume between the ramparts and the roofs.

I pace through the hollow streets, trying to escape the town's stifling embrace. I can smell the sea on the night air. No good. Gods, Pompey is dead, headless on a beach in Egypt . . .

There is an open space after all: the forum. It has a fountain at one end, a temple at the other, and in between, the memories of yesterday's market—trampled rinds of fruit, discarded lettuce leaves, a heap of dung. An uncovered sewer runs clattering among the stones to one side, a colonnade deepens the darkness on the other, where my troops have bivouacked. They are rolled in their cloaks now, asleep.

In the middle of the forum waits a huddle of townspeople, surrounded by my guards. The hostages. The guard snaps to attention, the townspeople whisper and moan like ghosts, holding out their hands to me. One man stands still in this bouquet of misery. His cloak is drawn up around his mouth, his eyes are staring straight ahead, ignoring me. A Stoic. "Treat good fortune and ill as if they were the same thing." I used to have a tutor who drummed that into me.

"Good evening, chief magistrate." I have recognized him, in spite of the cloak.

"Praetor." He bows. He seems to have grown in stature since this morning, when he sweated and twisted his hands in my room. It must be the starlight, washing palely over the stones that makes him seem taller. Either that or this new-found calm.

"What are you doing here, magistrate? Didn't you have a hostage to send? No son? No daughter? No nagging wife you'd like to see the last of?" I am laughing, but I doubt he finds this very funny. In fact, on the word "Son" he has winced like a man biting down on a decayed tooth. So. No love lost there. I wonder what happened to the boy. Dead, probably. Too bad. And now the old man must wait out his fate as best he can. Well, he's not doing too badly. I snap my fingers for the guard to bring me a chair. "It's pleasant talking to you, magistrate."

"I'm glad of that, praetor." Suspecting irony, I peer at him, ready to be angry, but he seems, oddly enough, perfectly sincere.

"Why is that?"

"Conversation distracts the mind." In the dark he smiles.

I lean back in my chair and stretch out my legs. "Distracts it from what?"

"From death."

Oh, yes. "So it does," I say, grinning at him. "Do you think you are going to die?"

He is not afraid of me now. "It is definitely a possibility," he says, very gently.

"It comes to us all, magistrate. Definitely."

"Yes, of course it does, praetor. I don't know what you plan to do with us—you and the people you are waiting for—but the circumstances—"

"What do you know about the people I am waiting for?" I sit up.

"Nothing, praetor, nothing at all. Of course I don't know . . . But there must be someone on the road that you don't want . . . that you would rather not . . ."

Just so. There is a detachment of cavalry out there; I have not forgotten it. It is riding through the fringes of mind all the time we talk, all the time since the news came. It has a hoofbeat like the beating of my heart, the hammer of blood in my ears. Now that my anger is subsiding I hear it more clearly than ever.

And I can see, very clearly. When Pompey fell on that quay in Egypt more was betrayed than just a general. All the rest of us, our hopes, our lives . . . The little magistrate is right: in this situation, death is definitely a possibility.

"Are you afraid, magistrate?" I ask, pulling back my lips in a smile that has not much amusement in it.

He thinks, his round cheeks working and his forehead puckered. "No. I don't think so."

"Why not? If you think it's likely."

He looks around the little forum. His town. No doubt he was born here—what, fifty years ago? Perhaps he has been to Rome a few times, for the voting if he thought it was important enough. Possibly he served on some general's staff in a war. Other than that I doubt he has left this place at all. This flyblown, dusty hole is all of life to him. The colonnade and the Temple of Mars, the fountain, the dirty stones—they are to him what the huge magnificence of Rome is to me. It's pathetic, this miserable, deprived, confined existence—and now, of course, he will lose it, without ever knowing better.

But I am wrong. There is more in his life than this forum, and the uninteresting little town it serves. He is looking up. Overhead the stars sparkle and foam in their silent rush. Heroes, gods, monsters, beautiful courtesans, warrior queens, all tumbling together over the roofs. Their light falls on his fat, shining face, and he smiles. He is still smiling when he turns to me. "Afraid? I was, you know. But not any more. I don't know why. It just doesn't seem so terrible—death, I mean. I have done what I could. The gods will let me go in peace."

"Done what you could?"

He is suddenly afraid again. He says nothing but stares with his eyes wide.

"Never mind," I say, getting up. The chair scrapes on the stones, a little sound, of disgust. He has betrayed me, too, with his fear. I thought he knew something. . . .

"Good night, praetor." He does not sound frightened now. In fact, there is pity in his voice.

I turn abruptly, surprised at his tone. "What did you mean, you have done what you could?"

"I'm sorry praetor. I can't tell you that." His voice is, oddly, full of genuine regret.

I reach for my sword. "Indeed you can, magistrate," I cry. The bronze blade glitters in the starlight as if it were silver. The point makes a nick at his throat and a drop of blood runs black along the ridge. Sweat pearls his forehead and his upper lip, and his eyes are like mercury, gleaming uneasily in the darkness.

"No," he says softly, and the pity in his voice is stronger.

We stand there a long moment at opposite ends of my weapon. "I've done what I have to do, praetor," he repeats. "It's nothing to do with you."

"I'll be the judge of that." I am grinning ferociously down the blade. "What is it? You sent a messenger, did you? Sneaked someone out before the gate was barred?"

"No, praetor, nothing like that."

The guards stir. "Nothing like that, praetor," they whisper. "No one could have gotten out."

"Well, it's easy enough to find out. What are hostages for, after all? Bring me the next magistrate—what do you call him? The senior man after this one. Have we some fire? That will get us an answer, don't you think?"

The hostages moan and hold out their hands. "Don't praetor . . . Don't . . . He didn't send anyone . . ." The hands reach out of darkness, clutching at me, begging . . .

"Quiet! Get back or I'll cut them off. Do you understand?"

The hands are snatched back and there is silence until a voice whispers, "Praetor, the chief magistrate has hidden his son in his house, and come instead."

"It's true," they all wail at the same time.

"Is it?" I have turned to the magistrate.

He is looking at me, still with that unwinking calm, but he says nothing.

"Praetor." The voice of his accuser comes, soft in the starlight. "The boy is hiding among the slaves. The magistrate disguised him—"

The little man is ridiculous no matter what he does. Now, though his eyes are wide and he does not flinch, two fat, shining tears have pooled up in them and spilled over. They run down his cheeks leaving a path like a snail's on his plump skin. Yet there is something more—as always with him— something to respect, for he says nothing and does not even glance toward his tormentor.

"Well, magistrate?" I am growing impatient. "You've hidden your son among the slaves, have you? And come in his place?"

"You said if you had no one to send you must come yourself. I had no one to send."

"Oh, didn't you? We'll see about that." My voice is roaring like the wind in my ears. "Bring me this boy."

The guards draw up at attention. "Well?" I shout, angry beyond any explanation. "What are you waiting for? Go and get him."

A couple of them run off, but I am not watching them. The little magistrate has taken my attention. He has begun to cry in earnest now. His head bows down and tears rush from his eyes. His nose runs, his shoulders hunch over and shake.

"Afraid now, magistrate?" My anger has not abated. It is scorching me, as if I were lying staked out somewhere in the desert under the sun.

The little magistrate lifts his head. "Afraid? No, praetor, I don't think I am. I am just very . . . sad." He wipes his eyes and nose busily on his toga. "Well, I must try to be braver for my boy—"

"Shut up!" I cry and he looks at me, startled. There is silence while we wait. The sun still beats down on me, the night breeze does not cool me, my cheeks are hot and my blood fiery. Gods, how dare he? To defy me, when I gave explicit orders . . . And pounding in the back of my head, louder than ever, the galloping of the cavalry's hooves, closer and closer . . . Into the forum come the soldiers, dragging between them a youth about sixteen years old.

"Is that your son?" I demand over the thundering in my ears. "I thought you were talking about a child. Someone . . . seven years old or so."

The magistrate is astonished at me. His betrayer among

the hostages whispers, "Praetor, that's the right one. That's his son."

My soldiers have brought him before me. He can hardly stand upright, but he turns his head over his shoulder, trying to see his father. The magistrate, eyes dry now, gives him a little smile. The boy, obviously encouraged, stands straighter now.

"Boy, look at *me*," I shout.

He pulls himself up in some pathetic imitation of a soldier's snap to attention, except that he is trembling all over like a wet dog, and his knobby young shoulders will not stay straight. Behind him his father's eyes have filled again, but he is looking proudly at his son through his tears.

The pounding in my head is worse; I can hear the approaching troops as plainly as if they were in the forum with us. "Boy," I roar over the noise. "Did your father send a messenger out of town?"

He opens his mouth wide with shock and tries to turn his head.

"*Don't* look at your father. Look at me. Did he? He did. I know it, don't bother to lie. Some servant who knows a secret way out of town. Am I right?" My sword is glittering again. The light plays on it; it jumps slightly in my sweaty grip, in time to the thunder of my heartbeat. My neck is stiff with rage. I do not remember when I have been so ready for action, so eager for it . . .

"Praetor," a voice whispers out of the silent huddle of hostages. "Ask the boy where his father buried his money."

The boy, wide-eyed with terror, turns to his father, who opens his arms and folds him into them. The two of them make a group together as still as a marble statue in the starlight, except that a tremor runs down the boy's back, and the magistrate blinks away his tears.

"He buried it in the garden, praetor," the voice insists. "A fortune. He's a rich man—"

"Gods!" I shout, my breath ripping from my body. "I'll have no more of this!" I am rushing forward, blinded as if by blood in my eyes. My heart slams in my body. Before me there are eyes, liquid and shining in the starlight, mouths open like holes. A man is kneeling on the stones. "Praetor," he screams. "I meant no—" But my sword is out. My shoulder thrusts, the sword goes in. A moment's obstruction, a swift grating on the bone, then deep . . . Ahh, gods. A long discharge of fury. I am shaking. My knees are weak.

There are buildings around me again, solid, the stars shine, the night breeze blows. The hostages are screaming, straining away from me against the ring of guards. My sword is so heavy it is ready to drop from my hand. Black and hot, blood drips from it. On the ground at my feet three bodies lie. Three? Gods, I must have been out of my mind.

"Centurion, take them away." I am overcome by a great weariness.

"But, they're not all dead."

"No? This one is." I turn him over with my foot. The whisperer. A substantial man, a member of the town's senate, no doubt, for he is wearing a toga with dark bands. An additional stripe runs down from his chest under his arm. No, that is the rent in the fabric where my sword went in, the flood of bleeding when I drew it out. I can smell it, as hot as molten copper on the cool air. I remember that now. I grin without pleasure over my clenched teeth.

"But these two are not," the centurion says. "You never touched them. You just shoved them aside when you charged the other one."

"Shoved them aside?"

The hostages are sighing now; some are weeping softly. "Yes, praetor," an old man says. "You knocked the chief magistrate down with your elbow. The boy I didn't see, but—"

"Yes, yes," they whisper. "He fainted. They fell together, praetor."

"Do you want me to take them away?" the centurion asks.

No. Let them be, there on the stones. They will be all right, together.

I have a flask of wine on the table, and someone's pretty Greek pottery cups, but I don't want much. One cupful, mixed with water, refreshes me. Odd when I think what I used to drink.

Odd, too, that the scene outside seems to have dropped from my memory. My throat aches where my voice tore at it in my rage, and I am tired, though the ponderous weariness that oppressed me when I saw the bodies on the ground has passed. I have killed a man who was begging for mercy: not a very Roman thing to do, though I had reasons for my act. I was defending . . . What? I don't know for sure. A good man and his son, certainly. A part of myself? That too. The past? Surely, the past . . .

The worst is averted. By some great good fortune I did not kill the little magistrate, though by Hercules I almost did. "You knocked him down with your elbow, praetor." Indeed. I suppose it was not apparent, but it was the magistrate I lunged for. His eyes, shining like quicksilver in the starlight. The boy in his embrace. At the last moment I turned aside; my sword found another home. I don't know why, nor am I sure why I feel that a god deserves a sacrifice for that. Well, he will get one; he has only to be patient for a very little while.

It does not trouble me now, the troops somewhere on the road, the poor mutilated body lying on a beach in Egypt. What difference does it make? An hour, a day, a year: it all comes to this in the end. And meanwhile there is the beauty of the night, the richness of the air cooling as the night deepens, heavy with the scents of summer and underlaid by the first hint of an autumnal frost. The chair, solid, is holding me, the kitchen table, its scrapes and scars touched as if by a jeweler's art to beauty under the lamplight, the cream-colored square of paper . . .

Far away, out on the road, a puff of air brings the perfume of earth and leaves; on the picket line behind the forum a horse shifts sleepily and lets out a soft neigh of recognition. Someone has gone to see if everything is all right. And though it surprises me to say it, everything is.

XVII

Midnight. A late moon, a quarter slice, is rising over a set
of distant hills, spilling out its light. Under it the landscape
is acquiring depth. A row of cypresses, tall and narrow, de-
taches itself from the mountains and stands free. The road
runs, no longer just a pale strip but rutted and pocked, out
from beneath the abrupt blackness of the wall. The town has
become a collection of volumes half-perceived, dark cubes
like dice tossed down around the curling rim of the sea.

In the harbor the ship has appeared again, this time riding
against the swiftly flowing spangle of the waves. It mocks me
like a memory; it cannot be ignored. Pompey. In a way he
was greater than the man who surpassed him: nobler, more
dignified, with an authority that nearly amounted to the maj-
esty of a king. Oh, he was a stupid man and brought upon
himself all the frustration and confusion of his last few years,
the sordid disgrace of his end, but that goes without saying,
it does not affect the magnificence of his personality. An ox
is less intelligent than a dog, but it is nobler all the same.
And Caesar, for all his brilliance and wit, will never understand that simple fact. He will die alone, when his time comes,
and I do not think he will find two old friends to risk a
tyrant's wrath and sit beside his bones.

Yet all the same, Caesar . . . Ah, gods, when I think of what
he was! Surely there has never been a man to equal him.
When he left that day in March for Gaul we could not have
guessed that it would be nearly nine years before we saw him
again. Yet in that time, not one day passed when someone
did not speak his name. Why? He was not an important man,
not really. He wasn't a Pompey or a Crassus, or even a Cato,
who had an illustrious name. Yet when he left, the city
changed. It was as if something had gone out of our lives
with him, the city we had known had been swept up in the

185

snap and billow of his cloak, like the dust of the road as he marched away.

The city changed, and not for the better. It was empty now. Cicero had gone, into an exile from which he sent back letters of such despair and grief it cracked your heart to read them. Cato had abandoned his familiar places in the Curia and the Forum for the island of Cyprus. My friends had disappeared. Curio was on an extended tour with his father, Publius Crassus was serving with Caesar in Gaul, Antony commanding a wing of cavalry in Palestine. Brutus had become his uncle Cato's assistant and sailed with him. Even the tribune Vatinius—not a friend, but at least a familiar face—had taken his swollen neck and popping eyes and slithered off to Gaul in a cloud of violet perfume.

At a party I met Catullus, but he was with Helvius Cinna, one of his political friends, and they talked of nothing but going to Bithynia with their patron, Gaius Memmius, as soon as he took up the governorship there. They were in good spirits, and sure they were going to get rich.

It was not only that people were missing. All over the city friendships that had held together for years fell apart, women dismissed their lovers and took new ones, political alliances dissolved. A young matron, wife of a tribune said, "It's as if a god has left us," and indeed it was. Rome was like a chariot pulled by a team: now that the driver had stepped down the harness was tangled, the horses pulled in all directions, the body caromed wildly from side to side. Had Caesar really done so much? No one would have said so, not even I, but without him it was plain that we were heading for a smash.

Everything was changing. One day my father called me into his study.

"Sit down." He spoke with his usual brusque distaste. I sat, and I might add, I waited. It was one of my father's rude gestures to demonstrate his power over me; in the course of the years I had developed a technique to deal with it. I kept a respectful look on my face, but behind it I went on thinking of the work I had been doing when he summoned me. So it was that he had been speaking for a while before I really

186

noticed, and a bit longer before the meaning of what he was saying sank in.

". . . The property near Leptis Magna will need new irrigation channels within a year, but you will know what to do about that. The warehouses in Ostia you can continue with as we have been, but you'd better think about leasing at least ten thousand square feet more. Valerius Maximus has some space that might be suitable, but you will have to see that he doesn't cheat you over the price. As for—"

"Are you telling me that you want me to take care of these things? By myself?"

"Of course. Haven't you been listening? How else are you going to run the businesses without me?"

In fact I had been handling most of the work of the grain farms and brokerages for more than a year, but my father had never commented on this fact; indeed, he had not seemed to notice. He still treated me as if I were a child or an exceptionally backward clerk that he hadn't gotten around to selling yet.

His eye glowed like a coal, and I clenched my teeth for an outbreak of his rage, but his passion cooled, his eye went dull and dim, and he spoke feebly. "I've done as much as I can. I have to leave it in your hands now. My health . . ." It was true that he had been growing weaker, and his movements were slowed by pain in his joints, but he had never said anything, and I had not cared to open the subject. He didn't care much for it himself, for he fell silent and glared at me like a tethered eagle.

"All right, father. I'll take care of everything."

"You do it properly, or I'll know the reason why."

"Of course," I agreed, but I resolved that he would know nothing about it at all.

I had thought when I got my hands on all our property that I would see that my father had been keeping back huge sums. It would have been like him to do that, and call it "financial prudence," or some such thing. To my surprise this proved not to be the case. The farms and warehouses, the brokerage commissions and so on were all healthy enough, but there was no great surplus of money anywhere.

My father took out some for his own expenses and for his household—more than I expected, though I could not really call him extravagant—and of course, that had to continue. I resolved, in fact, never to let it diminish, no matter what problems I might have. I did not want my father to say I had not done as well by him as he had himself.

Beyond that there was my rather meager allowance, and a few other expenses—pensions to old freedmen and their families, that sort of thing. They took up most of the rest. Certainly there was not enough left to cover what I already owed, let alone to enable me to increase what I spent. I stared at this depressing fact for several days before I could bring myself to accept it. It meant I was going to have to go on borrowing, and when those debts came due, borrow again to pay them off. I was no closer to financial independence than I had ever been, and I had far heavier responsibilities. And of course, I constantly worried about money.

In those years I lived the life of a successful young lawyer with a future in politics. I did favors for everybody, though mostly still for Crassus, who paid well in cash and assistance, and was always willing to lend. Now the favors were a little larger than when I had been a boy: I prosecuted my patrons' enemies in the courts and defended their friends—and since I have a quick tongue and was so well taught, I usually won. In addition, I carried confidential messages, and sat in on meetings where plans were discussed.

I carried a sword, too, when that was needed, and in those years it increasingly was. The violence that had begun when Caesar was consul grew once he had left. Clodius the tribune roamed the city with his gangs: no one was safe. In the streets there were encounters all the time—many mornings the city awoke to find bodies choking the gutters, or floating, broken, on the current downstream in the river. It was usually conservatives who were attacked, though sometimes all that was necessary was to be prosperous and well-dressed, for Clodius drew his support from the most bitter and disaffected of the lower classes, and he led them with a drunken lack of discrimination against anyone he disliked.

It got to the point that men went about with bodyguards

even in the Forum, and more than once there were riots, in which dozens of men were left for dead. Clodius swelled and swaggered and grew proud. No one was safe from him, and there was nothing he denied himself.

At that time I was fairly close to him, for one of the consequences of my success was that important women made much of me. And one of the most important was Clodius' sister Clodia. I had been her lover since shortly after I won my first case. I did not delude myself that I was the only one. She liked a lot of young men around, to dance with at her parties, and to entertain the influential senators she invited. A lot of political business was transacted at those dinners, and most of it to the advantage of her family.

I used to go and wait for her in the rose and gold bedroom where the nymphs and Cupids floated on the wall, and the swan-shaped stands held up the lamps. Rose-scented oil burned in them at night.

Sometimes I went in the afternoon, if she had sent a message. Often I had to wait then, too. But she was a great lady, and as beautiful as she was powerful, so I did not mind it— at least not as much as waiting in Crassus' drafty atrium, or the cloakroom of the Curia. It was as much a part of my career as those duties were.

Then one afternoon I did not find her, though I waited. At last, growing angry, I got up to go. As I stalked in fury past a row of cubicles, a maid came out of one. Through the open door I saw the room—a servant's room, poor and sordid. On the bed a woman was sprawled, naked, her legs parted and her head thrown back in sleep. It was Clodia. I saw her hair, strewn across the pillow, her slack mouth open as she breathed. Beside her lay her brother, snoring drunkenly, his hand between her thighs. Even in his sleep he was fingering the little folds of crimson flesh.

"Oh, gods," I muttered, cold with fear. There is nothing more strongly forbidden to mortal man than this. I stared as on that rumpled bed, Clodia murmured in her sleep and turned to embrace her brother.

At that I pulled myself together and hurried away. My heart was hammering, my flesh was cold and sweating. I thought, even to have seen that means trouble. The gods will punish me. Well, perhaps they have.

After that, I sought my pleasures elsewhere, and my political interests. But I wondered. Sometimes in my mind's eye I saw Caesar, the day Clodia's husband died. He stood in the corner of the room with Clodius, watching the progress of the old man's illness. Once he had reached out and let his hand fall on Clodius' shoulder. Was it a signal? I do not know. But I remembered how desperate Caesar had been in those days, though few suspected it. A province was necessary to him, a rich one. Well, Metellus had died and left Gaul vacant. A fortunate coincidence, wouldn't you say?

Could Caesar have seen something like what I did and taken advantage of it? Was anyone that cool? For myself the horror of that scene stayed with me for days. My flesh crept on my bones when I thought of it. I covered my head and prayed at the family shrine for an hour at a time. I did not go to a priest for cleansing, for even if I had known which one to go to, I could no more have spoken of what I saw than I could have flown. Yet I imagine I am a reasonably cool man. I had seen a lot by then, and I knew the ways of the world. Could Caesar have used such knowledge?

Well, perhaps. There is no proof even that Metellus did not die a natural death, though Cicero was sure that he hadn't. And to go further . . .

Yet I did not think that I was the only one who knew about the incest. Catullus knew. His bitterness and pain, his recklessness, all might have told me. But as it happens, there is another kind of evidence. He wrote a poem. It did not circulate, but I saw it after his death among his papers . . .

DOCUMENT APPENDED

**Lesbius is beautiful. Why not? when Lesbia
prefers him
to you and all your kin, Catullus.
What do you care? This beauty could buy and sell you in
the Forum**

if he could find three guarantors to take a friendly
greeting
from his lips.

He always called her Lesbia in his poems, after the poet
Sappho of Lesbos. And of course, "Pulcher" was their family
name—it means "Beautiful." It was clear who was meant, and
what Catullus was accusing him of.

So I left Clodia. She did not understand, and I was certainly not going to tell her why. She was angry. In a short
time, I was her enemy, hers and her brother's. I tried to stay
clear of them, but it was impossible. In those days Clodius
and his army of malcontents came close to ruling the city by
terror. The exile of Cicero had been only a preliminary, to
clear the ground for their rampage. They burned and looted,
they assaulted and murdered. No one was safe. They tore
Rome apart. It went on for months.

At last, in his arrogance, Clodius attacked Pompey. A slave
was arrested with a knife, which under torture he admitted
was intended for the Great Man. It came from Clodius. Pompey hid out in his country house again. I laughed, thinking
how he must regret participating in that ceremony in the
Temple of Castor when Clodius was adopted into a plebeian
family. He complained loudly, and he arranged to be away
from the city for a while.

More effective than that, he called a meeting of the powers
that had allowed Clodius to act so freely. They convened in
Luca, the last town in Gaul as you come down out of the
mountains. There Crassus and Caesar met him, each with
their retinues. It was a display of power the like of which
that little town has never seen before or since. Two hundred
senators and dignitaries crammed into it; there were so many
lictors waiting for their magistrates that the streets were impassable. Catullus, on his way home from Bithynia, saw them
there and wrote to me about it.

There, in that hotbed of pomp and power watered by the
money Caesar was bringing home from Gaul, the three men
renewed the compact I had heard them make under the
grape arbor the night of the Saturnalia. Pompey got a command in Spain and a fancy commission to be in charge of

191

the grain supply in the city; Crassus got Parthia in the Middle East and the possibility of a nice little war; Caesar got the renewal of his command in Gaul for five more years. It was as cut and dried as that. And, at Pompey's urging, they agreed to cut Clodius loose.

The results were visible immediately. When the Senate, trying to pull itself together in the face of nearly total anarchy, found a tribune, named Titus Annius Milo, who was willing to lead armed men against Clodius, they were not prevented from helping him with money or the use of their slaves, or whatever he needed. When I joined him, none of my patrons minded. In fact, Crassus encouraged me. It was plain that his two colleagues agreed.

So I found myself seeing action as if I were a soldier in Gaul after all, except that the men I met at the end of my sword were Romans as often as not—idlers, criminals, drunkards—the dregs of a city nearly choked with such sediment. There were engagements—hand-to-hand fighting among the tenement blocks, or in the squares. Once there was a battle in the Forum itself. I went down to find that Cicero's brother had been attacked by Clodius' men and left for dead. I managed to fight off the few who were left. After that encounter the slaves wiped the blood from the paving stones with sponges, and the main sewer overflowed, it was so choked with bodies.

That was enough for the Senate. Not long after they called Cicero back from exile, hoping he could restore order.

Clodius fought back. His sister prosecuted me for attempting to murder her—a silly business. Why would I have tried to buy poison from one of her friends if I intended to use it to kill her? And if I had tried, why would I have failed? Cicero defended me with his usual style, not the least intimidated. He had guessed about Clodia's incest, too, and mentioned it in court.

Gods, her face when he did! She went so pale I thought she was going to faint. That night she left the city, a ruined woman. I am sure the evidence was everywhere. Her servants would have talked under torture, for instance; they usually do. She could not have survived a prosecution. The death is an ugly one, I believe. They sew you in a sack and throw you into the sea. Let the water wash away the pollution of your life, for neither earth nor heaven will have you.

Clodia's effort to harm me was the last gasp of the power of the Clodians, though her brother did not quite realize it yet. But Milo was growing more effective. One night out on the Appian Way, they met. There was a brawl, and Clodius was killed. I was a tribune that year and could not legally leave the city, so I went in secret, but I was there, and I can swear that it was Clodius' men who started the fight.

But when it was all over and Clodius' body was brought back to the city his friends thought it was murder. There were a lot of them, especially among the plebeians. They rallied in the Forum, and in their rage and grief carried the body to the Curia where they made a pyre of the benches and the railings.

When the next morning dawned the Curia had been burned, and several nearby buildings were damaged. Elsewhere in the city the houses of prominent conservatives were sending smoke into the air, and a rain of ash and sour, greasy smuts fell everywhere. There were dead men in the alleys and the squares; the rioting continued for days.

They had to bring in Pompey and his troops to quiet things down. He set his chair on the steps of the Temple of Saturn; I saw him sitting there day after day as calm as a statue and as magnificent as a god. He wore his uniform, his scarlet cape and his beautiful gold-worked breastplate. I thought, if Caesar thinks he can rival this, he has his work cut out for him.

Powerful as the Senate had been they were not strong enough to get Milo off, and he was prosecuted for the murder of Clodius. Cicero did his best to defend him, but when Pompey brought in his troops there was a riot in the Forum, and even that great voice could not rise above the tumult. He did not complete his speech, and Milo had to run for the city gate.

Cicero, courageous as always, published the speech he would have given had he been allowed. It didn't do much to improve Milo's temper. From his exile in Gaul he wrote back,

"It's a good thing you never delivered this speech. If you had I wouldn't have the opportunity to taste the famous mullets of Massilia." It was the closest that flinty Milo ever came to wit.

"And at that it's not much closer than Massilia is to Rome." Cicero smiled, but as soon as I turned away his shoulders slumped with weariness and he rubbed the bridge of his nose.

In those days, as I say, I was getting well-known in the city. I had a reputation as a young man capable in any situation. I was a good speaker—even a very good one—and could generally tell which way the political wind was blowing, too, without having to ask an auger. Nor was I too squeamish to be useful. More than once Pompey or Crassus asked me to take on a confidential errand. I must have done well enough, because they next asked me together.

It was a serious matter. They had taken a bribe from Ptolemy, the Pharaoh, though of course nobody mentioned that. Caesar was reportedly the one who had arranged it, though all three of them were busily trying to get a commission from the Senate to go to Egypt and restore him to his throne. All three of them were angling for it, though Caesar, of course, less actively, since he was still in Gaul. It would have made quite an opportunity for one or the other of them, no question about it: Egypt is the richest place in the world.

The trouble was Ptolemy had managed to make himself hated by his people. When they found out that he was sending envoys to Rome they got up a delegation themselves under a very distinguished philosopher named Dio, from Alexandria, the capital. Crassus, when he told me about it, looked worse than usual. His long face was tragic, his eyes haunted by despair. "It's the *embarrassment*," he moaned. as if he were naming a disease.

I tried to look reassuring, my best bedside manner. "The thing is," he went on, eyeing me to see if I understood, "it would be so much better if this delegation didn't actually get to Rome . . ."

There didn't seem to be anything to say to this, so I waited. At last Crassus let out a deep sigh and, reaching into an alabaster box, pulled out a purse. It clinked when he set it before me, too heavily for silver. I looked at it for a while. "Where are they now?" I asked.

"Puteoli, in the south." He did not even smile. I left him staring at his antique desk as if someone had just told him it was a fake.

I can't say I was pleased by this, but equally I cannot see that I had much choice. I rode out of town at the head of a small column of men from my household—reliable freedmen and some of my less reliable slaves—feeling that I had no freedom to choose my actions. All the way to Puteoli I could feel a hand on my back, propelling me.

When the philosopher and his delegation appeared I went out to meet them with my men. They were unarmed. I made no threats, I simply told them their presence was not required in Rome. A few of them protested but my herdsmen made sure that they did not do it again. They are ugly looking brutes; it was enough for them to step forward and show their cudgels and swords. One man resisted, and I had to order them to knock him down. In my rage at my own lack of freedom, I felt as if the wood was falling on my head too.

I detest the use of force. It is inelegant, and inefficient. Many times it provokes just the opposite reaction from that which is intended. There can be no better example than what happened next. A few of the envoys continued to Rome. I did not think they constituted much of a threat—their numbers were much diminished and they didn't look very impressive. I even told Crassus so when he called me into his study, or at least I tried to, but the melancholy man was angry now and would not listen.

"I told you to get rid of these people. You know what I mean. I don't want any mistakes this time. And do it now."

"Excuse me, Marcus Licinius, but are you sure? It's dangerous, you know—"

"I've paid you enough to cover that," he said insolently.

I had to keep my temper, of course—he had paid me enough for that, at least. "I don't mean for me. I know my business. If I do this for you, no one will ever know I was involved. But that's not the case for you. Everyone's already talking about the bribe. If you do this too, you will—"

"Oh, I see. You want more money." He gave me a bitter look as he took another bag out of the box. "Here. Do it now."

So of course, I did. Not so much for the gold, though I don't expect to be believed, but because I couldn't risk the permanent anger of Crassus and Pompey. I hired some men in the lowest part of the city, and for a sum that seemed remarkably small to me they agreed to take care of the matter. A few days later the bodies of the delegation were found floating in the Tiber.

The outcry was terrible. To the already ripe and savory scandal of the bribe was added the far more juicy tidbit of murder. The prestige of Pompey and Crassus never recovered. To the end of their lives they were diminished men. The Senate refused to send either of them to Egypt, in spite of the pressure they brought to bear, and the whole effort was a waste—or worse. In politics force is a dangerous tool. You wouldn't think so, for nothing seems simpler or more clear cut, but it has to be used very delicately. Even for a man like Caesar, whose judgment is superb, it is a difficult weapon to wield. If you pick up a sword, other men may do the same, and you may not be able to control the situation any more.

I came out of it all right. Clodia tried to make something of it, but she was the only one. She included it among the accusations she brought against me in court. Crassus, a better speaker than his melancholy manner suggested, got it dismissed as a tale invited by a scorned woman's spite. Well, there wasn't much evidence; I know how to do these things, though I don't like them much.

Crassus took up the command in Parthia that Caesar had arranged for him, and he and his sons went out there in the hopes of finding a war to equal Caesar's great one in Gaul. Perhaps if he had, he would have made people forget the scandal, but Crassus was not the general Caesar was. He suffered a terrible defeat. Poor man, he lived just long enough to see his son's head held up to him on a pole from the enemy lines.

This death bothered me more than I can explain. Publius Crassus was not the first among my friends to die, but his death was the worst so far. The image haunted me. I saw it as Crassus himself must have, the staring eyes, the blood, the open mouth. And the old man, already burdened by a sorrow no one understood, was faced in the last moments of his life with one that everyone could.

I of all people ought to have been glad, for Crassus' death freed me. He was the only person who knew of my involvement with the Alexandrians; I no longer had to worry that some day politics might make him betray me. And his death left me free. I had no patron now, I could do what I liked. I ought to have celebrated like a manumitted slave, but instead I was haunted and upset, and my bad dreams returned. Sometimes in them I was a general in a town under siege; they were holding up my father's head. That was bad enough. But sometimes the head on the pole turned out to be my own. From that I awoke in such a sweat of horror that nothing could calm me.

I don't know why I was so sensitive, for as I said, Publius Crassus was not the first of my friends to die. That was Catullus. A sad business. He had been living with Clodia in a small villa outside of town. She was a proud woman, and I think her humiliation at Cicero's hands was more than she could endure. Nor could she bear the loss of her position and the wreck of her ambitions. In those circumstances it was natural for her to retire to the country and live in quiet luxury among her gardens and her fishponds.

Perhaps, too, the exposure of her love for her brother in the light of ordinary day shocked her. Their relationship must have looked very different by the time Cicero got through with his speech. He mocked her cruelly, you know. Well, I don't have to tell you, the speech is very famous. "Your brother, who is in these *affairs* the most sophisticated man in the world, who loves you most of all, who—I don't know, but I believe—when he was a little boy and afraid of the dark, used to creep into his bigger sister's bed . . ." And so on, until all of Rome was laughing at her. No wonder she disappeared.

One day, coming back into the city after a visit to some farms of ours nearby, I saw her, standing in the market square of a little town on the outskirts of Rome. She had a basket over her arm, and only the old serving woman to accompany her. Her black hair was blowing in the wind, snowflakes were tangled in it, her cheeks were bright with cold.

"Hello, Clodia," I said, reining my horse in beside her. "Doing your own marketing now?"

She turned to me a face so closed and stiff it might have been made of marble, but she did not speak.

"May I take you home?" I did not like to see a woman of her station in the village market.

She led me, still wordless, to her house. I could not believe it when I saw it. The wind came through the cracks in the walls, the braziers were empty and cold. There was only one chair in the room, and it was rickety. The place was a ruin. I think, in some strange way her mind was too.

"Are you all right, Clodia?" I asked.

She did not say a word. Simply, she let fall her cloak. Then, leading me to the bedroom, she took off the rest of her clothes.

She was ill, so thin her skin was milky and bluish and her ribs showed. But nothing could make her less than beautiful, or less than accomplished in bed. She made love with a kind of intensity that made me very uneasy. She pursued love-making, she drowned herself in it, she swallowed sex as if it were medicine, and she wanted more. At last, chilled and rather dismayed by her avidity, I excused myself and left. I made the servant take some money for her mistress but it did not make me feel much better. Even the knowledge that she had wanted me and not I her made little difference. I had taken advantage of someone not in a position to know better—it was almost like violating a child. I felt a little sick myself.

In the end I sent a messenger to Catullus, and told him where she was. He had always loved her; I thought he might want to help her in her distress. When, some time later, Vatinius came to me and asked me where he was, I was able to tell him that Catullus was living with Clodia in the village. I think he hoped that her condition was improving.

The trouble was he was not in much better shape himself. He had come back from Bithynia with a cough that did not disappear even in full summer; in the exceptional cold of the winter that year it grew worse. That miserable house cannot have done much to help. He should have gone south to Rhegium or Sicily and taken a cure, but he did not want to leave her. The weather went on getting worse and worse. They were isolated in the village for days by icy roads and blowing snow. Catullus did not survive. I had to go and fetch his body for his father, and take him home to Verona.

I didn't see Clodia again. I found Catullus by torchlight in the swirling snow. He was slumped at the bottom of a wall—he must have been too ill to get back to his house. There was only time to get him into the wagon before he coughed himself to death. Blood pooled in his mouth and ran down to soak his clothes. Poor Catullus. A dreadful end.

It was a sad time. The only thing that enlivened it was Caesar's success in Gaul and the envy and rage it caused at home. He made sure of that. He was writing a book, and bits of it came back to us with all the fascination of exotic lands and heroic events. "All Gaul is divided into three parts," he wrote, and we felt for a moment as if we were there.

His dispatches were eagerly read, and violently condemned. Once Cato made a speech in the Senate demanding that Caesar be turned over to the Gauls because he had attacked them under a truce. There was a riot over that. You might as well demand that we give Jupiter back to the Etruscans. Whatever is necessary is fair in war, I thought—never mind that Cato called Caesar's behavior "unRoman." I had to laugh.

A poem of Catullus' went around the city after that business. Even after he was dead these little verses circulated, doing their damage to Caesar's reputation and causing a lot of talk.

DOCUMENT APPENDED

**Nothing about you interests me, Caesar,
and I have no wish to please.
I wouldn't even send to know
on which side of you your face is.**

Oh, I missed him when he was gone.

I missed the others too: Publius Crassus who was never coming home, Antony, now Caesar's second-in-command in Gaul, Milo exiled to Massilia, all the rest. I had my work and my pleasures, but they weren't enough. I wanted something else, I didn't know what.

I had grown; I was no longer a boy just starting out, I was now a well-known advocate, a figure in the city. Crassus, my patron, was dead and I was free to take any cases I wanted. I chose well. I was good, and everybody knew it. I demolished Quintus Rufus, the patrician who had been so condescending to me at my first trial, so badly I ended up having to support the poor idiot with a pension for the rest of his life. Well, his mother begged me to, and I couldn't bring myself to refuse. It didn't do me any harm when the story got around, either.

I had held office, as tribune, and people knew me. In the street I was recognized and when I walked through the Forum my train of supporters was as long as any of the younger men's—even the great aristocrats, with their hereditary clients. I was ready, for what I didn't know, but I could feel it. My time had come.

BOOK FOUR

XVIII

A breath of air from the windows has touched my skin, chilling it, making me push back the paper and stand, stretching as if I had been asleep. On a hook Philo has hung my cloak. Wrapping it around my shoulders, I go to look out.

The road is still empty, but in the moonlight a few leaves are sifting across it. It is autumn, the year is ending. Onc night soon a frost will come, blackening the last grapes on the vines, furring the ruts with silver, painting the rusty oak leaves gold. A beautiful sight, but I will not be here to see it. I will have gone, taken the ship the gods has so generously provided . . .

LAST REPORT OF MARCUS CAELIUS RUFUS
PRAETOR PEREGRINUS OF ROME . . .

One morning I went down to the Forum with my escort. It was the spring of the year I was running for aedile and I was early. It was a damp morning, though not cold. As the sun peeled back the edge of darkness and poked through the buildings, I saw that someone had brought a gang of workmen down in front of the Temple of Vesta. They were laying out pegs and flags and unloading carts of lumber. A crowd was already collecting to watch. I strolled closer. Anything new in the Forum is interesting, and besides, these idlers are voters.

The crews were working pretty hard; I saw that the reason was the overseer, a tall man in the corner, waving his arms vigorously.

"Look, Marcus Caelius," my freedman Philo said. "He's wearing a black toga. Are they getting ready for a funeral, then?"

I shrugged. I hadn't heard of the death of anyone important enough to merit a funeral in the Forum. "Go and find out, " I said.

Philo took a few steps, then stopped. "What's the matter with you?" I shouted. At the same time the overseer turned and caught sight of me.

I couldn't believe my eyes. "Curio! When did you get back. What's been happening to you? You look wonderful. By Hercules, how are you?"

He was grinning at me shyly around his huge front teeth. He didn't look much changed by his absence; his hair still curled all over his head, his eyes were still gentle and contemplative, and guarded by his long eyelashes. He looked as girlish, not to say maidenly, as ever.

"What does all this mean? Is someone dead?"

"M-my father. I came back specially because they wrote to m-me that he had . . ." Then he was unable to speak at all, and I put my arms around him again. After a while he felt better, and he wiped his eyes with the hem of his black wool toga. It was so finely made it would have looked well on a woman. I had forgotten how rich he was.

"I'm getting m-married, Caelius," he announced with a shy smile.

"You are?"

"You're surprised?"

"What? Oh, of course not? Who's the lucky girl?" Some delicate and well-bred child no doubt, raised in the country and kept as innocent as milk. They'd be a pair, the two of them—you'd hardly be able to tell them apart.

"I'm m-marrying Fulvia," he said, obviously expecting me to know the name. After a moment, I did.

"But she's *Clodius'* wife."

"No, Caelius, his widow. She's been alone a long time now."

"But she's older than you . . ." I stopped, horrified at the thought that I might be offending him, but he only smiled and said serenely, "She's a wonderful woman, Caelius. She knows everything about politics. She'll be a great help to m-me."

He was right. After Clodia left Rome there was no woman in the city who knew more. "And she has so much money, too," I said.

He laughed. "Well, actually, yes. This all costs quite a bit, you know." He waved his hand at the construction. "Actually, I've had to borrow. But father is worth it."

"Is he, indeed."

"Oh, m-my dear," he murmured, as if I were the one who had suffered the loss. I said a few formal things about regret and so on. In fact, I had liked Curio's father quite a bit, in spite of his conservative politics. And Curio's obvious attachment to him must have meant something. I wondered about it sometimes.

"That young Curio is spending money like water on his father's funeral," my own father said. He had come back from a meeting at a friend's house, and it had tired him out. Impatiently he gestured me to give him my arm. "Foolish waste."

"Curio has his reasons."

He stopped and looked at me. Once he would have looked down, once level, now he had to look upward, but the glance had always been the same, bitter, angry, commanding. I know he would rather have had another kind of son, a more obedient one perhaps, or more loving . . . Well, I would have preferred a different father. It hadn't been much good for either of us . . .

"What reason could that boy have for throwing his money away?" he was muttering now. "Wants to be aedile, is that it? Thinks a big display will help him?"

"Well, it won't hurt," I snapped. "Possibly if I had more to spend on my own candidacy I'd have a better chance of winning myself. Besides, Curio was very fond of his father."

"Old Curio wouldn't have liked it," he said with a sourness worthy of Cato himself. "Curio was a very sound man."

"Some fathers would be glad to help their sons, even with their deaths. Licicnius Calvus' father committed suicide so as not to taint his son's career when he was accused of a crime."

He said nothing, but his eye flashed at me like a bolt of lightning. "When I go, I don't want you throwing your money away like this."

I couldn't help it; I burst out laughing. "I won't. Don't you

205

worry about that." But when I recovered myself I was talking to an empty room.

The funeral games Curio held for his father were famous, and talked about for a long time. In the Forum he built two stages that could be converted into one by some complicated mechanism. On this he produced plays, recitations, mimes. He hired a famous Greek tragedian to impersonate his father during the ceremonies. The actor, Xanthius, had made himself so like the elder Curio that people gasped when they saw him. Curio sat beside him throughout the whole performance, dignified and solemn, and was only once overcome by emotion. People commented on it—how brave he was, how Roman, how pious, to commemorate his father so richly. So the whole thing was worth what he spent.

A month later he married Fulvia. I went to his wedding. We ate and got drunk and danced, so that it seemed as if the old days had come back. It was a moment of great happiness. I thought how Catullus would have enjoyed it, and suddenly, in the midst of all that celebration I was struck by a feeling of sorrow and isolation I cannot explain.

I still cannot explain it. But sometimes since then it has come over me—as now, for example—as chill and damp as a fog. My hands and feet grow cold, my bones ache like an old man's, a wind sighs in my ears. What does it mean? I have never known, but with it comes anxiety, unease, restlessness. I scrape back my chair, and, snatching up my cloak, head for the stairs.

Outside, the night is as peaceful as ever. Nothing has moved. The ship still lies on a sea as flat as a silver tray. Only its reflection, riding upside down on its shadow, seems to tremble, as if it felt the impulse of a ghostly wind. Soon, I say to it in my mind. I'm almost finished here. Then we will go.

In the town the streets are as bright as ever under a quiet sky; the moon is hidden behind the roofs, but it seems to me that if I broke off a corner of a building I would find the stucco underneath soaked through with starlight.

The magistrate is still standing with his arms around his

son, the only figures upright among the sleeping hostages. He says good evening to me, and the boy's eyes slide toward me, though he does not lift his head from his father's shoulder, nor does he speak.

"Magistrate, I want to talk to you."

"I can tell you nothing." The boy gazes at him with admiration.

"Pompey is dead." It is a risk, but a small one. What can he do? My troops still control the town, and even if he were to try to make a break, lead a rebellion, whatever, it will be too late. I haven't much hope of keeping the news from him long enough to make a difference, once I leave this town.

"How did he die, praetor?" the little magistrate asks. If he had anything riding on the answer, he does not show it. I explain about the murder on the quay in Egypt, the decapitated body left with its two guardians on the beach. Like everyone else's who hears this story, the magistrate's eyes fill up with tears, but he does not turn his head away.

"That must make it very difficult for you, praetor."

So he has guessed, or figured out, what I am doing here. Does he suspect the cavalry on the road? Perhaps. He is certainly not as stupid as he looks.

"Where is Caesar now?" he asks. A very pertinent question.

"In Egypt."

"You could go to him, you know." He is urging me, gently, and his arms pull closer around his son. I do not know why, but I feel as if he is embracing me, too. "Caesar is a generous man, praetor. We are not really his clients here in Thurii; he does not owe us anything. But you see the baths over there? A beautiful building, isn't it?"

Well it wouldn't knock your eye out in Rome, but it's impressive enough for a little place like this.

"Caesar built it for us, out of money he sent from Gaul. He didn't have to do that. But he said in his letter that we ought to have something, for there were men from our town in his legions, and they deserved well of him. Well, praetor, men from Thurii have served all over the world, but no one has ever built us a bath before."

I nodded, not wanting to tell him that there was hardly a municipality in Italy that had not benefited from Caesar's generosity. It had helped too—every one of them was grateful, and when the time came, they had showed it.

Perhaps if I had told him, he wouldn't have cared. "Don't think I don't know why he did it, praetor. He wanted our votes in Rome. Why shouldn't he? Didn't Pompey and all the other politicians want our support, even the ones who were supposed to be our patrons? But Caesar was willing to do something for us, first, before we had done anything for him at all. Indeed, praetor, he never asked us for a thing. We were glad to be his friends."

Poor Thurii. I hope he remembers them now that he does not need their help. Now that he does not need anyone's help any more.

"I doubt Caesar would be very glad to see me just now, magistrate," I confess.

He considers this. It is odd how clearly you can see him thinking. He is wondering what I have done to alienate Caesar. As the question occurs to him, once again his arms tighten around his son. He knows what it is to anger the powerful. But there is no sign of all this in his answer.

"Praetor, I don't think that matters. Caesar will welcome you. If there are differences between you, no matter what they are, he will ignore them, or forgive. In the past he always has. Whole towns have been pardoned, if they asked. He has a merciful and gentle nature."

It's not nature, it's policy, I want to say, but I don't. "Perhaps you're right, magistrate." I want to believe him, that's the thing. Sitting there in that drench of starlight, listening as on the stillness of the night comes the voice of a rooster, awakened, surely before its time—oh, gods, surely before its time—I want to believe the little magistrate more than anything in the world.

The night is still as dark as it was, the stars glitter like frost in the October sky. They have not dimmed in an approaching dawn, have they? I don't think they have. It is not morning, it is still night.

Go to Caesar. He will pardon you. Well, perhaps he would. My freedman Philo, removing my cloak, adds, "You went to him once before." Well, it's true. I did.

Certainly going to Caesar did not occur to me right away. I was doing well enough. I was running for aedile, and I thought I had a good chance. Of course I was deeply in debt—I would say that altogether I owed about two and a half million sesterces, which I couldn't hope to recoup until I became a praetor and had a province to administer. But for that you have to be forty; I was only thirty-one. Well, what could I do? I closed my eyes and went on. It's impossible to make a political career in Rome without spending money, that's all there is to it.

In those days I was close to Cicero, he helped me with my candidacies in his usual tireless way. He was always available to make a speech, to call on a powerful senator, to lend a couple of thousand, and his advice on politics was the soundest in Rome. When he had to go out to the provinces as a governor he asked me to be his political correspondent, and send him all the news—which I faithfully did, feeling honored at the compliment to my perspicacity. I didn't even mind the expense of sending a man out to Cilicia now and then.

DOCUMENT APPENDED

CAELIUS TO CICERO, GREETINGS

Nothing, but *nothing*, has happened unless you want me to write you this—as I'm sure you do: young Corneficius is engaged to marry the daughter of Orestilla. Paulla Valeria has divorced her husband without even giving a reason, the *day* he was supposed to get back from his province. She will marry D. Brutus. She sent back all her clothes and jewelry. A lot more of this unbelievable kind of thing has been happening in your absence. Servius Ocella would have convinced no one that he was capable of adultery if he hadn't been caught in the act, twice in three days. Where, you ask? By Hercules, I leave it to you to find out. It doesn't displease me at all, a general having to ask around about who was caught in whose bed . . .

MARCUS TULLIUS CICERO, PROCONSUL, TO MARCUS CAELIUS,

Benita Kane Jaro

GREETINGS

What? Do you think that is what I commissioned you to send—news of the gladiatorial contests and the postponements of trials, Chrestus' burglary, and such things that if I were in Rome nobody would have the impertinence to waste my time with? How are things with you? What is happening with the elections? Is there any news from Gaul? What does the Senate say about the present situation, and has anyone done anything . . .

Of course he knew it was a joke, and I sent him all the real news that I could find. Not that there was much. Rumors about Caesar in Gaul, rumors even about him, nothing much in the Senate. Really, Chrestus' burglary was the most interesting event of the month.

He was grateful, though. At my request he promised to send me some wild animals to use in the games if I was elected aedile. That was a big help to me. And once he passed on a request from Caesar that I support a bill to allow him to keep his command in Gaul a little longer than planned. He needed the immunity from prosecution it gave him—he was afraid Cato and the others would go after him for what he had done in his first consulship. And he didn't want any debate in the Senate about it either—he knew they had not forgiven him for the humiliation he had inflicted on them.

I was willing enough to support the bill. It was the year I was tribune, and all the other nine tribunes were supporting it too. But Cicero was so scrupulous, so careful of my welfare that he checked with Pompey first before he asked me, to be sure I would not make an enemy of the Great Man. Not that I cared. Pompey's reputation had slipped so far from the days when he first returned from the east you could hardly find ten men in the Senate who admired him any more.

It was all his own fault. His shabby dealings, his dissembling, his clumsy attempts at political manipulation, all gave the impression of a man who was deceitful and disingenuous and thought too highly of himself to play by the rules.

Perhaps he thought all politicians acted that way. If so, no wonder he felt he was too good for electoral life. But he was

210

wrong: the best politicians don't do those things, and instead of looking like a man above politics, he looked like one a long way below it. Even people who had once thought him the greatest man our state had ever produced were disquieted now. Even so, it was probably more prudent not to offend him, so I was glad enough that Cicero got his endorsement for what very quickly became known as "The Law of Ten Tribunes." I was glad to see it pass.

Curio too was running for aedile that year—a disadvantage to me. He was so much richer than I, and I knew he would make a big splash with his games. He had panthers for the wild animal combats, too. I felt I had to do as well, and wrote to Cicero.

DOCUMENT APPENDED

CAELIUS TO CICERO, GREETINGS

. . . Also, about the panthers: you should get some experienced hunters to catch them, and see that they are transported to me . . .

CICERO TO CAELIUS

All the panthers in my province have migrated across the border. They complain that here I make war on them and do not allow them to live in peace. But never mind, I will still try . . .

Curio's election as aedile was assured, but he wasn't very happy about it. "M-my dear, such a useless office. I mean, what can you do? You're such a very junior m-magistrate, aren't you? I know you get a seat in the Senate, but that's not m-much, is it?"

It seemed like quite a lot to me; I was counting on the office to make me really well known to the voters. I had wanted those animals of Cicero's very badly for that. When a tribune-elect was disqualified for bribery, Curio ran for his seat, and got it. He gave me his panthers, too—good friend that he was.

I must have made an impression on someone, for one day in the Forum a man tried to bribe me. It was just a hint: could I use a little extra help? Who wanted to help me? I asked, always ready to listen to a constituent. The man, a Spaniard with banking interests, showed me his white teeth. "A friend," he said.

He didn't say whose friend, his or mine, so I declined without regret, remembering the tribune-elect whom Curio had replaced.

Curio was a good tribune, both sagacious and brave. Nothing frightened him, not even making an enemy of a powerful man, and he sailed into the fight that was brewing up over Caesar's proposed return like a gallant little war-trireme among the huge, five banked galleys.

When the Senate, under the direction of a pair of rabidly anti-Caesarian consuls, voted that after the first of March they would put off all other business and discuss only Caesar's removal from his command, Curio's name was prominent on the list of supporters. When they went further and declared that any attempt to obstruct the discussion—even the perfectly legal veto of the tribunes—would be regarded as an act of hostility to the Republic, and that a decree to that effect would immediately be drafted and set before the Senate and the people, Curio signed that too, though of course, two tribunes vetoed it on the spot.

He was outspoken, making his orations in the Forum to bring himself before the voters as a man opposed to what he called "Caesar's unconstitutional aims." He told the people that he would resist any attempt to award Caesar a triumph— though the gods know that if anyone ever deserved one it was Caesar—or to prolong Caesar's command. "He's been up there for nine years," he cried, all trace of a stammer gone. "If he hasn't conquered and pacified it by now, we need a new general, not honors for the old one." There were roars of approval for this. It was a point he raised several times.

Once he brought Pompey before the Plebeian Assembly

and asked him about the law the Senate had just passed. "What will happen if some tribune does try to veto the discussion on March first?" Pompey drew himself up to his full height and said it came to the same thing if Caesar refused to obey the Senate or if they got someone to veto the expressed wish of that body.

"And what if he thinks he can run for consul, and keep his army at the same time?"

"What if my young son thinks he can hit me over the shoulders with a stick?" Pompey boomed.

Well, that was the end of that alliance. It was plain that Pompey didn't want Caesar in office after the first of March. It was *very* plain; in fact, Caesar could make it out from as far away as Ravenna, where he had installed himself for the winter with a legion he had brought down over the Alps. He said he needed the troops to protect the region. Not many believed him, least of all Curio, who denounced him in the Forum again.

Towards the end of the year there was an incident. The consul Marcellus had a man from the town of Novum Comum whipped for some crime, I forget what. It's illegal to visit a Roman citizen with corporal punishment, and one of Caesar's acts during his consulship was to make the people of Novum Comum Roman citizens. So this was a way for Marcellus to show that he denied the legality of Caesar's consulship. In fact, when the man complained, Marcellus told him to show his stripes to Caesar.

For days there was great excitement in Rome. There were rumors that Caesar would never endure the insult, and was marching on the city with an army. It wasn't true, and in a short time it all blew over, but it served to mark the force of the wind that was blowing down on us from the Alps.

Around that time, too, I heard a rumor. Caesar, it was whispered, had bribed one of the consuls-elect. It had cost him thirty-six million sesterces. I wondered what Caesar thought he could get for so much money, What I did not realize then—perhaps nobody did—was that to Caesar it no longer seemed very much.

The consul-elect was not the only person he was offering

money to. It got around; some of it even came to me. A man approached me in the lobby of the Curia one morning with an offer. This time I recognized him. "Tell Caesar from me that I would not be interested," I said, wondering if I ought to have him thrown out. I was angry. What did Caesar take me for? I was a Roman, and an officer of the State. I would be no man's slave. Let him take his money and—

The more I thought of it the angrier I got, until it occurred to me that there had been nothing personal in it. Caesar was probably trying it on everyone. After all, he had nothing to lose, and probably some were ready to accept. I had a good laugh picturing to myself Caesar's surprise when he saw who had been caught in his net, and forgot about the matter.

On the tenth of December Curio took office as tribune, followed, on January first by my swearing in as aedile. We got drunk on both occasions to celebrate: it seemed a cheerful moment. "Well, m-my dear, we have a lot to do," Curio sighed late in the evening over the empty dishes and the wine-stained linen. We were alone, we had not wanted any company, and as soon as the meal had been served Curio had sent the servants to bed.

"How bad is it, Curio? What do you think?"

"It's a tricky situation, m-my dear. No one wants to back down."

"We're heading for a confrontation, " I said, meaning to warn him. "On the first of March someone is going to have to back down."

He said nothing, but drank some more wine. In those days we were thirsty all the time. It was anxiety I suppose.

"How far do you think it will go?" I asked. Silence. He poured us out more wine. "How far?" I asked. "More violence? Worse?"

He looked up at me then; his eyes were shaded by his long lashes, and his face looked unspeakably sad. But he said nothing, and to this day I do not know what he was thinking.

On the first of March the discussion of the consular provinces began. The presiding consul—the one Caesar *hadn't* bribed—opened with a speech. He seemed to hurl his words into a breathless hush. "It is the prerogative of the Senate to appoint generals and governors, and to arrange the disposition of armies, and the fate of the provinces. The Senate, not the generals in the field. Caesar must be relieved of his command immediately; his province must be divided into two again, as it was in the past, and governed by two men. They should be sent to take over as soon as possible—" and so on.

When he had finished he looked around. On three sides the benches stared back at him. For a long moment there was silence, but you could feel the air tingling. You could almost see it. Only the dust motes, trapped in a shaft of sunshine from the high, grilled window, moved along their appointed course in the quiet.

Then an uproar broke out, conservatives whistling and stamping, clapping as if they were at the theater. Caesar's friends, booing and hissing, cried out that a great wrong was being done. Men who only hoped for peace, or at least for an end to this dangerous bickering, were trying to quiet both groups.

Into this pandemonium to my astonishment, Curio rose, unwinding his tall, nervous shape. He was saying something. You could see his lips move, and his face had flushed bright pink, but no sound came to me over the roar of the senators. Finally the conservative consul shouted them down, and Curio began to speak.

He was always so surprising. He seemed as slight as a girl; and his manner was so affected, his expression so anxious and so sweet. Yet when he spoke it was a Roman voice that came out of him—logical and incisive, firm and grave.

Now his proposal was very simple. He said only that fair was fair, and Romans had always been just men. If Caesar must lay down his arms, then Pompey must lay down his, too.

At this the Senate burst into cries of joy. "A compromise," they shouted. Smiling modestly Curio came back and took his seat, gazing at his hands which he folded in his lap. I looked at him in wonderment. Could he really believe that what he had proposed was *fair*? Pompey had been given his command by a full and legal vote of the Senate; two years before it had been extended, again in the fullest form of the law, for five more years. He was not obliged, therefore, to give it up for three years to come. Caesar, on the other hand, was asking to keep his command beyond its legal expiration, and to run for office while he still had it—unprecedented measures, extra-legal, unconstitutional.

Yet here was neutral Curio, proposing to put Caesar on the same footing as the honest, if somewhat obtuse, Pompey. No wonder I stared. Nor was anything clearer when Curio, feeling my eyes on him, turned to me and making sure that no one saw, brought down his beautiful eyelashes in a secret wink.

All over the city Curio made speeches about his "compromise." And all over the city men greeted it like a message of hope. In the bars and baths they praised Curio for his courage. Once a crowd carried him home on their shoulders, like a famous gladiator after a successful bout. Perhaps they understood more than I gave them credit for: several people pointed out to me that it was no small thing for a man to risk offending Pompey.

Curio had forced Pompey into an awkward position all right. The measure was so popular the Great Man began to waver and temporize, saying one day that Caesar didn't have to give up his troops before November—a ridiculous date, no more legal that the one Caesar was asking for, but no more useful to him than the current one—and the next that he was sending as his share of the army that was being raised to fight the Parthians a legion he had already lent to Caesar.

All that this maneuvering did, I'm sorry to say, was to make Pompey look foolish and cheap. it was quite a contrast with Caesar, who obediently sent the legion—but before it went he gave every man in it a gift of a thousand sesterces—a year's pay. I blinked when I heard that. It came to nearly five million sesterces, just for one legion, that wasn't even his any more.

In those days I thought I was beginning to have an idea of the goal toward which all this was tending. Well, I did, but I didn't believe it. That's the trouble. Everyone saw, and no one believed. To this day you will find people who will tell you that Caesar was carried along by the flow of events, or merely took advantage of them as they came up, or was forced to act in response to circumstances. Nonsense. He *created* those circumstances, and if events flowed in a direction favorable to him, it was because he dug the channels for them. If they didn't, he dug again.

I'll give you an example. He had so much money he must not have been able to count it. Gaul was a rich province and he had been looting it for nearly ten years. Desperate men began to make their way to his winter quarters in Ravenna—those young bankrupts from good, or goodish, families, who had run through their inheritances and gotten into trouble with the moneylenders. They flocked to Caesar, hoping to use their influence, or their families', in return for his cash. He had plenty. He could have helped them if he wanted to.

Yet when they came he would smile regretfully and tell them no. "I can't help," he would murmur. The situation was painful to him, he said, it reminded him of his youth, when Catiline the aristocratic revolutionary had tried to take over the state and abolish all debts. Well, abolition of debts was a good idea. He had the deepest sympathy for these young men—he had been broke himself once. It was just that there was nothing he could do right now. "What you need," he would say, and his silver laugh would ring out over the wintery landscape, "is a civil war."

I had this story from Mark Antony, back in Rome to run for the tribuneship, for which he was now old enough to be eligible. His round face was leathery from the sun, he was bearded, his hair was long. He looked like his ancestor Hercules, and from the stories that circulated in the city of his exploits in Palestine and Gaul, he resembled him in strength and courage, too.

In addition to the tribuneship he had decided to try for a vacancy in the College of Augurs. His election cost Caesar quite a sum of money, I think, and Caesar travelled around Northern Italy campaigning for his young adjutant.

I had a lot of work, and one of my cases around this time was the defense of an elder statesman called Appius Claudius. Pompey got me the job. Claudius was, in fact, Clodia

Metelli's oldest brother. He was charged with corruption in a province he had administered. I got him off, and he got himself elected censor, on the strength of his spotless reputation and his friendship with Pompey. So I thought I had done myself some good. I never liked having enemies, especially among such a powerful clan as the Claudians.

Unfortunately one of Appius Claudius' first acts as censor was to purge the rolls of Senate. The censors are supposed to remove men whose extravagant, immoral, or illegal lives make them unfit to sit in the Curia. Unfortunately, Appius' definition of unfitness included all of Pompey's enemies—well, everyone who wasn't his friend—and Appius put Curio's name on the list.

"He can't do this!" Curio flushed a delicate pink. "I m-mean, can he?"

"No, of course not. No one will stand for it," I said. "Just because you have protested against some of Caesar's policies, and Caesar and Pompey are friends . . ."

Antony was laughing like a sewer, a friend named Dolabella, whom I was trying to marry off to Cicero's daughter, was reading the list on a couch in the corner. "Do you know who else he's put down? It's practically a roster of the city's best families. What does he think he's doing?"

"We'll see, won't we? " I said.

And we did. The next day Appius Clodius stood up in the Curia and insisted on reading his list. The consuls, shocked like everyone else, tired to prevent him, for if he read it there would be no appeal, and the names would be stricken from the roll of the Senate. It was no use; Appius was adamant. I stood up in my place and told him what I thought of him— at the top of my voice, because as usual the Senate was in an uproar. He heard me, though. I could see him turn toward me. All around me men were yelling, and fistfights had broken out. Curio was shouting—an amazing sight; Appius, purple in the face, shouted back at him like a cabbage seller in the market place. Curio reached out a long arm and grabbed Appius by the toga. A most comical look of dismay came over his features—the toga had torn in his hand. He must have been stronger than he thought; he was obviously stronger than he *looked*. The whole Senate burst out laughing. Appius retreated, silenced and disgraced, his list unread.

Well, that was the end of my friendship with Appius. He owed me money, too, for my expenses defending him during his trial, which he wouldn't repay. He declared—or rather, he didn't declare—a secret war on me. Not so secret that several people didn't tell me about it, and I could see for myself that he had evil thoughts about me.

Then I discovered that he was tampering with the College of Augurs. That was just too much. I had helped Antony get elected to that. You can say what you like about Antony, and perhaps his politics are too extreme and he is inclined to think that Caesar is the solution to everything, but I had my obligations. Antony had been my friend for years. Appius had no right to interfere. If he wanted to make an enemy of Caesar, that was his affair, but he had no right to get at him through Antony and me.

So pretty soon I was the enemy of Appius. The stupid man, mouthing his platitudes and grimacing like a Barbary ape, got one of his friends to indict me under the Scantinian Law. If you can believe that. And just at the moment when the games I was putting on as part of my duties as aedile were making a big noise in the city. It was nothing more than an attempt to ruin my career. The Scantinian Law—are you ready for this?—forbids intercourse with freeborn boys.

It's an old principle of our system that turn about is fair play, and if you can convict your accuser on the same charge, you go free without the trouble and expense—and risk—of a trial. I thought it was worth a try, so, no sooner had the words come out of Appius' mouth, than I stood up in front of the praetor and swore that I had evidence that Appius had committed the same crime.

Never have I seen a luckier hit. Appius turned so white I thought he was going to faint. The spectators applauded, and he had to be led away, the jeers of the crowd in his ears, and my laughter as well. He must have been as guilty as a slave with a box of money under his bed. Freeborn boys, indeed. I was glad that I had exposed him.

After that he hated me more than ever, of course. He never stopped harassing me with lawsuits and nuisances of one kind or another. I said goodbye to my money, and to the good will among the Claudians that I had generated by practically saving the old pederast's life in court. Really, there was no dealing, in those days, with the conservatives. Lines were drawing up; positions were hardening. Men voted in the Senate for party reasons, and no one remembered the obligations of friendship, or even of family. Slowly the conviction grew on me that we were forgetting more than that.

In those days I walked in the city again, as I had when I was a boy. It was part of my job, and I am happy to say that I was able to do something for Rome. There were some merchants who were taking water from the municipal system without paying—I was glad to be able to put a stop to that. And I was glad to discover that I was well known. People spoke to me on the streets, and most had heard of my feud with Appius. Most of them approved, but most of them were afraid.

"Aedile," their voices whispered out at me from street corners, "what is going to happen? Will there be a war?"

"I don't know," I said, but I thought sometimes that there was almost nothing that stood between us and one. There was violence everywhere in the city—small incidents that may or may not have had anything to do with politics. A cloud of tension hung over every conversation, and the smallest remark was enough to set off a brawl.

Around that time Antony began to keep a bodyguard with him when he went out. "I'm not in office yet," he explained. "Not until after the tenth of December. I have no protection till then."

"What are you afraid of?" I asked. Certainly the kind of small fights I had seen in the poorer parts of town would not affect him.

"I'm a friend of Curio's, you know."

"Why should that make you want a bodyguard?"

He shrugged and wouldn't say any more, but he was really

worried. He even posted those men outside his door when he was at home.

Soon after that a man approached me with an offer of assistance. He came up to me in the Forum as if he knew me; my nomenclator whispered his name in my ear, but I did not recognize it. But he was polite enough, at least at first. "Marcus Caelius Rufus, if you have a moment?"

"Certainly. What can I do for you?" Always the perfect young politician.

"A friend of mine has been admiring you for some time. He wants to help you." It wasn't the first time someone had said that to me.

"If it's Caesar, tell him I've already said no. Thank him, but inform him that the answer hasn't changed."

That should have been the end of it, but it was disquieting to see how bold this kind of thing had gotten. "You need money," he persisted.

"I do?"

He favored me with a breath like a whiff of rotting cheese. "Oh, yes. You've got problems, haven't you? A lot of people know about it. It's getting more difficult, isn't it?" And he went on to enumerate them. I was shocked; I don't think even Philo, my confidential secretary, was better acquainted with my affairs.

"Who sent you?" I demanded.

He smiled. "Let's just say someone who wants to help."

"Well, whoever it is, tell him I'm not interested," I shouted, furious. "I won't be bought and sold like a slave."

He had the nerve to be angry. "It isn't in your interest to refuse," he hissed at me.

"Tell whoever it is that I said no." I waved to my clerks and freedmen to chase the fellow off. But it worried me. What did he mean, it wasn't in my interest to refuse? It might have been nothing. But all the same I began to wonder if I ought to go around with a bodyguard myself.

There were some who didn't see what was coming. I suppose there are always men too stiff-necked to bend their eyes to the facts, like Cato, or to busy with their own selfish pursuits to look around, like Appius. And there are always one or two who try to stave off what is coming long past the point where it could possibly do any good.

I thought in those days that was what Curio was doing. He tried everything. He proposed a scheme for the construction and maintenance of roads, It would have given Caesar immunity for five years, like a magistrate. And, more to the point, it would have done the same for anyone he appointed. A neat solution to Caesar's problem it seemed to me—immunity, but no army. Curio's conservative opponents voted it down.

Next he showed up Pompey for the power-hungry hypocrite he was. Pompey wrote to the Senate that he had never sought office, but had had it thrust on him. He had only accepted because he felt a desire to serve his country, and he would be glad to return the powers they had forced upon him by law, and which he had so unwillingly assumed, any time they asked for them back. This he would do, even though his command still had years to run. Of course, Caesar would have to renounce his command, too.

At that Curio was on his feet. His slender height flickered like a flame in the shadows of the Curia. This was not merely fanciful: he was shaking so hard I could see the involuntary movement. Oh, gods, I thought in an agony of sympathy, he's nervous.

It was Curio's finest speech. All his life he might have been preparing for it. His voice flowed from him like a spring, pure and powerful with a bite in it like icy water. His anger showed, and his contempt, but he controlled them; he mastered the minds of the senators easily and confidently. Like the audience at a concert, they were swept along.

Yet Curio did not even seem to realize that we were there. It was to Pompey—absent from the Senate as all generals with active commands must be—that the undammed force of Curio's eloquence was directed. You could almost see the Great Man, seated as he had often been in the front row, listening with his usual massive calm. Curio addressed him directly. "You have promised you will lay down your arms when Caesar puts down his. Well, promises are not sufficient. Retire from your command *now.* Caesar cannot be disarmed until you do. It is a danger to the Republic," he cried, "that private men have public quarrels. It would not be advisable, nor good for Caesar, or the people of Rome, that a unique command should be held by one man, even if that man is you. Instead, each should have power against the other, in case one should try violence against the commonwealth."

All over the Curia there were cries of agreement, as men heard for the first time their fears openly expressed. And there was no doubt that what Curio was saying embodied the feelings of a large number of men, who had never felt easy with Pompey's five-year command and had only voted for it out of anxiety about the public safety. Once Caesar remarked that the men who opposed him were in the minority in the country; well it was true in the sense that most of them hoped to avert a war. And to those hopes, Curio spoke, giving them strength by the power of his voice, though his body shuddered with the effort and his upraised hand shook.

"And what about this man who had only taken power out of a desire to serve his country?" he cried. "Was it a good idea to trust him? He was not what he said he was. From his earliest youth he had only one ambition, to get control of the country." He, Curio, would demonstrate this. And one by one he held up the greatest moments of Pompey's life—his victories, his triumphs, his offices. I had the illusion that he was shining a light on them in which they had never been seen before. Most of the Senate must have had the same illusion, for they cried out in agreement and there were moans of fear from the back.

Curio ignored them. He was coming to the highest point of his speech. "You are a danger to every man here today, and to all we love, honor, protect." All over the Curia heads turned to Pompey's empty chair. "And unless you lay down your command now, *now* when you have the fear of Caesar before your eyes, then I say to you Gnaeus Pompeius Magnus, that you are lying, and you will never lay it down at all."

There was a silence. In it Curio turned toward his audience, as if aware of us for the first time. His shoulders drooped, his head hung. "Gentlemen," he panted, "I move that Pompey and Caesar both be required to resign their commissions and surrender their armies to the Senate, and

if they do not, they shall be pubic enemies, and armies shall
be sent out against them both."

Someone was on his feet to second the motion, but he was
too late. Slowly Marcellus, one of the consuls, rose. Behind
him I could swear that Pompey was standing up, majestic as
a mountain. You could almost feel the ground quake around
him, and the Senate twittered like birds flying up in shrill
dismay.

Marcellus raised his hand in imitation of Pompey's huge
dignity. "Young man, you have gone too far. You have put
yourself in danger."

"What danger, consul?" Curio cried. "Are you threatening me?"

"Take it as you wish."

"I am a tribune," Curio was shouting. "Must I remind you,
my person is sacred."

Marcellus closed his mouth with a snap. There was a feeling in the air as if the Curia was going to burst into flame.

It certainly burst into sound. Men were shouting that Pompey should lay down his command before Caesar, that Caesar
should do it first, or both together, that Pompey was a danger
to the Republic, or Caesar was, or neither. "One at a time,"
the consul roared, but it was a long time before anyone could
listen and longer still before they could vote. In the end, three
hundred and seventy senators voted to save the Republic by
Curio's clever "compromise." Only twenty-two—Cato and his
friends prominent among them—stuck to the law and voted
to allow Pompey to keep his entirely legal command after
Caesar laid down his. "The meeting is adjourned," the consul
cried. He was nearly screaming in an effort to suppress his
pain. "Enjoy your victory. And have Caesar for a master."

"What happened?" I asked Curio. "Why did you change
your mind? I thought you hated Caesar. You were such a
strong opponent of his."

"Aren't I still?" He was smiling but the arm that reached
out for the wine dipper trembled. I looked closer. His whole
body thrummed like a lute string.

"Curio does not agree with Caesar's policies." His wife Fulvia spoke up suddenly from the end of the couches. She was

a plain woman—as much as very rich women ever are plain—
with a formidable jaw. She looked like a general disguised
for some reason under an elaborate coiffure.

She gave me a look of hatred—well, it was no wonder. She
knew I was the enemy of her first husband Clodius. Curio
never allowed her animosity to make the slightest difference
between us, for he was always loyal to his friends, but sometimes I thought when I saw her that she would just as soon
put a knife between my ribs as serve my dinner. Now she
was scowling at me. I wasn't having any of that.

"Well, you wouldn't have guessed it today," I said. "Your
husband came out so strongly against Pompey you'd have
thought he was in Caesar's pay."

"I?" Curio cried. He seemed shocked. I remembered that
Caesar had insulted him. Curio looked like a girl, but he
resented an injury like the aristocrat he was.

I laughed aloud. To my surprise, Fulvia echoed me, letting
out an unexpectedly feminine peal of amusement. After a
moment, Curio joined in.

The next day there was a rumor in the Forum that Caesar
had crossed the boundary of his province and was marching
through Northern Italy. There were crowds shouting in the
Forum all morning, and a frantic and hasty meeting of the
Senate. Marcellus moved that the legions collected for the
Parthian War and waiting at Capua should be used against
Caesar. Curio was the first to oppose him.

"There is no army marching on us. There is not one word
of truth in that report," he cried.

Marcellus was no Cato. "Tribune," he said, lowering his
head like a bull about to charge, "if I am prevented from
insuring the public safety by your veto, or by some deluded
vote you encourage, I will do it on my own authority as consul." With that he took his lictors and tramped out to Pompey's house.

We found him there a few hours later. He had presented
his sword to Pompey, telling him that he and his colleague
in the consulship commanded him to march against Caesar
immediately. He was to use the legions at Capua, or anywhere

else, and Marcellus authorized him to recruit more if he wished.

It was hard to tell what Pompey made of this. He must have been gratified, but he was too experienced a military commander to jump at it. He said he would do what Marcellus wanted "unless we can do better." No one knew what he meant.

Curio could do very little. His term as tribune was expiring and he only had time to make one speech in the Forum, to the anxious and unsettled crowd. He demanded that the consuls issue a proclamation saying that no one had to obey the conscription unless they wanted to. Then, worried about his safety now that his office wouldn't protect him, he left in a chariot to join Caesar. He was in his winter quarters in Ravenna. The day after he left, along with eight others, Antony and Cassius were sworn in as tribunes.

There was a man who stood outside the Curia all day, dressed in a military uniform. He was a centurion, sent by Caesar to report on the proceedings of the Senate. When this man heard that the Senate had refused to grant Caesar an extension of his command, he slapped his sword and said, "This will give it to him."

Pompey could not come into the city, but he kept close by in his house out in the suburbs. He made no preparations for war. "But what will you do if Caesar marches against the city?" he was asked. "Do not trouble yourselves," the Great Man boomed, beaming like the sun with confidence and good will. "I have only to stamp my foot, and all over Italy troops will spring up to follow me."

It was the dead time of winter, between the installation of the new tribunes and the expiration of the offices of the other magistrates. The days were short and cold, the quick wind of December snapped at my heels. Under the gray skies the city appeared almost deserted. People avoided the Forum entirely now. In fact all public places were poorly attended. Shops closed early, even before the brief day drew down;

there were shutters drawn in every street no matter what hour you walked there.

Even the Saturnalia did nothing to help. The great annual festival came and went practically unnoticed: a few slaves romped in the streets, a few half-hearted garlands of greens drooped from the balconies of the apartment blocks, the little candles people gave as gifts appeared in the shops, where they gathered dust all month.

There were no parties now. Curio was with Caesar in Ravenna, Antony and Cassius and the rest of the crowd holed up in their houses waiting for the stalemate to lift, though Antony made an inflammatory speech in the Senate, denouncing Pompey for tyranny and suppression of freedom when the Senate had called him in to keep order after Clodius had died. This livened things up considerably, since it made all the conservatives hopping mad.

I ran into Antony in the baths one afternoon. The room was warm. Steam curled off the pool in rags, winding itself among the pillars and up under the painted scenery of the ceiling, but even so the place was nearly empty. Antony's brazen voice blared out as we splashed a little together. "It's a secret. Caesar has sent orders to two legions and twenty-two cohorts up in Gaul to march down to Italy."

I looked around apprehensively, but there was nobody to hear, just a slave or two sweeping up. "Why?"

"Why? Are you kidding? Pompey might march on him any day, and he has only one legion with him now in Ravenna. One. What do they think he's going to do with one legion? Conquer Italy? Don't make me laugh."

"Compromise is still possible," I said keeping my voice low in the vain hope of making him do the same. "Curio thinks it is, anyway."

"Well, it's not." He brought his weather-beaten face close to mine. "It's time you thought of yourself. Which side are you going to be on?"

An idea came to me. "Antony, have you taken money from Caesar?"

"Of course. My share when we were in Gaul."

"No, I mean . . ."

"A bribe? What do you think I am?" He was very angry. "Who do you think you are?" I saw him reach for his sword, then remember he was naked. His eye swiveled as he searched for his clothes.

Finally I calmed him down, explaining about the people who had approached me. "You can't blame Caesar for that," he said. His crazy laugh rang out over the water. "There are always men like that around. How do you know they really came from Caesar?"

"I don't, of course."

"Right. So ignore them. Make up your own mind. You'd better. You have to decide where you're going to stand when the war comes."

"Perhaps it won't come to that." I tried to sound sure of myself, but the chill and the grayness of the day seemed to have gotten into everything, and I feared that it would.

I had a letter from Cicero on his way home from his province.

DOCUMENT APPENDED

Formiae, December 26

Your guess that I would see Pompey before coming to Rome is a fact. On December 25 he caught up with me at Lavernium. We came to Formiae together and from the eighth hour until evening we talked. You asked whether there is hope of making peace. I gathered from Pompey's complete and meticulous examination of the subject that he does not even want it.

He holds the view that even if Caesar is elected consul without dismissing his troops first, the Republic will be undermined, and he believes that when Caesar hears of the thorough preparations against him he will renounce his hope of the consulship this year and retain possession of his province and his army . . .

In the Saturnalia I went to see my parents. There was a party for the servants, small and quiet, since my parents were past the age for festivities. We exchanged our gifts and ate our meal, waiting on the maids and footmen as tradition demands. Afterwards my father and I sat up drinking our wine in his study. I was surprised, as always, to see how frail he had grown. His hair was white, and his chest was concave. The skin on his upper arms, once as smooth and hard as bronze, fell in folds like a woman's linen dress.

"What do you think of the political situation?" he asked me. Since my service as tribune and aedile he had begun to regard me as some sort of authority on politics. I answered as well as I could, though it made me uneasy.

He listened carefully. "You don't see much hope, do you?"

"No."

"What do you plan to do?"

"About what, father?"

"Well, which side are you going to be on?"

"Oh. I don't know."

"Then hadn't you better decide?" He spoke with all his old fire and bite, and I was going to be angry, but he had put his hand on my arm to steady himself as he rose. His weight had grown so slight it was like a child's touch. I don't know why, but my eyes stung and my throat went tight.

"I suppose you're right, father. I ought to make some kind of decision."

"Good boy," he said.

It was the first meeting of the Senate after the New Year. We had all been up to the temple of Jupiter to swear in the new magistrates; I, like the other outgoing ones, had renounced my office and taken the oath that I had discharged it faithfully. Now we were sitting in the Senate, listening to Lentulus, the new consul, droning on as dully as the old.

Suddenly the door of the Curia burst open. It clanged against the wall, echoing so that the lights trembled and the shadows darted around the room. Into the doorway strode a tall figure, cloaked and hooded and covered with dust from the road. For a moment I thought Caesar had come to address us and my heart began to hammer in my chest.

The man in the doorway stepped forward. Whoever he was he walked with a fine, brisk, military pace, confident and swift. It wasn't Caesar—how could it be?—but it was someone so like him as to be his double. Or his ghost.

"I have here a m-message from Caesar," the apparition said. He flung back his hood, and Curio's handsome face looked out at us. He stood straight, though he was obviously exhausted; his eyes, peering out through the grime of the road, shone with intelligence. He looked older. Perhaps it was just that he no longer trembled.

Lentulus was scarlet. "I will not read a letter from Caesar."

"Consul," Curio said firmly, "I have ridden eighty miles a day for three solid days to bring you this dispatch. I thought you m-might not want to read it, so I waited until the Senate was in session to present it to you. So I don't see how you can avoid it. I don't want to be rude, but you *will* read it."

Lentulus was swearing, working himself up to making threats. "You have no status here," he screamed. "I did not give you permission to address us." He looked over toward his lictors.

"Read it. As tribune I demand that you read it." It was Antony, springing to his feet as he let out his brass-toned bellow.

"Second that," cried Cassius, right behind him. The Curia shuddered with noise.

"Overruled," Lentulus was shouting into the uproar, but of course there were no grounds for that. A tribune may compel a consul to read a letter if he wishes, and two of them may presumably do it twice as surely, though they may have to wait for the room to quiet down enough for them to do it.

"I, Gaius Julius Caesar, Proconsul and Imperator, send greetings to the Senate of Rome. Um. Umm. Skip that. And—"

"Read it all," Antony shouted in a thunderous voice, and again Cassius was behind him.

So Lentulus did. It was a long document, as long as a book, and it seemed to unroll very slowly. Caesar began with a list of benefits he had conferred on Rome—and there were many. Lentulus grew hoarse and had to refresh himself with water, while the Senate waited in murmurous silence.

"I have been charged with crimes," the letter continued.

"Let me answer my accusers." Which he did. In their seats the senators drooped as Lentulus droned wearily on.

At noon we stopped for a break. Men walked around to stretch their legs; those who lived nearby went home to eat, the rest of us had servants bring us something. No one spoke much; it was as if we had made an agreement not to discuss the letter until it was read—an occurrence I was beginning to doubt I would live to see. The one bright spot was Curio, as always. He hurled himself into the seat left vacant by the man next to me. Sighing, "Oh, m-my dear, these *people*," he proceeded to give me an account of his visit to Caesar, including Caesar's warmest greetings to me.

At last, somewhere near mid-afternoon, Lentulus came to the gold: Caesar proposed that the Senate respect the Law of Ten Tribunes and let him keep his provinces—both of them—until he had been safely installed as consul again. If the Senate did not wish to do that, he would lay down his command, if Pompey did, too.

There were shouts that people would be afraid or ashamed to give their real opinions. Lentulus, raising his head hopefully, seemed about to order a delay.

"Vote," roared Antony, and several others seconded him.

"Very well." Lentulus gave him a look of murderous hate. "All who think Pompey should give up his command, stand over there. All who think he shouldn't, on the other side, by the benches . . ." We got up and shuffled down the aisle, Curio leading. All four hundred or so senators trooped over to the side to proclaim their opinion that Pompey should not have to lay down his arms. They were watched by the sardonic eyes of the non-voting tribunes, Antony and Cassius.

"The motion fails," Lentulus cried, triumphant. "Now, how many think Caesar should give up his legions?"

"Stand back," I murmured and Curio laughed. In a moment we were standing alone, the only two opposed.

"The motion is carried."

"Vetoed," shouted Antony and Cassius in one voice.

"Now what?" I murmured to Curio, for we seemed to be at a standstill. Antony was on his feet again, ready to authorize a discussion of Caesar's letter. Before he could speak, three other tribunes had risen, the light of veto shining in their

231

eyes. "All right, all right," Lentulus shouted. "We'll discuss the situation in general terms only." He seemed surprised when Antony did not veto that.

"I'll speak first. Presiding consul's prerogative," Lentulus announced. "I just want to say that if the Senate stands firm against Caesar I will too. But if you cave in to him, as you have in the past, I'm not going to be the only one to hold out. I have my own interests to consider. Believe me, I know how to curry favor with Caesar as well as anyone. Don't think I'm going to throw away my career while the rest of you get fat on money from Gaul—"

He was followed by Scipio, Pompey's father-in-law. No one doubted that what he said came directly from the big, golden house in the suburbs where Pompey sat. Scipio said that Pompey was prepared to do anything necessary to help the Senate, if they asked him *now*, but if they delayed, or tried again to compromise, they would cry outside his gates later in vain. He would not come. He would not even listen.

Scipio's manner was if anything more threatening than Lentulus', and the Senate adjourned and shuffled out very oppressed and unhappy. Curio and I went out with them into the early winter twilight. "It's the crisis," I said, and I could not understand how it had blown up on us so suddenly.

"Yes," said Curio, "and it's been a long time coming."

The next day the debate continued, to no purpose that I could see except to make everybody angrier than before, and to bring us closer to the brink. That evening when the Senate adjourned, Pompey invited the whole body out to his house. Obedient to this siren call, we went: the lines of litters and wagons stretched out along the road, lanterns winked like fireflies in the freezing drizzle.

When we got there it was to find that Pompey was ready for war. He made a speech demanding the loyalty of those he called the "waverers," and announcing that he was bringing in cohorts from the two legions in Capua. So I left. I wasn't ready to enlist in Pompey's army, not yet, anyway.

Others, perhaps more realistic, or with less hope, kept going back for the next several days. The Senate was not meeting because of the Festival of the Crossroads, and the accompanying games. The holiday served as a reason—or a pretext—to allow both Pompey and the Caesarians to politic as frantically as they could.

Both of them called on me. The Pompeians, as stiff and condescending as their master, informed me that it was my duty to vote on their side; the Caesarians told me that it was in my interest to choose theirs. "Caesar means to abolish debts," one man said, and dug me in the ribs. Well, I know there were men who listened to this, so perhaps it worked. Polls were taken constantly of the factions, and letters flew back and forth all over Italy.

We had one last chance, and I think everybody knew it. It was Cicero. On the fourth of January he arrived outside the city, home at last from his governorship. He had a letter from Caesar asking him to try to arrange something—anything— that would preserve the peace.

For a day or two it looked as if he might succeed. Pompey was willing to listen to his old friend; so, presumably was Caesar. The trouble was the conservatives. When the Senate met again after the Festival, under the freezing eyes of the cohorts Pompey had stationed in the Forum, they were as thickly packed and as belligerent as wasps. Under the leadership of Cato and Appius and a couple of others, they refused even to consider the compromise Cicero had so carefully worked out. Cato cried bitterly that even if Caesar accepted it, he would not. "Remember his first consulship. We will not be deceived a second time by Caesar." All the conservatives buzzed their approval.

A couple of Caesar's friends tried at least to get them to allow a message to be sent to Caesar, telling him of the reception his letter had gotten. They gave their word to go to Ravenna and back in six days. "It can be done," they urged, and from his place, Curio got up. "Yes, it can," he drawled.

So our time came down to six days, and that was the most we could hope for, but even that the Senate refused. It took them two days of debate. Then, on the seventh of January, they issued their Ultimate Decree.

Lentulus proposed it: "All magistrates, and former magis-

trates holding military commands near the city, are authorized to take *any steps necessary* to defend the Republic."

"He can't mean it," I shouted to Curio over the noise, but
he was absorbed in some calculation or contemplation of his
own and did not seem to hear. "The last time the Senate
passed the Ultimate Decree was when Cicero was consul. To
put down Catiline's rebellion. The city was about to be
torched, and the slaves set free and armed. This is hardly
the same kind of situation."

"No." He smiled bleakly, still absorbed.

Down in front Antony and Cassius were shouting that they
would veto the motion if the consul put it to a vote. Lentulus
did not answer. Presently a small silence accumulated around
them. It spread, until even the back benches were quiet.
Everyone was waiting for something, I didn't know what.
Lentulus seemed to be holding his breath.

Into the tingling quiet came the sound of military feet
tramping up to the door, and an officer's voice shouting some
muffled command. The marching footsteps halted, equipment jingled briefly, and the silence resumed.

Lentulus looked at Antony and Cassius. "You'd better leave,
if you don't want trouble. Get out. Immediately."

"Trouble? Are you threatening us?" Antony roared, and
Cassius cried out, "Oh Gods, the city, the city." He meant, I
think, that a sacrilege was being committed, as indeed it was.
His voice was perfectly sincere: he was not thinking of the
danger to himself, but only that the gods might be angry at
Rome. Shocked, we watched. I don't think anyone in that
whole room breathed.

"Yes, tribune, I'm threatening you," Lentulus drawled sar-
castically. "If you don't get out of here now, I'll have you
put out. And if that doesn't stop you from obstructing this
assembly I'll go further than that." Suddenly he was shouting, dancing up and down in a frenzy of hatred. "Get out!
Get out!" He raised his hand as if to summon the troops.

Antony's handsome face flushed. He took a step toward
Lentulus, but Cassius was holding him back. They hesitated
a moment longer, standing there together, facing the consul.
Something, a noise from outside, a whispered word, I don't
know what, decided them, and Antony and Cassius turned

on their heels together and strode out of the building. Beside me Curio whispered, "I'll have a wagon at the Flaminian Gate at midnight, if you want to come." He got up and went out after his friends. I waited only long enough to see the Senate pass the Decree against Caesar before I followed him.

My first impulse had been to join Antony and Cassius, but the sight of the Forum somehow arrested me. A squad of Pompey's troops marched through, javelins glistening. There were flowers trampled in the puddles. A veil of rain trailed over the buildings down at the other end, where a crowd was just disappearing. I could hear Antony shouting over the patter of the rain, and the fading mutter of the crowd's agreement, like thunder rumbling in the hills. I don't know why, on such a miserable day, but the scene struck me as beautiful.

I thought about Curio's plan. If I went, the first thing that would happen was that my creditors would try to seize my property. Well, perhaps I could prevent them, if I juggled some things. There was a shipment of wheat due from North Africa as soon as the weather improved; it might be possible to defer . . . to rearrange . . . If I paid a little here, borrowed some more there . . . ? Why not? I'd been doing it for years.

Philo could handle some of it, he was an experienced man, clever and careful . . . But the rest? I would be gone. There would be no way to keep it all up in the air.

And how long would it take? Months? Years? What would happen to the businesses, the properties? I couldn't guess. Of course, if Caesar won, there would be no problem. Presumably he would make up to me whatever I lost. And if, as they hinted, he really planned to abolish debts, there would be no problem at all. If he won.

The city lay as bare as a skeleton, the white stucco walls had a ghostly shine in the wet, the trees rattled in the wind like bones. How could I decide? The advantages of each course of action seemed exactly balanced by the other; the disadvantages weighed the same. Over and over my mind turned them, through the wet streets where the shadows lay as deep as the pools. I walked through the city, my footsteps ringing on the stones, alone. No human being passed me, no lighted window shone. By the Circus Maximus the pigeons awoke and cooed, a bear, dreaming of a festival, shook the floor of his cage. Someone had sacrificed on the Capitoline Hill; I saw the altar fire from down below, no bigger than a spark. I wondered if it had been Curio, asking for luck from Capitoline Jupiter. And still I could not decide.

The rain was passing, followed by a cold wind that was scouring the clouds from the sky, revealing the stars. I drew my cloak up around my ears and urged the bearers to go faster. Their heels jolted on the road. Puddles glimmered among the mournful reeds, far away, on the horizon, mountains lay in a long, liquid wash of darkness.

Soon enough we came to a small villa. Dogs barked, a door flew open, light spilled out onto the stones. A huge shape blocked the doorway, shouting unintelligibly. "Cicero!" I reached out, and his arms went around me in an embrace.

"Come in, come in," he cried. "Tell me all the latest from Rome."

He had a table set up before the couch; there was food on it, scraps of bread, and little plates of cheese and ham and vegetables in olive oil, gleaming golden in the lamplight.

"I've interrupted your meal," I said.

"What? Oh, no, I was just trying to work out the situation. See. Here—this is Caesar, up in Ravenna with one legion. This salt cellar. These crumbs of bread are Caesar's other legions in Gaul, under Trebonius. And this—what is it? Oh, the soup. Do you want some? No? Well, that's Pompey with two, here in Italy, at Capua. There are some more—"

"They've passed it," I said.

"The Ultimate Decree?"

I nodded.

The breath went out of him, and he sat down, hard, on the couch. For a long time he said nothing. Then he raised his hand and swept the table clean.

"What shall I do?" I asked him. "They're willing to take me, if I want to go. Curio urges me to, in fact. You know Curio and his enthusiasms."

It was late; the table and its debris had been cleared away, fresh charcoal was heaped on the braziers. We lay on our couches with wine cups in our hands, but we had not drunk much. He was always moderate in his habits, and I had a decision to make.

"Do you want to go?"

I shrugged. "What is there for me in Rome? The enmity of the conservatives, so that I have no real possibility for advancement. Having to watch men inferior to myself in ability get the better jobs . . ."

He smiled. "Surely there's more to be said in Rome's favor? You love Rome. Why, we could hardly keep you in the house when you lived with us, you were so anxious to be out in the city. You used to go out over the garden wall at night, didn't you?"

"You know about that?"

"You were young. But you still love the city."

"Yes, but what good does it do me? I have to think of my own career. What would be best for me. Caesar is offering opportunities, reward for services, debt relief. I *have* debts. It's cost me money to work for the conservatives."

"Public service isn't supposed to be lucrative, you know."

"It had better be. I can't afford to stay in it if it isn't." I was angry. "Look," I said, raising my voice. "You have to look at this rationally—"

"Can you look at it rationally?" he asked gently. "I would have thought a lot of other things came into it too."

"Like what?"

"Like standing up for something you love, no matter what the consequences. Like defending something because it's right, and fighting something because it's wrong. Like being a Roman and honoring your word. You swore to uphold the constitution, you know. You were a magistrate."

"That's all right in peacetime." I was shouting with fury at his obtuseness. "Right and wrong, doing the honorable thing, all those luxuries. But in war there's only one question."

"Really?" he asked softly. "What is that?"

I looked at the table, swept clean and gleaming. The pieces had been cleared away. I was icy with fury now. "That's easy," I said. "Which side is going to win."

At the Flaminian Gate Curio was waiting, slumped on the

seat of the wagon. Two slaves, muffled to the eyes, held the heads of the horses, but Curio was not wrapped up. He was so drunk I doubt if he'd have felt the cold in an Alpine village, let alone on a January night in Rome. Nevertheless he was glad to see me.

"What time is it?" he whispered.

"Midnight." I climbed up on the seat beside him.

He smiled a sweet, joyful grin, like a boy let out of school. "All right, m-my dear. Let's go."

"But Antony and Cassius—where are they?"

"Here." It was one of the slaves, pulling himself into the back of the wagon. He pushed back his travelling hat to reveal a heavy chin and a sharp, strong nose.

I laughed. "Gods. Antony." Behind him Cassius briefly unwound himself from his cloak and gave me a grin. "Here," I said. "Is everyone drunk but me? Give me that wine flask."

We lurched off heading north and east. Curio had packed food and wine; at the first milestone a number of his men joined us, riding ahead or behind in the darkness. We ate and drank; presently we began to sing.

Once a messenger passed us on the road heading toward Rome. Antony and Cassius ducked down, hiding themselves among the packing cases and the jars of wine, but the messenger noticed nothing and hurried on his way.

Slowly the road began to climb. The stars overhead glittered like frost. The wind blew in my face. I fell into a dream. I was a boy again; I had opened the door in the garden wall. The grass rustled, the air smelled sweet, a vast distance spread out under the dome of the sky. Far away mountains rose, their cool breath swept over me, on its way to the sea. I ran to meet it. "This is the road that runs past our property, Curio," I said. "I used to climb up on it when I was a boy, and wonder what was on this side of the mountains."

"Now you know, m-my dear," he murmured.

That night we stopped at a little villa up among the peaks. Snow lay in patches on the stony ground and stalks of dead grass whistled dismally. I was exhausted and very drunk by then; I fell into bed just as the first light of dawn was staining the high boulders. "Well," I said aloud as my head touched the bolster. "I've done it. I've left Rome."

I was nearly asleep before I remembered that I had not told my father that I was going. Oh, well, I thought, he won't care. I'll send a message in the morning. On that thought I slept.

Two days later we arrived at Ariminum, the last town in Roman Italy before the border with Gaul. We had travelled fast and none of us looked very prepossessing. Cassius and Antony still wore the dress of slaves; Curio and I, unshaven, hung-over and unbathed, were nearly as bad.

"We look good enough for this town anyway," Cassius said, looking around. It was true. Ariminum is a bare, windswept place, smelling of the sea. Sand blows in the streets, trees are few and stunted, around the market hangs the odor of fish.

"Do you want to wait here until we can get a m-message to Caesar?" Curio asked doubtfully.

"I doubt there's a place in this town I'd care to stay," I said.

They agreed. "I'd rather camp on the ground," Antony sneered, letting out his too-loud laugh.

Curio shot him an uneasy glance. "The border is a little stream. There's a hill there, beside the road. I don't think m-many people will pass, and they won't be curious about us . . ."

We were back in the wagon before he had finished speaking.

Night had fallen when we arrived. "Are you sure this is right?" I asked Curio. Somewhere I could hear water chattering as it ran. A breeze played among reeds.

"Oh, certainly, m-my dear." He directed his men and the servants, while Antony and Cassius, drunk again, impeded them with suggestions and demands. Soon there was a fire, but too low to reveal much—just a scrap of landscape: the slope of a low hill, the grass kept short by grazing animals, the parapet of a small stone bridge. Up on the hill a lone oak spread out its branches. "Come on," I said to Curio. "Let's sit up there. I'm getting awfully tired of Cassius and Antony." He grinned, showing his huge, yellow teeth.

"Oh, m-my dear, I know what you m-mean. What a m-misfortune, to m-make a revolution with m-men like that."

The fire had died. Antony and Cassius were rolled in their cloaks asleep.

"How many legions has Caesar with him in Ravenna?" I asked.

"One."

Only one, I thought. "And Pompey has how many?"

"As m-many as he can raise. Probably it will work out to about ten. Plus the two waiting at Capua that he got from Caesar, of course."

Of course. "And you still think Caesar will come?"

In the starlight I saw him smile.

"Curio, why did you change your mind? You used to hate Caesar so much. Everybody noticed it. People said he insulted you, or something. Yet here you are, waiting for . . ." I did not finish my thought. "Why did you come?"

I don't know what I expected. Some political explanation, perhaps, or one of his stories about Caesar's mysterious and impressive character, But I was wrong. He laughed a little, quietly, to himself. "Oh, m-my dear. Why did I come? Because I took a bribe, of course."

"You what?"

"Caesar paid m-my debts. I had such a lot. M-my father's funeral—It was an expensive business, you know. And he offered, you see."

"How much was it?"

"I don't know, m-my dear. I just sent the bills to him. Anyway, *you* m-must know."

"Why should I know?"

"Well, you m-must have cost him nearly as m-much."

There was a small animal hunting among the reeds, a fox perhaps. I could hear the rustling—I could almost trace its passage.

"I didn't take a bribe," I said.

The fox had found something; there was a sharp rattle of the reeds and a tiny, broken cry.

Curio looked at me in consternation. "Oh, m-my dear. If you didn't, why are you here?"

He was looking at me, with one eyebrow raised. I smiled, thinking I knew where he had learned that trick. Suddenly a great longing came over me. The golden hair, the light voice with its silvery tone, the fine intelligent eyes. "Oh, I don't know. I suppose it was just that something useful could be made out of the situation."

Curio seemed impressed. "Oh, m-my dear. What a very *cool* way to look at it," he said.

"Curio," I asked. "What's this river called?"

The breeze ruffled the bare branches overhead; the stream murmured and sang. In the reeds a heron awoke and began to search the margin of the water. It was nearly dawn.

"It's called the Rubicon," Curio said.

It was morning before Caesar appeared. "There he is," Antony shouted.

"Antony's drunk again," Cassius said, but even if he was his eyes were better than ours, for presently a distant cloud of dust appeared where the road emerged between two low ridges. It drew nearer, resolving itself into a chariot, travelling fast, followed by several horsemen, and at a longer interval, a large troop of cavalry.

"He's coming from Ravenna, " mumbled Antony. "He must have gotten lost on the way."

"How do you know that?" Curio drawled, amused.

"Look." Antony pointed with his hawk's nose. "He's got mules pulling that chariot. He must have commandeered them from some civilian—if he'd been in camp he'd have taken horses."

Curio laughed. For myself I was too intent on the road to join in. I was straining my eyes for the first sight of him . . .

The hoofbeats approached, a rumor, a drumbeat, a tattoo. Then the dust-cloud, glittering in the morning sun. At last I saw the flash of gilt hair, the tall, slender figure, flexible as a whip, standing alone in the chariot, behind the foaming mules.

We were shouting, dancing up and down on the hill, waving and laughing. Antony had tears on his cheeks, and he was not ashamed of them. Gods, so did I. "Caesar!" we shouted, and beside me Curio said quietly, "I knew he'd come."

There was a pause while the day seemed to hover around us. Caesar had halted, drawing up the chariot to stand on the crown of the road. He gazed at the river and the bridge. His cohorts had stopped, his friends had reined in their mounts, waiting. For a long moment we held our breath. Nothing moved. There was no sound.

"Well, my friends we can still draw back. But once we cross, then we will have to fight it out." Caesar's voice came to us clearly on the still air. I had forgotten how light and friendly and easy it was. Oh, gods, I thought, and my hands were sweating. He'd better cross. What will happen to us if he doesn't? But my heart was dancing, my head was light. I felt drunk again, though I was sober. All the time the unnatural silence continued; even the noisy little river was quiet.

Caesar, too, seemed held in suspension. Still in the chariot, he had turned back to the bridge, thinking deeply. Then, slowly, he lifted his head and looked away down the bank. What has he seen? I tried to ask Curio, but the mysterious injunction against sound still rested on the world, and I could not speak. The river bank stretched away, empty, among the tall grasses; motionless sheep speckled a distant hillside. They all seemed to be looking toward the same place.

Then I heard it. In that vast stillness, a note, then another, a third. Perhaps it was the wind moving among the reeds that called forth that low sequence of tones, though I felt no movement in the air; perhaps a shepherd had blown a tune on his pipes . . . But I saw—and others did, too, for I asked them later—I saw—

It was a huge figure, and very beautiful. Light came from it, so that I could hardly see—Oh, gods, it was radiant. I thought it was—well, I don't know. But I thought the legs were furred and ended in hooves, the torso like man's. The head was clothed in a sun-like dazzle. It sat on the river bank, playing a shepherd's pipe. The sound was made up of all the noises of the day, of water murmuring, the click of stones, branches scraping against one another, the sheep on the hill, the groan of the earth, the whispered conversation of the grass, all woven into that wonderful spill of notes. Gods, I heard them as clearly as I hear this little town beginning to wake in the deepest dark before morning. It was real. I know it was. A soldier ran forward, splashing across the stream, to hand the enormous figure a trumpet. The god stood up and blew a blast.

"The die is cast," Caesar shouted into the reverberations of that tremendous summons, and, slapping the reins on the backs of the mules, he thundered across the bridge.

We ran to embrace him. "Caelius, how good of you to come," he found time to say, and rested his hand briefly on my shoulder. He looked wonderful: he was energetic and healthy, his body both thinner and more muscular than before, his dark eyes shone with their old brilliant light, but his hair was sparser and paler, and his skin was peeling across his nose. He looked like a man who has been living hard, and with whom it agreed.

"Welcome, welcome," he cried, and I knew I was. I looked around as he continued on to throw his arms around Antony and thump him on the back. His soldiers were coming across the bridge now. They were singing. My heart lifted up to see them tramping in their ordered rows toward us, under the great gold eagle on its pole.

Gods, they were a magnificent sight. Caesar's army. They looked hard-bitten and competent, tough men all of them, but not starving or ill-used. Whatever they thought of this march and its consequences, they had undertaken it cheerfully enough. They were loyal, and I thought they had reason to be. I was glad to see it. I was one of them now.

We followed Caesar into Ariminum where he mustered the legion just outside the town. He made a speech, showing Antony and Cassius in their humiliating dress as slaves, making much of the condition of Curio and me. "These distinguished men," he called us.

He told them how the tribunes had been threatened with harm. "In the past the rights of tribunes have been defended with arms. Now it is with arms that they have tried to take these rights away . . ." The soldiers roared like a crowd at the games.

Caesar paced in front of them, his tunic flapping over his thigh with a brisk little snap, his thinning hair floating above his head. "Pompey has been seduced and led astray," he shouted. He, Caesar, had always supported the great general. He had helped him in any way he could to attain his great honors and dignities. I saw smiles at that, and a kind of relief among the troops. Well, I think a number of them must have served with Pompey, and the Great Man was always very popular with soldiers.

Meanwhile Caesar was occupying the higher ground with a list of the wrongs done to him—including the last, the Senate's Ultimate Decree. "It used to be that this decree was used when the city was in danger of destruction—the temples seized on the high places, the fires set and waiting for the torch. But none of that had happened now, nothing like that has even been thought of."

Low growls were coming from his soldiers now, and cries of anger or dismay. "Avenge your commander," Caesar cried. "The general who has led you with honor, with success, for nine long years, Defend the dignity and good name of the man with whom you have conquered Germany and pacified Gaul. Do not let—"

But the soldiers had had enough. They let out a roar, the trumpets blared, the standards dipped and rose, and the whole legion, Caesar leading, marched into Ariminum, with the four of us at its head.

BOOK FIVE

XIX

It was a year before I saw the city again. I thought of it constantly. Sometimes I seemed to see it from a distance, as I had the first time, winking lights among the dark shapes of trees, a river of gold winding through the darkness. Sometimes I walked in its streets and saw the houses of my friends, lamps lit for a party, music spilling out. On other occasions it was the Forum I strolled in, or the Curia, the baths, the temples, the bars. I was with my friends, the ones who had died, those still alive, or alone, I was with women I had known or wished I had. I thought of my triumphs in court, and my losses. It didn't make any difference, it was all the city.

Sometimes I dreamed I was there; sometimes I only wished I was. In the snows of the Alps, in the parching heat of Spain, the city was always with me. Even now I cannot quite believe that I will never see it again.

Yet for me the city is gone. It was gone as soon as we crossed the river, though I did not know it. Caesar had committed himself, Curio and I without further thought hurled our own interests after him. We were going to conquer all of Italy with one legion. It is a tribute to our enthusiasm, and to the peculiar greatness of Caesar, that we never doubted we could.

As soon as we left Rome the Senate put Pompey in charge of its defense and urged him to recruit as many men as possible immediately. "Stamp now," someone called out to him, reminding him that once he had said that he had only to stamp his foot and all over Italy men would come flocking to his banners. He could raise, we calculated, about ten legions eventually, but they were far from springing up out of the ground like dragon's teeth. It was going to take some time.

Announcing that the city was indefensible, Pompey forced

the Senate to leave practically in a body and follow him to Brundisium, where he planned to embark for the east. He had thousands of loyal followers among the kingdoms there, and millions in aid. He would rearm, and with an army like a plague of locusts he would come marching back, victorious, to Italy.

The Senate, very unhappy about this, had no choice but to go with him, for in the meantime, we had been marching down the east side of the Italian peninsula, mopping up the little towns on the way. Generally we met no resistance at all, and often we had a joyful and exuberant welcome. Caesar took great care to treat everyone with gentleness, rewarding surrender with friendship and pardoning resistance, even when it did not seem in his interest. But it always was, for word got around, and all down the peninsula we were met with open gates. We were making for Brundisium, to try and prevent Pompey's escape.

We were very few to make a revolution. It is not just that we had only one legion: Caesar had more in Gaul. He had already sent for them from Ariminum. We would be a large army eventually. Large enough to have a chance now, since Pompey was not going to fight immediately.

No, what struck me was how thin Caesar's support was among the upper classes. Normally a general has dozens of young men around him, serving as adjutants and petty commanders, learning the business of war and making contacts that would last them all their lives. Cicero did his military service with Pompey's father, for instance. I had Quintus Pompeius Rufus. As I say a governor or a general has dozens of these people around him. But Caesar had only us.

He needed us badly, too. Within days he had sent Antony over the Apennines to Arretium which controls the route north. Curio he took with him to command half his troops, for a conservative senator was holed up in Corfinium, a town on the eastern slopes of the mountains. He was blocking the way to Brundisium—where Pompey had already arrived and was assembling a fleet to take him east. Cassius he told to get ready to go to Spain.

I waited, my eyes constantly on him as he flicked around

the camp like a spark in a draft, now here, now there, everywhere at once. He flashed with energy, grinned with joy, his cloak bellied out like a sail in his speed. Gods, one legion and a handful of disgruntled junior magistrates, to conquer all of Italy. In those days, watching him, I was sure Caesar could do it alone.

One night he came into my tent. I was undressed, trying in fact to take a bath that my servant Philo had heated for me. The draft of cold air as he lifted the tent flap made me turn around. "Oh, excuse me. I mean, I didn't see . . ." I reached for a cloak, nearly overturning the portable leather tub.

"That's all right, Caelius." He was smiling and his dark eyes were studying me with an expression I couldn't read. "At ease. Go on with what you were doing."

But I couldn't. It didn't seem soldierly somehow. I clambered out of the tub and began to towel myself off.

"Caelius, I haven't talked to you about a reward yet. I know that you have debts . . ." His eyes followed me.

"That's all right."

His eyes went over my nakedness again. He smiled. "I'm glad you're here. I'd like to make some tangible gesture to show it."

"I didn't come for that." I was embarrassed. I wished I could hide behind the towel.

"I'm aware of that. But a man who comes to me of his own free will deserves more, not less, than men I have to buy." His eyes were twinkling now, the skin at the corners had wrinkled up in a grin. "Besides, it's a very good example for any others who might be thinking about joining us, don't you see?"

"Well, yes. I suppose it is."

He was pleased with me. "Well, then. You have debts—"

"Rather a lot of them, I'm afraid. It cost me quite a bit to become aedile. And then the games on top of it . . ."

"I know." He flicked me a grin. He did—he had been deeper in debt than I was at my age.

I had finished with the towel and was standing with my

hands on my hips, thinking. "Is it true that you plan to abolish debts when you return to Rome?

He was looking at me with that unfathomable look, and his tongue passed over his lips. "What? Oh, yes. I told people that. It's a necessary step, as I see it. You keep yourself in good shape, Marcus. That's important for a soldier."

"Thank you. Well, if you're going to abolish debts altogether, I can wait. I've got a good man in charge in the city, and I can keep things going. Most of the men I owe money to went with Pompey anyway."

"I see." His eyes held mine. "And is there nothing else you need?"

"Well, there is one thing—I want to run for City Praetor when we get back. But I don't see where I'll get the money. And of course, I'm too young." I reached across for my woolen tunic. the servant was holding out for me. "I mean if the law is strictly observed . . ."

"Praetor? I don't see why not." Something made him catch his breath; he sounded like a man who has been running.

"City Praetor. It's important to me. It's the most senior praetorship—" My voice must have been muffled by the tunic as I pulled it over my head, for he repeated, "City praetor?" When I poked my head out, he had turned away, and was fiddling with some objects on the table. Even from the back he looked disappointed, though I couldn't imagine why.

"Is it a problem?" I asked. "Because I think I ought to know about it now, if it is."

"No, no, it's all right. I'll see you become a praetor. The age thing shouldn't make any difference. Not if we win."

"City Praetor," I insisted.

"Caelius." Having made up his mind, he spoke briskly now. "I have a job I want you to do. There's some trouble in a town called Intemilium, that guards the road to Gaul, just at the foot of the Alps. Some sort of rebellion. That road must be kept open—Trebonius, my senior legate, is bringing down my armies, and they must not be delayed." He was all business. He did not look at me any more, but studied the maps on the table. "I can't afford a disaffected town on that road. Will you take care of it for me?"

"Of course," I cried, leaving off buckling my breastplate

in my pleasure at the prospect of action and a command of my own.

"Take four cohorts—two thousand men is all I can spare. But there may be some loyal people up there. I can't tell what the situation is exactly."

"I'll take care of it."

"I'm sure you will." He smiled then. "Take care of *yourself*, Marcus. I'll see you when you get back."

So I went to Intemilium, in Southern Gaul, where the Alps come down and touch the sea, falling in broken terraces to a crumbling coast. It was a cold year; the snow lay deep over mountainside and road, the walls of the town wore a crown of white. I kept the road open with crews shovelling more or less constantly, and though the weather made problems for us, particularly with supplies, it solved several others. The Gauls of Intemilium must never have had a clear idea of how many we were, for we were hidden behind a screen of flakes. It must have made life inside the town harder to endure than a normal siege.

Tactically Intemilium was not a difficult problem—it was only a matter of waiting for hunger or cold to do its work. Every now and then I sent a foray, or a team of sappers. I really didn't care much if they had any success, I only wanted to remind Intemilium of our strength. I had plenty of time.

So I sat before Intemilium in a waste of snow, while everywhere else the world went on and life happened to other people. Pompey evaded Caesar's blockade of Brundisium and fled to Greece with almost the entire conservative faction, the majority of the Senate. Cicero met Caesar at his country house in Arpinum, and refused to go to Rome as Caesar's friend when Caesar entered the abandoned city.

DOCUMENT APPENDED

CICERO TO CAELIUS, GREETINGS

I spoke so as to make Caesar respect me rather than feel grateful to me, and I remained firm that I did not want to go to the city. I was mistaken when I thought he would be

easy to deal with—I have never seen anyone less so. He said over and over that I had judged and condemned him and that if I did not come, the rest of the men of substance who hadn't gone with Pompey would be reluctant to. I argued that my situation was different from theirs. After much talk, "Come then and talk about peace," he said.

"At my own discretion?"

"Should I prescribe to you?" he asked, surprised.

"If I speak I will say that the Senate should not have approved sending your army into Spain, or Pompey's into Greece. Moreover, I will publicly lament what has happened to Pompey."

"I truly do not want you to say that."

"So I thought. And for that reason I do not want to come. For if I come, I must speak out on these subjects, for I cannot keep silent about them. If not, I cannot come."

The end was, as he was looking for a way to conclude our talk, that I would think about it. It wasn't possible to refuse. On that note we went our separate ways. I believe that as a result of this, Caesar has no love for me, but I like myself, which hasn't happened for a while. But I see no end to this evil. I do not doubt that I have offended Caesar and I must act quickly and with discretion . . .

For the rest, oh, gods, what a following he has with him. The walking dead! How can you stand it? The worst collection of ruffians and bankrupts I ever saw . . .

Caesar, no doubt regretting Cicero's attitude, went on to Rome. There he set up a new government out of his best friends in the Plebeian Assembly and those senators who had stayed behind to brave the chaos when Pompey left. It was legally summoned by Antony and Cassius, who were still tribunes. To every voter in Rome, Caesar promised a free measure of grain and oil, and a gift of three hundred sesterces. There was, I understand, jubilation in the city at the announcement.

There was one unfortunate incident. I had a letter from Curio about it, nearly incoherent with excuses. I was just trying to make it out when someone called me. A bear had been seen above the camp.

"Nonsense. It's too early in the year for bears. Don't they hibernate or something?" But they were sure. Cursing, I snatched up the letter and went out.

It was a still night. The stars glittered across the roof of the sky, the distant sea shone like black marble. A vast white landscape surrounded me, tumbled with inky shadows where anything could have hidden. Shapes were disguised by the snow and the hard white light. I found I could read by it, it was so bright.

A tribune had vetoed Caesar's proposal to take over the Treasury, he had gone so far as to stand guard over the doors personally. Caesar, taking an army inside the city limits as an advertisement of the fact that a state of emergency was in force and the constitution suspended, marched right up to the Temple of Saturn at the head of the column and threatened to kill the tribune if he didn't get out of the way.

Just then a centurion called me, his voice low. "Legate, look. Up there. The bear."

"What? Oh, the bear." I peered through the dazzle. "I don't think it's anything, centurion. Just a bush covered with snow or some such thing." How could he have done it? To threaten a tribune, when that had been the reason he had gone to war in the first place? And he had violated a temple to do it.

"Legate," they were calling again, their voices softly echoing among the rocks. "There it is again."

Up on the hillside a shape was standing. It seemed to sway in that uncertain brightness. As I watched it disappeared. "That was just a breeze shaking a branch," I said.

"But legate, there is no breeze." I hardly heard. In my mind I was with Caesar. I looked at the letter again. "He was so angry, my dear. I really thought he was going to run the tribune through. But then he thought better of it, and remembered that mercy and gentleness are better policy."

Well, possibly. But I thought the anger might have been policy just as much. It might have suited him to let people think he was carried away. Because he needed that money very badly. What he had from Gaul was not going to last forever—not at the rate he was spending. Besides, if he left the Treasury untouched his enemies would have seized it as soon as he turned his back.

"There must have been something here, legate," the centurion said respectfully, showing me something that looked like tracks. Well, it might have been a bear. I doubled the guard just in case, and went back to finish my letter.

Caesar had removed fifteen thousand bars of gold, thirty thousand pieces of silver, thirty million sesterces in coin. Well, it would have been stupid to leave it behind, and Caesar was never stupid.

All the same it appeared from what Curio wrote that it had undone all the good work of his gifts to the people. They were so upset that Caesar had to cancel his farewell speech and leave Rome sooner than he had planned. He was heading north, toward Spain, where he intended to engage Pompey's legates and their legions and prevent a war behind his back. I had orders to have the gates of Intemilium open when he arrived.

Well, I got busy. I arranged my cohorts in a closer circle around the walls, I blocked up the streams, I closed the roads. I also let it be known that anyone who opened the gates to us would be favorably treated. It had been almost two months that they had been sitting in their cold and empty houses, hearing us outside; it didn't take much longer for them to decide where the better course lay.

I was anxious, I admit it. I could hear Caesar marching at my back, and I wanted to be sure he was pleased with me, so perhaps I was a little harsh with the Intemilii when they surrendered. But following Caesar's example, I forgave them very quickly and made sure those who were not part of the rebellion did not suffer. All in all I felt I had done very well for my first single command. Caesar thought so, too, for he wrote me in glowing terms. The letter warmed even Intemilium in February.

There was one moment, like the bear, I suppose. In itself it doesn't mean much, but it keeps coming back to me. Trebonius, Caesar's legate, brought down the army from Northern Gaul. They came along the road one morning, gray figures silently materializing out of the mist and snow. Their standards floated over them, the eagles soared.

Rank after rank of veterans paraded past, their faces set and grim, their eyes hard. Officers rode up and down the line on horses furred with winter coats, the steam of breath hung over all of them.

They looked invincible; they looked as hard as bronze. All the time they marched I watched them, sitting beside Trebonius on my best thoroughbred. It took hours. Then they were gone, dissolved into the grayness of the day, leaving behind the mutter of marching feet on an empty road, the patches of puddles reflecting the overcast sky. Gods, I thought, I'm glad I was born a Roman, to see this day.

Cato can say what he likes, there is something about power that is as beautiful as a naked sword. Men are right to love it. Well, perhaps not. I don't think I know any more. I thought so then. And even now I cannot deny that it is beautiful. Leave it at that.

XX

In the spring Caesar came north and accepted the surrender of Intemilium, And mine as well, I nearly wrote, for I was glad to see him, and very ready to go on. I was bored with my tiny conquest, and around Caesar, you had to admit, there was always excitement . . .

He did not disappoint me. We marched west to Massilia, where we besieged that great city and blockaded its harbor, but the Massiliotes resisted more strongly than we expected and we could not stay long. The army in Spain was in trouble; it was necessary to get to it quickly.

So Caesar left behind a siege force of three legions, and twelve war-ships he had built farther up the Rhone; the legions he put under Trebonius' command, and the fleet under a very experienced and successful admiral.

It was exhausting, a life full of movement and event, colored with purple and scarlet, with blood and bronze and leather, with the deep browns of the wooden siege towers and catapults, the creak of ropes, the thud of stones, white plumes and mudstains, voices, tramping feet, trumpets, screams. The blue sky of spring arched over us, the sea sparkled like hammered metal.

Success in Italy had changed the people around Caesar. Once a handful of us had taken every town in Italy, now dozens, hundreds, of men hung around Caesar's tent, getting in the way and taking up everybody's time. It was like the atrium of a consul, some mornings. And what people! I saw what Cicero meant now. I've seen more respectable looking men playing dice in the back room of a public bath and hiding the evidence when the aedile walks in. Bankrupts and notorious profligates, drunks and incompetents—all the men who had gone through their family's money and now had to live on their wits, such as they were, had flocked to Caesar's banner like a convocation of sparrows, to quarrel over the pickings and hinder the ones who were doing the work.

Caesar, too, had changed. His face was bitter and angry, and he swore under his breath. He spoke often of the Senate, and I thought he felt that they had robbed him by leaving Italy, deprived him of victory he was still sure he would win. In any case, he had lost the exaltation that had animated him after the Rubicon, and though he still flashed and glittered around the camp he was more often lit with sparks of anger than of joy.

There was one consolation: for a short time I had Curio's company again. He was his usual laughing self, telling me all the news from home, but a shadow hid in his eyes and his drawl sounded hollow in his throat.

"Is something the matter?" I asked him one night when we had dined in Caesar's tent.

"It's Cicero. I'm worried about him. I fear that he m-may—"

"What is it? Is he ill?"

He shook his head, and though I asked him again he would say nothing more. The next day he pretended he had been too drunk to remember the conversation.

It was wonderful to see him again, but he left much too soon with a force to secure our food supplies in Sicily. He sent back dispatches and a letter or two for me.

DOCUMENT APPENDED

CURIO TO CAELIUS, GREETINGS

. . . my dear, they saw us coming and just fell down on their faces. Well, not literally after the first few days, but you know what I mean. Cato, who had been in charge of the province before, announced that he could not ask Romans to fight Romans, and abandoned the place to us without a single blow. I was quite *pleased*, you can imagine. I've written to tell Caesar how much grain I can send, and all that dreary stuff, but the *main* thing is, it's really *fun* being a conqueror, and so popular, because I didn't kill anyone. The Sicilians can't do enough for me. Gifts pour in—money,

jewelry, works of art, slaves, anything they imagine I might want. And really my dear, their taste is exquisite. Anyway the whole thing is an absolute *shriek* . . .

I had a few laughs myself at this picture of Curio as a conqueror, but of course, it was an exaggeration. Caesar must have been pleased with what his money bought for he sent Curio a more difficult assignment: he was to take two legions to North Africa and prevent a local king named Juba from going over to Pompey. This was likely, since he hated both the Curios and Caesar. I thought myself that Curio was just the right man to send: under his silly manner he was all brilliance and dedication.

I got drunk with a couple of the more tolerable of my fellow officers that night to celebrate on Curio's behalf, but I did not have much time to think of him. By the time I received his letter we were already on the road to Spain.

We camped that night among the high bare passes of the Pyrenees in a long valley, the far end of which was closed by a waterfall. The air was clear, with that peculiar soft distinctness of Southern Gaul that polishes every leaf and blade with light and makes the mountain peaks seem so close. We were nine hundred or so, an escort of cavalry to protect Caesar, for the legions had been sent ahead.

The valley was full of the quiet bustle of dawn when I heard Caesar come flying out of his tent, shouting my name. "Did you have anything to do with this?" He was so angry he could hardly say, "Good morning."

"With what, general?"

He had a packet of letters in his hands, which he thrust at me. One was from Cicero, polite and neutral, but the other was from Antony. He wrote that Cicero was planning to leave Italy and go over to Pompey in Greece.

"What do you know about this?" he demanded.

"Nothing, nothing at all."

"You talked to him before you came to me at Ariminum."

"Yes. And he sent messages for you saying how much he hoped for peace, and how he'd always respected you—"

"And did he tell you that he was planning to do this to me? Stab me in the back?"

"No, of course not. He said he was going to his country house and was going to stay neutral. He wouldn't go to Rome, but he wouldn't try to go to Pompey either. It was the best I could do. I tried to get him to come with me—"

"No, he wouldn't do that," he said with great bitterness. The long light of morning filtered through the cooking fires. It touched the bones of his skull; his nostrils, flared in anger, the muscles bunched over his jaw.

"Surely it can't matter so much? Cicero was never a powerful man, really—not like Pompey or some of the others. How many soldiers could he raise? It can't be a significant number, not compared with what Pompey has out there. Why, Pompey has six legions here alone." This was the word we had from Fabius, who was just then confronting those legions in the south. In the end, I might as well say, it turned out that there were actually seven, though only five were harassing Fabius so badly. The other two were in the west.

Caesar was staring at me as if I were beneath contempt. "It's not that he has men, or that he doesn't. It's that it makes me look bad."

He always cared about things like that. He had warned Catullus to stop writing satirical poems against him.

"A man like Cicero, eloquent, impressive, can sway a lot of people," he was saying. "And if he deserts me for Pompey his example will cost me . . ."

"He's been Pompey's friend all his life."

He looked at me in icy rage. "He implied he was mine, too."

"I think he tried to be."

Very carefully he said, "I've written to Antony. I've told him to make sure that no one leaves Italy without my permission. Now I want you to write to him—to your *friend*. To Cicero. Make it absolutely clear to him. Do you understand?"

I felt a jolt in my chest. "Make what clear, exactly?" In the high air I was suddenly very cold.

"I'll have someone get rid of him if he keeps this up," Caesar said.

DOCUMENTS APPENDED

ANTONY, TRIBUNE OF THE PLEBEIANS AND
PROPRAETOR,
TO CICERO, GENERAL
GREETINGS

If I did not care for you, and more than you think, I
would not have paid attention to the rumors which are being spread about you, especially since I thought they were
false. That you are going overseas I cannot bring myself to
believe, all the more since you have a family. So I want you
to be convinced that I hold no one dearer than you except
Caesar, and I believe Caesar puts Cicero among his greatest
friends. Therefore Cicero, my friend, I beg you not to trust
the honor of a man who may give you a gift but injures you
first, and on the other hand, not to run away from one who
though he cannot feel affection for you—I cannot conceal
that fact from you—still wishes for you to be safe, and emi-
nent, as always.

I have applied myself to the task of sending you this
letter so that you will know what a concern your life and
your reputation are to me.

CAESAR, GENERAL, SENDS GREETING TO CICERO,
GENERAL

Although I believe that you will do nothing blindly or
recklessly, nevertheless I have been so upset by the talk that
I judge it best to write to you and for the sake of our friendship ask you not to leave Italy now that everything is leaning towards me, when you did not go when everything
opposed me. Certainly you will do a grave injury to our
friendship. People will think I have done something you
condemn, which is the worst thing you can do to me. I beg
you not to do this. As a final thought: what befits a good
man, and a good citizen, more than to stay out of civil con-
flicts? Quite a few men we know would have if they could
but had to participate because they were in danger, but you

may look everywhere in my life and find nothing but evidence of my friendship. I think you will find it is more honorable to stay away from the dispute. April 16, on the march.

I wrote, too:

CAELIUS TO CICERO, GREETINGS

Hideously shocked by your letter, which showed that you had some desperate plan without saying explicitly what it was—though you reveal enough of what sort of thing you are contemplating—I am writing this letter at *once*. For the sake of your future and your children Cicero, I pray, I beg you: decide nothing to endanger your safety or your health. Yes, gods and men and our friendship all will testify that I told you this before, and it was not a hasty suggestion. After I met Caesar and learned what his feelings are likely to be after he wins, I gave you *certainties*. If you suppose that Caesar's policy will be the same as before and he will make peace and let his adversaries go, you are mistaken: to me he has said nothing that is not bloody, cruel and violent. He left Rome very angry with the Senate. By Hercules, there will be no room for an appeal to his mercy.

As I once told you—in peacetime it is possible to think about which side is right, but in civil war there is only one question: who is going to win. I do not think there can be any doubt about that now.

Finally, think of this. Any offense delay could give you have already given. To offend a *victorious* Caesar, when you did nothing to harm him when our fortunes were in doubt, and to join in flight those whom you refused to follow when they stood up to him, is the depths of stupidity.

If I cannot convince you completely, at least wait for word to get back to you from Spain—which I assure you will be ours as soon as Caesar gets close enough. What your friends hope for once they have lost Spain I do not know, and what you are planning by joining such a hopeless crew I cannot discover.

Again and again, Cicero, think, before you bring *total*

ruin on you and your family. Do not, knowingly and with eyes open, put yourself in a position from which you *cannot* escape . . . April 16, on the march with Caesar.

MARCUS TULLIUS CICERO, GENERAL, SENDS GREETINGS
TO MARCUS CAELIUS RUFUS, CURULE AEDILE

Great sorrow would have taken hold of me when I read your letter, if thought had not pushed away anything worrying, and permanent despair had not hardened my mind to new pain. . . . I am surprised that you—who ought to know me inside out—could have been led to think me either so reckless that I would abandon a cause raised up by fortune for one that she has cast down and is nearly prostrate, or so unstable as to spill out the accumulated good will of a man at the height of his power. That would be to fail myself and my principles, and to intervene in what I had always and from the beginning avoided—a civil war.

What, therefore, is my "desperate plan"? I have never even *thought* of leaving the country without the approval of your friends. But you know my small country estates, I will live on them and not be troublesome to my friends. But because I am more comfortable at the seashore, a number of people are moved to the suspicion that I intend to get on a ship—well, perhaps I would want to, after all, if I could sail toward peace. But to war who would ever want to sail?

Nor did they terrify me, those ideas that you put forward most loyally and lovingly, to inspire me with fear. I am glad my family is a concern to you. If there is to be anything left at all of the Republic I will leave to them an ample legacy in the memory of my name. If there is to be nothing at all, their fate will not be different from their fellow citizens. But perhaps I am raving, and everything will come to a better conclusion than I see now . . . May 3, from my villa at Cumae.

This last reached me among the folds of land south of the mountains. We were following a rushing river down towards

Fabius' camp. It was a few days' march way through a bare and rather hilly country just coming into the first green of early summer. There were crops in the fields but they were far from ready to harvest, and to my eyes looked sparse and stunted. It was not like the richness of Italy. I don't know the reason—there was plenty of water: streams filled with melting snow from the Pyrenees cut the rolling plain, making crossing sometimes difficult. The people in the tiny settlements watched us with hostile eyes. Well, they were mostly from tribes friendly to Pompey, I think.

In the circumstances, this letter from Cicero reassured me, and I rode through this sullen country watching Caesar's scarlet and bronze back in high enough spirits. I was looking forward to action. I suppose I did not trouble to read the letter very carefully; If I had, perhaps I would have seen—guessed, really—how false it was. On the day that he wrote that letter to me, Cicero wrote another to his closest friend. It came into my hands later, but I will attach it in the usual way.

DOCUMENT APPENDED

I pondered over the matter of Caelius' letter. It is possible that it is a mere ruse, and that Caesar dictated it, so I wrote back to him doing away with all reason for suspicion.

Antony goes around in public with an actress in an open litter, as if she was his wife. His friends—male and female—go with him, seven other litters' worth. What a spectacle! See what a disgraceful death we are dying here, and doubt if you can whether when Caesar returns, *either victor or vanquished*, he will perpetrate a massacre.

What am I to do? I would rather be conquered with Pompey than conquer with Caesar—but Pompey as he used to be, not Pompey as he is now, who runs away before he knows from whom he is running, or where to, who betrays us and abandons his country. Well, if I wanted to be conquered, I am. I am weighed down with sorrow. The sun itself seems to have fallen out of the universe.

Yet I cannot stay. Everywhere I am watched. I must sneak away on some cargo ship. *I must not allow it to appear that I let myself be hindered.* Sometimes I think it would be pref-

**erable if I received some damage, however bitter, from Cae-
sar's party, so that people can see how I am hated by the
tyrant . . .**

Though I had no idea of it at the time, the day I received
Cicero's last letter to me—the one designed to "do away with
all reason for suspicion"—Cicero had already set sail from
Italy to join his old friend Pompey in the east.

I didn't like to think about Cicero just then. There was a
reason. I believed Caesar's threats. Indeed, he repeated them,
then and on several occasions later. Once he even called a
muster of his soldiers in front of his tent to address us on
the subject of what he would do when he got back to Rome.

That was when we were already encamped with Fabius'
legions near the town of Ilerda. Two of Pompey's generals,
Afranius and Petreius, with their five legions, occupied the
high ground in front of us. We could see them, just as they
could see us: the palisaded rectangle of the camp, the long
rows of tents laid out in perfect order with the standards of
each cohort at the head of its square.

Ilerda is on a point where one of those swift Spanish
streams joins a main river; where they come together they
make a noise like cymbals, and the wind blows all the time.
It is a terrible country, like no other I have ever seen.
Scorched, bare, bitter, it looks as if the rage of a god has
passed over it. Furious little rivers slice through stone the
color of blood or ashes, hills pile up, steeper and more broken as you go. Far away in the south, purple mountains brood
over the desolation.

A horrible place—I wouldn't like to be lost out there, I
thought. We were drawn up in our ranks to listen to Caesar.
The wind blew, the standards fluttered, the trumpets blared.
Caesar addressed us that day about a number of things. He
began with what we could expect of Afranius and Petreius—
two very experienced generals, whom he did not underesti-
mate, though he was confident of victory. From there he went
on to what he would do when we won.

He made me shudder when he talked about Rome. There
would be blood in the streets, trials, executions, confiscations.

"This is war," he cried, his voice carrying over the thunder of the river and the shriek of the wind. "And whatever is needed to win it I will do." The rabble he was calling his legates cheered.

I looked about again to the camp of the enemy and beyond that to the shattered mountains in the south. Tears of anger stung my eyes. Cicero, I thought, and for a moment I saw the Forum just in the evening when the lamps are being lit.

Afterwards in my tent I thought that Pompey and his friends would be no better if they won—indeed, they might even be worse. No one had ever claimed that they had any desire to abolish debts, or help the poor. Well, if they got their hands on me—Appius and Cato and that crowd—it didn't bear thinking of. My father and mother on the streets, our goods sold up, me exiled on some trumped up charge— at best. My finances alone would make a feast for them, they'd fall on me like wasps at a honey jar. For a moment I envied Publius Crassus and Catullus. At least they were out of it. Their choices had been made, it had all worked out for them one way or another. They were safe.

For some days we sat opposite the army of Afranius and Petreius, they on their hill commanding the one permanent bridge over the river, we on a rise a little to the west, farther from the water. Caesar was waiting for a column from Gaul, something like six thousand cavalry and native auxiliaries— archers and slingers mainly, plus a large number of Roman citizens from the towns in Gaul.

Our army was so large already that our animals had eaten all the grass on our side of the river, and the people had consumed the available grain. Our foragers had to cross the river by two wooden bridges upstream that Fabius had constructed while he was waiting for us. It was a long way to go, but we needed the food we could get on the other side.

Then one night of thunder and rain, we awoke to hear a tremendous noise as if the heavens were crashing to the earth around us. "Gods, what is that?" I cried, flinging myself out of my tent only to find the entire camp milling in the streets shouting the same question.

It was the river. Somewhere upstream the storm had fallen

with even more violence; snow from the mountains, added to tons of rainwater, had swollen the river. Now it came down like an army, foaming in its narrow channel. I saw the corpse of an ox float by, bobbing like a toy. Boulders tossed in the rushing water, the planks and piles of Fabius' bridges swirled by on the dirty water like twigs. We stood watching, open-mouthed. We were so awed by the sight I don't think we understood what it meant for some time.

The river continued high and the weather bad. We tried to repair the bridges, but it was no use; the water swept everything away. We lost two men, crushed between a floating log and a support they were trying to lower into place. Two more were yanked abruptly under the surface and never reappeared. Worse, we made no progress.

Afranius and Petreius crossed the river freely by their stone bridge; their cohorts harassed our bridge-building efforts. Lined up on the opposite bank, they rained javelins and stones onto us. We lost several men by this form of attack because we couldn't send men across to chase them away. Presently we got word that Afranius and Petreius were attacking the column we had been waiting for from Gaul. The column had managed to retreat to safety, thanks to their cavalry, but two hundred men were killed, along with some horses and slaves. It was plain that they would not be able to come to us until we could send them an escort.

Perhaps that was just as well, for we had not enough food in our camp even for ourselves. A measure of grain that usually sold for four sesterces now went for two hundred; even so my servants often came back from the market outside the ramparts empty-handed. Ordinary soldiers began to starve: two hundred sesterces is nearly three months' pay.

We slaughtered a number of draft oxen—they ate more than we could afford—and some villages where the tribesmen were friendly to us sent some cattle, but they were not enough. Many of the men, weakened by hunger to begin with, suffered cramps of the belly and a debilitating flux from the unaccustomed diet of meat. At muster every morning the gaps in the line were longer and more noticeable until the few of us who were left stood up virtually alone.

There was not much work to do. I lay on my bed by the

hour, gazing at the leather roof overhead. I cannot remember now what, if anything, I thought about. I let the time pass over me, floating with it as if on a stream. I did not feel hungry any more. I didn't feel much of anything at all.

My servants were concerned and tried to rouse me to activity, but I waved them away. My valet had a hollow look; I remember I thought that if I tapped him he would echo. His hair had fallen out, and his flesh had sunk on his bones. Then one day I caught sight of myself reflected in the bronze shine of my helmet. I looked hollow, too.

One afternoon Caesar summoned me to his tent. We had not seen much of him for a day or two—there was a rumor that he was sick. He had a recurring illness, contracted when he hid in the marsh country from Sulla's men when he was young. He had once or twice fallen to the ground and threshed his arms and legs in a frightening way, but he had been better soon after. He never referred to those incidents, and no one liked to bring them up. In Rome an attack of this illness would have cancelled an election, so he did not like people to know.

If he had been enduring such an episode now, it was not apparent. He was reclining on one elbow on a couch as if he were going to dine. For a moment my stomach contracted and my head swam with hope. But the table in front of him was spread with notes and itineraries, lists and books instead of food. When I looked closer I saw that he, too, had the hollow look, and the arm he reached out to indicate the couch in front of him was thinner than usual. I should have known that he would not eat better than the rest of us.

"Well, Caelius. Welcome to the gates. Take a seat." His grin shone as brightly as ever, but the skin stretched so tightly over the cheekbones, the feverish eyes had sunk so deep he looked like a skeleton.

"The gates?"

"Of Hades, of course. That's where we stand, wouldn't you say? It won't be long before they open for us. We can't get across the river and there is nothing left to eat here."

"Then are we ... finished, do you think?" My mouth went dry.

"Do you care?"

"I'm sorry. I . . . I don't think I understand."

He flicked me with his death's-head smile. "Are you afraid to die, Caelius?"

"I don't know," I said after a while. "Are you?"

His brilliant eyes looked through the gates to another country beyond. "I think it's the end of struggle. The end of pain."

"A good thing, then."

He studied that distant landscape. "No. Not good. Not bad. Just the end."

I don't believe him; indeed the more I think about it the less I do. I have known many men who feared death and one or two who sought it, but I don't think I ever met another who didn't care at all.

"I'll have good company there, anyway," he said, coming back. "Here, have a little wine—only a little. I find I get drunk very quickly these days. The doctor tells me it's an effect of starvation." He leaned across and poured me a lot of hot water and a few drops of wine as scarlet as blood. As he handed me the cup his fingers rested for a moment on mine.

"Good company? What company is that?" I was looking into his eyes. I saw them light up as if someone had moved a lamp near a window in the dusk. Nervously I looked away. "You mean the army, don't you?" I was gabbling, not sure why I was so uncomfortable. "Well, I can certainly understand that. You've been through so much with this army. Over the Alps, and through Gaul. Across the Rhine. Even to Britain. Tell me, is it true about the British that—?"

He was no longer listening. His eyes had gone to the papers on his table. He was staring at them with peculiar intensity, like a ferret waiting to pounce. He lifted one, pushed aside another. "Britain," he muttered. I thought he had forgotten me, but presently he said, "Caelius, take a detail and get me some twigs and branches. You'll need an escort." He spoke impersonally. I might have been anyone now.

"Twigs and branches?" I wondered if he thought we were going to eat them.

"Twigs. About like this." He measured a circle with his thumb and forefinger. "And make them as long as you can, and flexible. Willow or something. Oh, and for the escort:

take a lot—at least two hundred men. And cavalry. This is important."

I got to my feet slowly, so as not to black out. "What is this for?"

"We want to cross a river, don't we? Well, We're going to build some boats."

"Out of twigs?"

He laughed. "More or less. When I was in Britain I saw them making quite adequate vessels out of thin strips of wood with hides stretched over them. I don't see why it wouldn't work here. Well, enough of this. We have a lot of work to do." He was already striding toward the tent-flap, calling for Fabius, every line of his hard, thin body alive with energy and purpose.

We built the British boats, as Caesar had ordered, working behind the camp, out of sight of the enemy. Then we lashed each one across a pair of wagons and hauled them twenty miles upstream to a suitable place. Caesar sent men across in them bit by bit, until he had fortified a hill opposite us. That would prevent Afranius and Petreius from harassing us. Free to work now, the engineers threw up a temporary bridge; in quick order a legion crossed, and very shortly the Gallic column with its supplies and travellers from Rome came filing down the peninsula to us, still in the main camp in Ilerda.

Sons of knights and senators arrived with them—travelling out to serve as adjuncts as if this were an ordinary war. I spent a couple of evenings in my tent with my acquaintances among them catching up on the news from home. They brought letters—the ones I have already appended to this report. What had happened to Cicero was still unknown; they believed him to be at his country house.

We also had news of the war. Caesar's admiral in Massilia had captured the Massiliote fleet. The town was far from surrender, but this was, all the same, an important victory, and the word was obviously getting around. The local tribes began to come over to us. All day their envoys filled the camp, dressed in their outlandish clothes and chattering in their

269

gaudy dialects. They left behind their young sons as hostages; their gifts of cattle lowed all day from outside the ramparts.

All this was not lost on Afranius and Petreius. Now that our cavalry could cross the river they were having trouble getting their own supplies, and I suppose it didn't take a military genius to see that their position was only going to get worse. Caesar was digging trenches to carry away some of the still violent flow of the river. Very soon we would have a ford and would not have to depend on that one bridge upstream. Both banks of the river would be ours then.

We began to notice preparations for departure in the enemy camp on the hill. Then one afternoon we saw them muster. "Are they going to attack?" A military tribune asked me as we peered through the hot summer shimmer, trying to make out what they were doing.

They were not. We heard a trumpet call, the ranks turned a quarter of a circle to form a column, and they began to march.

"How many?" I shouted.

"Two legions." It was Caesar coming up to study the channel we were digging. But the water was still too high. He set his lips with displeasure and turned to go back to his tent. He did not waste another glance on his departing enemy.

"He's beaten this time," the military tribune said. "No one could finish that ford in time. Well, it's no disgrace to be beaten by nature—at least he'll be able to say that Pompey never conquered him. You'll see. He'll ask for terms in the morning."

The next morning the rest of Afranius and Petreius' army marched across the stone bridge, leaving behind two cohorts to guard their camp. Caesar called a conference in his tent.

"The scouts have reported the construction of a bridge and some ships about thirty miles downstream. Obviously our friends across the way plan to take the war farther south, where they have allies among the local tribes." He was worried. "The thing is, can we prevent them?"

The chief engineer stepped forward. "Well, the river is still very high. The cavalry could cross it now even with the ford

270

not quite complete, but the infantry . . . I just don't know, general. The current is very swift and the water is nearly over a man's shoulders. I don't see how we can."

"Can we use the bridge upstream?"

Fabius stepped forward. "General, think of the terrain south of here. It's some of the roughest country we've ever seen—broken land rising to mountains. It's clear that whoever can get to those mountains can command the whole theater. If we have to go forty miles out of our way over the bridge—"

I never saw Caesar waste time disputing a fact. "Come outside. I want to look at that ford."

As soon as I saw it, I knew it was hopeless. The river rushed between its rocky banks with its force almost undiminished. Black as Lethe, and as cold, it hurled itself in a frenzy downstream, smashing against its walls.

Caesar contemplated it for some time, his eyes growing darker like a sky clouding over. He looked away to the south; I could see him studying the line of mountains with its one great visible peak. Then his eyes returned to watch the last legion of Afranius and Petreius' army as it tramped across the bridge. His mouth tightened, but he said nothing.

As usual when he went out in the camp he had attracted a crowd of soldiers. Now they began to mutter and rumble, a sound like the river. Caesar ignored them and went back into his tent. As soon as he had gone the men formed themselves into clumps and clusters and began to talk. I could see their gestures of anger and indignation, I could see the bitterness in their weathered faces. I was bitter myself. It seemed a long way to come to be beaten.

I was trying to make a will when the delegation came to me an hour later. They shuffled into my tent uneasily, grizzled veterans—mostly centurions—with the marks of many years of campaigning on their faces, and the scars of their bravery on their muscular arms. "Legate," their spokesman said, "we have come from the men. They want to cross the river. They're ready. They want a fight, legate, and a quick war. Will you go to the general for us and tell him so?"

How could I refuse, seeing who they were? I could not

even tell them that it would make no difference. We were beaten, and we had to face it.

When I got to Caesar's tent, it was to find a whole congregation of such heroes, and my fellow legates representing more, all charged with the same message. In the middle, Caesar listened, his tall, golden form lit with happiness like a candle.

So we crossed. The weaker of the men, and those who would admit to being afraid, stayed behind to guard the camp—an honorable job in a hostile country. The rest of us forded that river out of Hell.

The drivers on their pack horses posted themselves above and below the crossing, the one line to break the force of the water with their bodies, the other to catch anyone who was swept down to them. Some were. The water was so cold you lost all sensation as soon as you stepped into it, and the force of the current so swift it tended to knock you off your feet. But the horsemen were courageous and alert, the men helped one another, and in the end we crossed without losing even one soldier. On the far bank we formed up and immediately marched south; within an hour we had caught up with the enemy. I cannot imagine anything in their lives ever amazed Afranius and Petreius as much.

We pursued them across that awful country, and though they tried to elude us—even, shamefully, attempting to escape by night without the trumpet calls by which a Roman army signals its departure—we were the first to the mountain passes. We had to clamber up the rocks to get to them, one man hauling up his neighbor until we were all at the top. Then we had to do the same, to lower ourselves down to the other side. But it was done at last. Afranius and Petreius were forced to camp in a very disadvantageous position on a hill, while we occupied the base of the great peak we had seen from Ilerda.

Late in the afternoon four cohorts of light-armed infantry detached themselves from the main body of Afranius and Petreius' army and marched away toward the knee of the mountain. Caesar, informed of this, came running, and

waved a squadron of cavalry after them. He shouted something and the plume of the squadron leader's helmet dipped;
he raised his arm in a quick Gallic salute. Then he wheeled
his horse and rode away.

I found myself pressed against the temporary rampart beside Caesar. The whole army ranged itself along the walls to
watch. Across the way, on the low hill, Pompey's troops had
done the same.

The four cohorts marched quickly in good order, looking
very smart. Their standards rose above them, straight and
proud, their ranks were even, their equipment shone. The
cavalry, darting after them had that improvised air that Gallic
horsemen have, especially when they're travelling fast, and
the noise of their hoofbeats came rolling over the plain to us
with a perceptible delay.

Very soon they had surrounded the Afranians, who
formed themselves into a square and unslung their weapons.
They carried the small shield and the thin javelin that throws
well, but they could not hold out against the riders who now
circled them in a dizzying flow. Round and round the cavalry
swept, tightening the noose as the javelins were spent. One
or two horsemen fell, horses reared up screaming against
the bitter red rocks with spears in their sides, but the damage
to the square was much worse. By twos, by handfuls, by dozens, the light-armed infantry were dying. Their bodies fell
forward, breaking the lines of their square; behind them
more men, exposed, died, too.

Up on the walls of the Pompeian camp there were groans
and shouts, as if the cavalry's spears had pierced them, too.
Our own men cried aloud in sympathy. "Call back the cavalry," someone begged, but Caesar stood like a stone. I do
not think he even heard.

It was impossible to watch. There were two thousand men
who marched out of Afranius and Petreius' camp. Of them
all, not one survived. Blood had splashed on the chests of
the horses, and their riders were red to the arms. The thick,
metallic smell of it choked the dust of that burnt and broken
ground. I had tears on my cheeks; many others did, too. In
the Pompeian camp there were sobs and shouts, and rising
above them the piercing wail of the camp-followers.

Through it all Caesar stood beside me. He did not move, nor did he say a word. Only when the grim work was done did he speak. Turning to me he said, "The circumstances are now favorable for dealing with this business successfully." And to my horror, he smiled.

Well, you will say, it's not much. It was war, and what did I expect? I was no innocent. I had even seen men die. But not two thousand, given no chance to surrender, cut down like a field of wheat in that barren place, before their comrade's eyes, and all so that Caesar could say, "The circumstances are now favorable for dealing with this business successfully." The coldness of it appalled me, the ruthless, unRoman savagery. I watched Caesar stroll away as if I had never seen him before. And indeed, perhaps I never had.

They weren't Romans, of course. Those four cohorts had been Spanish auxiliaries attached to the Pompeian army. Dear gods, what difference does that make? I saw their blood. It was as red as anybody else's.

Cato used to speak of Caesar's murders in Gaul. "He has conquered by the deaths of two million people. He has broken his word to them, attacked people protected by a truce, practiced hideous cruelties on them—" His voice would rise to a high-pitched irritating whine, like a wasp on a summer day. Like a wasp I used to brush it aside.

Now I could not. Now I remembered a town in Gaul called Uxellodunum. It had resisted Caesar. Why not? They were only defending their homes. Caesar wished to make an example of them. He thought if he simply slaughtered them the rest of Gaul would not be sufficiently impressed. So instead he lined them up, every male left alive—and it was a large town—at the end of the siege. And he cut off their hands, turning them loose to wander around the countryside, surviving as best they could—if they wanted to. I imagine it is difficult to kill yourself, if you have no hands.

Cato said that Caesar ought to be turned over to the people of Gaul to be punished as they saw fit for these crimes. If not, he shrilled, our own gods would turn away from us in disgust. Well, perhaps they have. That night in my tent in Spain, it was disgust I felt, though I don't claim the moral discernment of a god. I just kept seeing those men, thrust through. Their blood shot up in fountains before my eyes, the smell of it clung to my clothes. Through it all Caesar kept saying, "The circumstances are now favorable . . ." and flicking his smile at me. I kept my servant running for more wine, but the only result was to make me send him for the basin, too. I heaved over it for hours, it seemed, but I could not purge myself of what I had seen. It was a long time before I slept.

The next day a strange heaviness hung over the camp. In the brutal heat the Spanish women collected the bodies from the plain; the corpses had already begun to smell and the stench hung over us, punctuated by the cries of carrion birds disturbed at their feeding.

Up on the hill Afranius and Petreius' army huddled raggedly around their insignia, without order or discipline, keeping terrified eyes on the cavalry, which pressed them unmercifully. Our men watched, rumbling unhappily.

Toward noon the grumbling resolved itself into anger, and the men ran for their officers. I had ten or twelve of these excited centurions and military tribunes in my tent before the noon meal was over. They were going to Caesar; they wanted me to come. "We'll tell him he has to set up a battle. If he doesn't let the men fight now, they won't when he wants them to."

"What about yesterday?" I demanded, sickened. "Does that mean nothing to you?"

Their eyes lighted up and their faces broke out into smiles. "Yesterday was just what we needed, legate. The Pompeians couldn't even go to help their friends. Look at them. They're softened up now. The war could be over today."

It was like listening to wolves howling in a forest. Gods, it was worse. They were lower than wolves—jackals perhaps, gloating over the corpses of an army. "Get out of my tent," I shouted, not caring if they were angry or thought I was feeble. When they were gone the air seemed cleaner, as if a breeze had rinsed it.

It turned out that several other officers refused to go to Caesar, too. It was never held against us; on the contrary, Caesar was grateful, because it had not been his intention to march against the Pompeians. He told the men so at a muster, pacing back and forth with his usual vigorous step, gesturing with his usual energy. And as always, the men watched as if they could not take their eyes away.

Once I had been like them, fascinated as a bird by those movements, but not that day. That day it was all hollow. I stood at attention, sweating in my leather breastplate, as Caesar told us that he felt only kindness toward his fellow citizens, and would not harm them at all if he could help it.

All around us that landscape of dun and blood looked on like the audience at a play. Caesar's pale hair flickered before it, his words echoed off the flat, uncomprehending hills. He looked like an actor to me now. His hypocrisy was evident, and behind the wide cheekbones and the white-toothed grin, the contours of a skeleton's head peeked out. His compassion for his fellow citizens, indeed. He knew what he was doing. "Why should I lose even one of you—you who have served me so faithfully? Why should I risk even that you might be wounded?"

"It's our job to fight," they shouted back.

He was as quick as ever. "Yes, and it's a generals' to win by strategy as much as by the swords of their troops." Besides, he added, had they asked themselves *why* the Pompeians had made such a desperate effort to break out? They were safe enough up there on their hillside. Well, the answer was simple. They had no water.

It did not content the men, but it did calm things down. As they dispersed, still muttering, Caesar came up to me. He put his hand on my arm and looked into my eyes. "Thank you for your support. You'll see, this is the best way. The troops forget that this is a *civil* war. We're going to have to live with the results. It'll be remembered in our favor that we were merciful when we had the chance."

"Yes, general." I spoke with my best military discipline and reserve, but he noticed nothing.

"Give the order to withdraw the camp a quarter of a mile

276

or so, will you, Marcus? We'll find a less intimidating position, let the other side think things over a little in peace."

"Yes, general."

He smiled again. "Good man. I knew I could count on you. I know who my friends are."

XXI

As soon as they saw us moving off Afranius and Petreius moved their camp, too. We built our new camp on a slope opposite them, as close as the land allowed, and constructed a trench and a rampart. Caesar had posted me to block every possible route south.

The next day our cavalry cut down the Pompeian's water carriers. We were so close we could hear the consternation when the news was brought to the opposite camp and the frantic blowing of trumpets and tramp of feet as they tried to determine how to deal with the threat. It was not long before their plan became clear. Stringing out their cavalry and auxiliaries to supplement the regular legions, they made a defensive wall of troops all the way down to the river. Then behind it they began to dig. Afranius and Petreius rode out to supervise the work.

"What on earth are they doing?" I demanded, ducking out of my tent to watch.

My tribune answered me. "Legate, they're trying to dig a channel to bring water to their camp."

"Oh, gods, they can't mean it." I didn't know whether to laugh at the absurdity of this plan or weep at its desperation.

"Look, legate. Up there." Across the way men were coming out of their camp, calling over the distance to us. At first there were only a few, then dozens, then half of the Pompeians' army came pouring down the hill, waving to their friends and relatives among us. Caesar had come out to watch; at his signal we opened the gate, and our own men went across the narrow valley to welcome their fellow citizens.

Everyone had friends in the opposite camp, even people like me, who didn't think we did. Some men from Interamnia found me in the press and insisted I go back with them to their tent. So, getting a ham and some jars of wine and as

278

much water as my servants could carry, I climbed up the main street of the Pompeians' camp, to what was rapidly becoming a party. On the way crowds of men stopped me. They recognized me for an officer by the way I wore my sword on my left side—they knew I never carried a shield. "Why did Caesar spare us yesterday?" they wanted to know.

"He doesn't want to harm his fellow citizens."

"But we're fighting him."

"He's noticed that."

The soldiers laughed, and one of the men from Interamnia, made bolder by his connection with me, asked. "Can we trust him, legate? Is he acting in good faith?"

"He's acting, all right," I said bitterly, but they were clamoring around me and I doubt they heard. "If we surrender will he punish us? Will he have us killed? Does he think we're traitors?"

I didn't know what to tell them. Rage and pain boiled up in me and I doubted I could speak at all. Fortunately, I didn't have to, for Fabius, Caesar's chief legate, was striding past in a lisping cloud of Spanish auxiliaries, who were clients of his family. "Caesar will welcome you," he cried. "He will treat you as your citizenship demands, with honor and courtesy. Isn't that so, Marcus Caelius?"

"I see very little point in the events of the last few days if he doesn't."

"That's right," Fabius said, taking this for agreement. "You can have confidence in Caesar." He bent his smooth dark head in a diplomat's bow and walked away.

My Interamnians murmured around me. "Oh, legate we made a mistake. We should have gone with Caesar from the beginning." I had to swear to intercede with Caesar on their behalf before they would cheer up enough to enjoy their feast.

About the seventh hour of the day, a delegation went to Caesar. We all came out of the tents to watch as they shimmered in the midday heat across the shallow valley. They were led by a friend of Afranius' young son, and they were wearing the white headbands of men who ask a favor.

Their leader called out when they were still some distance

from Caesar's camp. "General, we have come to surrender. We are sorry we ever opposed you and we'd like to make up for our mistake. If you allow we will bring our standards over to you at once, and send the senior centurions to make the arrangements."

Caesar rushed forward and embraced him around the shoulders. "Of course, my dear fellow, of course. You are all welcome. I couldn't be more pleased."

"But, Caesar . . . We . . . we do not wish anyone ever to say that we betrayed our generals, you see. Or that we came here contemplating any crime against them. Do you understand, general, how we feel about that? We cannot come unless you can give us assurances that no harm will come to them."

At that Afranius' son knelt down. "In the name of the most holy gods," he said, and his clear young voice carried like a flute across the valley, "spare my father, Caesar. He is a good man, and only doing his duty." It was plainly sincere, a pretty and touching scene, and Caesar played it for all it was worth. He lifted the boy to his feet and clasped him in his arms as if he were his own son.

At that the two camps went wild. Cheering broke out, everyone hugged everyone else, there were smiles and tears, and shouts of approval. "He's a great man," my friends from Interamnia assured me, hoarse from shouting.

We were making a considerable noise, of course, and it was not long before it attracted Afranius and Petreius. Afranius heard it first and came back to camp, not unduly worried that I could see. Someone must have warned him what was going on. His son came up to him, still in his suppliant's headdress. They spoke briefly and Afranius got down off his horse to embrace the boy. "He'll accept the surrender, then," my Interamnians whispered, relieved.

I opened my mouth to answer, but at that moment there was a tremendous clatter of horses' hooves and a roar of shouting down the way. Petreius and some of his household cavalry were charging down on us, spears lowered and swords flashing. "Gods," I cried, "they're going to resist. Caesarians, to me. To me."

There was no time to run. Beside me ten men had clustered, "We can make it. Stick together. If we separate, they'll hunt us down." We put our backs together and wrapped our cloaks around our arms for shields. I felt my sword jolt into my hand as step by step we fought our way backwards, between the tents and out into the open space. In front of us all was confusion. Men were running everywhere, horses neighed, other groups like ours fought the attacking cavalry. They seemed to have been joined by infantry, I don't know where from.

At the rampart we had to fight again, but there was someone there—one of the Interamnians, by Hercules. He let us out. I wish I knew his name: I would mention it if I could. He died for his kindness to us, brought down by an arrow from Petreius' cavalry, before we could get to him to help.

But he had saved us. We were out. Other men were running down the slope beside us. At the gate the sentries thumped us on the back, hugged us, wept. "Lucius. Where is Lucius?" someone was shouting, over and over. "Gaius Aricius? From Bonnonia? Has anyone seen him?" There were other names, other towns, but for many of them, no answer came. We were among the last groups to get out. Though we waited by the gate until darkness began to fall, not many more came through.

Caesar waited with us. Like ours, his eyes never left the camp across the way. Once, just before dusk, we heard orders and the tramp of marching feet, followed by a long cry, eerie and full of pain, as if the whole army up there was suffering. Caesar never flinched. "They're executing men over there," I heard him say to Fabius, who was standing with him.

"Ours or their own?" Fabius said, but Caesar only shrugged.

When it was fully dark we got our answer. It was a thick night, moonless and sweltering. The frogs were loud by the river; crickets sawed the silence. Just below me a voice said softly, "Let us in. Dear heaven, friends, let us in."

Some of our men, hidden by their countrymen or relatives in their tents had now sneaked through the Pompeians' ramparts, and under cover of the dark had made it across to us. They were only a few. Caesar questioned every one, but the others must have been captured or killed.

Petreius had mustered out the army and made every soldier swear an oath of allegiance. The first person he had compelled to do this was Afranius, the second, Afranius' son. Then he demanded that they surrender our men to him; those that were given up he executed in front of his army.

When Caesar heard this he ordered all the Afranians out of our camp. "They won't surrender now. Not with the new oath."

"And not with those punishments before their eyes," Fabius added.

Caesar lifted his shoulders indifferently.

A few of Afranius' military tribunes and senior centurions asked to stay with us. Caesar, embracing them, agreed, giving them the same rank in our army.

So we waited again. It didn't take long. Petreius and Afranius must have realized their position was deteriorating, and the food and water situation growing desperate, for they broke their camp and set out back toward Ilerda. Caesar immediately sent the cavalry after them, and followed with the legions. The Pompeians had to stop in a very unfavorable place—no water still, and not much natural defense.

"Let them alone," Caesar ordered. "There's no need for a fight. The ground will do it for us." So desperate did he think they were he expected them to try to get away during the night, and did not even let us put up our tents.

For two days we watched the Pompeians struggle with the difficulties of their situation. They built outworks and moved their camp a few thousand paces to a safer spot, but they were still without water. They sent out the whole army to drink, but could not afford foragers for food.

Day and night their transport oxen bellowed in thirsty misery, day and night men slipped from their camp and came to ours across the ditch we had dug to keep the Pompeians in. The torment of the cattle kept us awake, and we grew snappish and surly.

At last there was silence over the way. "They've killed their transport," Caesar said. "If they're going anywhere, they'll have to leave their equipment behind." There was neither triumph nor dismay in his voice; it was all business to him, and he strode around our camp with the same light, energetic step he had always used.

That night the Pompeian camp was quiet, but I did not sleep any better than the previous nights. There was a kind of tension in the air, as if a storm was beginning somewhere over the mountains. The silence raised the hair on my arms and sent my blood tingling. I ate no dinner, but pushed my plate away untouched. The heat seemed suffocating.

Just before midnight Caesar put his head inside my tent. "Still up? It won't be long now."

I offered him a drink. "Well, here's to the god who looks after us." He smiled as he poured out a little on the mosaic floor of my tent.

"Has a god been looking after us?"

"Oh, yes. Surely. This business is coming to a better conclusion that I hoped. You brought me luck, did you know that?"

"I did?"

"When you didn't come to my tent that day, with all the others, to ask me to attack the Pompeians. I knew I wasn't going to, but I never expected anyone else to see the situation as I did. They don't, usually; I don't know why that is."

It was because he was so much more brilliant than anyone else, that was why, but I wasn't going to tell him so. Nor was I going to admit that I hadn't seen any situation at all—I was just too angry over the slaughter of the Spanish auxiliaries to go with the others.

He did not notice. He was in a strange mood: relaxed, rather pleased with himself, but alert, as if he were on the watch for something. I had never seen him so willing to confide.

"Do you believe in luck?" I asked, wiping the sweat from my upper lip. His eyes followed the gesture.

"Oh, yes. I'm a soldier. I've seen too often now a small chance will make a battle go one way or another. Look, if you hadn't mentioned Britain to me, would I have thought of those twig and hide boats? Or thought of them in time? Who can say? If that isn't luck, I don't know what is."

He smiled again and reached across to clasp my hand. I felt the nervous strength in his long fingers, the heat of his palm. His eyes were on me, like a touch. "Caelius," he said, and his voice caught in his throat.

He was cool and silver in the shadowy lamplight of my tent; like water in the desert, he seemed to be surrounded by freshness. His eyes glowed with a greenish bloom, his hair lay along his elegant skull like precious metal. He had stood and watched while two thousand men died at his orders; he had said, "The situation is now favorable for dealing with this business successfully." He leaned toward me. "My luck is still with me," he growled in that same throaty tone, and he slid his hand along my arm.

"What's the matter?" he asked. "Your hand is cold."

He sprawled on the couch, as easy as a mountain lion sunning himself on a rock. He was watching me, and he was excited. I could see the unmistakable sign swelling under his tunic. He looked into my eyes. "I'm going to win, Caelius. Everything I want I will get." He leaned the rest of the way across and thrust his mouth down on mine.

"No," I cried, leaping backward as if a whip had touched me.

He was as unruffled as ever. "Why not? You want it, too."

"No. No, I don't. I don't care for that sort of thing . . ."

"Nonsense. You've been in love with me since we met." He slid his hand down my belly and grasped me by my erect and overheated penis. "You see?" he said, and kissed me again.

I don't know how I got away. Protesting, I backed out of his embrace, my face flaming, my eyes hot, like a child about to burst into tears. Clumsily I swore that I was loyal to him, that I admired him—I think I used the phrase "prodigious accomplishments"—and all the time I could feel the heat of his hand, on my arm, on my groin, as if he were still holding me.

He was surprised, but that was all the emotion he showed. He lay back on his couch, still faintly smiling, one eyebrow arched until it nearly touched his hair. His dark eyes with their odd, pale shine were fixed on me as I stumbled through my recitation. Presently he picked up a wine cup and sipped from it. It struck me that he was assessing me, like a consul judging a contestant at the games. I staggered on, trying to make clear what has never had any explanation, and growing angry as I did. My voice wobbled on, without me.

He put down the cup with a deliberate little click. "Well, Caelius, I see I've come at a bad moment. You seem to be in some confusion of mind."

"Yes, I think I must be. Please, don't . . . I mean . . ."

He laughed. "Don't trouble yourself." He nodded very slightly at my fading erection. "I always get what I want. If not now, later. Good night." He sauntered away into the night, still laughing. I think it was the most frightening sound I have ever heard.

I picked up the couch I must have at some point over-turned and sat down to think about my situation. It seemed to me about as bad as Afranius and Petreius'. Worse. I was hundreds of miles from Rome. I had with me five or six freedmen and servants. Perhaps a hundred men from my estates would be loyal to me and perhaps a hundred more from the region around Interamnia who were serving in the army would remain neutral or come over to me. If I tried to make a break for it, I had between me and Rome Caesar's army presently sitting before the intransigent walls of Massilia. Attempting to go around would take me through the territories of barbarous tribes, about whom I knew little. They, however, would know me. I am, after all, the man who retook Intemilium.

I sent for a couple of my servants; on some pretext I kept them busy in my tent. Then I sat and thought. If I could get through, I could go to Cicero, take refuge there as I had once long ago, on the morning of the Women's Festival. In one of Cicero's country houses I would have the protection of his household as well as my own. Say what you like about Cicero, he was far too Roman to give a friend up to murder, no matter what it cost him.

But then, Cicero had problems of his own. The most recent letters I had—I did not yet know that he had left Italy to go to Pompey—showed that he was contemplating some desperate measure of his own. I did not want to add to his danger by my presence; much less did I want his rashness to contribute to my own.

So Cicero was out. Our own estates in Interamnia could provide some protection, and perhaps a thousand men, some of whom I could hire. Not enough to confront a victorious Antony, in charge of Italy. And all this supposed I could get to Italy in the first place.

Of course I could go to Pompey, if I could find the means. But would he welcome me? I had enemies in that camp, too. People like Appius Claudius would poison his mind against me. And I had nothing to bring with me to make Pompey see that I was worth more than what Appius would say.

Besides, it was all depressingly clear that Pompey's cause was not doing very well. We—Caesar—had just defeated a huge army of Pompey's supporters, and would be free to carry the war into Greece as soon as Massilia surrendered. That could not take long now. Was it worth it to leave one place of danger to go to a worse? For if Pompey lost and his men surrendered, surely Caesar would hate me worse than before. No, Pompey was not the answer, haven of peace though he at that moment appeared.

Towards morning I remembered Curio. Away in Africa with his legions, he would certainly welcome me. He was Caesar's man, but the claims of old friendship are sacred. By Hercules, even Caesar, however angry he might be, *must* be, would understand why Curio would have to help me. Of course he would.

And no one could be angry with Curio for long. In my mind I saw the long face with the prominent teeth and the round eyes. Yes, Curio was the answer. I felt so sure of it, I drank enough wine to put myself to sleep and went to bed. I kept the servants in the tent though and I took the precaution of laying my unsheathed sword beside me on my couch.

In the morning Afranius and Petreius surrendered. They asked for a private conference, but Caesar insisted that it take place in front of the armies, so they were drawn up and allowed to watch from the ramparts of the two camps. The generals met in the middle, surrounded by their legates.

I went with Caesar and his escort: I had been ordered to do so. Fabius had given me the message at first light. Caesar did not appear to notice me, but once when his eye caught mine, he winked. I nearly choked.

Caesar discharged Afranius and Petreius' legions without penalty or punishment, saying that those who lived in Spain could go immediately, while those who lived in Gaul or Italy could march with us to the other side of Massilia, where they could go to their homes.

I thought I might slip away with the Spaniards, for there were some who were heading for the coast with Afranius and Petreius. A ship could be found to take me to Curio. But in the end I did not have the opportunity. Whether by chance or because he guessed what was in my mind, Caesar kept me busy with tasks where I was constantly under someone's eye—Fabius' or another legate's or his own. He did not, by the smallest flicker of an expression, show that anything had passed between us, and he treated me with the impersonal pleasantness he gave to everyone. Nor did he lessen my responsibilities or my rank. But I did not trust him, especially when he was so cool, and I waited for my chance to escape.

Did not trust him? Waited for my chance to escape? Dear gods, I was in a fever of rage and fear. I could not sleep, but paced in my stifling tent until my lungs rebelled, Then I paced outside, under a sky flaming with stars, my mind a turmoil. Escape? Dear gods, I would have killed him if I could.

More than once I found myself outside his tent, my hand on the hilt of my sword. Only the sentry's voice brought me back to myself. I stumbled and swore, I drank until I passed out, but nothing erased the images in my mind, the sensations on my skin. I saw his body stretched out on the couch. His erection was plain. I saw him reach across the table to me, felt his hand on my arm, heard him whisper, "Why not? You want it, too." The dark eyes looked into mine, the fine, long mouth came down, the hand descended . . . Gods, I would have killed him then and not cared if I died for it.

But I couldn't get near him. Once he accepted the surrender of Afranius and Petreius, I never saw him alone. It looked accidental; perhaps it was. He is not a god, he couldn't have known everything. It may be that he never suspected what I felt. All the way back to Massilia he rode in a group of legates and military tribunes who had come over to him with the surrender of the Pompeians. When we camped at night, these men were with him.

By that time I was feeling a little cooler. The turbulence of my emotions had calmed a little; I had a plan now. I had written to Curio. "Let us take a couple of legions and set up on our own in some corner of the world that no one knows about. In Africa, perhaps? We could live like kings. And no one would disturb us, with two legions. Anyway, it wouldn't be worth anyone's trouble to try.

"By Hercules, Curio, how great it would be. Forget politics, forget ambition. What good did they ever do us? Are we happier? Are we even better off? No, of course not. Let us go and live like philosophers in the peace and beauty of the countryside, and cultivate our minds. Doesn't it appeal to you? It does to me . . ." And so on. I meant it, though. I went over it in my mind, again and again as we rode, I dreamed of it at night. In those days, the thought of Curio was all that kept me sane.

BOOK SIX

XXII

It is late. The rooster has crowed again far away in the country, the herald of an unwanted day. A breeze has begun to blow; the shutter on the seaward side trembles against the wall. The sky is still in darkness, but one by one the stars are going out, slain under the advancing day.

It is time to think. The garrison will arrive this morning. There's no getting around that. Shall we fight? A delaying action? For of course it can be no more than that. I see no advantage in it. What I'll do is this. I'll send the hostages down with Philo, as if we were going to negotiate our surrender. In the meantime, I will slip down to the ship that is waiting, there on the sea, as calm and beautiful as a migrating swan. Truly it is the gift of a god.

While Philo is out on the road with the Spanish troops. I will be safely away, and trouble the world no more. Let the great do what they like with it: destroy it, improve it, loot it for their own benefit. I will not care. I will occupy myself with—with agriculture. Yes, that's it. Perhaps I'll culitvate the fine small olives I saw growing in the hills around Massilia. The fruit was tiny but the flavor winy and strong . . .

Perhaps I'll get married. I'll have children. Educate my sons. Do all the things I've never had time for. After all, I am thirty-four; it's a good age to settle down. I'll live the decent and time-honored life of a Roman country gentleman. Yes, indeed. Why not? Who has more right?

In the meantime, the breeze comes in at the window, the shutter knocks. On the night air floats the tang of the sea, the first hint of dew. I must finish this report. Well, there is still time.

**LAST REPORT OF MARCUS CAELIUS RUFUS
PRAETOR PERGRINUS OF ROME . . .**

For whom am I writing this? I do not even know.

. . . the thought of Curio was all that kept me sane. That was what I wrote. It makes me laugh to see it. Sane? I suppose I thought I was. My mind seemed to me as clear as cool water. Now, looking back on it, I see that I was never more mistaken in my life.

It was a good time for Caesar and his army. When we had been there only a short time, Massilia surrendered. Loyal ally and friend of Rome for hundreds of years, she suffered the fate of all who oppose Caesar: harsh terms and a bitter peace. Poor city. She gave up her treasure—which was vast, her arms, her territory, what was left of her fleet, her colonies along the coast and in the interior of the beautiful country she had controlled. Her walls were thrown down and her streets and squares laid open to Caesar, who rode through them, smiling faintly, to the tears and moans of the populace. The point, unintentional and coincidental as it was, was not lost on me.

Still Caesar did nothing to me. Sometimes I caught him watching me; he would flick his razor-sharp smile, and I wondered what he was remembering, what he thought. But he made no effort to talk to me alone, nor to be nearer to me in any way. I continued to receive assignments: was it by accident that none of them was very important or interesting, and that none gave me the opportunity to win distinction or advancement? Perhaps it even was.

I used to study him under my lids. He looked happy. Well, he had conquered Spain and the last hold-out in Gaul, his legate Curio had secured him a food supply and was working on pacifying North Africa, he was on his way home to an Italy that lay as open to him as poor Massilia. There did not seem to be anything that could hinder him now.

Then, within twenty-four hours, three things happened. The first affected me more than it did Caesar, though it made him very angry. Word had arrived in our camp that Cicero had slipped through the guard Antony had set, and gone to Pompey. Caesar said nothing when he heard, but his face went blank and stiff, like marble, and his eyes looked suddenly uninhabited. It's a good thing he's gone, I thought. Caesar would kill him now, if he got his hands on him. I felt a kick of anxiety under the ribs, then a flood of relief.

Later, when I thought about it, I was sad. For Rome. I couldn't imagine the city without Cicero. Indeed, though I have seen it, I still can't. The Forum must echo to his eloquence, the Curia witness his dignity, his courage, his honor. Up on the Palatine Hill his mansion must be thronged with all the people who wanted his help, for his kindness never failed, his generosity flowed without cease. Gods, something went out of Rome when Cicero left. What Caesar conquered was not the country he had set out to win.

That day also the Ninth Legion mutinied in a town called Placentia, just over the mountains on the peninsula of Italy. The soldiers were unhappy about back pay and bonuses. Caesar, taking the bulk of the army—which was going to Italy anyway—rapidly marched to the camp. In no time he had put down the mutiny and arrested the leaders. They hardly resisted. It was as if, seeing him, they no longer wanted to; like children, once they knew he would come to them their complaints disappeared.

But Caesar did not feel the same. He drew up the army with the Ninth in front, surrounded by the others, and announced that he would punish them in the traditional way. At that there were cries and sobs, and half the Ninth fell to its knees. The other legions, pleading, groaned as if they had been struck. Fabius went so white I thought he was going to faint, and a man behind me forgot his discipline and burst into speech.

"What does he mean, 'the traditional way'?" I asked.

"Decimation," the man said. He looked as green as an apple, and polished by a film of sweat. "Every tenth man in the legion will be killed."

"What if they weren't the ones involved?"

"Doesn't matter."

"But that's five hundred men." I felt sick myself.

The Ninth was on the ground now, begging and weeping, apologizing. They seemed to be trying to crawl under the dust.

"Citizens," Caesar reproved them. "This is unseemly. Take your punishment."

They wailed as if the word had hurt them. "Citizens?" they cried. "No. No. We are Caesar's soldiers." The began to recite the history of their service under him, like a lover trying to remind his mistress of happier days.

In the end he let them surrender one hundred and twenty leaders of the rebellion. Of these he executed twelve. The Ninth watched, stony-eyed, and went back to their tents in silence. It was impossible to know what they felt. Perhaps they were frightened by Caesar's harshness, though they themselves were hard-bitten men. More likely they thought they had been justly treated. It is possible even that they were grateful. I don't know. I watched the detail carry off the corpses of the twelve who had been so unlucky, and my stomach heaved.

The next day a messenger arrived in camp with dispatches from North Africa. Another victory, I thought.

But if so it was only for a god who did not favor us. Curio had miscalculated; his army had been trapped and heavily attacked. The odds were very bad. Curio had a chance to get away, but he had not taken it. "M-my dears, " he had cried, "I'll never be able to look Caesar in the face again," and he had plunged back into the fighting. A short time later he fell, pierced by an enemy javelin.

The rest of his army perished with him, except for a few men who clambered aboard the overloaded transport ships. The messenger said that the soldiers chose from among themselves who was to go—the fathers of large families— and they watched calmly as they sailed away.

Gods, poor Curio. Dead in the desert. It was for him the jackals howled, not for me.

I went back to my tent and pulled my toga over my head. For nine days I did not move. I mourned him as if he had been my brother; he was closer to me even than that. By day the sun shone on the leather roof, and the air around me glowed like honey. By night the lamplight picked out the objects that had travelled with me all that long distance from Rome and back. My eyes went over them and did not see.

Outside the tent I heard the sounds of the camp, the trumpet calls, the voices passing, the tramp of feet. Still I sat; my eyes were hot and dry, my chest tight. I could not cry. I felt sorrow, but my body was as tense as if anger were gripping me. I did not sleep.

Once Caesar called with five of his officers, a formal gesture of condolence. They ranged themselves on the chairs, very stiff and correct, and very sad, keeping me company with their silence. As they left, Caesar patted me on the shoulder, his fingers playing for a moment with the lobe of my ear. I managed not to leap to my feet and strike him dead.

I sat. And after a while I began to think.

Curio was gone. He was my last friend, my final hope. Now I was alone, and there was nowhere to go. Pompey was a lost cause; Caesar was so plainly going to win. The man who had done everything so superbly right in Spain couldn't be beaten. I had to face it—it was a simple fact. Curio had.

And if that was true it followed that I was going to have to accommodate myself to Caesar. No matter how I felt. And really, I thought, is that so terrible? Why was I in such a lather of rage? Because Caesar was attracted to me? A lot of men would have envied me that. "I always get what I want," Caesar had said. Perhaps he did. In any case it was clear that he intended to get me.

At that I got up and paced around the tent, in the process reminding myself of Curio again. My breath caught painfully in my chest, my eyes swelled and burned. Oh, gods, dead in the sand with the animals gnawing at his bones . . .

When the fit had passed, I thought of myself again. I had promises from Caesar. He would abolish debts, without which help I could not live; he would make me City Praetor and see to it that after my time in office I got a good command. On the other hand, if he were my enemy, my property would be seized, my parents dispossessed, my income shut off. In poverty I would have to struggle . . .

So, what did it matter what I felt? I could master my emotions, couldn't I? Caesar had, over and over: it was what gave him the power to conquer the world. Silvery and cool he had defied Sulla; he had not turned an immaculate blond hair when the crosses had gone up for his pirate friends; without a flicker he had condemned two thousand to die. Well, I thought, if he can, I can, too. I got to my feet and went to look for him, the man who controlled my fate. I believe I thought at that point that what I was doing was the most reasonable thing in the world.

The tent Caesar used was scraped and scarred with hard use. He was not like some generals, who travel with gardeners to train ivy to grow over theirs and painters and decorators to make the inside look like home. Caesar had an ordinary military tent with a flagpole in front and a rope to hold back the flap.

"Come in Caelius," he cried, putting his arms around me. "I've been waiting for you . . ."

I stepped forward into his embrace. As he leaned toward me to kiss me, I told him the truth. "Yes," I said. "I had to come."

XXIII

LAST REPORT OF MARCUS CAELIUS RUFUS
PRAETOR PEREGRINUS OF ROME . . .

For whom? For whom?

There is very little more to say. I betrayed myself when I went to Caesar, and the gods saw to it that I paid. He used me as he wished, as if I had been a child or a slave, and I could do nothing about it. Once in the past I had refused a bribe in order to keep my independence. I could have saved myself the trouble. I lost it all the same.

All that month as we travelled down to Rome he had me as a man has a woman, and all that time I told myself that I was as cool and as clear as he was. But it was not true. I was seething with rage, furious, sick with confusion and anger and despair. And I did not know it. That was the strangest part of all.

I was full of energy; I have never had such strength, such need for movement. I walked, I rode, I saw to my men and equipment, I argued with my colleagues, and I planned for my return to Rome, but all the time, my eyes were fixed on something I could not see, my mind was somewhere I cannot now recall.

Most nights, it seemed to me, I was called to Caesar's tent, or asked by a wink to stay behind when the others left. Then I would lie on the couch: I think I memorized every carved and painted acanthus leaf and touch of gilt on that creaking bed, while Caesar's hands and voice and body were everywhere on mine.

Those few nights that I was left to myself I did not sleep. Instead, unnaturally alert and active, I sat up drinking, holding imaginary conversations with Caesar in which we solved the problems of the city, and with them of my finances and my career. In those lengthening autumn nights I saw Rome laid out in front of me as never before. The markets: "Really, they need better regulation," I said, and proposed several plans to him; the great open space of the Forum—"Expanded," he said. "Oh, yes, we will build. I think a temple to my ancestors . . ." The streets of the poor districts, cluttered with life, lay before my eyes like lines of writing, "When I am City Praetor—when you have made me City Praetor—I will do something to help those poor men," I cried in the solitude of my tent.

"Yes," he said, and his green eyes gleamed.

By day I was alone with him only occasionally. When I tried to talk to him about the future he always agreed, amiably, easily, with everything I said, but when I pressed him for details of his plans he stopped my mouth with his.

There had been a battle at sea and my friend Dolabella, in charge of Caesar's fleet, had been defeated. Gaius Antonius, Mark Antony's brother, going to his rescue, had himself been forced to take refuge on an island and surrender fifteen cohorts he was transporting. Altogether, between them they lost forty ships and several thousand men. Caesar went around looking haggard, and he wanted my company more than ever.

At the end of the month we rode down the last miles with the army at our backs. The sky flamed. Far away over the plain I could see the city massed on the darkness of its hills, the golden river running between.

XXIV

Caesar had his plans, about which he didn't consult me; he had a view of the city which was not like mine. Nor did it much resemble what I believed it to be. The first thing he did was hold elections for consul. Well, it was important. In a way, it was what the whole war was about. He was elected, of course—with a colleague called Publius Servilius, an old friend. There wasn't anybody left in the city to oppose him.

He then held the elections for the other offices. I went down to the Forum to drop my ballot in the urn along with everyone else, so I had it directly, like a public slap in the face. Caesar's legate from Gaul, Trebonius, had been chosen City Praetor; I was made only Praetor Peregrinus, a junior office responsible for hearing the cases of foreigners in court.

Face flaming from this public humiliation, I went to see Caesar. I could not get in, there was such a crush of well-wishers at his door. I had to have my people shout that I was a praetor-elect before a way was cleared for me. So when I was ushered in it was with half my complaint stolen from me.

"My dear Caelius, Trebonius has been with me for ten years or more," Caesar said, squeezing my arm. "He really does have a prior claim. And he's a good officer. Steady and experienced. He'll do what I want."

"You promised me."

He seemed surprised, and his eyebrow rose. "I have kept my promise. I made you a praetor."

"You said City Praetor."

"Well, no, I didn't. You said that. I only agreed to make you a praetor. Isn't that so? You see?" But to soften the blow he arranged for me to buy a house near the Flaminian Gate, very cheaply. It had belonged to one of his opponents. This point, like others, I understood, as perhaps he had intended I should.

I could have sold the house, of course, except that it was impossible to sell anything then. No one was brave enough to buy in such unsettled times. All day men stood in the Forum calling to passers-by like whores, except that what they were so desperately trying to sell were the family farms, the workshops, brickyards, marble quarries, the blocks of city property, even their homes. There were no takers. More than one man went home and fell on his sword, unwilling to watch the suffering of his family.

"If you are having difficulties," my father said, "your mother and I can certainly get along on less."

"There's no need for that, father," I said airily. "Everything is fine. Do you think you entrusted the management of the businesses to a fool?"

But he had, for I was bankrupt, like the rest of the city. There just simply was no money. I went through the books a dozen times, a hundred, my eyes burning with sleep-lessness, but the river of gold had slowed to a trickle and the drought was growing worse. I couldn't make a payment on a mortgage, I couldn't borrow more to cover what I owed, there wasn't any way to sell off anything. And those who owed money to me—few enough, heaven knows—were in the same position.

"There's got to be money somewhere," I insisted. My temper had grown short and I was angry.

"Yes, praetor," Philo said.

"There have to be men who are profiting by this."

"Yes, praetor."

"All I have to do is find out where they are."

"Yes, praetor."

"Oh, Hercules," I shouted, throwing down my pen. "At least disagree with me so I'll know there are two of us here, Philo."

He looked at me with terrified eyes. "Yes, praetor."

I went to Caesar. "Now is the time to abolish debts."

"I have it in hand, Caelius. I appreciate your concern."

He announced a plan. Anyone who owed money could have his property evaluated by a board, which Caesar would appoint. His creditors would have to accept the property instead of money, and at the pre-war price, which the board would establish. Anything a debtor had already paid in interest would be deducted from the principle he owed.

This Caesar announced in the Forum one rainy December afternoon, to the rather puzzled and resentful silence of a large crowd. It didn't seem to me that these measures would do much good. "Too little," I said, and the men round me nodded. "Too late."

"It'll save me about twenty-five percent," one man said.

"That's a help, surely."

His eyes looked sick, like a beaten slave's. "Twenty-five percent of nothing is still nothing, praetor."

He was right. When I went home I saw that I was in the same position. Things had been bad so long that every property I owned had mortgages and second mortgages, every bill had come due three or four times, every payment owed to me had been suspended, usually for good.

"It's a mess, Philo," I moaned. Gods, it was like being tangled in a serpent: the more I struggled, the tighter I was bound. The confusion was impossible. All I could say for sure was that there was no money coming in, and no prospect of any for a long time to come.

"He has done nothing to help me," I cried one night, exasperated beyond bearing. "It has all been for nothing."

I felt his hands on me, his body penetrating mine—all for nothing, no help, no change, no improvement. I pushed back my chair to go to him, once again.

The stars are gone. Over the eastern rim of the harbor, light is beginning to seep into the sky.

He would not see me. He was too busy. There were thousands of petitions demanding his ear, applications, disputes, irregularities, vacancies in the Senate, political exiles to be recalled, preparations for the war in Greece. "Perhaps in a day or two," one of his secretaries said; he was sure I would understand.

"A day or two?" A parade of men was coming out the door, so I had to stand back. Knights. Moneylenders. They were smiling with satisfaction. Of course. I went back anyway. What could I do?

"Wait a few days more," the secretaries counselled me, but in a few days Caesar had celebrated the Latin Festival on the Alban Mount and marched away to Greece.

As usual, the city was empty without him. The Curia droned in its dust-moted irrelevance like a beehive in summer, the Forum echoed hollowly when you strolled through. In the vacant streets the little boys played the Troy Game, Caesar against Pompey. Caesar always won. Oh, the city adored him; in its ruin it seemed to love him more than ever.

A half a month later I became Praetor Peregrinus. By that time I had heard more in the city of its extreme financial suffering. If a man can die of a fever, a city can contract a kind of monetary disease, which kills it just as surely. Rome muttered and buzzed, mumbled and whispered, in a delirium of debt. What could I do? Trebonius, the City Praetor, was administering Caesar's law, but it wasn't strengthening the patient—not enough, not that I could see. Rome was clearly dying. I had to do something.

Finally, desperate, I took my magistrate's chair, and placed it next to Trebonius' on the steps of the Temple of Saturn in the Forum. There was a crowd below. I may not have served ten years in Gaul with Caesar like Trebonius, but I have not wasted my time either. I was pretty well known and had a large following—larger since I had been spreading my views on debt around the city.

"I, Marcus Caelius Rufus, Praetor Peregrinus of the city of Rome, announce that as of today, any man who wants to appeal against the rulings of Caesar's board may step forward. I will do what I can for him."

The men in line to speak to Trebonius looked around anxiously at the large crowd. One or two shrugged helplessly. The mob below muttered, and Trebonius' lictors suddenly became very noticeable.

"Come on. I'll protect you. I have men here, too. See?" It did no good. They did not dare, and I could not help them. I went home, discouraged and upset.

"Never mind," my father said that night at dinner. I had

gone to pay my obligatory call on my parents, a thing I tried to do every few days or so. I still found the money to keep them as they were accustomed, don't ask me how because I have no idea.

"They'll come tomorrow," he said.

"You think so?"

"Yes, of course they will. What you're proposing is the only way out of this." His hands shook and his head wobbled on a neck that now resembled a stalk, but I was desperate enough to find comfort even from such a feeble source. And his eyes were as shrewd as ever.

All right, if they wouldn't take the risk for a favorable hearing to an appeal, I would go further. I announced from the Rostra that I would defer all payments on debts without interest for six years. "That ought to be enough time to settle this civil war and get everything back to normal," I said, and the walls around the Forum echoed my words. "Back to normal. Back to normal."

The crowd cheered, and I was encouraged, but Trebonius, growing anxious about all this, was making disapproving noises, and the other magistrates were muttering their agreement.

Trebonius. That oaf. He occupied himself in the next few days making speeches against me all over the city—not that he got much of a reception. And I had my revenge. I had a chair made, just like his official one, except that it had a seat made out of leather. It looked pretty odd, I can tell you. When I set it out for him with a flourish on the steps of the tribunal, there was a laugh that sent the pigeons into the air. Trebonius flushed angrily. His father had been some kind of dealer in hides. The joke was not lost on the crowd, and my speeches were better attended than ever.

I used to walk in those days. Well, they are not so long ago, though it seems as if I have been with this rag-bag army for years. It is only a few months. February then, October now, and I have not seen the city in between. But in those days I walked it, as I had when I left to go to Caesar. This time it was leaving me, and we both knew it.

The city I walked through did not look like Rome any more. Before it had been populous, but there had been order in it. In one street the shops of a dozen sandal makers had been open to the sun, full of purpose and activity; in another a barber had set out his chair, a college of priests was chanting, a woman sang as she filled a jug at the public water fountain. Children had gone back and forth to school, servants to market, men to the Forum or to work. Shutters had opened in the morning, lights had bloomed behind them when it got dark. There was washing hung out on lines on the roofs of the tenement buildings, there was gambling in the bars, and everywhere voices raised and footsteps passing.

Now with the war all this had stopped. The shops were closed, the markets abandoned, the schools shut down. There was no way to tell day from night. Sometimes windows were shuttered in the sunlight, sometimes the lights burned all day long.

Yet there was motion everywhere. Crowds surged back and forth in the streets and turned slowly through the squares, but it was all random, chaotic, senseless movement. You could see it in the eyes of the men and women on that strange promenade. They had no purpose. They were just there. They moved because they had nothing else to do. One place was as good as another to them, and they were hungry in both. It was terrible to see, like watching some force of nature, a flow of lava, an avalanche; its mindlessness was shocking. The meaning had gone out of life.

Meaning had left every part over the city, especially politics, which is the heart of Roman life. All the old faces had disappeared, all the old voices were stilled. There was no Cato, nagging us like a grandmother, no Cicero reminding us of our nobility in measured eloquence; the vast presence that had been Pompey was removed, leaving us oddly exposed, as if one of our walls had been breached.

The old nobility was gone, the pompous senators of distinguished lineage, the descendants of men who had fought with Scipio against Hannibal, or with Manlius against the Celts. By the gods, some of them had ancestors who had fought with Romulus against the Sabines, and built the city afterwards. I never thought I would miss them, but I did. Where they had strolled our history had walked too; in their debates the issues that had troubled us for generations were argued. However futilely and to however little purpose, they were part of the continuity of the city's life.

Now in their places drunks and thugs packed the Senate, friends of Caesar's he had made rich and promoted to fill the numbers of that deserted body. Offices were held by men who had no right to them save that Caesar had awarded them. It was not only that they had no grasp of affairs—indeed a lot of the old senators hadn't either—but that they didn't even care. They came to their new dignities still hung over from the night before. More than once in the Senate the public slaves had to mop the place up because someone had been sick; one of the praetors let an actress sit in his lap while he administered justice in a court of law.

Even the colleges of priests were filled with Caesar's friends. They too reduced their offices to babble, to the chaos that was so noticeable everywhere. They were too careless to chant the prayers correctly, for they did not understand their significance. Nor did they trouble to find out.

Over all this the dull uniformity of the winter sky spread its diffuse light, so that for the first time the city looked drab to me. The buildings had neither shadows nor highlights to give them form. They floated, looking immaterial, gray on the gray air.

At first I thought that this was what always happened when Caesar went away; he took everything with him. I had felt it before. I wished as I always had for him to come back and restore us to what we had been before he left. But slowly it dawned on me that this chaos was what Caesar had created. It was the state that he preferred. This had been the vision of Rome that he had worked for all along, this gray confusion where nothing was better than anything else, and things had value only in so far as he could make use of them. This to him was what the city on the river, burning golden in the evening light, had been to me.

And gradually the odd conviction came on me that Caesar loved destruction because he had always believed it to be the foundation of the world. He had never outgrown the view of that poor, sick, desperate boy, hunted by Sulla's thugs and hiding in the marshes with a new bed every night. To him there was nothing in life that endured, no safety, no help, no consolation in anything, and therefore, there was nothing worth protecting. Faithful to this vision, he had worked all his life to destroy, without even realizing it.

Now anyone could see it. He had written it on the world. When you looked at the dying city under that washed out winter sun, you were looking at the inside of his mind.

Then came the news of Caesar's defeat at Dyrrhachium. Pompey, superb general that he was, that he had always been of course, broke through Caesar's lines and put his army to flight. Caesar's demoralized troops spread across the Thessalian plain in a retreat that only the presence of his friends in Rome prevented us from calling a rout. It did not seem likely that Caesar could bring it together again, and if Pompey pursued his advantage the war might be over in a month.

That night I walked much farther than usual, out past the suburbs and into a region of isolated farms, with here and there a little country town. My mind was in confusion so deep I did not know where I was. The night lapped over me, it concealed me, but I paced as if I were at the bottom of the sea.

After a while I came to a town I recognized, a tiny place huddled behind its shutters with uncivil distrustfulness. I wandered around it: here was the market, there a shabby little bar. Here the wind had come down like a funnel, laden with snow, in a winter of exceptional cold. It was only a memory now. On a wall there were some marks—they might have been lines of a poem, written in charcoal, run together and faded by years of sun and rain. All the same I could just make them out:

Nothing about you interests me, Caesar,
and I have no wish to please.
I wouldn't even send to know
on which side of you your face is.

It was the last of his poems against Caesar, the one he had

written after Caesar had warned him to stop. Catullus had hated Caesar—well, put it this way. He had taken him seriously, long before the rest of us did.

I remembered a story that had gone around, how Caesar had invited him to dinner one night, up in Luca when he was governor of Gaul, and asked him to stop writing verses against an old family friend. I had never questioned it, but now I wondered if "asked" was the exactly right word.

In any case Catullus had not stopped, for here was the poem. Damaging in itself, it seemed to me that it announced worse. Catullus meant to go on publishing the corruption of the hero of Gaul, the treachery of the man who destroyed the constitution. And standing there on that winter night it occurred to me to wonder for the first time why all those years ago Vatinius had wanted to know where Catullus was. Vatinius who was Caesar's ape, and Caesar's dog. Vatinius who almost certainly strangled the informer Vettius for his patron—if Caesar didn't do it himself—when Vettius had named some conspirators who were too close to Caesar. I wondered how I had failed to notice this before.

Waving my servants forward with the torch, I bent down. There at the bottom of the wall, where I had found Catullus lying that night years before, was a discolored spot, a stain the size of my palm. It wasn't evidence, I know that, but all the same it was possible. . . . It looked like blood.

I passed on, walking now through smoke and flame as my servants held up the light. In a short time I came to the villa, still solitary behind its heavy gates. I pulled the rope, expecting nothing. In the old days she had kept only one servant, who was deaf. But a door man in a smart, clean tunic peered through the gate at me. I gave him my name, and my rank. He looked over my shoulder at my lictors and torchmen, and then he drew back the bolt.

Inside the house was different, too. The walls were plastered and painted, and tapestries hung from some of them; pieces of furniture, polished and graceful, gleamed around the walls. I sat on a bench and waited. There wasn't any hurry; I might as well be there as anywhere, it didn't matter to me. There was light here, and clarity: I had had enough of the night.

Presently I hear a rustling noise; a curtain was pulled back with a gentle clash of rings. A woman stood there, looking at me.

"Hello, Clodia," I said.

She had been beautiful once, the most beautiful woman in Rome. She was, I guessed, in her fifties now, and still handsome, though her slenderness had thickened and her hair was more gray than black. But her eyes were still the same. They used to say in Rome, before she was disgraced and destroyed, that she had the brightest eyes in the city. Well, she still did. Dark, intelligent, shrewd and hostile, they contemplated me as they always had.

"Don't talk too loudly. You'll wake the girl."

I searched my memory, but I could recall no girl. "Your daughter?"

"My niece. My brother's child. By his wife." Her black eyes snapped and flared. I saw that her anger was implacable . . . She had not forgotten anything; nothing had mellowed or tamed her.

"I am not responsible. The lawsuit was your idea, I can't help what Cicero . . . And your brother's death. That wasn't me, either. That was Milo. And you had your revenge for it. Milo is still in exile."

The torchlight illuminated her magisterial contempt. She wasn't interested in such details. "You were there. You helped."

"Clodia, can't we be friends? I have a certain amount of power and influence. I could help you. You don't have to live like this."

"Is that what you think friendship is? Power and influence?" It amused her, and she smiled. Gods, she was still beautiful, but her anger burned. Why have I come? I thought, and then I remembered the night outside.

Suddenly it was too much for me. It swept over me: I was alone, my friends were dead, my patron ruined, my money gone. I had chosen the losing side in a civil war, and I did not know what would happen to me. I had a feeling that my life was nearly over. "Clodia," I cried, "I loved you once—"

"Loved me?" Her laughter rained down on me like a shower of sparks.

"Oh, yes, of course I did. You were so lovely. I wanted—"

"You wanted. You wanted to emulate your friend Catullus, that was all. Your only wish was to go where he had been before." She looked around that poor, provincial room as if she were thinking that she liked it. Clodia Metelli, who used to live at the top of the Palatine Hill, at the best address in Rome. "Not many men are capable of love for a woman. You are not one of the ones who are."

"But Clodia, that's not true." I was anxious to prove it to her; suddenly the night was there, a darkness spreading between us like a lake. I spoke against it, trying to make it recede and my voice was louder than I intended.

Her contempt swept over me like a fire. "Even my beauty was only a token for you, a coin to buy the world's good opinion for yourself. You never cared for me, you were never interested in me, not even in bed. The only person you—"

I leaped to my feet. The black night was lapping at them. "Oh, no. No—"

"The only person you ever wanted to make love to was Gaius Julius Caesar. You were in love with him. The whole city knew it, people used to talk about it at dinner parties, how your eyes never left him . . . There's nothing to be ashamed of—I was infatuated myself, for a while. And he paid for the privilege by helping my brother and me. What do you think bought me my freedom from my husband?" Her anger was everywhere in that room, beating against the walls like a tide; it flowed out after me as I ran into the street.

She was still laughing when the gate slammed shut behind me. From far away, deep in the house, I heard a child awake and cry.

Well, naturally she lied—anything to make me look bad. All that long walk home I told myself that, but I was seething with rage all the same. How dare she? I was a praetor of Rome. And to say I was in love with Julius Caesar . . . It was absurd, irresponsible. People ought to be punished for such talk. What if she repeated it in the city? Well, if she did, I would see to it that she never had a chance to say anything in her life again. The law would help me, I was not helpless against her. No woman had the power, the right, to detract from the dignity of a magistrate. I could shut that red, mocking mouth, close those brilliant black eyes. There was some good in my office after all. And it was such a lie, such a disgusting, repellent, hideous untruth . . .

The next day I packed the Forum with my men and announced that I would see to it that all debts were immediately abolished, and all payment for rent on houses and apartments remitted for one year. Trebonius, still smarting from the joke about the leather chair, tried to shut me up; my men grew angry and there was a riot. Well, a heavy scuffle. A few people were hurt, anyway. I didn't care. Laughing savagely, I threw myself into the fight, while Trebonius himself ran to fetch the consul.

When they finally hauled me up before the Senate I was dishevelled and out of breath, and I had a swelling rising above one eye, but I felt better than I had in days. They expelled me from the Senate, of course, and deprived me of my office. I'm not surprised, in view of the things I called them. Servilius, the consul, forbade me to come near the Curia. As if that were a punishment. Just to make it stick, they passed the Ultimate Decree against me, suspending my civil rights. I suppose they expected me to take myself off into exile to protect myself.

I marched outside and climbed up the Rostra to address what was by now a very large and interested audience. I was still laughing. Servilius, of course, couldn't allow that, and sent his lictors to arrest me. I got away, dashing through the Forum and out toward the Circus Maximus, but Sevilius' men were close behind me.

It's death or exile for you, Caelius, I thought, running hard. I looked back over my shoulder. It made me unwary, and before I knew it I had caromed into a cage of animals waiting in the square by the Circus for some game or other. There was a crash, and from the animals such a roar and chatter and screech you would have thought all the demons of the underworld were loose and had gotten between me and Servilius' men. "Well, why not?" I shouted with laughter, and darting between the cages, pulled open the doors. Out poured the animals in a cacophony, a confusion, the like of which you never saw before. A lion eyed me mistrustfully before jumping down from his platform, three huge aurochs from Dacia lowed and shook their horns, a sad-eyed bear waddled out into that crowd of liberated beasts with the deliberate dignity of an ancient Roman king.

So I escaped. That night I issued a statement saying I was going to Caesar to get redress. I slipped out of the city one step ahead of the lictors. But I did not go to Caesar. Instead I went home to Interamnia, and raised the army I have with me now. I wrote to Milo, my old friend still in exile, and for a time he joined me, bringing a thousand men of his household with him, but Milo was killed at a siege over a month ago, and his men were captured. Since then I have been alone.

It's odd, you know. I was in a hurry and didn't notice, but the night that I left Rome it was by the same gate that I had first come in, when I was sixteen years old. It was my first and my last glimpse of the city.

No, not quite the last. Let me be accurate here. A report, no matter who it is for, must be correct. That night as I raced along the road, heading for Interamnia and the men of my farms and workshops, just as my wagon was beginning to climb up the mountains the horses snorted and shied to the left. I glanced to the right of the road. There in the darkness stood the bear, risen to his great height on his hind legs, his small, shining eyes watching me. It seemed to me that he nodded. Then he lowered himself and lumbered away into the night. I looked back, and far away, just on the edge of sight, the lights of the city winked and flickered among the trees. As I watched one or two went out, then more, then almost all of them, and the city was absorbed into the darkness, and disappeared.

It is dawn outside. Color has come into the world—one color. A transparent blue like water, filling up every space, tinting every object. You can see quite well in it, except that you cannot see far, and the world is still very dark. But close at hand everything is stained with the deep, vibrant light. A wall looms up, unnaturally close to the window, a street goes rapidly away like a tunnel into night; the tang of the sea is suddenly very close and strong.

Did I mean to go to Caesar? I could have, once I escaped from the city. The road was the same. Up over the mountains, down toward the sea, and the wind lifting my hair as I drove. The door was open, and in the vast spaces of the night I could travel towards whatever I wished. I could have taken a ship at Brundisium or Ancona or Ariminum, I could have sailed to Greece to join him in his flight from the victorious Pompey—

That is nonsense. I never intended to do that. Go to Caesar? I hated Caesar now. And when the bear halted my horses on the road, I had time to think, and I admitted it. I watched the last lights wink out in Rome far away. Then I chucked to my team and started down the slope to my home. The wind blew in my face, the world stretched itself out under my wheels, but now I had nowhere else to go but back where I began. Go to Caesar? Clodia with her laughter had slammed that last door in my face.

Was it true? Was I in love with him? He had said so once himself. Was he right? I thought of his hands on my body, the flick of his cruel mouth, the dark eyes with their strange bloom of light . . . Gods, how he used me, and how, when I had done for him what he required he no longer had any use for me at all. Did I love him? He treats men like counters in a game, without regard for their strengths and weaknesses except as he can gain advantage from them. The odd thing is, he uses himself in exactly the same way. Caesar is to Caesar just another man who can serve his purposes. When he no longer does, will Caesar get rid of him? Perhaps he will.

Who could love a man like that? Not I. I hated him. Long ago, when I met him in the Forum, I met an evil destiny. He was like a knife that opened a wound I did not even notice, but ever since my life has been bleeding away, first slowly, now with terrifying speed. All I have left now is a futile escape and a forced retirement, somewhere far from Rome.

It is the same for all of us. An entire generation. We weren't worth much, most of us: we loved good times and spending money, and most of us did not have very high ideals. How often we thought our own good and the good of the city were the same, I wouldn't like to say. We were not our ancestors, that's for sure. But we were their heirs. We were free men. We did what we liked and didn't care who it pleased, we spoke our own minds in the Forum, we fought our own elections, and when the voting came, no one could ever tell us which name to put on the ballot. Now all that is finished, and all of us are gone.

Curio is dead, and Catullus, Publius Crassus died in Asia, with his father. Clodius had his throat cut in a gutter; Milo, his killer, was brought down by a stone hurled from the wall of a country town. Pompey is betrayed and butchered. The others, the hundreds of others, are scattered and destroyed. I am the only one left, and my life has almost leaked away. And all because we knew Gaius Julius Caesar, and were his friends.

Oh, yes, he is dangerous, even to himself: cruel and treacherous, violent, deceitful, cold. That mocking smile. Those brilliant eyes. He put his hand on my arm, and I was like a slave, whose freedom is lost and who is helpless in his grip.

The darkness is lifting, the blue fading. The town, tumbled around its harbor, has emerged into the first gray. I can see the water now, lapping on the stony curve of shingle, over the eastern edge of the harbor colors are beginning to show in the sky, a faint rose, then the first flush of gold. In a moment the sun will rise. The day is almost here.

Was I in love with him?
That smile. Those eyes. That hand on my arm.
Yes. I was.

XXV

LAST REPORT OF MARCUS CAELIUS RUFUS
PRAETOR PEREGRINUS OF ROME . . .

Dawn light is flooding through the eastern window, the pigeons are calling, one or two are fluttering on the sill. The roofs shine like copper, the sea is aquamarine, the buildings of the town are chalky gold and deep yellow ochre. Sparks of light run along the wind-ruffle the breeze is making on the sea.

Out on the road the shadow of the wall is deep and cool, but farther out the stones shine in the morning sun, and the leaves rustle. Have they turned to bronze already? They look it.

My room has filled with people: servants bringing food, scouts with their report, Philo, herding the hostages before him. "One thing at a time." I have to shout above the noise. Slowly the room clears.

First the scouts. The cavalry on the road will be here in an hour. It does not appear that they are aware of us yet. Well, it gives us a little time to maneuver. It might be possible to bargain with them, buy ourselves off.

Philo looks doubtful. "We don't have that much money left, praetor—"

"We have enough. And we have other goods as well." I give him a smile that doesn't feel very good-humored. He flinches, so I suppose it isn't. "There are the hostages. Go on, bring them in. What are they, waiting outside? Let's see what they will fetch, from a troop of Caesar's cavalry. It ought to be enough to let us get away on the ship and set up somewhere else . . ."

"Yes, praetor. Perhaps we can hope for a good outcome after all."

314

Luxuriously I stretch and rise to my feet. Out the window—

There is something in the view from the window that disturbs my eye. Something wrong. Pigeons, sky, rooftops, my soldiers in the forum around their cooking fires, my legate speaking to the guard. All correct. Beyond that, the town's streets—vacant, as they are supposed to be. The harbor. The sea, dancing with light.

The sea is empty. The ship is gone.

I am on my feet, staring, but it is true. The ship is gone. "I have been betrayed," I cry out, and indeed a blow seems to have struck me, so heavily that it buckles my knees. "Betrayed."

I am shouting, pounding on the table, calling on the guard. The sea is as empty as a plate at a cancelled feast. There is nothing there but the light, flashing and glittering in the early morning sun. The trireme is gone; it might never have existed at all. Gods. Where is my escape? My future on our estates in North Africa, my olive trees, my philosophy, my sons? Where is the long succession of peaceful days, the simple existence of a retired Roman gentleman of educated tastes? Gods, I am robbed. Someone has stolen half my life.

And I know who the villain is: Philo.

Trembling, he kneels before me. The javelins of the guard are at his throat. The hostages, like sheep, have followed him back into the room and are gazing at me out of round, stupefied eyes. The chief magistrate puts his arms around his son again, to protect him from my wrath.

"Philo," I say in terrible voice, "prepare to die."

Philo warbles in his terror like a bird.

"You failed to put the guard I told you to on the ship."

His color is like clay, it cannot get worse, but he sways as if the blood is draining from his head. He looks as if he is going to faint. His eyes are turning up; I can see the whites. He stinks abominably; the creature has dirtied himself.

"Guards, pour water on him. I want him conscious for this."

"Praetor. Marcus Caelius Rufus." Philo is weeping. "You never told me to post a guard on the ship."

"Of course I did. When I told you to have the light put

out. Remember the light? It was bothering me, and it made me think someone might see. I told you then. No, not then. Wait. You left too fast. I had to go after you. I stopped to talk to the chief magistrate here, but certainly I must have told you then to—"

"No, praetor, no you didn't," he moans softly.

"Praetor." It is the chief magistrate. He is nearly as gray as Philo. "If that is when you think you gave the order, you are mistaken. We saw this man hurry though the forum, on his way down to the harbor. Then you came, and there was . . . well, our little incident. You remember, I'm sure." I remember. I almost killed him and his son. "And afterwards," he is going on, his fat face sweating, his brown eyes as anxious as a dog's. "Afterwards you went right back to your room here. Perhaps you spoke to this man earlier or later, but not then . . ."

He is right. I did not find Philo, I did not deliver my message. I was distracted, by—never mind that now. But it is the second time the little magistrate has prevented me from doing an injustice.

I am betrayed. Betrayed by my anger, my rage, my ungovernable emotions, my failure to understand what was important in my life. I used to think I was like Caesar, a cool man. I was wrong. I am boiling, I am seething with emotion, there is nothing cool about me anywhere. I am the warmest man I have ever met, the least like Caesar of us all. I admired him. I wanted to be just like him. I was dazzled by his superb self-control. I remember that I tried to imitate him, and how I argued about it with Curio, with Catullus. They could not understand. Well, I'm not so sure I understand myself, any more.

All I am sure of is that I was wrong. I thought I acted from calculation, from a pure and rational consideration of my advantage. I had not. Not in one single case. Not when I betrayed Catullus to go to bed with his beloved Clodia— for though I said it was for my career, it was really, as she saw so clearly, out of jealousy of him; not when I joined Milo against the Clodians, because I loved Cicero and hated my failure to love Clodia.

I fought Crassus' battles out of love of excitement and action, I rejected my father out of fear and refused affection. I never married, not because I was too busy, but because my love was given elsewhere, though I never guessed where. Worst of all, I thought I went to Caesar because I believed that he would win. The real reason I cannot even now bring myself to admit . . . Yes. Because I loved him. No, not loved exactly. Because I wanted him. That, at last, is the truth. I went to Caesar for a pure animal lust, a sexual desire, like a beast in rut. I mistook my nature, right from the start, and it has destroyed my life.

But my mistake, bad as it is, is not as bad as Caesar's. For he is not a cool man either. Perhaps no one really is. Caesar with his devastated youth, his bitter capture, his terrible experiences, is hotter than any of us. Yet Caesar believes in his emotionless judgment, and out of that error he has destroyed not himself but the whole world.

There remains the army on the road. Well, I will have to try my luck with them. Bargain if I can, get some kind of safe-conduct, some permission to go away on the promise that I never try to return to Italy or see Rome again. I have thought of taking the hostages with me as a guarantee of my passage, but the little magistrate has earned more than that from me. No, I will ride out of the city gates and meet that army alone.

THURII   OCTOBER 2, 706 A. U. C.
LAST REPORT OF MARCUS CAELIUS RUFUS
PRAETOR PEREGRINUS OF ROME . . .

My report is done. It only remains to address it and send it off. But to whom? There is no one. Everyone I ever cared for is gone.

A long time ago when I was a boy in our house in Interamnia, I used to stand before the door in the garden wall. I would reach up and lift the latch, the door would open, and before me would stretch the vast liberty of the world.

The wind blew toward me. There was news in it, of forests

317

and fields, seas and mountains, roads, farms, houses, animals, men. I would follow it, over mountains and flower-starred plains, until one evening, far in the distance, on a mass of dark hills, the lights of a city would twinkle among moving branches, a river of gold would flow under a burning sky.

In a moment I will tell them to go and open the gates in the wall below me. I will ride out and meet my fate on the road. And who knows? It may be that the breeze will be blowing, and somewhere, after a long time, I will come to the city again.

THURII   OCTOBER 2, 706 A. U. C.
LAST REPORT OF MARCUS CAELIUS RUFUS
PRAETOR PEREGRINUS OF ROME . . .
FROM MARCUS CAELIUS RUFUS TO HIS FATHER.
GREETINGS.
AND MUCH LOVE. AT LAST.

NOTES

HISTORY IN THIS BOOK

Most of the people in this novel are real, and this account of their lives is based on those that have come down to us from the ancient historians—men contemporary or nearly contemporary with the events leading to the breakup of the Roman Republic and the establishment of the Empire under the Caesars. There are several histories written by the participants themselves, notably Caesar's books about the war in Gaul, and the books published under his name but probably written by his aide, about the civil war. Livy's history and Sallust's, Appian's and Dio Cassius', are all worth reading for the narrative sweep they bring to their accounts. Two famous biographies of Caesar: Plutarch's portrait in the *Parallel Lives*, and Suetonius' in *The Lives of the Caesars* are, in addition to their importance as history, remarkable examples of the biographer's art.

As always the greatest detail comes from Cicero's letters and speeches, so many of which, by a great good fortune, have been preserved. They are remarkable to read. Packed with gossip, rumor, jokes, information, deep feeling and shrewd intelligence, they must surely be one of the most amazing objects the sea of history has cast up on the shores of our lives. Nothing in the writing of these novels has given me more pleasure than to read them. Several of them are quoted in this book.

Marcus Caelius Rufus was born in 82 B. C., and died in 48, according to Saint Jerome. His wit and charm were well known in antiquity, and the letters I have quoted in this text are really his, as is the fragment of the speech against Antonius Hybrida. (Most of the other documents are real, too, though I have invented some when I needed them.)

Julius Caesar's career is also well documented. His bisexuality was well known, and widely disapproved. Roman attitudes toward homosexuality are difficult to decipher. The references we have are all extremely negative, but what they condemn seem to be effeminacy and extravagance, not homosexuality in itself. What this means is difficult to say.

In any case, however widely homosexuality may be accepted in a society, there must always be individuals who, for one reason or another, do not share the prevailing sentiments. That Caelius was one of them is entirely my own invention. We know nothing of his own preferences, except that he appears to have been a lover of Clodia Metelli. Antony's purchase, with Curio, of young slave boys is historically attested and the presumption is that they wanted the boys for sex. Curio was excoriated for his feminine mannerisms—Cicero called him "Curiola"—"Little Miss Curio"—and spoke to him about the damage he was doing to his reputation. Caesar was widely condemned for his affairs with men, though again it may be because he was supposed to have accepted a passive role in them, out of ambition.

Julius Caesar was in his own time, and remains to this day, one of the most controversial figures who ever lived. His bisexuality is only part of his mystery. Every age, every country, every culture, has seen him differently. It is one of the strangenesses of studying a time so remote from our own to discover that we are all prisoners of our culture; we read into history what our own experience allows us.

One illustration may suffice: in the nineteenth century Caesar's abrupt way with the constitution seemed much more benign, even praiseworthy, than it did to historians who had lived through the dictatorships in Europe in the twentieth. Yet it would be a mistake not to realize that these earlier historians saw things to which we are blinded by our limitations, or to think that we finally know the truth. We are caught in our time, just as surely as they were in theirs, and the only thing that is certain is that the future will see the past differently.

THE DOOR IN THE WALL

A WORD ABOUT TWO WORDS

Two words common in Caesar's time have come into modern English, but they are so often misused they may to be taking on a new set of meanings, so I thought I ought to explain them. In Caesar's time, and for long after, *cohort* was a military term denoting a unit of around five hundred men. Nowadays people speak of a cohort and mean only one person, a companion, usually shady. I suppose this use arose from the fact that cohorts often served as escorts and bodyguards for generals and emperors.

At Placentia Caesar threatened to *decimate* the Ninth Legion for its mutiny. He meant, as the word shows, that he intended to kill one man in ten in it. It was a terrible punishment, for almost five hundred men would have been executed, but it is not as terrible as the modern interpretation makes it seem. *Decimated* nowadays is used as a synonym for *completely destroyed.*

WHAT HAPPENED AFTER

Marcus Caelius Rufus and his friends formed a revolutionary generation; like others in history its fate was not happy. Very few of the people mentioned in these books lived long.

Caelius was killed by the wing of cavalry he went out to meet, to the sorrow of his friends. Cicero is on record as saying he deserved "a longer life and a better fate." Cato committed suicide rather than surrender the town of Utica in North Africa to Caesar, who was himself assassinated in Rome four years after the conclusion of this book. Marcus Junius Brutus led the assassins, though he had been Caesar's friend; in ancient times there was even a rumor that he was Caesar's son. The Cassius of that conspiracy was probably a cousin of the tribune in this book. Neither of them survived the war.

Catullus' friend Calvus died at the age of thirty, of unknown causes; another, Helvius Cinna, who went with him to Bithynia, was killed by the Roman mob the day of Caesar's assassination. They mistook him for another man of the same name who had been involved in the plot, and though he protested his innocence, they tore him apart.

Mark Antony survived the assassination of Caesar, and, joining forces with Caesar's nephew and heir, Octavian, made war on the conspirators. But after that their relationship was troubled and broke out in war. Antony committed suicide on the death of his ally and lover, Cleopatra, when the war was lost. Octavian became the Emperor Augustus.

Cicero, though he was not part of the conspiracy of the Ides of March, supported the assassins. His speeches against Antony did the general great harm and when Antony and Octavian had conquered, Antony persuaded Octavian to allow Cicero to be murdered. Cicero died with heroic stoicism, having received the news that his brother had already been assassinated. It is said that Augustus always regretted his part in this crime. Years later he is supposed to have come across a relative of his reading a volume of Cicero's works. The youth, naturally, was frightened that the Emperor had caught him with a subversive volume, but Augustus reassured him, saying that Cicero had been a great patriot. He then had all of the statues of Mark Antony in Rome pulled down, and forbade any member of the Antonius family ever to take the name Marcus again.

Cicero's enemy Clodia disappeared from history before the end of these books. There is a reference in a late letter of Cicero's suggesting she may have been alive and in prosperous circumstances at that point, but that is all we know.

Clodius' rich and aristocratic wife Fulvia, who married Curio after Clodius' murder, was left a widow again on the death of Curio in North Africa. True to her penchant for radical politicians, she next married Mark Antony, by whom she had two sons. She is said to have hated Cicero, and when he was dead she had his head and hands cut off and the bloody trophy brought to her as proof that he could do her husband no more harm. This story is not substantiated. In any case, her marriage to Antony cannot have been happy, and she was forced to go to Greece, where she died not long after. Her son by Publius Clodius had a political career later, her daughter by him, Claudia, was briefly married to Augustus, her son by Curio was executed by Octavian. Her two sons by Antony had important political careers in opposition to Augustus, which were not successful. One of them was killed by Augustus, and the other, already under sentence of death, committed suicide.

Terentia, Cicero's wife and the mother of his two children, was divorced by her husband for financial dishonesty in the year this book ends. She married the historian Sallust and then, later, another man. Her family was aristocratic and well-to-do. She had a very long life—she died at the age of 103.

About Philo, though he was a real person, we know nothing. Tiro, the secretary of Cicero, is famous. He invented a form of shorthand. Surviving his former master and friend, he was the editor of some of his speeches and the author of a number of books, including a biography of Cicero.

PS 3560 .A5368 D66 1994

Jaro, Benita Kane.

The door in the wall

WITHDRAWN